THE WEDDING PLANNER'S BIG DAY

BY
CARA COLTER

This is a work of fiction. Names, characters, places, locations and incidents are purely fictional and bear no relationship to any real life individuals, living or dead, or to any actual places, business establishments, locations, events or incidents. Any resemblance is entirely coincidental.

First Published in Great Britain 2016
By Mills & Boon, an imprint of HarperCollins*Publishers*
1 London Bridge Street, London, SE1 9GF

ISBN: 978-0-263-91976-9

23-0416

Our policy is to use papers that are natural, renewable and recyclable products and made from wood grown in sustainable forests. The logging and manufacturing processes conform to the legal environmental regulations of the country of origin.

Printed and bound in Spain
by CPI, Barcelona

"A girl like you does not kiss a guy like me!"

Becky could ask what Drew meant by a girl like her, but she already knew that he thought she was small-town and naive and hopelessly out of her depth, and not just in the ocean, either. What she wanted to know was what the last half of that sentence meant.

"What do you mean a guy like you?" she asked. Her voice was husky from the salt and from something else. Desire. Desire was burning like a white-hot coal in her belly. It was brand-new, it was embarrassing and it was wonderful.

"Look, Becky, I'm the kind of guy your mother used to warn you about."

"The kind who would jump in the water without a thought for his own safety to save someone else?"

"Not that kind!"

"What kind of guy, then?" she asked, gently curious. "Self-centered. Here for a good time. Commitment-phobic. Good-time Charlie. Confirmed bachelor. They write whole articles about guys like me in your bridal magazines. And not about how to catch me, either. How to give a guy like me a wide berth."

He glanced at her. She bit her lip and his gaze rested there, hot with memory, until he made himself look away.

"It was just a kiss," she pointed out mildly, "not a posting of the banns."

"You're in shock," he said.

If she was, she hoped she could experience it again, and soon!

'A girl like you does not kiss a guy like me!'

[illegible] wanted to know [illegible] [illegible] knew [illegible] [illegible] and not just in the [illegible] wanted to know was what the last [illegible] someone [illegible]

'Why do you want [illegible]?' she asked. [illegible] [illegible] and [illegible] else. Desire [illegible] [illegible] [illegible]

'[illegible] the kind of [illegible] something [illegible]'

'Think about [illegible] in the way [illegible] for [illegible] to see someone else?'

'[illegible] kind.'

'What [illegible]?' she asked [illegible] [illegible] good time. Commitment [illegible] [illegible] [illegible] [illegible] magazines. And not about how to [illegible], rather how to [illegible]'

He [illegible] [illegible] [illegible] away.

[illegible] a [illegible] and a [illegible]

'[illegible]' he [illegible]

[illegible] she [illegible] again [illegible]

Cara Colter shares her life in beautiful British Columbia, Canada, with her husband, nine horses and one small Pomeranian with a large attitude. She loves to hear from readers, and you can learn more about her and contact her through Facebook.

To all those readers who have made the past thirty years such an incredible journey.

CHAPTER ONE

"No."

A paper fluttered down on her temporary desk, slowly floating past Becky English's sunburned nose. She looked up, and tried not to let her reaction to what she saw—or rather, whom she saw—show on her face.

The rich and utterly sexy timbre of the voice should have prepared her, but it hadn't. The man was gorgeous. Bristling with bad humor, but gorgeous, nonetheless.

He stood at least six feet tall, and his casual dress, a dark green sports shirt and pressed sand-colored shorts, showed off a beautifully made male body. He had the rugged look of a man who spent a great deal of time out of doors. There was no sunburn on his perfectly shaped nose!

He had a deep chest, a flat stomach and the narrow hips of a gunslinger. His limbs, relaxed, were sleekly muscled and hinted at easy strength.

The stranger's face was mesmerizing. His hair, dark brown and curling, touched the collar of his shirt. His eyes were as blue as the Caribbean Sea that Becky could just glimpse out the open patio door over the incredible broadness of his shoulder.

Unlike that sea, his eyes did not look warm and inviting. In fact, there was that hint of a gunslinger, again, something cool and formidable in his uncompromising gaze. The look in his eyes did not detract, not in the least, from the fact that his features were astoundingly perfect.

"And no," he said.

Another piece of paper drifted down onto her desk, this one landing on the keyboard of her laptop.

"And to this one?" he said. "Especially no."

And then a final sheet glided down, hit the lip of the desk, forcing her to grab it before it slid to the floor.

Becky stared at him, rather than the paper in her hand. A bead of sweat trickled down from his temple and followed the line of his face, slowly, slowly, slowly down to the slope of a perfect jaw, where he swiped at it impatiently.

It was hot here on the small, privately owned Caribbean island of Sainte Simone. Becky resisted a temptation to swipe at her own sweaty brow with the back of her arm.

She found her voice. "Excuse me? And you are?"

He raised an arrogant eyebrow at her, which made her rush to answer for him.

"You must be one of Allie's Hollywood friends," Becky decided.

It seemed to her that only people in Allie's field of work, acting on the big screen, achieved the physical beauty and perfection of the man in front of her. Only they seemed to be able to carry off that rather unsettling I-own-the-earth confidence that mere mortals had no hope of achieving. Besides, it was more than evident how the camera would love the gorgeous planes of his face, the line of his nose, the fullness of his lips…

"Are you?" she asked.

This was exactly why she had needed a guest list, but no, Allie had been adamant about that. She was looking after the guest list herself, and she did not want a single soul—up to and including her event planner, apparently—knowing the names of all the famous people who would be attending her wedding.

The man before Becky actually snorted in disgust, which was no kind of answer. Snorted. How could that possibly sound sexy?

"Of course, you are very early," Becky told him, trying for a stern note. Why was her heart beating like that, as if she had just run a sprint? "The wedding isn't for two weeks."

It was probably exactly what she should be expecting. People with too much money and too much time on their hands were just going to start showing up on Sainte Simone whenever they pleased.

"I'm Drew Jordan."

She must have looked as blank as she felt.

"The head carpenter for this circus."

Drew. Jordan. Of course! How could she not have registered that? She was actually expecting him. He was the brother of Joe, the groom.

Well, he might be the head carpenter, but she was the ringmaster, and she was going to have to establish that fact, and fast.

"Please do not refer to Allie Ambrosia's wedding as a circus," the ringmaster said sternly. Becky was under strict orders word of the wedding was not to get out. She was not even sure that was possible, with two hundred guests, but if it did get out, she did not want it being referred to as a circus by the hired help. The paparazzi would pounce on that little morsel of insider information just a little too gleefully.

There was that utterly sexy snort again.

"It is," she continued, just as sternly, "going to be the event of the century."

She was quoting the bride-to-be, Hollywood's latest "it" girl, Allie Ambrosia. She tried not to show that she, Becky English, small-town nobody, was just a little intimidated that she had been chosen to pull off that event of the century.

She now remembered Allie warning her about this very man who stood in front of her.

Allie had said, *My future brother-in-law is going to head up construction. He's a bit of a stick-in-the-mud. He's a few years older than Joe, but he acts, like, seventy-five. I find him quite cranky. He's the bear-with-the-sore-bottom type. Which explains why* he *isn't married.*

So, this was the future brother-in-law, standing in front of Becky, looking nothing at all like a stick-in-the-mud, or like a seventy-five-year-old. The bear-with-the-sore-bottom part was debatable.

With all those facts in hand, why was the one that stood out the fact that Drew Jordan was not married? And why would Becky care about that, at all?

Becky had learned there was an unexpected perk of being a wedding planner. She had named her company, with a touch of whimsy and a whole lot of wistfulness, Happily-Ever-After. However, her career choice had quickly killed what shreds of her romantic illusions had remained after the bitter end to her long engagement. She would be the first to admit she'd had far too many fairy-tale fantasies way back when she had been very young and hopelessly naive.

Flustered—here was a man who made a woman want to believe, all over again, in happy endings—but certainly not wanting to show it, Becky picked up the last paper Drew Jordan had cast down in front of her, the *especially no* one.

It was her own handiwork that had been cast so dismissively in front of her. Her careful, if somewhat rudimentary, drawing had a big black X right through the whole thing.

"But this is the pavilion!" she said. "Where are we supposed to seat two hundred guests for dinner?"

"The location is fine."

Was she supposed to thank him for that? Somehow words, even sarcastic ones, were lost to her. She sputtered ineffectually.

"You can still have dinner at the same place, on the front lawn in front of this monstrosity. Just no pavilion."

"This monstrosity is a castle," Becky said firmly. Okay, she, too, had thought when she had first stepped off the private plane that had whisked her here that the medieval stone structure looked strangely out of place amidst the palms and tropical flowers. But over the past few days, it had been growing on her. The thick walls kept it deliciously cool inside and every room she had peeked in had the luxurious feel of a five-star hotel.

Besides, the monstrosity was big enough to host two hundred guests for the weeklong extravaganza that Allie wanted for her wedding, and monstrosities like that were very hard, indeed, to find.

With the exception of an on-site carpenter, the island getaway came completely staffed with people who were accustomed to hosting remarkable events. The owner was record mogul Bart Lung, and many a musical extravaganza had been held here. The very famous fund-raising documentary *We Are the Globe*, with its huge cast of musical royalty, had been completely filmed and recorded here.

But apparently all those people had eaten in the very expansive castle dining room, which Allie had said with a sniff would not do. She had her heart set on alfresco for her wedding feast.

"Are you saying you can't build me a pavilion?" Becky tried for an intimidating, you-can-be-replaced tone of voice.

"Not can't. Won't. You have two weeks to get ready for the circus, not two years."

He was not the least intimidated by her, and she suspected it was not just because he was the groom's brother. She suspected it would take a great deal to intimidate Drew Jordan. He had that don't-mess-with-me look about his eyes, a set to his admittedly sexy mouth that said he was far more accustomed to giving orders than to taking them.

She debated asking him, again, not to call it a circus, but that went right along with not being able to intimidate him. Becky could tell by the stubborn set of his jaw that she might as well save her breath. She decided levelheaded reason would win the day.

"It's a temporary structure," she explained, the epitome of calm, "and it's imperative. What if we get inclement weather that day?"

Drew tilted his head at her and studied her for long enough that it was disconcerting.

"What?" she demanded.

"I'm trying to figure out if you're part of her Cinderella group or not."

Becky lifted her chin. Okay, so she wasn't Hollywood gorgeous like Allie was, and today—sweaty, casual and sporting a sunburned nose—might not be her best day ever, but why would it be debatable whether she was part of Allie's Cinderella group or not?

She didn't even know what that was. Why did she want to belong to it, or at least seem as if she could?

"What's a Cinderella group?" she asked.

"Total disconnect from reality," he said, nodding at the plan in her hand. "You can't build a pavilion that seats two hundred on an island where supplies have to be barged in. Not in two weeks, probably not even in two years."

"It's temporary," she protested. "It's creating an illusion, like a movie set."

"You're not one of her group," he decided firmly, even though Becky had just clearly demonstrated her expertise about movie sets.

"How do you know?"

"Imperative," he said. *"Inclement."* His lips twitched, and she was aware it was her use of the language that both amused him and told him she was not part of Allie's regular set. Really? She should not be relieved that it was vocabulary and not her looks that had set her apart from Allie's gang.

"Anyway, *inclement* weather—"

Was he making fun of her?

"—is highly unlikely. I Googled it."

She glanced at her laptop screen, which was already open on Google.

"This side of this island gets three days of rain per year," he told her. "In the last forty-two years of record-keeping, would you care to guess how often it has rained on the Big Day, June the third?"

The way he said *Big Day* was in no way preferable to *circus*.

Becky glared at him to make it look as if she was annoyed that he had beat her to the facts. She drew her computer to her, as if she had no intention of taking his word for it, as if she needed to check the details of the June third weather report herself.

Her fingers, acting entirely on their own volition, without any kind of approval from her mind, typed in D-r-e-w J-o-r-d-a-n.

CHAPTER TWO

DREW REGARDED BECKY ENGLISH thoughtfully. He had expected a high-powered and sophisticated West Coast event specialist. Instead, the woman before him, with her sunburned nose and pulled-back hair, barely looked as if she was legal age.

In fact, she looked like an athletic teenager getting ready to go to practice with the high school cheer squad. Since she so obviously was not the image of the professional woman he'd expected, his first impression had been that she must be a young Hollywood hanger-on, being rewarded for loyalty to Allie Ambrosia with a job she was probably not qualified to do.

But no, the woman in front of him had nothing of slick Hollywood about her. The vocabulary threw his initial assessment. The way she talked—with the earnestness of a student preparing for the Scripps National Spelling Bee—made him think that the bookworm geeky girl had been crossed with the high school cheerleader. Who would have expected that to be such an intriguing combination?

Becky's hair was a sandy shade of brown that looked virgin, as if it had never been touched by dye or blond highlights. It looked as if she had spent about thirty seconds on it this morning, scraping it back from her face and capturing it in an elastic band. It was a rather nondescript shade of brown, yet so glossy with good health, Drew felt a startling desire to touch it.

Her eyes were plain old brown, without a drop of makeup around them to make them appear larger, or wider, or darker, or greener. Her skin was pale, which would have been considered unfashionable in the land of endless summer that he came from. Even after only a few days in the tropics, most of which he suspected had been spent inside, the tip of her nose and her cheeks were glowing pink, and she was showing signs of freckling. There was a bit of a sunburn on her slender shoulders.

Her teeth were a touch crooked, one of the front ones ever so slightly overlapping the other one. It was oddly endearing. He couldn't help but notice, as men do, that she was as flat as a board.

Drew Jordan's developments were mostly in Los Angeles. People there—especially people who could afford to buy in his subdivisions—were about the furthest thing from *real* that he could think of.

The women he dealt with had the tiny noses and fat lips, the fake tans and the unwrinkled foreheads. They had every shade of blond hair and the astonishingly inflated breast lines. Their eyes were widened into a look of surgically induced perpetual surprise and their teeth were so white you needed sunglasses on to protect you from smiles.

Drew was not sure when he had become used to it all, but suddenly it seemed very evident to him why he had. There was something about all that fakeness that was *safe* to a dyed-in-the-wool bachelor such as himself.

The cheerleader bookworm girl behind the desk radiated something that was oddly threatening. In a world that seemed to celebrate phony everything, she seemed as if she was 100 percent real.

She was wearing a plain white tank top, and if he leaned forward just a little bit he could see cutoff shorts. Peeking out from under the desk was a pair of sneakers with startling pink laces in them.

"How did you get mixed up with Allie?" he asked. "You do not look the way I would expect a high-profile Hollywood event planner to look."

"How would you expect one to look?" she countered, insulted.

"Not, um, wholesome."

She frowned.

"Take it as a compliment," he suggested.

She looked uncertain about that, but marshaled herself.

"I've run a very successful event planning company for several years," she said with a proud toss of her head.

"In Los Angeles," he said with flat disbelief.

"Well, no, not exactly."

He waited.

She looked flustered, which he enjoyed way more than he should have. She glared at him. "My company serves Moose Run and the surrounding areas."

Was she kidding? It sounded like a name Hollywood would invent to conjure visions of a quaintly rural and charming America that hardly existed anymore. But, no, she had that cute and geeky earnestness about her.

Still, he had to ask. "Moose Run? Seriously?"

"Look it up on Google," she snapped.

"Where is it? The mountains of Appalachia?"

"I said look it up on Google."

But when he crossed his arms over his chest and raised an eyebrow at her, she caved.

"Michigan," she said tersely. "It's a farm community in Michigan. It has a population of about fourteen thousand. Of course, my company serves the surrounding areas, as well."

"Ah. Of course."

"Don't say *ah* like that!"

"Like what?" he said, genuinely baffled.

"Like *that explains everything.*"

"It does. It explains everything about you."

"It does not explain everything about me!" she said. "In fact, it says very little about me."

There were little pink spots appearing on her cheeks, above the sunburned spots.

"Okay," he said, and put up his hands in mock surrender. Really, he should have left it there. He should keep it all business, let her know what she could and couldn't do construction wise with severe time restraints, and that was it. His job done.

But Drew was enjoying flustering her, and the little pink spots on her cheeks.

"How old are you?" he asked.

She folded her arms over her own chest—battle stations—and squinted at him. "That is an inappropriate question. How old are you?" she snapped back.

"I'm thirty-one," he said easily. "I only asked because you look sixteen, but not even Allie would be ridiculous enough to hire a sixteen-year-old to put together this cir—event—would she?"

"I'm twenty-three and Allie is not ridiculous!"

"She isn't?"

His brother's future wife had managed to arrange her very busy schedule—she was shooting a movie in Spain—to grant Drew an audience, once, on a brief return to LA, shortly after Joe had phoned and told him with shy and breathless excitement he was getting married.

Drew had not been happy about the announcement. His brother was twenty-one. To date, Joe hadn't made many major decisions without consulting Drew, though Drew had been opposed to the movie-set building and Joe had gone ahead anyway.

And look where that had led. Because, in a hushed tone of complete reverence, Joe had told Drew *who* he was marrying.

Drew's unhappiness had deepened. He had shared it with Joe. His normally easygoing, amenable brother had yelled at him.

Quit trying to control me. Can't you just be happy for me?

And then Joe, who was usually happy-go-lucky and sunny in nature, had hung up on him. Their conversations since then had been brief and clipped.

Drew had agreed to meet Joe here and help with a few construction projects for the wedding, but he had a secret agenda. He needed to spend time with his brother. Face-to-face time. If he managed to talk some sense into him, all the better.

"I don't suppose Joe is here yet?" he asked Becky with elaborate casualness.

"No." She consulted a thick agenda book. "I have him arriving tomorrow morning, first thing. And Allie arriving the day of the wedding."

Perfect. If he could get Joe away from Allie's influence, his mission—to stop the wedding, or at least reschedule it until cooler heads prevailed—seemed to have a better chance of succeeding.

Drew liked to think he could read people—the woman in front of him being a case in point. But he had come away from his meeting with Allie Ambrosia feeling a disconcerting sense of not being able to read her at all.

Where's my brother? Drew had demanded.

Allie Ambrosia had blinked at him. *No need to make it sound like a kidnapping.*

Which, of course, was exactly what Drew had been feeling it was, and that Allie Ambrosia was solely responsible for the new Joe, who could hang up on his brother and then ignore all his attempts to get in touch with him.

"Allie Ambrosia is sensitive and brilliant and sweet."

Drew watched Becky with interest as the blaze of color deepened over her sunburn. She was going to rise to defend someone she perceived as the underdog, and that told him almost as much about her as the fact that she hailed from Moose Run, Michigan.

Drew was just not sure who would think of Allie Ambrosia as the underdog. He may have been frustrated about his inability to read his future sister-in-law, but neither *sensitive* nor *sweet* would have made his short list of descriptive adjectives. Though they probably would have for Becky, even after such a short acquaintance.

Allie? Brilliant, maybe. Though if she was it had not shown in her vocabulary. Still, he'd been aware of the possibility of great cunning. She had seemed to Drew to be able to play whatever role she wanted, the real person, whoever and whatever that was, hidden behind eyes so astonishingly emerald he'd wondered if she enhanced the color with contact lenses.

He'd come away from Allie frustrated. He had agreed to build some things for the damn wedding, hoping, he supposed, that this seeming capitulation to his brother's plans would open the door to communication between them and he could talk some sense into Joe.

He'd have his chance tomorrow. Today, he could unabashedly probe the secrets of the woman his brother had decided to marry.

"And you would know Allie is sensitive and brilliant and sweet, why?" he asked Becky, trying not to let on just how pleased he was to have found someone who actually seemed to know Allie.

"We went to school together."

Better still. Someone who knew Allie *before* she'd caught her big break playing Peggy in a sleeper of a movie called *Apple Mountain.*

"Allie Ambrosia grew up in Moose Run, Michigan?" He prodded her along. "That is not in the official biography."

He thought Becky was going to clam up, careful about saying anything about her boss and old school chum, but her need to defend won out.

"Her Moose Run memories may not be her fondest ones," Becky offered, a bit reluctantly.

"I must say Allie has come a long way from Moose Run," he said.

"How do you know? How well do you know Allie?"

"I admit I'm assuming, since I hardly know her at all," Drew said. "This is what I know. She's had a whirlwind relationship with my little brother, who is building a set on one of her movies. They've known each other weeks, not months. And suddenly they are getting married. It can't last, and this is an awful lot of money and time and trouble to go to for something that can't last."

"You're cynical," she said, as if that was a bad thing.

"We can't all come from Moose Run, Michigan."

She squinted at him, not rising to defend herself, but staying focused on him, which made him very uncomfortable. "You are really upset that they are getting married."

He wasn't sure he liked that amount of perception. He didn't say anything.

"Actually, I think you don't like weddings, period."

"What is this, a party trick? You can read my mind?" He intended it to sound funny, but he could hear a certain amount of defensiveness in his tone.

"So, it's true then."

"Big deal. Lots of men don't like weddings."

"Why is that?"

He frowned at her. He wanted to ferret out some facts about Allie, or talk about construction. He was comfortable talking about construction, even on an ill-conceived project like this. He was a problem solver. He was not comfortable discussing feelings, which an aversion to weddings came dangerously close to.

"They just don't like them," he said stubbornly. "Okay, I don't like them."

"I'm curious about who made you your brother's keeper," she said. "Shouldn't your parents be talking to him about this?"

"Our parents are dead."

When something softened in her face, he deliberately hardened himself against it.

"Oh," Becky said quietly, "I'm so sorry. So you, as older brother, are concerned, and at the same time have volunteered to help out. That's very sweet."

"Let's get something straight right now. There is nothing sweet about me."

"So why did you agree to help at all?"

He shrugged. "Brothers help each other."

Joe's really upset by your reaction to our wedding, Allie had told him. *If you agreed to head up the construction, he would see it was just an initial reaction of surprise and that of course you want what is best for your own brother.*

Oh, he wanted what was best for Joe, all right. Something must have flashed across Drew's face, because Becky's brow lowered.

"Are you going to try to stop the wedding?" she asked suspiciously.

Had he telegraphed his intention to Allie, as well? "Joe's all grown up, and capable of making up his own mind. But so am I. And it seems like a crazy, impulsive decision he's made."

"You didn't answer the question."

"You'd think he would have asked me what I thought," Drew offered grimly.

A certain measure of pain escaped in that statement, and so he frowned at Becky, daring her to give him sympathy.

Thankfully, she did not even try. "Is this why I can't have the pavilion? Are you trying to sabotage the whole thing?"

"No," he said curtly. "I'll do what I can to give my brother and his beloved a perfect day. If he comes to his senses before then—" He lifted a shoulder.

"If he changes his mind, that would be a great deal of time and money down the tubes," Becky said.

Drew lifted his shoulder again. "I'm sure you would still get paid."

"That's hardly the point!"

"It's the whole point of running a business." He glanced at her and sighed. "Please don't tell me you do it for love."

Love.

Except for what he felt for his brother, his world was comfortably devoid of that pesky emotion. He was sorry he'd even mentioned the word in front of Becky English.

CHAPTER THREE

"SINCE YOU BROUGHT it up," Becky said solemnly, "I got the impression from Allie that she and your brother are head over heels in love with one another."

"Humph." There was no question his brother was over the moon, way past the point where he could be counted on to make a rational decision. Allie was more difficult to interpret. Allie was an actress. She pretended for a living. It seemed to Drew his brother's odds of getting hurt were pretty good.

"Joe could have done worse," Becky said, quietly. "She's a beautiful, successful woman."

"Yeah, there's that."

"There's that cynicism again."

Cynical. Yes, that described Drew Jordan to an absolute T. And he liked being around people who were as hard-edged as him. Didn't he?

"Look, my brother is twenty-one years old. That's a little young to be making this kind of decision."

"You know, despite your barely contained scorn for Moose Run, Michigan, it's a traditional place where they love nothing more than a wedding. I've planned dozens of them."

Drew had to bite his tongue to keep from crushing her with a sarcastic *Dozens?*

"I've been around this for a while," she continued. "Take it from me. Age is no guarantee of whether a marriage is going to work out."

"He's known her about eight weeks, as far as I can tell!" He was confiding his doubts to a complete stranger, which was not like him. It was even more unlike him to be hoping this wet-behind-the-ears country girl from Moose Run, Michigan, might be able to shed some light on his brother's mysterious, flawed decision-making process. This was why he liked being around people as *not* sweet as himself. There was no probing of the secrets of life.

"That doesn't seem to reflect on how the marriage is going to work out, either."

"Well, what does then?"

"When I figure it out, I'm going to bottle it and sell it," she said. There was that earnestness again. "But I've planned the weddings of lots of young people who are still together. Young people have big dreams and lots of energy. You need that to buy your first house and have your first baby, and juggle three jobs and—"

"Baby?" Drew said, horrified. "Is she pregnant?" That would explain his brother's rush to the altar of love.

"I don't think so," Becky said.

"But you don't know for certain."

"It's none of my business. Or yours. But even if she is, lots of those kinds of marriages make it, too. I've planned weddings for people who have known each other for weeks, and weddings for people who have known each other for years. I planned one wedding for a couple who had lived together for sixteen years. They were getting a divorce six months later. But I've seen lots of marriages that work."

"And how long has your business been running?"

"Two years," she said.

For some reason, Drew was careful not to be quite as sarcastic as he wanted to be. "So, you've seen lots that work for two years. Two years is hardly a testament to a solid relationship."

"You can tell," she said stubbornly. "Some people are going to be in love forever."

Her tone sounded faintly wistful. Something uncomfortable shivered along his spine. He had a feeling he was looking at one of those forever kinds of girls. The kind who were not safe to be around at all.

Though it would take more than a sweet girl from Moose Run to penetrate the armor around his hard heart. He felt impatient with himself for the direction of his thoughts. Wasn't it proof that she was already penetrating something since they were having this discussion that had nothing to do with her unrealistic building plans?

Drew shook off the feeling and fixed Becky with a particularly hard look.

"Sheesh, maybe you are a member of the Cinderella club, after all."

"Despite the fact I run a company called Happily-Ever-After—"

He closed his eyes. "That's as bad as Moose Run."

"It is a great name for an event planning company."

"I think I'm getting a headache."

"But despite my company name, I have long since given up on fairy tales."

He opened his eyes and looked at her. "Uh-huh," he said, loading those two syllables with doubt.

"I have!"

"Lady, even before I heard the name of your company, I could tell that you have 'I'm waiting for my prince to come' written all over you."

"I do not."

"You've had a heartbreak."

"I haven't," she said. She was a terrible liar.

"Maybe it wasn't quite a heartbreak. A romantic disappointment."

"Now who is playing the mind reader?"

"Aha! I was right, then."

She glared at him.

"You'll get over it. And then you'll be in the prince market all over again."

"I won't."

"I'm not him, by the way."

"Not who?"

"Your prince."

"Of all the audacious, egotistical, ridiculous—"

"Just saying. I'm not anybody's prince."

"You know what? It is more than evident you could not be mistaken for Prince Charming even if you had a crown on your head and tights and golden slippers!"

Now that he'd established some boundaries, he felt he could tease her just a little. "Please tell me you don't like men who wear tights."

"What kind of man I like is none of your business!"

"Correct. It's just that we will be working in close proximity. My shirt has been known to come off. It has been known to make women swoon." He smiled.

He was enjoying this way more than he had a right

to, but it was having the desired effect, putting up a nice big wall between them, and he hadn't even had to barge in the construction material to do it.

"I'm not just *getting* a headache," she said. "I've had one since you marched through my door."

"Oh, great," he said. "There's nothing I like as much as a little competition. Let's see who can give who a bigger headache."

"The only way I could give you a bigger headache than the one you are giving me is if I smashed this lamp over your head."

Her hand actually came to rest on a rather heavy-looking brass lamp on the corner of her desk. It was evident to him that she would have loved to do just that if she wasn't such a prim-and-proper type.

"I'm bringing out the worst in you," he said with satisfaction. She looked at her hand, resting on the lamp, and looked so appalled with herself that Drew did the thing he least wanted to do. He laughed.

Becky snatched her hand back from the brass lamp, annoyed with herself, miffed that she was providing amusement for the very cocky Mr. Drew Jordan. She was not the type who smashed people over the head with lamps. Previously, she had not even been the type who would have ever thought about such a thing. She had dealt with some of the world's—or at least Michigan's—worst Bridezillas, and never once had she laid hand to lamp. It was one of the things she prided herself in. She kept her cool.

But Drew Jordan had that look of a man who could turn a girl inside out before she even knew what had hit her. He could make a woman who trusted her cool suddenly aware that fingers of heat were licking away inside her, begging for release. And it was disturbing that he knew it!

He was laughing at her. It was super annoying that instead of being properly indignant, steeling herself against attractions that he was as aware of as she was, she could not help but notice how cute he was when he laughed—that sternness stripped from his face, an almost boyish mischievousness lurking underneath.

She frowned at her computer screen, pretending she was getting down to business and that she had called up the weather to double-check his facts. Instead, she learned her head of construction was also the head of a multimillion-dollar Los Angeles development company.

The bride's future brother-in-law was not an out-of-work tradesman that Becky could threaten to fire. He ran a huge development company in California. No wonder he seemed to be impatient at being pressed into the service of his very famous soon-to-be sister-in-law.

No wonder he'd been professional enough to Google the weather. Becky wondered why she hadn't thought of doing that. It was nearly the first thing she did for every event.

It was probably because she was being snowed under by Allie's never-ending requests. Just now she was trying to find a way to honor Allie's casually thrown-out email, received that morning, which requested freshly planted lavender tulips—picture attached—to line the outdoor aisle she would walk down toward her husband-to-be.

Google, that knowledge reservoir of all things, told

Becky she could not have lavender tulips—or any kind of tulip for that matter—in the tropics in June.

What Google confirmed for her now was not the upcoming weather forecast or the impossibility of lavender tulips, but that Drew Jordan was used to million-dollar budgets.

Becky, on the other hand, had started shaking when she had opened the promised deposit check from Allie. Up until then, it had seemed to her that maybe she was being made the butt of a joke. But that check—made out to Happily-Ever-After—had been for more money than she had ever seen in her life.

With trembling fingers she had dialed the private cell number Allie had provided.

"Is this the budget?"

"No, silly, just the deposit."

"What exactly is your budget?" Becky had asked. Her voice had been shaking as badly as her fingers.

"Limitless," Allie had said casually. "And I fully intend to exceed it. You don't think I'm going to be outdone by Roland Strump's daughter, do you?"

"Allie, maybe you should hire whoever did the Strump wedding, I—"

"Nonsense. Have fun with it, for Pete's sake. Haven't you ever had fun? I hope you and Drew don't manage to bring down the mood of the whole wedding. Sourpusses."

Sourpuss? She was studious to be sure, but sour? Becky had put down the phone contemplating that. Had she ever had fun? Even at Happily-Ever-After, planning fun events for other people was very serious business, indeed.

Well, now she knew who Drew was. And Allie had

been right when it came to him. He could definitely be a sourpuss! It was more worrying that he planned to take off his shirt. She had to get back to business.

"Mr. Jordan—"

"Drew is fine. And what should I call you?"

Barnum. "Becky is fine. We can't just throw a bunch of tables out on the front lawn as if this were the church picnic."

"We're back to that headache." His lips twitched. "I'm afraid my experience with church picnics has been limited."

Yes, it was evident he was all devilish charm and dark seduction, while it was written all over her that that was what she came from: church picnics and 4-H clubs, a place where the Fourth of July fireworks were *the* event of the year.

She shifted her attention to the second *no.* "And we absolutely need some sort of dance floor. Have you ever tried to dance on grass? Or sand?"

"I'm afraid," Drew said, "that falls outside of the realm of my experience, too. And you?"

"Oh, you know," she said. "We like to dust up our heels after the church picnic."

He nodded, as if that was more than evident to him and he had missed her sarcasm completely.

She focused on his third veto. She looked at her clumsy drawing of a small gazebo on the beach. She had envisioned Allie and Joe saying their vows under it, while their guests sat in beautiful lightweight chairs looking at them and the sea beyond them.

"And what's your complaint with this one?"

"I'll forgive you this oversight because of where you are from."

"Oversight?"

"I wouldn't really expect a girl from Michigan to have foreseen this. The *wedding*—" he managed to fill that single word with a great deal of contempt "—according to my notes, is supposed to take place at 4:00 p.m. on June third."

"Correct."

"If you Google the tide chart for that day, you'll see that your gazebo would have water lapping up to the third stair. I'm not really given to omens, but I would probably see that as one."

She was feeling very tired of Google, except in the context of learning about him. It seemed to her he was the kind of man who brought out the weakness in a woman, even one who had been made as cynical as she had been. Because she felt she could ogle him all day long. And he knew it, she reminded herself.

"So," she said, a little more sharply than intended, "what do you suggest?"

"If we scratch the pavilion for two hundred—"

"I can get more people to help you."

He went on as if she hadn't spoken. "I can probably build you a rudimentary gazebo at a different location."

"What about the dance floor?"

"I'll think about it."

He said that as if he were the boss, not her. From what she had glimpsed about him on the internet he was very used to being in charge. And he obviously knew his stuff, and was good with details. He had spotted the weather and the tides, after all. Really, she should be grateful. What if her bride had marched down her tulip-lined aisle—or whatever the aisle ended up being lined with—to a wedding gazebo that was slowly being swallowed by water?

It bothered her to even think it, but Drew Jordan was right. That would have been a terrible omen.

Still, gratitude was not what Becky felt. Not at all.

"You are winning the headache contest by a country mile," she told him.

"I'm no kind of expert on the country," he said, without regret, "but I am competitive."

"What did Allie tell you? Are you in charge of construction?"

"Absolutely."

He said it too quickly and with that self-assured smile of a man way too used to having his own way, particularly with the opposite sex.

"I'm going to have to call Allie and see what that means," Becky said, steeling herself against that smile. "I'm happy to leave construction to you, but I think I should have the final word on what we are putting up and where."

"I'm okay with that. As long as it's reasonable."

"I'm sure we define that differently."

He flashed his teeth at her again. "I'm sure we do."

"Would it help you do your job if I brought more people on-site? Carpenters and such?"

"That's a great idea, but I don't work with strangers. Joe and I have worked together a lot. He'll be here tomorrow."

"That wouldn't be very romantic, him building the stuff for his own wedding."

"Or you could see it as him putting an investment and some effort into his own wedding."

She sighed. "You want him here so you can try to bully him out of getting married."

"I resent the implication I would bully him."

But Becky was stunned to see doubt flash across those self-confident features. "He isn't talking to you, is he?" Becky guessed softly.

She could tell Drew was not accustomed to this level of perception. He didn't like it one little bit.

"I have one of my teams arriving soon. And Joe. I'm here a day early to do some initial assessments. What I need is for you to pick the site for the exchange of vows so that I can put together a plan. We don't have as much time as you think."

Which was truly frightening, because she did not think they had any time at all. Becky looked at her desk: flowers to be ordered, ceremony details to be finalized, accommodations to be organized, boat schedules, food, not just for the wedding feast, but for the week to follow, and enough staff to pull off pampering two hundred people.

"And don't forget fireworks," she added.

"Excuse me?"

"Nothing," she muttered. She did not want to be thinking of fireworks around a man like Drew Jordan. Her eyes drifted to his lips. If she were ever to kiss someone like that, it would be the proverbial fireworks. And he knew it, too. That was why he was smiling evilly at her!

Suddenly, it felt like nothing in the world would be better than to get outside away from this desk—and from him—and see this beautiful island. So far, she had mostly experienced it by looking out her office window.

The sun would be going down soon. She could find a place to hold the wedding and watch the sun go down.

"Okay," she said. "I'll find a new site. I'll let you know as soon as I've got it."

"Let's do it together. That might save us some grief."

She was not sure that doing anything with him was going to save her some grief. She needed to get away from him…and the thoughts of fireworks he had caused.

CHAPTER FOUR

"I'D PREFER TO do it on my own," Becky said, even though it seemed ungracious to say so. She felt a need to establish who was running the cir—show.

"But here's the problem," Drew said with annoying and elaborate patience.

"Yes?"

"You'll pick a site on your own, and then I'll go look at it and say no, and so then you'll pick another site on your own, and I'll go look at it and say no."

She scowled at him. "You're being unnecessarily negative."

He shrugged. "I'm just making the point that we could, potentially, go on like that endlessly, and there is a bit of a time crunch here."

"I think you just like using the word *no*," she said grumpily.

"Yes," he said, deadpan, as if he was not being deliberately argumentative now.

She should argue that she was quite capable of picking the site by herself and that she had no doubt her next selection would be fine, but her first choice was not exactly proof of that. And besides, then who would be the argumentative one?

"It's too late today," Drew decided. "Joe's coming in on the first flight. Why don't we pick him up and the three of us will pick a site that works for the gazebo?"

"Yes, that would be fine," she said, aware her voice was snapping with ill grace. Really, it was an opportunity. Tomorrow morning she would not scrape her hair back into a careless ponytail. She would apply makeup to hide how her fair skin, fresh out of a Michigan winter, was already blotchy from the sun.

Should she wear her meet-the-potential-client suit, a cream-colored linen by a famous designer? That would certainly make a better impression than shorty-shorts and a sleeveless tank that could be mistaken for underwear!

But the following morning it was already hot, and there was no dry cleaner on the island to take a sweat-drenched dress to.

Aware she was putting way too much effort into her appearance, Becky donned white shorts and a sleeveless sun-yellow shirt. She put on makeup and left her hair down. And then she headed out of her room.

She met Drew on the staircase.

He looked unreasonably gorgeous!

"Good morning," she said. She was stupidly pleased by how his eyes trailed to her hair and her faintly glossed lips.

He returned her greeting gruffly and then went down the stairs in front of her, taking them two at a time. But he stopped and held open the main door for her. They were hit by a wall of heat.

"It's going to be even hotter in two weeks," Drew

told her, when he watched her pause and draw in her breath on the top stair of the castle.

“Must you be so negative?”

“Pragmatic,” he insisted. “Plus…”

“Don’t tell me. I already know. You looked it up. That’s how you know it will be even hotter in two weeks.”

He nodded, pleased with himself.

“Keep it up,” she warned him, “and you’ll have to present me with the prize. A king-size bottle of headache relief.”

They stood at the main door to the castle, huge half circles of granite forming a staircase down to a sparkling expanse of emerald lawn. The lawn was edged with a row of beautifully swaying palm trees, and beyond that was a crescent of powdery white sand beach.

“That beach looks so much less magical now that I know it’s going to be underwater at four o’clock on June the third.”

Drew glanced at Becky. She looked older and more sophisticated with her hair down and makeup on. She had gone from cute to attractive.

It occurred to Drew that Becky was the kind of woman who brought out things in a man that he would prefer to think he didn’t have. Around a woman like this a man could find himself wanting to protect himself—and her—from disappointments. That’s all he wanted for Joe, too, not to bully him but to protect him.

He’d hated that question, the one he hadn’t answered. Had he bullied his brother? He hoped not. But the sad truth was Joe had been seven when Drew, seventeen, was appointed his guardian. Drew had floundered, in way over his head, and he'd resorted to doing whatever needed to be done to get his little brother through childhood.

No wonder his brother was so hungry for love that he'd marry the first beautiful woman who blinked sideways at him.

Unless he could talk some sense into him. He cocked his head. He was pretty sure he could hear the plane coming.

"How hot is it supposed to be on June third?" she asked. He could hear the reluctance to even ask in her voice.

"You know that expression? Hotter than Hades—"

"Never mind. I get it. All the more reason that we really need the pavilion," she said. "We'll need protection from the sun. I planned to have the tables running this way, so everyone could just turn their heads and see the ocean as the sun is going down. The head table could be there, at the bottom of the stairs. Imagine the bride and groom coming down that staircase to join their guests."

Her voice had become quite dreamy. Had she really tried to tell him she was not a romantic? He knew he'd pegged it. She'd had some kind of setback in the romance department, but inside her was still a giddy girl with unrealistic dreams about her prince coming. He had to make sure she knew that was not him.

"Well, I already told you, you can't have that," he said gruffly. He did not enjoy puncturing her dream as much as he wanted to. He did not enjoy being mean as much as he would have liked. He told himself it was for her own good.

He was good at doing things for other people's own

good. You could ask Joe, though his clumsy attempts at parenting were no doubt part of why his brother was running off half-cocked to get married.

"I'm sure we can figure out something," Becky said of her pavilion dream.

"We? No, *we* can't."

This was better. They were going to talk about practicalities, as dream-puncturing as those could be!

The plane was circling now, and they moved toward the airstrip.

He continued, "What you're talking about is an open, expansive structure with huge unsupported spans. You'd need an architect and an engineer."

"I have a tent company I use at home," Becky said sadly, "but they are booked nearly a year in advance. I've tried a few others. Same story. Plus, the planes that can land here aren't big enough to carry that much canvas, and you have to book the supply barge. There's only one with a flat enough bottom to dock here. An unlimited budget can't get you what you might think."

"Unlimited?" He heard the horror in his voice.

She ignored him. "Are you sure I'd need an architect and an engineer, even for something so temporary?"

He slid her a look. She looked quite deflated by all this.

"Especially for something so temporary," he told her. "I'm sure the last thing Allie wants is to be making the news for the collapse of her wedding pavilion. I can almost see the headlines now. 'Three dead, one hundred and eighty-seven injured, event planner and building contractor missing.'"

He heard her little gasp and glanced at her. She was blushing profusely.

"Not missing like *that*," he said.

"Like what?" she choked.

"Like whatever thought is making you blush like that."

"I'm not blushing. The sun has this effect on me."

"Sheesh," he said, as if she had not denied the blush at all. "It's not as if I said that while catastrophe unfolded all around them, the event planner and the contractor went missing *together*."

"I said I wasn't blushing! I never would have thought about us together in any way." Her blush deepened.

He watched her. "You aren't quite the actress that your employer is."

"I am not thinking of us together," she insisted. Her voice was just a little shrill. He realized he quite enjoyed teasing her.

"No?" he said, silkily. "You and I seeking shelter under a palm frond while disaster unfolds all around us?"

Her eyes moved skittishly to his lips and then away. He took advantage of her looking away to study her lips in profile. They were plump little plums, ripe for picking. He was almost sorry he had started this. Almost.

"You're right. You are not a prince. You are evil," she decided, looking back at him. There was a bit of reluctant laughter lurking in her eyes.

He twirled an imaginary moustache. "Yes, I am. Just waiting for an innocent from Moose Run, Michigan, to cross my path so that in the event of a tropical storm, and a building collapse, I will still be entertained."

A little smile tugged at the lips he had just noticed were quite luscious. He was playing a dangerous game.

"Seriously," she said, and he had a feeling she was

the type who did not indulge in lighthearted banter for long, "Allie doesn't want any of this making the news. I'm sure she told you the whole wedding is top secret. She does not want helicopters buzzing her special day."

Drew felt a bit cynical about that. Anyone who wanted a top secret wedding did not invite two hundred people to it. Still, he decided, now might not be the best time to tell Becky a helicopter buzzing might be the least of her worries. When he'd left the States yesterday, all the entertainment shows had been buzzing with the rumors of Allie's engagement.

Was the famous actress using his brother—and everyone else, including small-town Becky English—to ensure Allie Ambrosia was front and center in the news just as her new movie was coming out?

Even though it went somewhat against his blunt nature, the thought that Becky might be being played made Drew soften his bad news a bit. "This close to the equator it's fully dark by six o'clock. The chance of heatstroke for your two hundred guests should be minimized by that."

They took a path through some dense vegetation. On the other side was the airstrip.

"Great," she said testily, though she was obviously relieved they were going to discuss benign things like the weather. "Maybe I can create a kind of 'room' feeling if I circle the area with torches and dress up the tables with linens and candles and flowers and hope for the best."

"Um, about the torches? And candles?" He squinted at the plane touching down on the runway.

"What?"

"According to Google, the trade winds seem to pick

up in the late afternoon. And early evening. Without any kind of structure to protect from the wind, I think they'll just blow out. Or worse."

"So, first you tell me I can't have a structure, and then you tell me all the problems I can expect because I don't have a structure?"

He shrugged. "One thing does tend to lead to another."

"If the wind is strong enough to blow out the candles, we could have other problems with it, too."

"Oh, yeah, absolutely. Tablecloths flying off tables. Women's dresses blowing up over their heads. Napkins catching fire. Flower arrangements being smashed. There's really a whole lot of things people should think about before planning their wedding on a remote island in the tropics."

Becky glared at him. "You know what? I barely know you and I hate you already."

He nodded. "I have that effect on a lot of people."

He watched the plane taxi toward them and grind to a halt in front of them.

"I'm sure you do," she said snippily.

"Does this mean our date under the palm frond is off?"

"It was never on!"

"You should think about it—the building collapsed, the tablecloths on fire, women's dresses blowing over their heads as they run shrieking..."

"Please stop."

But he couldn't. He could tell he very nearly had her where he wanted her. Why did he feel so driven to make little Miss Becky English angry? But also to make her laugh?

"And you and me under a palm frond, licking wedding cake off each other's fingers."

At first she looked appalled. But then a smile tickled her lips. And then she giggled. And then she was laughing. In a split second, every single thing about her seemed transformed. She went from plain to pretty.

Very pretty.

This was exactly what he had wanted: to glimpse what the cool Miss English would look like if she let go of control.

It was more dangerous than Drew had anticipated. It made him want to take it a step further, to make her laugh harder or to take those little lips underneath his and…

He reminded himself she was not the type of girl he usually invited out to play. Despite the fact she was being relied on to put on a very sophisticated event, there didn't seem to be any sophistication about her.

He had already figured out there was a heartbreak in her past. That was the only reason a girl as apple pie as her claimed to be jaundiced about romance. He could tell it wasn't just dealing with people's wedding insanity that had made her want to be cynical, even as it was all too evident she was not. He had seen the truth in the dreamy look when she had started talking about how she wanted it all to go.

He could tell by looking at her exactly what she needed, and it wasn't a job putting together other people's fantasies.

It was a husband who adored her. And three children. And a little house where she could sew curtains for the windows and tuck bright annuals into the flower beds every year.

It was whatever the perfect life in Moose Run, Michigan, looked like.

Drew knew he could never give her those things. Never. He'd experienced too much loss and too much responsibility in his life.

Still, there was one thing a guy as jaundiced as him did not want or need. To be stuck on a deserted island with a female whose laughter could turn her from a plain old garden-variety girl next door into a goddess in the blink of an eye.

He turned from her quickly and watched as the door of the plane opened. The crew got off, opened the cargo hold and began unloading stuff beside the runway.

He frowned. No Joe.

He took his phone out of his pocket and stabbed in a text message. He pushed Send, but the island did not have great service in all places. The message to his brother did not go through.

Becky was searching his face, which he carefully schooled not to show his disappointment.

"I guess we'll have to find that spot ourselves. Joe will probably come on the afternoon flight. Let's see what we can find this way."

Instead of following the lawn to where it dropped down to the beach, he followed it north to a line of palm trees. A nice wide trail dipped into them, and he took it.

"It's like jungle in here," she said.

"Think of the possibilities. Joe could swing down from a vine. In a loincloth. Allie could be waiting for him in a tree house, right here."

"No, no and especially no," she said.

He glanced behind him. She had stopped to look at

a bright red hibiscus. She plucked it off and tucked it behind her ear.

"In the tropics," he told her, "when you wear a flower behind your ear like that, it means you are available. You wouldn't want the cook getting the wrong idea."

She glared at him, plucked the flower out and put it behind her other ear.

"Now it means you're married."

"There's no winning, is there?" she asked lightly.

No, there wasn't. The flower looked very exotic in her hair. It made him very aware, again, of the enchantment of tropical islands. He turned quickly from her and made his way down the path.

After about five minutes in the deep shade of the jungle, they came out to another beach. It was exposed to the wind, which played in the petals of the flower above her ear, lifted her bangs from her face and pressed her shirt to her.

"Oh," she called, "it's beautiful."

She had to shout because unlike the beach the castle overlooked, this one was not in a protected cove.

It was a beautiful beach. A surfer would probably love it, but it would have to be a good surfer. There were rocky outcrops stretching into the water that looked like they would be painful to hit and hard to avoid.

"It's too loud," he said over the crashing of the waves. "They'd be shouting their vows."

He turned and went back into the shaded jungle. For some reason, he thought she would just follow him, and it took him a few minutes to realize he was alone.

He turned and looked. The delectable Miss Becky English was nowhere to be seen. He went back along the path, annoyed. Hadn't he made it perfectly clear they had time constraints?

When he got back out to the beach, his heart went into his throat. She had climbed up onto one of the rocky outcrops. She was standing there, bright as the sun in that yellow shirt, as a wave smashed on the rock just beneath her. Her hands were held out and her face lifted to the spray of white foam it created. With the flower in her hair, she looked more like a goddess than ever, performing some ritual to the sea.

Did she know nothing of the ocean? Of course she didn't. They had already established that. That, coming from Moose Run, there were things she could not know about.

"Get down from there," he shouted. "Becky, get down right now."

He could see the second wave building, bigger than the first that had hit the rock. The waves would come in sets. And the last wave in the set would be the biggest.

The wind swallowed his voice, though she turned and looked at him. She smiled and waved. He could see the surf rising behind her alarmingly. The second wave hit the rock. She turned away from him, and hugged herself in delight as the spray fell like thick mist all around her.

"Get away from there," he shouted. She turned and gave him a puzzled look. He started to run.

Becky had her back to the third wave when it hit. It hit the backs of her legs. Drew saw her mouth form a surprised O, and then her arms were flailing as she tried to regain her balance. The wave began pulling back, with at least as much force as it had come in with. It yanked her off the rock as if she were a rag doll.

CHAPTER FIVE

BECKY FELT THE shocked helplessness as her feet were jerked out from under her and she was swept off the rock. The water closed over her head and filled her mouth and nose. She popped back up like a cork, but her swimming skills were rudimentary, and she was not sure they would have helped her against the fury of the sea. She was being pulled out into what seemed to be an endless abyss. She tried frantically to swim back in toward shore. In seconds she was as exhausted as she had ever been.

I'm going to drown, she thought, stunned, choking on water and fear. How had this happened? One moment life had seemed so pleasant and beautiful and then…it was over.

Her life was going to be over. She waited, helplessly, for it to flash before her eyes. Instead, she found herself thinking that Drew had been right. It hadn't been a heartbreak. It had been a romantic disappointment. Ridiculous to think that right now, but on the other hand, right now seemed as good a time as any to be acutely and sadly aware of things she had missed.

"Hey!" His voice carried over the crashing of the sea. "Hang on."

Becky caught a glimpse of the rock she had fallen off. Drew was up there. And then she went under the water again.

When she surfaced, Drew was in the water, slashing through the roll of the waves toward her. "Don't panic," he called over the roar of the water pounding the rock outcropping.

She wanted to tell him it was too late for that. She was already panicked.

"Tread," he yelled. "Don't try to swim. Not yet. Look at my face. Nowhere else. Look at me."

Her eyes fastened on his face. There was strength and calm in his features, as if he did this every day. He was close to her now.

"I'm going to come to you," he shouted, "but you have to be calm first. If you panic, you will kill us both."

It seemed his words, and the utter strength and determination in his face, poured a honey of calm over her, despite the fact she was still bobbing like a cork in a ravaged sea. He seemed to see or sense the moment she stopped panicking, and he moved in close.

She nearly sobbed with relief when Drew reached out and touched her, then folded his arms around her and pulled her in tight to him. He was strong in the water—she suspected, abstractly, he was strong everywhere in his life—and she rested into his embrace, surrendering to his warmth. She could feel the power of him in his arms and where she was pressed into the wet slickness of his chest.

"Just let it carry you," he said. "Don't fight it anymore"

It seemed as if he could be talking about way more than water. It could be a message about life.

It seemed the water carried them out forever, but eventually it dumped them in a calmer place, just beyond where the waves began to crest. Becky could feel the water lose its grip on her, even as he refused to.

She never took her eyes off his face. Her mind seemed to grow calmer and calmer, even amused. If this was the last thing she would see, it told her, that wasn't so bad.

"Okay," he said, "can you swim?"

"Dog paddle." The water was not cold, but her voice was shaking.

"That will do. Swim that way. Do your best. I've got you if you get tired." He released her.

That way was not directly to the shore. He was asking her to swim parallel to the shore instead of in. But she tried to do as he asked. She was soon floundering, so tired she could not lift her arms.

"Roll over on your back," he said, and she did so willingly. His hand cupped her chin and she was being pulled through the water. He was an enormously strong swimmer.

"Okay, this is a good spot." He released her again and she came upright and treaded water. "Go toward shore. I've got you, I'm right with you."

She was scared to go back into the waves. It was too much. She was exhausted. But she glanced at his face once more and found her own courage there.

"Get on your tummy, flat as a board, watch for the next wave and ride it in. Watch for those rocks on the side."

She did as she was told. She knew she had no choice. She had to trust him completely. She felt the wave lift her up and drive her toward the shore at a stunning speed. And then it spit her out. She was lying in shallow water, but she could already feel the wave pulling at her, trying to drag her back in. She used what little strength she had left to scramble to her knees and crawl through the sugar pebbles of the sand.

Drew came and scooped her out of the water, lifted her to his chest and struggled out of the surf.

On the beach, above the foaming line of the ocean, he set her down on her back in the sun-warmed sand. For a moment she looked at the clear and endless blue of the sky. It was the very same sky it had been twenty minutes ago, but everything felt changed, some awareness sharp as glass within her. She rolled over onto her stomach and rested her head on her forearms. He flung himself onto the sand beside her, breathing hard.

"Did you just save my life?" she whispered. Her voice was hoarse. Her throat hurt from swallowing salt water. She felt drowsy and extraordinarily peaceful.

"You'll want to make sure this beach is posted before guests start arriving," he finally said, when he spoke.

"You didn't answer the question," she said, taking a peek at him over her folded arm. "Is that a habit with you?"

Drew didn't answer. She looked at him, feeling as if she was drinking him in, as if she could never get enough of looking at him. It was probably natural to feel that way after someone had just saved your life, and she did not try to make herself stop.

She was in a state of altered awareness. She could see the water beading on his eyelashes, and the sun streaming through his wet hair. She could see through his soaked shirt where it was plastered to his body.

"Did you just save my life?" she asked again.

"I think you Michigan girls should stay away from the ocean."

"Do you ever just answer a question, Drew Jordan? Did you save my life?"

He was silent again.

"You did," she finally answered for him.

She could not believe the gratitude she felt. To be alive. It was as if the life force was zinging inside her, making her every cell quiver.

"You risked yourself for me. I'm nearly a complete stranger."

"No, you're not. Winning the headache competition, by the way."

"By a country mile?"

"Oh, yeah."

"That was incredibly heroic." She was not going let him brush it off, though he was determined to.

"Don't make it something it wasn't. I'm nobody's hero."

Just like he had insisted earlier he was nobody's prince.

"Well," she insisted, "you're mine."

He snorted, that sexy, cynical sound he made that was all his own and she found, right now, lying here in the sand, alive, so aware of herself and him, that she liked that sound very much, despite herself.

"I've been around the ocean my whole life," he told her grimly. "I grew up surfing some pretty rough water. I knew what I was doing. Unlike you. That was incredibly stupid."

In her altered state, she was aware that he thought he could break the bond that had been cementing itself into place between them since the moment he had entered the water to rescue her.

"Life can change in a blink," he said sternly. "It can be over in a blink."

He was lecturing her. She suddenly *needed* him to know she could not let him brush it off like that. She needed him to know that the life force was flowing through her. She had an incredible sense of being alive.

"You were right," she said, softly.

There was that snort again. "Of course I'm right. You don't go climbing up on rocks when the surf is that high."

"Not about that. I mean, okay, about that, too, but I wasn't talking about that."

"What were you talking about?"

"It wasn't a heartbreak," Becky said. "It was a romantic disappointment."

"Huh?"

"That's what I thought of when I went into the water. I thought my whole life would flash before my eyes, but instead I thought of Jerry."

"Look, you're obviously in shock and we need to—"

"He was my high school sweetheart. We'd been together since I was seventeen. I'd always assumed we were going to get married. Everybody in the whole town thought we would get married. They called us Salt and Pepper."

"You know what? This will keep. I have to—"

"It won't keep. It's important. I have to say it before I forget it. Before this moment passes."

"Oh, sheesh," he said, his tone indicating he wanted nothing more than for this moment to pass.

"I wanted that. I wanted to be Salt and Pepper, *for-*

ever. My parents had split up the year before. It was awful. My dad owned a hardware store. One of his clerks. And him."

"Look, Becky, you are obviously rattled. You don't have to tell me this."

She could no more have stopped herself from telling him than she could have stopped those waves from pounding on the shore.

"They had a baby together. Suddenly, they were the family we had always been. That we were supposed to be. It was horrible, seeing them all over town, looking at each other. Pushing a baby carriage. I wanted it back. I wanted that feeling of being part of something back. Of belonging."

"Aw, Becky," he said softly. "That sucks. Really it does, but—"

But she had to tell all of it, was compelled to. "Jerry went away to school. My mom didn't have the money for college, and it seemed my dad had new priorities.

"I could see what the community needed, so I started my event company."

"Happily-Ever-After," he said. "Even though you had plenty of evidence of the exact opposite."

"It was way more successful than I had thought it could be. It was way more successful than Jerry thought it could be, too. The more successful I became, the less he liked me."

"Okay. Well. Some guys are like that."

"He broke up with me."

"Yeah, sorry, but now is not the time—"

"This is the reason it's important for me to say it right now. I understand something I didn't understand before. I thought my heart was broken. It is a terrible thing to suffer the humiliation of being ditched in a small town. It was a double humiliation for me. First my dad, and then this. But out there in the water, I felt glad. I felt if I had married him, I would have missed something. Something essential."

"Okay, um—"

"A grand passion."

He said a word under his breath that they disapproved of in Moose Run, Michigan.

"Salt and pepper?" She did a pretty good imitation of his snort. "Why settle for boring old salt and pepper when the world is full of so many glorious flavors?"

"Look, I think you've had a pretty bad shake-up. I don't have a clue what you are talking about, so—"

She knew she was making Drew Jordan wildly uncomfortable, but she didn't care. She planned to make him more uncomfortable yet. She leaned toward him. He stopped talking and watched her warily.

She needed to know if the life force was as intense in him right now as it was in her. She needed to take advantage of this second chance to be alive, to really live.

She touched Drew's back through the wetness of his shirt, and felt the sinewy strength there. The strength that had saved her.

She leaned closer yet. She touched her forehead to his, as if she could make him *feel* what was going on inside her, since words could not express it. He had a chance to move away from her. He did not. He was as caught in what was unfolding as she had been in the wave.

And then, she touched her lips to his, delicately, *needing* the connection to intensify.

His lips tasted of salt and strength and something

more powerful and more timeless than the ocean. That desire that people had within them, not just to live, but to go on.

For a moment, Drew was clearly stunned to find her lips on his. But then, he seemed to get whatever she was trying to tell him, in this primal language that seemed the only thing that could express the celebration of all that lived within her.

His lips answered hers. His tongue chased the ridges of her teeth, and then probed, gently, ever so gently…

It was Becky's turn to be stunned. It was everything she had hoped for. It was everything she had missed.

No, it was *more* than what she had hoped for, and more than what she could have ever imagined. A kiss was not simply a brushing of lips. No! It was a journey, it was a ride on pure energy, it was a connection, it was a discovery, it was an intertwining of the deepest parts of two people, of their souls.

Drew stopped kissing her with such abruptness that she felt forlorn, like a blanket had been jerked from her on a freezing night. He said Moose Run's most disapproved-of word again.

She *liked* the way he said that word, all naughty and nasty.

He found his feet and leaped up, staring down at her. He raked a hand through his hair, and water droplets scattered off his crumpled hair, sparkling like diamonds in the tropical heat. His shirt, crusted in golden sand, was clinging to his chest.

"Geez," he said. "What was that about?"

"I don't know," she said honestly. *But I liked it.*

"A girl like you does not kiss a guy like me!"

She could ask what he meant by a girl like her, but

she already knew that he thought she was small town and naive and hopelessly out of her depth, and not just in the ocean, either. What she wanted to know was what the last half of that sentence meant.

"What do you mean a guy like you?" she asked. Her voice was husky from the salt and from something else. Desire. Desire was burning like a white-hot coal in her belly. It was brand-new, it was embarrassing and it was wonderful.

"Look, Becky, I'm the kind of guy your mother used to warn you about."

Woo-hoo, she thought, but she didn't dare say it. Instead, she said, "The kind who would jump in the water without a thought for his own safety to save someone else?"

"Not that kind!"

She could point out to him that he obviously *was* that kind, and that the facts spoke for themselves, but she probed the deeper part of what was going on.

"What kind of guy then?" she asked, gently curious.

"Self-centered. Commitment-phobic. Good-time Charlie. Confirmed bachelor. They write whole articles about guys like me in your bridal magazines. And not about how to catch me, either. How to give a guy like me a wide berth."

"Just in case you didn't listen to your mother's warnings," she clarified.

He glanced at her. She bit her lip and his gaze rested there, hot with memory, until he seemed to make himself look away.

"I wouldn't have pictured you as any kind of expert about the content of bridal magazines," she said.

"That is not the point!"

"It was just a kiss," she pointed out mildly, "not a posting of the banns."

"You're in shock," he said.

If she was, she hoped she could experience it again, and soon!

CHAPTER SIX

DREW LOOKED AT Becky English. Sprawled out, belly down in the sand, she looked like a drowned rat, her hair plastered to her head, her yellow shirt plastered to her lithe body, both her shirt and her white shorts transparent in their wetness. For a drowned rat, and for a girl from Moose Run, Michigan, she had on surprisingly sexy underwear.

She looked like a drowned rat, and she was a small-town girl, but she sure as hell did not kiss like either one of those things. There had been nothing sweet or shy about that kiss!

It had been hungry enough to devour him.

But, Drew told himself sternly, she was exceedingly vulnerable. She was obviously stunned from what had just happened to her out there at the mercy of the ocean. It was possible she had banged her head riding that final wave in. The blow might have removed the filter from her brain that let her know what was, and what wasn't, appropriate.

But good grief, that kiss. He had to make sure nothing like that ever happened again! How was he going to be able to look at her without recalling the sweet, salty taste of her mouth? Without recalling the sweet welcome? Without recalling the flash of passion, the pull of which was at least as powerful as those waves?

"Becky," he said sternly, "don't make me your hero. I've been cast in that role before, and I stunk at it."

Drew had been seventeen when he became a parent to his brother. He had a sense of having grown up too fast and with too heavy a load. He was not interested in getting himself back into a situation where he was responsible for someone else's happiness and well-being. He didn't feel the evidence showed he had been that good at it.

"It was just a kiss," she said again, a bit too dreamily.

It wasn't just a kiss. If it had been just a kiss he would feel nothing, the same as he always did when he had just a kiss. He wouldn't be feeling this need to set her straight.

"When were you cast in that role before? How come you stank at it?" she asked softly. He noticed that, impossibly, the flower had survived in her hair. Its bright red petals were drooping sadly, kissing the tender flesh of her temple.

"This is not the time or the place," he said curtly before, in this weakened moment, in this contrived atmosphere of closeness, he threw himself down beside her, and let her save him, the way he had just saved her.

"Are you hurt?" he asked, cold and clinical. "Any bumps or bruises? Did you hit your head?"

Thankfully, she was distracted, and considered his question with an almost comical furrowing of her brow.

"I don't think I hit my head, but my leg hurts," she decided. "I think I scraped it on a rock coming in."

She rolled onto her back and then struggled to sit up. He peered over her shoulder. There was six inches of scrapes on the inside of her thigh, one of the marks looked quite deep and there was blood clumping in the sand that clung to it.

What was wrong with him? The first thing he should have done was check for injuries.

He stripped off his wet shirt and got down beside her. This was what was wrong with him. He was way too aware of her. The scent of the sea was clinging to her body, a body he was way too familiar with after having dragged her from the ocean and then accepted the invitation of her lips.

Becky was right. There was something exhilarating about snatching life back out of the jaws of death. That's why he was so aware of her on every level, not thinking with his customary pragmatism.

He brushed the sand away from her wound. He should have known touching the inner thigh of a girl like Becky English was going to be nothing like a man might have expected.

"Ow," she said, and her fingers dug into his shoulder and then lingered there. "Oh, my," she breathed. "You did warn me what would happen if you took your shirt off."

"I was kidding," he said tersely.

"No, you weren't. You were warning me off."

"How's that working for you, Drew?" he muttered to himself. He cleaned the sand away from her wound as best he could, then wrapped it in his soaked shirt.

She sighed with satisfaction like the geeky girl who had just gotten all the words right at the spelling bee. "Women adore you."

"Not ones as smart as you," he said. "Can you stand? We have to find a first aid kit. I think that's just a superficial scrape, but it's bleeding quite a lot and we need to get it looked after."

He helped her to her feet, still way too aware, steeling himself against the silky resilience of her skin. She swayed against him. Her wet curves were pressed into him, and her chin was pressed sharply into his chest as she looked up at him with huge, unblinking eyes.

Had he thought, just an hour ago, her eyes were ordinary brown? They weren't. They were like melted milk chocolate, deep and rich and inviting.

"You were right." She giggled. "I'm swooning."

"Let's hope it's not from blood loss. Can you walk?"

"Of course."

She didn't move.

He sighed and scooped her up, cradling her to his chest, one arm under her knees, the other across her back. She was lighter than he could have believed, and her softness pressed into him was making him way more vulnerable than the embraces of women he'd known who had far more in the curvy department.

"You're very masterful," she said, snuggling into him.

"In this day and age how can that be a good thing?"

"It's a secret longing."

He did not want to hear about her secret longings!

"If you don't believe me, read—"

"Stop it," he said grimly.

"I owe you my life."

"I said stop it."

"You are not the boss over me."

"That's what I was afraid of."

He carried her back along the path. She was small and light and it took no effort at all. At the castle, he found the kitchen, an enormous room that looked like the kind of well-appointed facility one would expect to find in a five-star hotel.

"Have you got a first aid attendant here?" Drew asked one of the kitchen staff, who went and fetched the chef.

The chef showed him through to an office adjoining the kitchen, and Drew settled Becky in a chair. The chef sent in a young man with a first aid kit. He was slender and golden-skinned with dark, dark hair and almond-shaped eyes that matched.

"I am Tandu," he said. "I am the medical man." His accent made it sound as if he had said *medicine man.*

Relived that he could back off from more physical contact with the delectable Miss Becky, Drew motioned to where she sat.

Tandu set down his first aid kit and crouched down in front of her. He carefully unwrapped Drew's wet shirt from her leg. He stared at Becky's injury for a moment, scrambled to his feet, picked up the first aid kit and thrust it at Drew.

"I do not do blood."

"What kind of first aid attendant doesn't—?"

But Tandu had already fled.

Drew, even more aware of her now that he had nearly escaped, went and found a pan of warm water, and then cleaned and dressed her wound, steeling himself to be as professional as possible.

Becky stared down at the dark head of the man kneeling at her feet. He pressed a warm, wet cloth against the tender skin of her inner thigh, and she gasped at the sensation that jolted through her like an electric shock.

He glanced up at her, then looked back to his task quickly. “Sorry,” he muttered. “I will try to make this as painless as possible.”

Despite the fact his touch was incredibly tender—or maybe because of it—it was one of the most deliciously painful experiences of Becky’s life. He carefully cleaned the scrapes, dabbed an ointment on them and then wound clean gauze around her leg.

She could feel a quiver within her building. There was going to be an earthquake if he didn’t finish soon! She longed to reach out and touch his hair, to brush the salt and sand from it. She reached out.

A pan dropped in the kitchen, and she felt reality crashing back in around her. She snatched her hand back, just as Drew glanced up.

“Are you okay?”

“Sure,” she said shakily, but she really wasn’t. What she felt like was a girl who had been very drunk, and who had done all kinds of uninhibited and crazy things, and was now coming to her senses.

She had kissed Drew Jordan shamelessly. She had shared all her secrets with him. She had blabbered that he was masterful, as if she enjoyed such a thing! Now she had nearly touched his hair, as if they were lovers instead of near strangers!

Okay, his hand upon her thigh was obviously creating confusion in the more primal cortexes of her brain, but she had to pull herself together.

“There,” he said, rocking back on his heels and studying the bandage around her thigh, “I think—”

She didn’t let him finish. She shot to her feet, gazed down at her bandaged thigh instead of at him. “Yes, yes, perfect,” she said. She sounded like a German engineer approving a mechanical drawing. Her thigh was tingling unmercifully, and she was pretty sure it was from his touch and not from the injury.

"I have to get to work," she said in a strangled voice.

He stood up. "You aren't going to work. You're going to rest for the afternoon."

"But I can't. I—"

"I'm telling you, you need to rest."

She thought, again, of telling him he was masterful. Good grief, she could feel the blush rising up her cheeks. She had probably created a monster.

In him and in herself.

"Go to bed," he said. Drew's voice was as caressing as his hand had been, and just as seductive. "Just for what is left of the afternoon. You'll be glad you did."

You did not discuss bed with a man like this! And especially not after he had just performed intimate rituals on your thigh! Particularly not after you had noticed his voice was seduction itself, all deep and warm and caressing.

You did not discuss bed with a man like this once you had come to your senses. She opened her mouth to tell him she would decide for herself what needed to be done. It would not involve the word *bed.* But before she could speak, he did.

"I'll go scout a spot for the wedding. Joe will be here in a while. By the time you wake up, we'll have it all taken care of."

All her resolve to take back the reins of her own life dissolved, instantly, like sugar into hot tea.

It felt as if she was going to start crying. When was the last time anything had been taken care of for her? After her father had left, her poor shattered mother had absconded on parenting. It felt as if Becky had been the one who looked after everything. Jerry had seemed to like her devoting herself to organizing his life. Even her career took advantage of the fact that Becky English was the one who looked after things, who tried valiantly to fix all and to achieve perfection. She took it all on… until the weight of it nearly crushed her.

Where had that thought come from? She *loved* her job. Putting together joyous and memorable occasions for others had soothed the pain of her father's abandonment, and had, thankfully, been enough to fill her world ever since the defection of Jerry from her personal landscape.

Or had been enough until less than twenty-four hours ago, when Drew Jordan had showed up in her life and showed her there was still such a thing as a hero.

She turned and fled before she did something really foolish. Like kissing him again.

Becky found that as much as she would have liked to rebel against his advice, she had no choice but to take it. Clear of the kitchen, her limbs felt like jelly, heavy and nearly shaking with exhaustion and delayed reaction to all the unexpected adventures of the day. It took every bit of remaining energy she had to climb the stone staircase that led to the wing of the castle with her room in it.

She went into its cool sanctuary and peeled off her wet clothes. It felt like too much effort to even find something else to put on. She left the clothes in a heap and crept under the cool sheets of the welcoming bed. Within seconds she was fast asleep.

She dreamed that someone was knocking on her door, and when she went to answer it, Drew Jordan was on the other side of it, a smile of pure welcome on his face. He reached for her, he pulled her close, his mouth dropped over hers…

Becky started awake. She was not sure what time it was, though the light suggested early evening, which meant she had frittered away a whole precious afternoon sleeping.

She wanted to leap from bed, but her body would not let her. She felt, again, like the girl who had had too much to drink. She tested each of her limbs. It was official. Her whole body hurt. Her head hurt. Her mouth and throat felt raw and dry. But mostly, she felt deeply ashamed. She had lost control, and she hated that.

Her door squeaked open.

"How you doing?"

She shot up in bed, pulled the sheet more tightly around herself. "What are you doing here?"

"I knocked. When there was no answer, I thought I'd better check on you. You slept a long time."

Drew Jordan looked just as he had in the dream—gorgeous. Though in real life there was no expression of tender welcome on his face. It did not look like he was thinking about sweeping her into his big strong arms.

In fact, he slipped into the room, but rested himself against the far wall—as far away from her as possible—those big, strong arms folded firmly across his chest. He was wearing a snowy-white T-shirt that showed off the sun-bronzed color of his arms, and khaki shorts that showed off the long, hard muscle of equally sun-bronzed legs.

"A long time?" She found her cell phone on the bedside table. "It's only five. That's not so bad."

"Um, maybe you should have a look at the date on there."

She frowned down at her phone. Her mouth fell open. "What? I slept an entire day? But I couldn't have! That's impossible."

She started to throw back the covers, then remembered she had slipped in between the sheets naked. She yanked them up around her chin.

"It was probably the best thing you could do. Your body knows what it needs."

She looked up at him. Her body, treacherous thing, did indeed know what it needed! And all of it involved him.

"If you would excuse me," she said, "I really need—"

Now her brain, treacherous thing, silently screamed *you*.

"Are you okay?"

No! It simply was not okay to be this aware of him, to yearn for his touch and his taste.

"I'm fine. Did your brother come?" she asked, desperate to distract him from her discomfort, and from the possibility of him discerning what was causing it.

"Nope. I can't seem to reach him on my phone, either."

"Oh, Drew," she said softly.

Her tone seemed to annoy him. "You don't really look fine," he decided.

"Okay, I'm not fine. I don't have time to sleep away a whole day. Despite all that rest, I feel as if I've been through the spin cycle of a giant washing machine. I hurt everywhere, worse than the worst hangover ever."

"You've had a hangover?" He said this with insulting incredulousness.

"Of course I have. Living in Moose Run isn't like taking vows to become a nun, you know."

"You would be wasted as a nun," he said, and his gaze went to her lips before he looked sharply away.

"Let's talk about that," she said.

"About you being wasted as a nun?" he asked, looking back at her, surprised.

"About the fact you think you would know such a thing about me. I don't normally act like that. I would never, under ordinary circumstances, kiss a person the way I kissed you. Naturally, I'm mortified."

He lifted an eyebrow.

"There was no need to throw myself at you, no matter how grateful and discombobulated I was."

His lips twitched.

"It's not funny," she told him sternly. "It's embarrassing."

"It's not your wanton and very un-nun-like behavior I was smiling about."

"Wanton?" she squeaked.

"It was the fact you used *discombobulated* in a sentence. I can't say as I've ever heard that before."

"Wanton?" she squeaked again.

"Sorry. Wanton is probably overstating it."

"Probably?"

"We don't all have your gift for picking exactly the right word," he said. He lifted a shoulder. "People do weird things when they are in shock. Let's move past it, okay?"

Actually, she would have preferred to find out exactly what he meant by wanton—it had been a little kiss really, it didn't even merit the humiliation she was feeling about it—but she didn't want to look like she was unwilling to move past it.

"Okay," she said grudgingly. "Though just for the

record, I want you to know I don't like masterful men. At all."

"No secret longing?"

He was teasing her! There was a residue of weakness in her, because she liked it, but it would be a mistake to let him know her weaknesses.

"As you have pointed out," Becky said coolly, "I was in shock. I said and did things that were completely alien to my nature. Now, let's move past it."

Something smoky happened to his eyes. His gaze stopped on her lips. She had the feeling he would dearly like to prove to her that some things were not as alien to her nature as she wanted them both to believe.

But he fended off the temptation, with apparent ease, pushing himself away from the wall and heading back for the door. "You have one less thing to worry about. I think I have the pavilion figured out."

"Really?" She would have leaped up and gave him a hug, except she was naked underneath the sheet, he already thought she was wanton enough, and she was not exposing anything to him, least of all not her longing to let other people look after things for a change. And to feel his embrace once more, his hard, hot muscles against her naked flesh.

"You do?" she squeaked, trying to find a place to put her gaze, anywhere but his hard, hot muscles.

"I thought about what you said, about creating an illusion. I started thinking about driving some posts, and suspending fabric from them. Something like a canopy bed."

She squinted at him. That urge to hold him, to feel him, to touch him, was there again, stronger. It was because he was looking after things, taking on a part of the burden without being asked. It was because he had listened to her.

Becky English, lying there in her bed, naked, with her sheet pulled up around her chin, studied her ceiling, so awfully aware that a woman could fall for a guy like him before she even knew what had happened to her.

CHAPTER SEVEN

THANKFULLY FOR BECKY, Drew Jordan had already warned her about guys like him.

"What does a confirmed bachelor know about canopy beds?" she said, keeping her gaze on the ceiling and her tone deliberately light. "No, never mind. I don't want to know. I think I'm still slightly discombobulated."

"Admit it."

She glanced over at him just as he grinned. His teeth were white and straight. He looked way too handsome. She returned her gaze to the ceiling. "I just did. I'm still slightly discombobulated."

"Not that! Admit it's brilliant."

She couldn't help but smile. And look at him again. "It is. It's brilliant. It will create that illusion of a room, and possibly provide some protection from the sun if we use fabric as a kind of ceiling. It has the potential to be exceedingly romantic, too. Which is why I'm surprised you came up with it."

"Hey, nobody is more surprised than me. Sadly, after traipsing all over the island this afternoon, I still haven't found a good site for the ceremony. But you might as well come see what's going on with the pavilion."

She should not appear too eager. But really? Pretending just felt like way too much effort. She would have to chalk it up to her near drowning and the other rattling events of the day. "Absolutely. Give me five minutes."

"Sure. I'll meet you on the front stairs."

Of course, it took Becky longer than five minutes. She had to shower off the remains of her adventure. She had sand in places she did not know sand could go. Her hair was destroyed. Her leg was a mess and she had to rewrap it after she was done. She had faint bruising appearing in the most unlikely places all over her body.

She put on her only pair of long pants—as uninspiring as they were in a lightweight grey tweed—and a long-sleeved shirt in a shade of hot pink that matched some of the flowers that bloomed in such abundance on this island. Her outfit covered the worst of the damage to her poor battered body, but there was nothing she could do about the emotional battering she was receiving. And it wasn't his fault. Drew Jordan was completely oblivious to the effect he was having on her.

Or accustomed to it!

Becky dabbed on a bit of makeup to try to hide the crescent moons from under her eyes. She looked exhausted. How was that possible after nearly twenty-four hours of sleep? At the last minute, she just touched a bit of gloss to her lips. It wasn't wrong to want him to look at them, but she hoped she would not be discombobulated enough to offer them to him again anytime in the near future.

"Or any future!" she told herself firmly.

She had pictured Drew waiting impatiently for her, but when she arrived at the front step, he had out a can of spray paint and was marking big X's on the grassy lawn in front of the castle.

Just when she was trying not to think of kisses anymore. What was this clumsy artwork on the lawn all about? An invitation? A declaration of love? A late Valentine?

"Marking where the posts should go," he told her, glancing toward her and then looking back at what he was doing. "Can you come stand right here and hold the tape measure?"

So much for a declaration of love! Good grief. She had always harbored this secret and very unrealistic side. She thought Jerry had cured her of her more fantastic romantic notions, but no, some were like little seeds inside her, waiting for the first hint of water and sun to sprout into full-fledged fairy tales. Being rescued from certain death by a very good-looking and extremely competent man who had so willingly put his own life on the line for her had obviously triggered her most fanciful longings.

She just needed to swat herself up the side of the head with the facts. She and Drew Jordan barely knew one another, and before she was swept off the rock they had been destined to butt heads.

She had to amend that: she barely knew Drew Jordan, but he knew her better than he should because she had blurted out her whole life story in a moment of terrible weakness. It was just more evidence that she must have hit her head somewhere in that debacle. Except for the fact she was useful for holding the tape measure, he hardly seemed aware that she was there.

Finally, he rolled up the tape measure. "What do you think?"

His X's formed a large rectangle. She could picture it already with a silken canopy and the posts swathed in fabric. She could picture the tables and the candles, and music and a beautiful bride and groom.

"I think it's going to be perfect," she breathed. And for the first time since she had taken on this job, she felt like maybe it would be.

How much of that had to do with the man who was, however reluctantly, helping her make it happen?

"Don't get your hopes up too high," he said. "Perfection is harder to achieve than you think. And we still have the evening tropical breezes to contend with. And I haven't found a ceremony site. It could go sideways yet."

"Especially if you talk to your brother?"

He rolled his shoulders. "There doesn't seem to be much chance of that happening. But there are a lot of things that could go sideways before the big day."

Yes, she had seen in recent history how quickly things could go sideways. In fact, when she looked at him, she was pretty sure Drew Jordan was the kind of man who could make your whole life go sideways with no effort on his part at all.

"Let's go see if we can find a place for the ceremony."

She *had* to go with him. It was her job. But tropical breezes seemed to be the least of her problems at the moment.

"I should be getting danger pay," she muttered to herself.

"Don't worry, I won't be letting you anywhere near any rocks."

No sense clarifying with him that was not where the danger she was worried about was coming from. Not at all.

They were almost at the edge of the lawn when a voice stopped them.

"Miss Becky. Mr. Drew."

They turned to see Tandu struggling across the lawn with a huge wicker basket. "So sorry, no good with blood. Take you to place for wedding vow now."

"Oh, did you tell him we were looking for a new ceremony site?" Becky asked. "That was smart."

"Naturally, I would like to take credit for being smart, but I didn't tell him. They must do weddings here all the time. He's used to this."

"Follow, follow," Tandu ordered.

They fell into step behind him, leaving the lawn and entering the deep, vibrant green of the jungle forest. Birds chattered and the breeze lifting huge leaves made a sound, too.

"Actually, the owner of the island told me they had hosted some huge events here, but never a wedding," Becky told Drew. "He's the music mogul, Bart Lung. He's a friend of Allie's. He's away on business but he'll be back for the wedding. He's very excited about it."

"Are you excited about meeting him?"

"I guess I hadn't really thought about it. We better catch up to Tandu, he's way ahead of us."

Drew contemplated what had just happened with a trace of self-loathing.

Are you excited about meeting him? As bad as asking the question was how much he had liked her answer. She genuinely seemed not to have given a thought to meeting Bart Lung.

But what had motivated Drew to ask such a question? Surely he hadn't been feeling a bit threatened about

Becky meeting the famously single and fabulously wealthy record broker? He couldn't possibly have felt the faintest little prickle of…jealousy.

He never felt jealous. He'd had women he had dated who had tried to make him jealous, and he'd been annoyed by how juvenile that felt. But at the heart of it, he knew they had wanted him to show what he couldn't: that he cared.

But he'd known from the moment she had instigated that kiss that Becky English was different from what his brother liked to call the rotating door of women in his life. The chemistry between them had been unexpected, but Drew had had chemistry before. He wasn't sure exactly what it was about the cheerleader-turned-event-planner that intrigued him, but he knew he had to get away from it.

Which was exactly why he had marched up to her room. He had two reasons, and two reasons only, to interact with her: the pavilion and the ceremony site. He'd promised his brother and Becky his help, and once the planning for his assigned tasks was solidly in place, he could minimize his interactions with her. He was about to get very busy with construction. That would leave much less time for contemplating the lovely Miss English.

"I hate to say it," he told Becky, looking at Tandu's back disappearing down a twisting path in front of them, "but I've already been over this stretch of the island. There is no—"

"This way, please." Tandu had stopped and was holding back thick jungle fronds. "Path overgrown a bit. I will tell gardening staff. Important for all to be ready for big day, eh?"

It was just a short walk, and the path opened onto a beautiful crescent of beach. Drew studied it from a construction point of view. He could see the high tide line, and it would be perfect for building a small pavilion and setting up chairs for the two hundred guests. Three large palms grew out of the center of the beach, their huge leathery leaves shading almost the entire area.

Becky, he could see, was looking at it from a far less practical standpoint than he was. She turned to look at him. Her eyes were shiny with delight, and those little plump lips were curved upward in the nicest smile.

Task completed! Drew told himself sternly. Pavilion, check. Wedding location, check. Missing brother…well, that had nothing to do with her. He had to get away from her—and her plump little lips—and *stay* away from her.

"It's perfect," he said. "Do you agree?"

She turned those shining eyes to him. "Agree?" she said softly. "Have you ever seen such a magical place in your whole life?"

He looked around with magic in mind rather than construction. He was not much of a magic kind of person, but he supposed he had not seen a place quite like this before. The whole beach was ringed with thick shrubs with dark green foliage. Tucked in amongst the foliage was an abundance of pale yellow and white flowers the size of cantaloupes. The flowers seemed to be emitting a perfume that was sweet and spicy at the same time. Unfortunately, that made him think of her lips again.

He glared at the sand, which was pure white and finer than sugar. They were in a cove of a small bay, and the water was striped in aqua shades of turquoise, all the way out to a reef, where the water turned dark navy blue, and the waves broke, white-capped, over rocks.

"Well," he said, "I'll just head back."

"Do you ever just answer a question?"

"Sit, sit," Tandu said from behind them.

Drew swung around to look at him. While he had been looking out toward the sea, Tandu had emptied the wicker basket he carried. There was a blanket set up in the sand, and laid out on it was a bottle of wine, beaded with sweat, two wineglasses and two plates. There was a platter of blackened chicken, fresh fruit and golden, steaming croissants.

"What the hell?" Drew asked.

"Sit, sit—amens...amens."

"I'm not following," Drew said. He saw that Becky had had no trouble whatsoever plopping herself down on the blanket. Had she forgotten she'd lost a whole day? She had to be seriously behind schedule.

"I make amens," Tandu said quietly, "for not doing first aid."

"Oh, *amends*," Drew said uncomfortably. "Really, it's not necessary at all. I have a ton of stuff to do. I'm not very hungry." This was a complete lie, though he had not realized quite how hungry he was until the food had *magically* appeared.

Tandu looked dejected that his offer was being refused.

"You very irritated with me," Tandu said sadly.

Becky caught his eye, lifted her shoulder—*come on, be a sport*—and patted the blanket. With a resigned shake of his head, Drew lowered himself onto the blanket. He bet if he ate one bite of this food that had been set out the spell would be complete.

"Look, I wasn't exactly irritated." This was as much a lie as the one about how he wasn't hungry, and he had a feeling Tandu was not easily fooled. "I was just a little surprised by a first aid man who doesn't like blood."

"Oh, yes," Tandu said happily. "Sit, sit, I fix."

"I am sitting. There's to nothing to fix." Except that Sainte Simone needed a new first aid attendant—before two hundred people descended on it would be good—but Drew found he did not have the heart to tell Tandu that.

Maybe the place was as magical as it looked, because he found himself unable to resist sitting beside Becky on the picnic blanket, though he told himself he had complied only because he did not want to disappoint Tandu, who had obviously misinterpreted his level of annoyance.

"I am not a first aid man," Tandu said. "Uh, how you say, medicine man? My family are healers. We see things."

"See things?" Drew asked. "I'm not following."

"Like a seer or a shaman?" Becky asked. She sounded thrilled.

Drew shot her a look. *Don't encourage him.* She ignored him. "Like what kind of things? Like the future?"

Drew groaned.

"Well, how did he know we needed a wedding site?" she challenged him.

"Because two hundred people are descending on this little piece of paradise for a marriage?"

She actually stuck one of her pointy little elbows in his ribs as if it was rude of him to point out the obvious.

"Yes, yes, like future," Tandu said, very pleased,

missing or ignoring Drew's skepticism and not seeing Becky's dig in his ribs. "See things."

"So what do you see for the wedding?" Becky asked eagerly, leaning forward, as if she was going to put a great deal of stock in the answer.

Tandu looked off into the distance. He suddenly did not look like a smiling servant in a white shirt. Not at all. His expression was intense, and when he turned his gaze back to them, his liquid brown eyes did not seem soft or merry anymore.

"Unexpected things," he said softly. "Lots of surprises. Very happy, very happy wedding. Everybody happy. Babies. Many, many babies in the future."

Becky clapped her hands with delight. "Drew, you're going to be an uncle."

"How very terrifying," he said drily. "Since you can see things, Tandu, when is my brother arriving?"

"Not when you expect," Tandu said, without hesitation.

"Thanks. Tell me something I don't know."

Tandu appeared to take that as a challenge. He gazed off into the distance again. Finally he spoke.

"Broken hearts mended," Tandu said with satisfaction.

"Whose broken hearts?" Becky asked, her eyes wide. "The bride? The groom?"

"For Pete's sake," Drew snapped.

Tandu did not look at him, but gazed steadily and silently at Becky.

"Oh," Becky said, embarrassed. "I don't have a broken heart."

Tandu cocked his head, considering. Drew found himself listening with uncomfortable intentness.

"You left your brokenness in the water," Tandu told Becky. "What you thought was true never was."

She gasped softly, then turned faintly accusing eyes to Drew. "Did you tell him what I said about Jerry?"

He was amazed how much it stung that she thought he would break her confidence. That accusing look in her eyes should be a good thing—it might cool the sparks that had leaped up between them.

But he couldn't leave well enough alone. "Of course not," he said.

"Well, then how did he know?"

"He's a seer," Drew reminded her with a certain amount of satisfaction.

Tandu seemed to have not heard one word of this conversation.

"But you need to swim," he told Becky. "Not be afraid of water. Water here very, very good swimming. Safe. Best swimming beach right here."

"Oh, that's a good idea," she said, turning her head to look at the inviting water, "but I'm not prepared."

"Prepared?" Tandu said, surprised. "What to prepare?"

"I don't have a swimming suit," Becky told him.

"At all?" Drew asked, despite himself. "Who comes to the Caribbean without a swimming suit?"

"I'm not here to play," she said with a stern toss of her head.

"God forbid," he said, but he could not help but feel she was a woman who seemed to take life way too seriously. Which, of course, was not his problem.

"I don't actually own a swimming suit," she said. "The nearest pool is a long way from Moose Run. We aren't close to a lake."

"Ha. Born with swimming suit," Tandu told her seriously. "Skin waterproof."

Drew watched with deep pleasure as the crimson crept up her neck to her cheeks. "Ha-ha," he said in an undertone, "that's what you get for encouraging him."

"You swim," Tandu told her. "Eat first, then swim. Mr. Drew help you."

"Naked swimming," Drew said. "Happy to help when I can. Tandu, do you see skinny-dipping in my future?"

There was that pointy little elbow in his ribs again, quite a bit harder than it had been the last time.

But before he could enjoy Becky's discomfort too much, suddenly Drew found himself pinned in Tandu's intense gaze. "The heart that is broken is yours, Mr. Drew?"

CHAPTER EIGHT

DREW JORDAN ORDERED himself to say no. No to magic. No to the light in Becky's eyes. And especially no to Tandu's highly invasive question. But instead of saying no, he found he couldn't speak at all, as if his throat was closing and his tongue was stuck to the roof of his mouth.

"They say a man is not given more than he can take, eh?" Tandu said.

If there was an expression on the face of the earth that Drew hated with his whole heart and soul it was that one, but he still found he could say nothing.

"But you were," Tandu said softly. "You were given more than you could take. You are a strong man. But not that strong, eh, Mr. Drew?"

His chest felt heavy. His throat felt as if it was closing. There was a weird stinging behind his eyes, as if he was allergic to the overwhelming scent of those flowers.

Without warning, he was back there.

He was seventeen years old. He was standing at the door of his house. It was the middle of the night. His feet and chest were bare and he had on pajama bottoms. He was blinking away sleep, trying to comprehend the stranger at the door of his house. The policeman said, "I'm sorry, son." And then Drew found out he wasn't anyone's son, not anymore.

Drew shook his head and looked at Tandu, fiercely.

"You heal now," Tandu said, not intimidated, as if it was an order. "You heal." And then suddenly Tandu was himself again, the easygoing grin on his face, his teeth impossibly perfect and white against the golden brown of his skin. His eyes were gentle and warm. "Eat, eat. Then swim. Then sunset."

And then he was gone.

"What was that about?" Becky asked him.

"I don't have a clue," he said. His voice sounded strange to him, choked and hoarse. "Creepy weirdness."

Becky was watching him as if she knew it was a lie. When had he become such a liar? He'd better give it up, he was terrible at it. He poured two glasses of wine, handed her one and tossed back the other. He set down the glass carefully.

"There. I've toasted the wedding spot. I'm going to go now." He didn't move.

"Have you?" she asked.

"Have I what? Toasted the wedding spot?"

"Had a heartbreak?" she asked softly, with concern.

And he felt, suddenly, as alone with his burdens as he had ever felt. He felt as if he could lay it all at her feet. He looked at the warmth and loveliness of her brushed-suede eyes. *You heal now.*

He reeled back from the invitation in her eyes. He was the most pragmatic of men. He was not under the enchantment of this beach, or Tandu's words, or her.

Not yet, an inner voice informed him cheerfully.

Not ever, he informed the inner voice with no cheer

at all. He was not touching that food with its potential to weaken him even further. And no more wine.

"People like me," he said, forcing a cavalier ease into his voice.

She leaned toward him.

"We don't have hearts to break. I'm leaving now." Still, he did not move.

She looked as if she wanted to argue with that, but she took one look at his face and very wisely turned her attention to the chicken. "Is this burned?" she asked, poking one of the pieces gingerly with her fingertip.

"I think it's jerked, a very famous way of cooking on these islands." It felt like a relief to focus on the chicken instead of what was going on inside himself.

She took a piece and nibbled it. Her expression changed to one of complete awe. "You have to try it," she insisted. "You have to try it and tell me if it isn't the best thing you have ever tasted. Just one bite before you go."

Despite knowing this food probably had a spell woven right into it, he threw caution to the wind, picked up a leg of chicken and chomped into it. Just a few hours ago it definitely would have been the best thing he had ever tasted. But now that he was under a spell, he saw things differently.

Because the blackened jerk chicken quite possibly might have been the best thing he'd ever tasted, if he hadn't very foolishly sampled her lips when she had offered them yesterday afternoon.

"You might as well stay and eat," she said. She reached over and refilled his empty wineglass. "It would be a shame to let it go to waste."

He was not staying here, eating enchanted food in

an enchanted cove with a woman who was clearly putting a spell on him. On the other hand, she was right. It would be a shame to let the food go to waste.

There was no such thing as spells, anyway. He picked up his second piece of chicken. He watched her delicately lick her fingertips.

"We don't have this kind of food in Moose Run," she said. "More's the pity."

"What kind of food do you have?" He was just being polite, he told himself, before he left her. He frowned. That second glass of wine could not be gone.

"We have two restaurants. We have the Main Street Diner which specializes in half-pound hamburgers and claims to have the best chocolate milk shake in all of Michigan."

"Claims?"

"I haven't tried all the chocolate milk shakes in Michigan," she said. "But believe me, I'm working on it."

He felt something relax within him. He should not be relaxing. He needed to keep his guard up. Still, he laughed at her earnest expression.

"And then we have Mr. Wang's All-You-Can-Eat Spectacular Smorgasbord."

"So, two restaurants. What else do you do for fun?"

She looked uncomfortable. It was none of his business, he told himself firmly. Why did he care if it was just as he'd suspected? She did not have nearly enough fun going on in her life. Not that it was any concern of his.

"Is there a movie theater?" he coaxed her.

"Yes. And don't forget the church picnic."

"And dancing on the grass," he supplied.

"I'm not much for the church socials, actually. I don't really like dancing."

"So what do you like?"

She hesitated, and then met his eyes. "I'm sure you are going to think I am the world's most boring person, but you know what I really do for fun?"

He felt as if he was holding his breath for some reason. Crazy to hope the answer was going to involve kissing. Not that anyone would consider that boring, would they? Was his wineglass full again? He took a sip.

"I read," she said, in a hushed whisper, as if she was in a confessional. She sighed. "I love to read."

What a relief! Reading, not kissing! It should have seemed faintly pathetic, but somehow, just like the rest of her, it seemed real. In an amusement park world where everyone was demanding to be entertained constantly, by bigger things and better amusements and wilder rides and greater spectacles, by things that stretched the bounds of what humans were intended to do, it seemed lovely that Becky had her own way of being in the world, and that something so simple as opening a book could make someone contented.

She was bracing herself, as if she expected him to be scornful. It made him wonder if the ex-beau had been one of those put-down kind of guys.

"I can actually picture you out in a hammock on a sunny afternoon," he said. "It sounds surprisingly nice."

"At this time of year, it's a favorite chair. On my front porch. We still have front porches in Moose Run."

He could picture a deeply shaded porch, and a sleepy street, and hear the sound of birds. This, too, struck him as deliciously simple in a complicated world. "What's your favorite book?" he asked.

"I have to pick one?" she asked with mock horror.

"Let me put it differently. If you had to recommend a book to someone who hardly ever reads, which one would it be?"

And somehow it was that easy. The food was disappearing and so was the wine, and she was telling him about her favorite books and authors, and he was telling her about surfing the big waves and riding his motorbike on the Pacific Coast Highway between LA and San Francisco.

The fight seemed to ease out of him, and the wariness. The urgent need to be somewhere else seemed silly. Drew felt himself relaxing. Why not enjoy it? It was no big deal. Tomorrow his crew would be here. He would immerse himself in his work. He could enjoy this last evening with Becky before that happened, couldn't he?

Who would have ever guessed it would be so easy to be with a man like this? Becky thought. The conversation was comfortable between them. There was so much work that needed to be done on Allie's wedding, and she had already lost a precious day. Still, she had never felt less inclined to do work.

But as comfortable as it all was, she could feel a little nudge of disappointment. How could they go from that electrifying kiss, to this?

Not that she wanted the danger of that kiss again, but she certainly didn't want him to think she was a dull small-town girl whose idea of an exciting evening was sitting out on her front porch reading until the fireflies came out.

Dinner was done. The wine bottle was lying on its

side, empty. All that was left of the chicken was bones, and all that was left of the croissants were a few golden crumbs. As she watched, Drew picked one of those up on his fingertip and popped it in his mouth.

How could such a small thing be so darned sexy?

In her long pants and long-sleeved shirt, Becky was suddenly aware of feeling way too warm. And overdressed. She was aware of being caught in the enchantment of Sainte Simone and this beautiful beach. She longed to be free of encumbrances.

Like clothing? she asked herself, appalled, but not appalled enough to stop the next words that came out of her mouth.

"Let's go for that swim after all," she said. She tried to sound casual, but her heart felt as if she had just finished running a marathon.

"I really need to go." He said it without any kind of conviction. "Are you going to swim in nature's bathing suit?"

"Don't be a pervert!"

"I'm not. Tandu suggested it. One-hundred-percent waterproof."

"Don't look," she said.

"Sure. I'll stop breathing while I'm at it."

What was she doing? she asked herself.

For once in her life, she was acting on a whim, that's what she was doing. For once in her life she was being bold, that's what she was doing. For once in her life, she was throwing convention to the wind, she was doing what she wanted to do. She was not leaving him with the impression she was a dull small-town girl who had spent her whole life with her nose buried in a book. Even if she had been!

She didn't want that to be the whole truth about her anymore, and not just because of him, either. Because the incident in the water yesterday, that moment when she had looked her own death in the face and somehow been spared, had left her with a longing for second chances.

She stood up and turned her back to him. Becky took a deep breath and peeled her shirt over her head, then unbuckled her slacks and stepped out of them. She had on her luxurious Rembrandt's Drawing brand underwear. The underwear was a matching set, a deep shade of turquoise not that different from the water. It was as fashionable as most bathing suits, and certainly more expensive.

She glanced over her shoulder, and his expression—stunned, appreciative, approving—made her run for the water. She splashed in up to her knees, and then threw herself in. The water closed over her head, and unlike yesterday afternoon, it felt wonderful in the heat of the early evening, cool and silky as a caress on her nearly naked skin.

She surfaced, then paddled out and found her footing when she was up to her neck in water, her underwear hidden from him. She turned to look at where he was still sitting on the blanket. Even from here, she could see the heat in his eyes.

Oh, girlfriend, she thought, *you do not know what you are playing with.* But the thing about letting a bolder side out was that it was very hard to stuff it back in, like trying to get a jack-in-the-box back in its container.

"Come in," she called. "It's glorious."

He stood up slowly and peeled his shirt off. She held

her breath. It was her turn to be stunned, appreciative and approving.

She had seen him without his shirt already when he had sacrificed it to doctor her leg. But this was different. She wasn't in shock, or in pain, or bleeding all over the place.

Becky was aware, as she had been when she had first laid eyes on him, that he was the most beautifully made of men. Broad shouldered and deep chested, muscular without being muscle-bound. He could be an actor or a model, because he had that mysterious something that made her—and probably every other woman on earth—feel as if she could look at him endlessly, drink in his masculine perfection as if he was a long, cool drink of water and she was dying of thirst.

Was he going to take off his shorts? She was aware she was holding her breath. But no, he kicked off his shoes and, with the khaki shorts safely in place, ran toward the water. Like she had done, he ran in up to about his thighs and then she watched as he dived beneath the surface.

"I didn't peg you for shy," she told him when he surfaced close to her.

He lifted an eyebrow at her.

"I've seen men's underwear before. I'm from Moose Run, not the convent."

"You've mentioned you weren't a nun once before," he said. "What's with the fascination with nuns?"

"You just seem to think because I'm small town I'm prim and proper. You didn't have to get your shorts all wet to save my sensibilities."

"I don't wear underwear."

Her mouth fell open. She could feel herself turning crimson. He laughed, delighted at her discomfort.

"How are your sensibilities doing now?" he asked her.

"Fine," she squeaked. But they both knew it was a lie, and he laughed.

"Come on," he said, shaking the droplets of water from his hair. "I'll race you to those rocks."

"That's ridiculous. I don't have a hope of winning."

"I know," he said fiendishly.

"I get a head start."

"All right."

"A big one."

"Okay, you tell me when I can go."

She paddled her way toward the rocks. When it seemed there was no chance he could catch her, she called, "Okay, go."

She could hear him coming up behind her. She paddled harder. He grabbed her foot!

"Hey!" She went under the water. He let go of her foot, and when she surfaced, he had surged by her and was touching the rock.

"You cheater," she said indignantly.

"You're the cheater. What kind of head start was that?"

"Watch who you are calling a cheater." She reached back her arm and splashed him, hard. He splashed her back. The war was on.

Tandu had been so right. She needed to leave whatever fear she had remaining in the water.

And looking at Drew's face, she realized, her fear was not about drowning. It was about caring for someone else, as if pain was an inherent ingredient to that.

Becky could see that if she had not let go enough in

life, neither had he. Seeing him like this, playful, his face alight with laugher and mischief, she realized he did carry some burden, like a weight, just as Tandu had suggested. Drew had put down his burden for a bit, out here in the water, and she was glad she had encouraged him to come swim with her.

She wondered what his terrible burden was. Could he really have been given more than he thought he could handle? He seemed so unbelievably strong. But then again, wasn't that what made strength, being challenged to your outer limits? She wondered if he would ever confide in her, but then he splashed her in the face and took off away from her, and she took chase, and the serious thoughts were gone.

A half hour later, exhausted, they dragged themselves up on the beach. Just as he had promised, the trades came up, and it was surprisingly chilly on her wet skin and underwear. She tried to pull her clothes over her wet underwear, but it was more difficult than she thought. Finally, with her clothes clinging to her uncomfortably, she turned to him.

He had pulled his shirt back on over his wet chest and was putting the picnic things back in the basket.

"We have to go," she said. "I feel guilty."

"Tut-tut," he said. "There's that nun thing again. But I have to go, too. My crew is arriving first thing in the morning. I'd like to have things set up so we can get right to work. You're a terrible influence on me, Sister English."

"Sister Simone, to you."

He didn't appear to be leaving, and neither did she.

"I am so far behind in what I need to get done," Becky said. "I didn't expect to be here this long. If I go to work right now, I can still make a few phone calls. What time do you think it is in New York?"

"Look what I just found."

Did he ever just answer the question?

He had been rummaging in the picnic basket and he held up two small mason jars that looked as if they were filled with whipped cream and strawberries.

"What is that?" Knowing the time in New York suddenly didn't seem important at all.

"I think it's dessert."

She licked her lips. He stared at them, before looking away.

"I guess a little dessert wouldn't hurt," she said. Her voice sounded funny, low and seductive, as if she had said something faintly naughty.

"Just sit in the sand," he suggested. "We'll wrap the picnic blanket over our shoulders. We might as well eat dessert and watch the sun go down. What's another half hour now?"

They were going to sit shoulder to shoulder under a blanket eating dessert and watching the sun go down? It was better than any book she had ever read! The time in New York—and all her other responsibilities—did a slow fade-out, as if it was the end of a movie.

CHAPTER NINE

BECKY PLUNKED HERSELF down like a dog at obedience class who was eager for a treat. Drew picked up the blanket and placed it carefully over her shoulders, then sat down in the sand beside her and pulled part of the blanket over his own shoulders. His shoulder felt warm and strong where her skin was touching it. The chill left her almost instantly.

He pried the lid off one of the jars and handed it to her with a spoon.

"Have you ever been to Hawaii?" He took the lid off the other jar.

"No, I'm sorry to say I haven't been. Have you?"

"I've done jobs there. It's very much like this, the climate, the foliage, the breathtaking beauty. Everything stops at sunset. Even if you're still working against an impossible deadline, you just stop and face the sun. It's like every single person stops and every single thing stops. This stillness comes over everything. It's like the deepest form of gratitude I've ever experienced. It's this thank-you to life."

"I feel that right now," she said, with soft reverence. "Maybe because I nearly drowned, I feel so intensely alive and so intensely grateful."

No need to mention sharing this evening with him might have something to do with feeling so intensely alive.

"Me, too," he said softly.

Was it because of her he felt this way? She could feel the heat of his shoulder where it was touching hers. She desperately wanted to kiss him again. She gobbled up strawberries and cream instead. It just made her long, even more intensely, for the sweetness of his lips.

"I am going to hell in a handbasket," she muttered, but still she snuggled under the blanket and looked at where the sun, now a huge orb of gold, was hovering over the ocean.

He shot her a look. "Why would you say that?"

Because she was enjoying him so much, when she, of all people, was so well versed in all the dangers of romance.

"Because I am sitting here watching the sun go down when I should be getting to work," she clarified with a half-truth. "I knew Allie's faith in me was misplaced."

"Why would you say that?"

"I'm just an unlikely choice for such a huge undertaking."

"So, why did she pick you, then?"

"I hadn't seen her, or even had a note from her, since she moved away from Moose Run." Becky sighed and pulled the blanket tighter around her shoulders. "Everyone in Moose Run claims to have been friends with Allison Anderson *before* she became Allie Ambrosia the movie star, but really they weren't. Allison was lonely and different, and many of those people who now claim to have been friends with her were actually exceptionally intolerant of her eccentricities.

"Her mom must have been one of the first internet daters. She came to Moose Run and moved in with Pierce Clemens, which anybody could have told her was a bad bet. Allie, with her body piercings and colorful hair and hippie skirts, was just way too exotic for Moose Run. She only lived there for two years, and she and I only had a nodding acquaintance for most of that time. We were in the same grade, but I was in advanced classes."

"That's a surprise," he teased drily.

"You could have knocked me over with a feather when I got an out-of-the-blue phone call from her a couple of weeks ago and she outlined her ambitious plans. She told me she was putting together a guest list of two hundred people and that she wanted it to be so much more than a wedding. She wants her guests to have an *experience.* The island was hers for an entire week after the wedding, and she wanted all the guests to stay and have fun, either relaxing or joining in on organized activities.

"You know what she suggested for activities? Volleyball tournaments and wienie roasts around a campfire at night, maybe fireworks! You're from there. Does that strike you as Hollywood?"

"No," he said. "Not at all. Hollywood would be Jet Skis during the day and designer dresses at night. It would be entertainment by Cirque and Shania and wine tasting and spa treatments on the beach."

"That's what I thought. But she was adamant about what she wanted. I couldn't help but think that Allie's ideas of fun, despite this exotic island setting, are those of a girl who had been largely excluded from the teen cliques who went together to the Fourth of July activities. She seems, talking to her, to be more in sync with the small-town tastes of Moose Run than with lifestyles of the rich and famous."

"It actually makes me like her more," he said reluctantly.

"I asked her if what she wanted was like summer camp for adults, to make sure I was getting it right. She said—" Becky imitated the famous actress's voice "—'Exactly! I knew I could count on you to get it right.'"

Drew chuckled at Becky's imitation of Allie, which encouraged her to be even more foolish. She did both voices, as if she was reading for several parts in a play.

"Allie, I'm not sure I'm up to this. My event company has become the go-to company for local weddings and anniversaries, but— 'Of course you are up to it, do you think I don't do my homework? You did that great party for the lawyer's kid. Ponies!'

"She said *ponies* with the same enthusiasm she said *fireworks* with," Becky told Drew ruefully. "I think she actually wanted ponies. So I said, 'Um…it would be hard to get ponies to an island—and how did you know that? About the party for Mr. Williams's son?' And she said, 'I do my research. I'm not quite as flaky as the roles I get might make you think.' Of course, I told her I never thought she was flaky, but she cut me off and told me she was sending a deposit. I tried to talk her out of it. I said a six-week timeline was way too short to throw together a wedding for two hundred people. I told her I would have to delegate all my current contracts to take it on. She just insisted. She said she would make it worth my while. I told her I just wasn't sure, and she said she was, and that I was perfect for the job."

"You were trying to get out of the opportunity of a lifetime?" Drew weighed in, amused.

"Was I ever. But then her lighthearted delivery kind of changed and she said I was the only reason she survived Moose Run at all. She asked me if I remembered the day we became friends."

"Did you?"

"Pretty hard to forget. A nasty group of boys had her backed into the corner in that horrid place at the high school where we used to all go to smoke.

"I mean, I didn't go there to smoke. I was Moose Run High's official Goody Two-shoes."

"No kidding," he said drily. "Do not elbow my ribs again. They are seriously bruised."

They sat there in companionable silence for a few minutes. The sun demanded their stillness and their silence. The sunset was at its most glorious now, painting the sky around it in shades of orange and pink that were reflecting on a band on the ocean, that seemed to lead a pathway of light right to them. Then the sun was gone, leaving only an amazing pastel palette staining the sky.

"Go on," he said.

Becky thought she was talking too much. Had they really drunk that whole bottle of wine between the two of them? Still, it felt nice to have someone to talk to, someone to listen.

"I was taking a shortcut to the library—"

"Naturally," he said with dry amusement.

"And I came across Bram Butler and his gang tormenting poor Allie. I told them to cut it out.

"Allie remembers me really giving it to them. She told me that for a long time she has always thought of me as having the spirit of a gladiator."

"I'll attest to that," he said. "I have the bruises on my ribs to prove it." And then his tone grew more serious. "And you never gave up in the water yesterday, either."

"That was because of you. Believe me, I am the little bookworm I told you I was earlier. I do not have the spirit of a gladiator."

Though she did have some kind of unexpected spirit of boldness that had made her, very uncharacteristically, rip off her clothes and go into the water.

"How many guys were there?"

"Hmm, it was years ago, but I think maybe four. No, five."

"What were they doing?"

"They kind of had her backed up against a wall. She was quite frightened. I think that stupid Bram was trying to kiss her. He's always been a jerk. He's my second cousin."

"And you just waded right in there, with five high school guys being jerks? That seems brave."

She could not allow herself to bask in his admiration, particularly since it was undeserved.

"I didn't exactly wade right in there. I used the Moose Run magic words."

"Which were?"

"Bram Butler, you stop it right now or I'll tell your mother."

He burst out laughing, and then so did she. She noticed that it had gotten quite dark. The wind had died. Already stars were rising in the sky.

"Allie and I hung out a bit after that," she said. "She was really interesting. At that time, she wanted to be a clothing designer. We used to hole up in my room and draw dresses."

"What kind of dresses?"

"Oh, you know. Prom. Evening. That kind of thing. Allie and her mom moved away shortly after that. She said we would keep in touch—that she would send me her new address and phone number—but she never did."

"You and Allie drew wedding dresses, didn't you?"

"What would make you say that?" Becky could feel a blush rising, but why should she have to apologize for her younger self?

"I'm trying to figure out if she has some kind of wedding fantasy that my brother just happened into."

"Lots of young women have romantic fantasies. And then someone comes along to disillusion them."

"Like your Jerry," he said. "Tell me about that."

"So little to tell," she said wryly. "We lived down the street from one another, we started the first grade together. When we were seventeen he asked me to go to the Fourth of July celebrations with him. He held my hand. We kissed. And there you have it, my whole future mapped out for me. We were just together after that. I wanted exactly what I grew up with, until my dad left. Up until then my family had been one of those solid, dull families that makes the world feel so, so safe.

"An illusion," she said sadly. "It all ended up being such an illusion, but I felt determined to prove it could be real. Jerry went away to college and I started my own business, and it just unraveled, bit by bit. It's quite humiliating to have a major breakup in a small town."

"I bet."

"When I think about it, the humiliation actually might have been a lot harder to handle than the fact that I was not going to share my life with Jerry. It was like a second blow. I had just barely gotten over being on the receiving end of the pitying looks over my dad's scandal."

"Are you okay with your dad's relationship now?"

"I wish I was. But they still live in Moose Run, and I have an adorable little sister who I am pathetically jealous of. They seem so happy. My mom is still a mess. Aside from working in the hardware store, she'd never even had a job."

"And you rushed in to become the family breadwinner," he said.

"It's not a bad thing, is it?"

"An admirable thing. And kind of sad."

His hand found hers and he gave it a squeeze. He didn't let go again.

"Were you thinking of Jerry when you were drawing those dresses?" he finally asked softly.

"No," she said slowly, "I don't think I was."

She suddenly remembered one dress in particular that Allie had drawn. *This is your wedding dress*, she had proclaimed, giving it to Becky.

It had been a confection, sweetheart neckline, fitted bodice, layers and layers and layers of filmy fabric flowing out in that full skirt with an impossible train. The dress had been the epitome of her every romantic notion. Becky had been able to picture herself in that dress, swirling in front of a mirror, giggling. But she had never, not even once, pictured herself in that dress walking down an aisle toward Jerry.

When Jerry had broken it to her that her "business was changing her"—in other words, he could not handle her success—and he wanted his ring back, she had never taken that drawing from where it was tucked in the back of one of her dresser drawers.

"I've talked too much," she said. "It must have been the wine."

"I don't think you talked too much."

"I usually don't confide in people so readily." She suddenly felt embarrassed. "Your name should be a clue."

"To?"

"You *drew* my secrets right out of me."

"Ah."

"We have to go now," she said.

"Yes, we do," he said.

"Before something happens," she said softly.

"Especially before that," he agreed just as softly.

Her hand was still in his. Their shoulders were touching. The breeze was lifting the leathery fronds of the palm trees and they were whispering songs without words. The sky was now almost completely black, and finding their way back was not going to be easy.

"Really," Becky said. "We need to go."

"Really," he agreed. "We do.

Neither of them moved.

CHAPTER TEN

DREW ORDERED HIMSELF to get up and leave this beach. But it was one of those completely irresistible moments: the stars winking on in the sky, their shoulders touching, the taste of strawberries and cream on his lips, the gentle lap of the waves against the shore, her small hand resting within the sanctuary of his larger one.

He turned slightly to look at her. She was turning to look at him.

It seemed like the most natural thing in the world to drop his head over hers, to taste her lips again.

Her arms came up and twined around his neck. Her lips were soft and pliant and welcoming.

He could taste everything she was in that kiss. She was bookish. And she was bold. She was simple, and she was complex. She was, above all else, a forever kind of girl.

It was that knowledge that made him untangle her hands from around his neck, to force his lips away from the soft promise of hers.

You heal now.

He swore under his breath, scrambled to his feet. "I'm sorry," he said.

"Are you?"

Well, not really. "Look, Becky, we have known each other for a shockingly short period of time. Obviously circumstances have made us feel things about each other a little too quickly."

She looked unconvinced.

"I mean, in Moose Run, you probably have a date or two before you kiss like that."

"What about in LA?"

He thought about how fast things could go in Los Angeles and how superficial that was, and how he was probably never going to be satisfied with it again. Less than forty-eight hours, and Becky English, bookworm, was changing everything in his world.

What was his world going to look like in two weeks if this kept up?

The answer was obvious. This could not keep up.

"Look, Becky, I obviously like you. And find you extremely attractive."

Did she look pleased? He did not want her to look pleased!

"There is obviously some kind of chemistry going on between us."

She looked even more pleased.

"But both of us have jobs to do. We have very little time to do those jobs in. We can't afford a, um, complication like this."

She stared at him, uncomprehending.

"It's not professional, Becky," he said gruffly. "Kissing on the job is not professional."

She looked as if he had slapped her. And then she just looked crushed.

"Oh," she stammered. "Of course, you're right."

He felt a terrible kind of self-loathing that she was taking it on, as if it were her fault.

She pulled herself together and jumped up, doing what he suspected she always did. Trying to fix the whole world. Her clothes were still wet. Her pink blouse looked as though red roses were blooming on it where it was clinging to that delectable set of underwear that he should never have seen, and was probably never going to be able to get out of his mind.

"I don't know what's gotten into me. It must still be the aftereffects of this afternoon. And the wine. I want you to know I don't usually rip my clothes off around men. In fact, that's extremely uncharacteristic. And I'm usually not such a blabbermouth. Not at all."

Her voice was wobbling terribly.

"No, it's not you," he rushed to tell her. "It's not. It's me, I—"

"I've given you the impression I'm—what did you call it earlier—wanton!"

"I told you at the time I was overstating it. I told you that was the wrong word."

She held up her hand, stopping him. "No, I take responsibility. You don't know how sorry I am."

And then she rushed by him, found the path through the darkened jungle and disappeared.

Perfect, he thought. He'd gotten rid of her before things got dangerously out of control. But it didn't feel perfect. He felt like a bigger jerk than the chicken they had eaten for supper.

She had fled up that path—away from him—with extreme haste, probably hoping to keep the truth from him. That she was crying.

But that's what I am, Drew told himself. He was a

jerk. Just ask his brother, who not only wasn't arriving on the island, but who also was not taking his phone calls.

The truth was, Drew Jordan sucked at relationships. It was good Becky had run off like that, for her own protection, and his. It would have been better if he could have thought of a way to make her believe it was his fault instead of hers, though.

Sitting there, alone, in the sand, nearly choking on his own self-loathing, Drew thought of his mother. He could picture her: the smile, the way she had made him feel, that way she had of cocking her head and listening so intently when he was telling her something. He realized the scent he had detected earlier had reminded him of her perfume.

The truth was, he was shocked to be thinking of her. Since that day he had become both parents to his younger brother, he had tried not to think of his mom and dad. It was just too painful. Losing them—everything, really, his whole world—was what life had given him that was too much to bear.

But the tears in Becky's eyes that she had been holding back so valiantly, and the scent in the air, made him think of his mother. Only in his mind, his mother wasn't cocking her head, listening intently to him with that soft look of wonder that only a mother can have for her offspring.

No, it felt as if his mother was somehow near him, but that her hands were on her hips and she was looking at him with total exasperation.

His mother, he knew, would never have approved of the fact he had made that decent, wholesome young woman from Moose Run, Michigan, cry. She would be really angry with him if he excused his behavior by saying, *But it was for her own good.* His mother, if she was here, would remind him of all the hurt that Becky had already suffered at the hands of men.

She would show him Becky, trying to keep her head up as her father pushed a stroller down the main street of Moose Run, as news got out that the wedding planner's own wedding was a bust.

Sitting there in the sand with the stars coming out over him, Drew felt he was facing some hard truths about himself. Would his mother even approve of the man he had become? Work-obsessed, so emotionally unavailable he had driven his brother right out of his life and into the first pair of soft arms that offered comfort. His mother wouldn't like it one bit that not only was he failing to protect his brother from certain disaster, his brother would not even talk to him.

"So," he asked out loud, "what would you have me do?"

Be a better man.

It wasn't her voice. It was just the gentle breeze stirring the palm fronds. It was just the waves lapping onshore. It was just the call of the night birds.

But is that what her voice had become? Everything? Was his mother's grace and goodness now in everything? Including him?

Drew scrambled out of the sand. He picked up the picnic basket and the blanket and began to run.

"Becky! Becky!"

When he caught up with her, he was breathless. She was walking fast, her head down.

"Becky," he said, and then softly, "Please."

She spun around. She stuck her chin up in the air.

But she could not hide the fact that he was right. She had been crying.

"I didn't mean to hurt your feelings," he said. "I'm the one in the wrong here, not you."

"Thank you," she said icily. "That is very chivalrous of you. However the facts speak for themselves."

Chivalrous. Who used that in a sentence? And why did it make him feel as if he wanted to set down the picnic basket, gather her in his arms and hold her hard?

"Facts?"

"Yes, facts," she said in that clipped tone of voice. "They speak for themselves."

"They do?"

She nodded earnestly. "It seems to me I've just dragged you along with my *wanton* behavior, kissing you, tearing off my clothes. You were correct. It is not professional. And it won't be happening again."

He knew that it not happening again was a good thing, so why did he feel such a sense of loss?

"Becky, I handled that badly."

"There's a good way to handle 'keep your lips off me'?"

He had made her feel rejected. He had done to her what every other man in her life had done to her: given her the message that somehow she didn't measure up, she wasn't good enough.

He rushed to try to repair the damage.

"It's not that I don't want your lips on me," he said. "I do. I mean I don't. I mean we can't. I mean I won't."

She cocked her head, and looked askance at him.

"Do I sound like an idiot?" he said.

"Yes," she said, unforgivingly.

"What I'm trying to say, Becky, is I'm not used to women like you."

"What kind of women are you used to?"

"Guess," he said in a low voice.

She did not appear to want to guess.

He raked his hand through his hair, trying desperately to think of a way to make her get it that would somehow erase those tearstains from her cheeks.

"I'm scared I'll hurt you," he said, his voice gravelly in his own ears. "I don't think it's a good idea to move this fast. Let's back up a step or two. Let's just be friends. First."

He had no idea where that *first* had come from. It implied there would be something following the friendship. But really, that was impossible. And he just had to get through what remained of two weeks without hurting her any more than he already had. He could play at being the better man for eleven damn days. He was almost sure of it.

"Do you ever answer a question?" she asked. "What kind of women are you used to?"

"Ones who are as shallow as me," he said.

"You aren't shallow!"

"You don't know that about me."

"I do," she said firmly.

He sucked in his breath and tried again. Why was she insisting on seeing him as a better man when he did not deserve that? "Ones who don't expect happily-ever-after."

"Oh."

"You see, Becky, my parents died when I was seventeen." *Shut up*, he ordered himself. *Stop it.* "It broke something in me. The sense of loss was just as Tandu said this afternoon. It was too great to bear. When I've had relationships, and it's true, I have, they have been deliberately superficial."

Becky went very still. Her eyes looked wide and beautiful in the starlight that filtered through the thick leaves of the jungle. She took a step toward him. And she reached up and laid the palm of her hand on his cheek.

Her touch was extraordinary. He had to shut his eyes against his reaction to the tenderness in it. In some ways it was more intimate than the kisses they had shared.

"Because you cannot handle one more loss," she guessed softly.

Drew opened his eyes and stared at Becky. It felt as if she could see his soul and was not the least frightened by what she saw there.

This was going sideways! He was not going to answer that. He could not. If he answered that, he would want to lay his head on her shoulder and feel her hand in his hair. He would want to suck up her tenderness like a dry sponge sucking up moisture. If he answered that he would become weak, instead of what he needed to be most.

He needed to be strong. Since he'd been seventeen years old, he had needed to be strong. And it wasn't until just this minute he was seeing that as a burden he wanted to lay down.

"I agree," she said softly, dropping her hand away from his cheek. "We just need to be friends."

His relief was abject. She got it. He was too damaged to be any good for a girl like her.

Only then she went and spoiled his relief by standing on her tiptoes and kissing him on the cheek where her hand had lay with such tender healing. She whispered something in his ear.

And he was pretty sure it was the word *first.*

And then she turned and scampered across the moonlit lawn to the castle door and disappeared inside it.

And he had to struggle not to touch his cheek, where the tenderness of her kiss lingered like a promise.

You heal now.

But he couldn't. He knew that. He could do his best to honor the man his mother had raised him to be, to not cause Becky any more harm, but he knew that his own salvation was beyond what he could hope for.

Because really in the end, for a man like him, wasn't hope the most dangerous thing of all?

CHAPTER ELEVEN

BECKY LISTENED TO the sound of hammers, the steady *ratta-tat-tat* riding the breeze through the open window of her office. When had that sound become like music to her?

She told herself, sternly, she could not give in to the temptation, but it was useless. It was as if a cord circled her waist and tugged her toward the window.

This morning, Drew's crew had arrived, but not his brother. They had arrived ready to work, and in hours the wedding pavilion was taking shape on the emerald green expanse of the front lawn. They'd dug holes and poured the cement they had mixed by hand out of bags. Then they had set the posts—which had arrived by helicopter—into those holes.

She had heard helicopters delivering supplies all morning. It sounded like a MASH unit around here.

Now she peeped out the window. In all that activity, her eyes sought him. Her heart went to her throat. Drew, facing the ocean, was straddling a beam. He had to be fifteen feet off the ground, his legs hanging into nothingness. He had a baseball cap on backward and his shirt off.

His skin was sun-kissed and perfect, his back broad

and powerful. He was a picture of male strength and confidence.

She could barely breathe he was so amazing to look at. It was also wonderful to be able to look at him without his being aware of it! She could study the sleek lines of his naked back at her leisure.

"You have work to do," she told herself. Drew, as if he sensed someone watching, turned and glanced over his shoulder, directly at her window. She drew back into the shadows, embarrassed, and pleased, too. Was he looking to glimpse her? Did it fill him with this same sense of delight? Anticipation? Longing?

Reluctantly, she turned her back to the scene, but only long enough to try to drag her desk over to the window. She could multitask. The desk was very heavy. She grunted with exertion.

"Miss Becky?" Tandu was standing in the doorway with a tray. "Why you miss lunch?"

"Oh, I—" For some reason she had felt shy about lunch, knowing that Drew and his crew would be eating in the dining room. Despite their agreement last night to be friends, her heart raced out of control when she thought of his rescue of her, and eating dinner with him on the picnic blanket last night, and swimming with him. But mostly, she thought of how their lips had met. Twice.

How was she going to choke down a sandwich around him? How was she going to behave appropriately with his crew looking on? Anybody with a heartbeat would take one look at her—them—and know that something primal was sizzling in the air between them.

This was what she had missed by being with Jerry

for so long. She had missed all the years when she should have been learning the delicate nuances of how to conduct a relationship with a member of the opposite sex.

Not that it was going to be a relationship. A friendship. She thought of Drew's lips. She wondered how a friendship was going to be possible.

There must be a happy medium between wanton and so shy she couldn't even eat lunch with him!

"What you doing?" Tandu asked, looking at the desk she had managed to move about three feet across the room.

"The breeze!" she said, too emphatically. "I thought I might get a better breeze if I moved the desk."

Tandu set down the lunch tray. With his help it was easier to wrestle the big piece of furniture into its new location.

He looked out the window. "Nice view," he said with wicked amusement. "Eat lunch, enjoy the view. Then you are needed at helicopter pad. Cargo arriving. Many, many boxes."

"I have a checklist. I'll be down shortly. And Tandu, could you think of a few places for wedding photographs? I mean, the beaches are lovely, but if I could preview a few places for the photographer, that would be wonderful."

"Know exactly the place," he said delightedly. "Waterfall."

"Yes!" she said.

"I'll draw you a map."

"Thank you. A waterfall!"

"Now eat. Enjoy the view."

She did eat, and she did enjoy the view. It was actually much easier to get to work when she could just glance up and watch Drew, rather than making a special trip away from her desk and to the window.

Later that afternoon, she headed down to the helicopter loading dock with her checklist and began sorting through the boxes and muttering to herself.

"Candles? Check. Centerpieces? Check."

"Hi there." She swung around.

Drew was watching her, a little smile playing across his handsome features.

"Hello." Oh, God, did she have to sound so formal and geeky?

"Do you always catch your tongue between your teeth like that when you are lost in thought?"

She hadn't been aware she was doing it, and pulled her tongue back into her mouth. He laughed. She blushed.

"The pavilion is looking great," she said, trying to think of something—anything—to say. She was as tongue-tied as if she were a teenager meeting her secret crush unexpectedly at the supermarket!

"Yeah, my guys are pretty amazing, aren't they?"

She had not really spared a glance to any of the other guys. "Amazing," she agreed.

"I just thought I'd check and see if the fabric for draping the pavilion has arrived. I need to come up with a method for hanging it."

"I'll look."

But he was already sorting through boxes, tossing them with easy strength. "This might be it. It's from a fabric store. There's quite a few boxes here." He took a box cutter out of his shirt pocket and slit open one of the boxes. "Come see."

She sidled over to him. She could feel the heat radiating off him as they stood side by side.

"Yes, that's it."

He hefted up one of the boxes onto his shoulder. "I'll send one of the guys over for the rest."

She stood there. That was going to be the whole encounter. *Very professional*, she congratulated herself.

"You want to come weigh in on how to put it up?" he called over his shoulder.

And she threw professionalism to the wind and scampered after him like a puppy who had been given a second chance at affection.

"Hey, guys," he called. "Team meeting. Fabric's here."

His guys, four of them, gathered around.

"Becky, Jared, Jason, Josh and Jimmy."

"The J series," one of them announced. "Brothers. I'm the good-looking one, Josh." He gave a little bow.

"But I'm the strong one," Jimmy announced.

"And I'm the smart one."

"I'm the romantic," Jared said, and stepped forward, picked up her hand and kissed it, to groans from his brothers. "You are a beauty, me lady. Do you happen to be available? I see no rings, so—"

"That's enough," Drew said.

His tone had no snap to it, at all, only firmness, but Becky did not miss how quickly Jared stepped back from her, or the surprised looks exchanged between the brothers.

She liked seeing Drew in this environment. It was obvious his crew of brothers didn't just respect him, they adored him. She soon saw why.

"Let's see what we have here," Drew said. He opened

a box and yards and yards of filmy white material spilled out onto the ground.

He was a natural leader, listening to all the brothers' suggestions about how to attach and drape the fabric to the pavilion poles they had worked all morning installing.

"How about you, Becky?" Drew asked her.

She was flattered that her opinion mattered, too. "I think you should put some kind of bar on those side beams. Long bars, like towel bars, and then thread the fabric through them."

"We have a winner," one of the guys shouted, and they all clapped and went back to work.

"I'll hang the first piece and you can see if it works," Drew said.

With amazing ingenuity he had fabricated a bar in no time. And then he shinnied up a ladder that was leaning on a post and attached the first bar to the beam. And then he did the same on the other side.

"The moment of truth," he called from up on the wall.

She opened the box and he leaned way down to take the fabric from her outstretched hand. Once he had it, he threaded it through the first bar, then came down from the ladder, trailing a line of wide fabric behind him. He went up the ladder on the other side of what would soon look like a pavilion, and threaded the fabric through there. The panel was about three feet wide and dozens of feet long. He came down to the ground and passed her the fabric end.

"You do it," he said.

She tugged on it until the fabric lifted toward the sky, and then began to tighten. Finally, the first panel was in place. The light, filmy, pure-white fabric formed a dreamy roof above them, floating walls on either side of them. Only it was better than walls and a roof because of the way the light was diffused through it, and the way it moved like a living thing in the most gentle of breezes.

"Just like a canopy bed," he told her with satisfaction.

"You know way too much about that," she teased him.

"Actually," he said, frowning at the fabric, "come to think of it, it doesn't really look like a canopy bed. It looks like—"

He snatched up the hem of fabric and draped it over his shoulder. "It looks like a toga."

She burst out laughing.

He struck a pose. "'To be or not to be…'" he said.

"I don't want to be a geek…" she began.

"Oh, go ahead—be a geek. It comes naturally to you."

That stung, but even with it stinging, she couldn't let *To be or not to be* go unchallenged. "'To be or not to be' is Shakespeare," she told him. "Not Nero."

"Well, hell," he said, "that's what makes it really hard for a dumb carpenter to go out with a smart girl."

She stared at him. "Are we going out?" she whispered.

"No! I just was pointing out more evidence of our incompatibility."

That stung even worse than being called a geek. "At least you got part of it right," she told him.

"Which part? The geek part?"

"I am not a geek!"

He shook his head sadly.

"That line? 'To be or not to be.' It's from a soliloquy in the play *Hamlet*. It's from a scene in the nunnery."

"The nunnery?" he said with satisfaction. "Don't *you* have a fascination?"

"No! You *think* I have a fascination. You are incorrect, just as you are incorrect about me being a geek."

"Yes, and being able to quote Shakespeare, chapter and verse, certainly made that point."

She giggled, and unraveled the fabric from around him.

"Hey! Give me back my toga. I already told you I don't wear underwear!

But it was her turn to play with the gauzy fabric. She inserted herself in the middle of it and twirled until she had made it into a long dress. Then she swathed some around her head, until only her eyes showed. Throwing inhibition to the wind, she swiveled her hips and did some things with her hands.

"Guess who I am?" she purred.

He frowned at her. "A bride?"

The thing he liked least!

"No, I'm not a bride," she snapped.

"A hula girl!"

"No."

"I give up. Stop doing that."

"I'm Mata Hari."

"Who? I asked you to stop."

"Why?"

"It's a little too sexy for the job site."

"A perfect imitation of Mata Hari, then," she said with glee. And she did not stop doing it. She was rather enjoying the look on his face.

"Who?"

"She was a spy. And a dancer."

He burst out laughing as if that was the most improbable thing he had ever heard. "How well versed was she in her Shakespeare?"

"She didn't have to be." Becky began to do a slow writhe with her hips. He didn't seem to think it was funny anymore.

In fact, the ease they had been enjoying—that sense of being a team and working together—evaporated.

He stepped back from her, as if he thought she was going to try kissing him again. She blushed.

"I have so much to do," she squeaked, suddenly feeling silly, and at the very same time, not silly at all.

"Me, too," he said.

But neither of them moved.

"Uh, boss, is this a bad time?"

Mata Hari dropped her veil with a little shriek of embarrassment.

"The guys were thinking maybe we could have a break? It's f—"

Drew stopped his worker with a look.

"It's flipping hot out here. We thought maybe we could go swimming and start again when it's not so hot out."

"Great idea," Drew said. "We all need cooling off, particularly Mata Hari here. You coming swimming, Becky?"

She knew she should say no. She had to say no. She didn't even have a proper bathing suit. Instead she unraveled herself from the yards of fabric, called, "Race you," ran down to the water and flung herself in completely clothed.

Drew's crew crashed into the water around her,

following her lead and just jumping in in shorts and T-shirts. They played a raucous game of tag in the water, and she was fully included, though she was very aware of Drew sending out a silent warning that no lines were to be crossed. And none were. It was like having five brothers.

And wouldn't that be the safest thing? Wasn't that what she and Drew had vowed they were going to do? Hadn't they both agreed they were going to retreat into a platonic relationship after the crazy-making sensation of those shared kisses?

What had she been thinking, playing Mata Hari? What kind of craziness was it that she wanted him to not see her exactly as she was: not a spy and dancer who could coax secrets out of unsuspecting men, but a book-loving girl from a small town in America?

After that frolic in the water, the J brothers included her as one of them. Over the next few days, whenever they broke from work to go swimming, one of them came and pounded on her office door and invited her to come.

Today, Josh knocked on the door.

"Swim time," he said.

"I just can't. I have to tie bows on two hundred chairs. And find a cool place to store three thousand potted lavender plants. And—"

Without a word, Josh came in, picked her up and tossed her over his shoulder like a sack of potatoes.

"Stop it. This is my good dress!" She pounded on his back, but of course, with her laughing so hard, he did not take her seriously. She was carried, kicking and screaming and pounding on his back, to the water, where she was unceremoniously dumped in.

"Hey, what the hell are you doing?" Drew demanded, arriving at the water's edge and fishing her out.

The fact that she was screaming with laughter had softened the protective look on his face.

Josh had lifted a big shoulder. "Boss, you said don't take no for an answer."

"No means no, boss," she inserted, barely able to breathe she was laughing so hard.

Drew gave them both an exasperated look, and turned away. Then he turned back, picked her up, raced out into the surf and dumped her again!

She rose from the water sputtering, still holding on to his neck, both their bodies sleek with salt water, her good dress completely ruined.

Gazing into the mischief-filled face of Drew Jordan, Becky was not certain she had ever felt so completely happy.

CHAPTER TWELVE

AFTER THAT BECKY was "in." She and the J's and Drew became a family. They took their meals together and they played together. Becky soon discovered this crew worked hard, and they played harder.

At every break and after work, the football came out. Or the Frisbee. Both games were played with rough-and-tumble delight at the water's edge. She wasn't sure how they could have any energy left, but they did.

The first few times she played, the brothers howled hysterically at both her efforts to throw and catch balls and Frisbees. They good-naturedly nicknamed her Barnside.

"Barnside?" she protested. "That's awful. I demand a new nickname. That is not flattering!"

"You have to earn a new nickname," Jimmy informed her seriously.

"Time to go back to work," Drew told them, after one coffee-break Frisbee session when poor Josh had to climb a palm tree to retrieve a Frisbee she'd thrown. He caught her arm as she turned to leave. "Not you."

"What?" she said.

"Have you heard anything from Allie recently?" he asked.

"The last I heard from her was a few days ago, when she okayed potted lavender instead of tulips." She scanned his face. "You still haven't heard from Joe?"

He shrugged. "It's no big deal."

But she could tell it was. "I'm sorry."

He obviously did not want to talk about his distress over his brother. Becky was aware that she felt disappointed. He was okay with their relationship—with being "friends" on a very light level.

Did he not trust her with his deeper issues?

Apparently not. Drew said, "It's time you learned how to throw a Frisbee. I consider it an essential life skill."

"How could I have missed that?" she asked drily. As much as she wanted to talk to him about his brother, having fun with him was just too tempting. Besides, maybe the lighthearted friendship growing between them would develop some depth, and some trust on his part, if she just gave it time.

"I'm not sure how you could have missed this important life skill," he said, "but it's time to lose 'Barnside.' They are calling you that because you could not hit the side of a barn with a Frisbee at twenty feet."

"At twenty feet? I could!"

"No," Drew informed her with a sad shake of his head, "you couldn't. You've now tossed two Frisbees out to sea, and Josh risked his life to rescue the other one out of the palm tree today. We can't be running out of Frisbees."

"That would be a crisis," she agreed, deadpan.

"I'm glad you understand the seriousness of it. Now, come here."

He placed her in front of him. He gave her a Frisbee. "Don't throw it. Not yet."

He wrapped his arms around her from behind, drawing her back into the powerful support of his chest. He laid his arm along her arm. "It's in the wrist, not the arm. Flick it, don't pitch it." He guided her throw.

Becky actually cackled with delight when it flew true, instead of her normal flub. Soon, he released her to try on her own, and then set up targets for her to throw at. The troubled look that had been on his face since he mentioned his brother evaporated.

Finally, he high-fived her, gave her a little kiss on the nose and headed back to his crew. She watched him go and then looked at the Frisbee in her hand.

How could such a small thing make it feel as if a whole new world was opening up to her? Of course, it wasn't the Frisbee, it was him.

It was being with him and being with his crew.

It occurred to Becky she felt the sense of belonging she had craved since the disintegration of her own family. They were all becoming a team. Drew and his crew were a building machine. The pavilion went up, and they designed and began to build the dance floor. And Becky loved the moments when she and Drew found themselves alone. It was so easy to talk to each other.

The conversation flowed between them so easily. And the laughter.

The hands-off policy had been a good one, even if it was making the tension build almost unbearably between them. It was like going on a diet that had an end date. Not that they had named an end date, but some kind of anticipation was building between them.

And meanwhile, her admiration for him did nothing but grow. He was a natural leader. He was funny. He was smart. She found herself making all kinds of excuses to be around him. She was pretty sure he was doing the same thing to be around her.

The days flew by until there were only three days until the wedding. The details were falling into place seamlessly, not just for the wedding but for the week following. The pagoda and dance floor were done, the wedding gazebo was almost completed, though it still had to be painted.

Usually when she did an event, as the day grew closer her excitement grew, too. But this time she had mixed feelings. In a way, Becky wished the wedding would never come. She had never loved her life as much as she did right now.

Today she was at the helipad looking at the latest shipment of goods. Again, there was a sense of things falling into place: candles in a large box, glass vases for the centerpieces made up of single white roses. She made a note as she instructed the staff member who had been assigned to help her where to put the boxes. Candles would need to be unwrapped and put in candle holders, glass vases cleaned to sparkling. The flowers—accompanied by their own florist—would arrive the evening before the wedding to guarantee freshness.

Then one large, rectangular box with a designer name on it caught her eye. It was the wedding dress. She had not been expecting it. She had assumed it would arrive with Allie.

And yet it made sense that it would need to be hung.

Becky plucked it from all the other boxes and, with some last-minute instructions, walked back to the castle with it. She brought it up to the suite that Allie would inhabit by herself the day before the wedding, and with her new husband after that.

The suite was amazing, so softly romantic it took Becky's breath away. She had a checklist for this room, too. It would be fully supplied with very expensive toiletries, plus fresh flowers would abound. She had chosen the linens from the castle supply room herself.

Becky set the box on the bed. A sticker in red caught her eye. They were instructions stating that the dress should be unpacked, taken out of its plastic protective bag and hung immediately upon arrival. And so Becky opened the box and lifted it out. She unzipped the bag, and carefully lifted the dress out.

Her hands gathered up a sea of white foam. The fabric was silk, so sensuous under her fingertips that Becky could feel the enchantment sewn right into the dress. There was a tall coatrack next to the mirror, and Becky hung the silk-wrapped hanger on a peg and stood back from it.

She could not believe what she was seeing. That long-ago dress that Allie had drawn and given to her, that drawing still living in the back of Becky's dresser drawer, had been brought to life.

The moment was enough to make a girl who had given up on magic believe in it all over again.

Except that's not what it did. Looking at the dress made Becky feel as though she was being stabbed with the shards of her own broken dreams. The dress shimmered with a future she had been robbed of. In every winking pearl, there seemed to be a promise: of someone to share life with, of laughter, of companionship, of passion, of "many babies," fat babies chortling and clapping their hands with glee.

Becky shook herself, as if she was trying to break free of the spell the dress was weaving around her. She wanted to tell herself that she was wrong. That this was not the dress that Allie had drawn on that afternoon of girlish delight all those years ago, not the drawing she had handed to her and said, *This is your wedding dress.*

But she still had that drawing. She had studied it too often now not to know every line of that breathtakingly romantic dress. She had dreamed of herself walking down the aisle in that dress one too many times. There was simply no mistaking which dress it was. Surely, Allie was not being deliberately cruel?

No, Allie had not kept a drawing of the dress. She had given the only existing drawing to Becky. Allie must have remembered it at a subliminal level. Why wouldn't she? The dress was exactly what every single girl dreamed of having one day.

But Becky still felt the tiniest niggle of doubt. What if Drew's cynicism was not misplaced? What if his brother was making a mistake? What if this whole wedding was some kind of publicity stunt orchestrated by Allie? The timing was perfect: Allie was just finishing filming one movie, and another was going to be released in theaters within weeks.

With trembling hands, Becky touched the fabric of the dress one more time. Then she turned and scurried from the room. She felt as if she was going to burst into tears, as if her every secret hope and dream had been shoved into her face and mocked. And then she bumped right into Drew and did what she least wanted to do. She burst into tears.

"Hey!" Drew eased Becky away from him. She was crying! If there was something worse than her laughing and being joyful and carefree, it was this. "What's the matter?"

"Nothing," she said. "I'm just tired. There's so much to do and—"

But he could tell she wasn't just tired. And from working with her for the past week, he could tell there was hardly anything she liked more than having a lot to do. Her strength was organizing, putting her formidable mind to problems that needed to be solved. No, something had upset her. How had he come to be able to read Becky English so accurately?

She was swiping at those tears, lifting her chin to him with fierce pride, backing away from a shoulder to cry on.

The wisest thing would be to let her. Let her go her own way and have a good cry about whatever, and not involve himself any more than he already had.

Who was he kidding? Just himself. He'd noticed his crew sending him sideways looks every time she was around. He'd noticed Tandu putting them together. He was already involved. Spending the past days with her had cemented that.

"You want to be upset together?" he asked her.

"I told you I'm not upset."

"Uh-huh."

"What are you upset about?"

He lifted a shoulder. "You're not telling, I'm not telling."

"Fine."

"Tandu asked me to give you this."

"How could Tandu have possibly known you were going to bump into me?" Becky asked, taking the paper from him.

"I don't know. The man's spooky. He seems to know things."

Becky squinted at the paper. "Sheesh."

"What?"

"It's a map. He promised it to me over a week ago. Apparently there's a waterfall that would make a great backdrop for wedding pictures. Can you figure out this drawing?"

She handed the map back to him. It looked like a child's map for a pirate's treasure. Drew looked at a big arrow, and the words, *Be careful this rock. Do not fall in water, please.*

"I'll come with you," he decided.

"Thank you," she said. "That's unnecessary." She snatched the map back and looked at it. "Which way is north?"

"I'll come."

The fight went out of her. "Do you ever get tired of being the big brother?"

He thought of how tired he was of leaving Joe messages to call him. He looked at her lips. He thought of how tired he was getting of this friendship between them.

"Suck it up, buttercup," he muttered to himself.

She sighed heavily. "If you have a fault, do you know what it is?"

"Please don't break it to me that I have a fault. Not right now."

"What happened?"

"I said I'm not talking about it, if you're not talking about it."

"Your fault is that you don't answer questions."

"Your fault is—" What was he going to say? Her

fault was that she made him think the kind of thoughts he had vowed he was never going to think? "Never mind. Let's go find that waterfall."

"I don't know," Becky said dubiously, after they had been walking twenty minutes. "This seems like kind of a tough walk at any time. I'm in a T-shirt and shorts and I'm overheating. What would it be like in a wedding dress?"

Drew glanced at her. Had she flinched when she said *wedding dress*?

"Maybe her royal highness, the princess Allie is expecting to be delivered to her photo op on a litter carried by two manservants," Drew grumbled. "I hope I'm not going to be one of them."

Becky laughed and took the hand he held back to her to help her scramble over a large boulder.

"Technically, that would be a sedan chair," she said, puffing.

"Huh?"

"A seat that two manservants can carry is sedan chair. Anything bigger is a litter."

He contemplated her. "How do you know this stuff?" he asked.

"That's what a lifetime of reading gets you, a brain teeming with useless information." She contemplated the rock. "Maybe we should just stop here. There's no way Allie can scramble over this rock in a wedding dress."

He contemplated the map. "I think it's only a few more steps. I'm pretty sure I can hear the falls. We might as well see it, even if Allie never will."

And he was right. Only a few steps more and they

pushed their way through a gateway of heavy leaves, as big and as wrinkled as elephant ears, and stood in an enchanted grotto.

"Oh, my," Becky breathed.

A frothing fountain of water poured over a twenty-foot cliff and dropped into a pool of pure green water. The pond was surrounded on all sides by lush green ferns and flowers. A large flat rock jutted out into the middle of it, like a platform.

"Perfect for pictures," she thought out loud. "But how are we going to get them here?"

"Wow," Drew said, apparently not the least bit interested in pictures. In a blink, he had stripped off his shirt and dived into the pond. He surfaced and shook his head. Diamonds of water flew. "It's wonderful," he called over the roar of the falls. "Get in."

Once again, there was the small problem of not having bathing attire.

And once again, she was caught in the spell of the island. She didn't care that she didn't have a bathing suit. She wanted to be unencumbered, not just by clothing, but by every single thought that had ever held her prisoner.

CHAPTER THIRTEEN

So AWARE OF the look on Drew's face as he watched her, Becky undid the buttons of her blouse, shrugged it off and then stepped out of her skirt.

When she saw the look on Drew's face, she congratulated herself on her investment in the ultra-sexy and exclusive Rembrandt's Drawing brand underwear. Today, her matching bra and panties were white with tiny red hearts all over them.

And then she stepped into the water. She wanted to dive like him, but because she was not that great a swimmer, she waded in up to her ankles first. The rocks were slipperier than she had expected. Her arms began to windmill.

And she fell, with a wonderful splash, into where he was waiting to catch her.

"The water is fantastic," Becky said, blinking up at him.

"Yes, it is."

She knew neither of them were talking about the water. He set her, it seemed with just a bit of reluctance, on her feet. She splashed him.

"Is that any way to thank me for rescuing you?"

"That is to let you know I did not need to be rescued!"

"Oh," he said. "You planned to fall in the water."

She giggled. "Yes, I did."

"Don't take up poker."

She splashed him again. He got a look on his face. She giggled and bolted away. He was after her in a flash. Soon the grotto was filled with the magic of their splashing and laughter. The days of playing with him—of feeling that sense of belonging—all seemed to have been leading to this. Becky had never felt so free, so wondrous, so aware as she did then.

Finally, exhausted, they hauled themselves out onto the warmth of the large, flat rock, and lay there on their stomachs, side-by-side, panting to catch their breaths.

"I'm indecent," she decided, without a touch of remorse.

"I prefer to think of it as wanton."

She laughed. The sun was coming through the greenery, dappled on his face. His eyelashes were tangled with water. She laid her hand—wantonly—on the firmness of his naked back. She could feel the warmth of him seeping into her hand. He closed his eyes, as if her touch had soothed something in him. His breathing slowed and deepened.

And then so did hers.

When she awoke, her hand was still on his back. He stirred and opened his eyes, looked at her and smiled.

She shivered with a longing so primal it shook her to the core. Drew's smile disappeared, and he found his feet in one catlike motion. As she sat up and hugged herself, chilled now, he retrieved his T-shirt. He came back and slid it over her head. Then he sat behind her, pulled her between the wedge of his legs and wrapped his arms around her until she stopped shivering.

The light was changing in the grotto and the magic deepened all around them.

"What were you upset about earlier?" he asked softly.

She sighed. "I unpacked Allie's wedding dress."

He sucked in his breath. "And what? You wished it was yours?"

"It was mine," she whispered. "It was the dress she drew for me one of those afternoons all those years ago."

"What? The very same dress? Maybe you're just remembering it wrong."

Was there any way to tell him she had kept that picture without seeming hopelessly pathetic?

"No," she said firmly. "It was that dress."

"Representing all your hopes and dreams," he said. "No wonder you were crying."

She felt a surge of tenderness for him that there was no mockery in his tone, but instead, a lovely empathy.

"It was just a shock. I am hoping it is just a weird coincidence. But I'm worried. I didn't know Allie that well when we were teenagers. I don't know her at all now. What if it's all some gigantic game? What if she's playing with everyone?"

"Exactly the same thing I was upset about," Drew confessed to her. "My brother was supposed to be here. He's not. I've called him twice a day, every day, since I got here to find out why. He won't return my calls. That isn't like him."

"Tell me what *is* like him," Becky said gently.

And suddenly he just wanted to unburden himself. He felt as if he had carried it all alone for so long, and he was not sure he could go one more step with the weight of it all. It felt as if it was crushing him.

He was not sure he had ever felt this relaxed or this at ease with another person. Drew had a deep sense of being able to trust this woman in front of him. It felt as if every day before this one—all those laughter-filled days of getting to know one another, of splashing and playing, and throwing Frisbees—had been leading to this.

He needed to think about that: that this wholesome woman, with her girl-next-door look, was really a Mata Hari, a temptress who could pull secrets from an unwilling man. But he didn't heed the warning that was flashing in the back of his brain like a red light telling of a train coming.

Drew just started to talk, and it felt as if a rock had been removed from a dam that had held back tons of water for years. Now it was all flowing toward that opening, trying to get out.

"When my parents died, I was seventeen. I wasn't even a mature seventeen. I was a superficial surfer dude, riding a wave through life."

Something happened to Becky's face. A softness came to it that was so real it almost stole the breath out of his chest. It was so different than the puffy-lipped coos of sympathy that he had received from women in the past when he'd made the mistake of sharing even small parts of his story.

This felt as if he could go lay his head on Becky's slender, naked shoulder, and rest there for a long, long time.

"I'm so sorry," she said quietly, "about the death of your parents. Both of them died at the same time?"

"It was a car accident." He could stop right there, but no, he just kept going. All those words he had never spoken felt as if they were now rushing to escape a building on fire, jostling with each other in their eagerness to be out.

"They had gone out to celebrate the anniversary of some friends. They never came home. A policeman arrived at the door and told me what had happened. Not their fault at all, a drunk driver..."

"Drew," she breathed softly. Somehow her hand found his, and the dam within him was even more compromised.

"You have never met a person more totally unqualified for the job of raising a seven-year-old brother than the seventeen-year-old me."

She squeezed his hand, as if she believed in the younger him, making him want to go on, to somehow dissuade this faith in him.

He cleared his throat. "It was me or foster care, so—" He rolled his shoulders.

"I think that's the bravest thing I ever heard," she said.

"No, it wasn't," he said fiercely. "Brave is when you have a choice. I didn't have any choice."

"You did," she insisted, as fierce as him. "You did have a choice and you chose love."

That word inserted into any conversation between them should have stopped it cold. But it didn't. In fact, it felt as if more of the wall around everything he held inside crumbled, as if her words were a wrecking ball seeking the weakest point in that dam.

"I love my brother," he said. "I just don't know if he knows how much I do."

"He can't be that big a fool," Becky said.

"I managed to finish out my year in high school and

then I found a job on a construction crew. I was tired all the time. And I never seemed to be able to make enough money. Joe sure wasn't wearing the designer clothes the rest of the kids had. I got mad if he asked. That's why he probably doesn't have a clue how I feel about him."

Becky's hand was squeezing his with unbelievable strength. It was as if her strength—who could have ever guessed this tiny woman beside him held so much strength?—was passing between them, right through the skin of her hand into his, entering his bloodstream.

"I put one foot in front of the other," Drew told her. "I did my best to raise my brother. But I was so scared of messing up that I think I was way too strict with him. I thought if I let him know how much I cared about him he would perceive it as weakness and I would lose control. Of him. Of life.

"I'd already seen what happened when I was not in control."

"Did you feel responsible for the death of your parents?" she asked. He could hear that she was startled by the question.

"I guess I asked myself, over and over, what I could have done. And the answer seemed to be, 'Never let anyone you love out of your sight. Never let go.' Most days, I felt as if I was hanging on by a thread.

"When he was a teen? I was not affectionate. I was like Genghis Khan, riding roughshod over the troops. The default answer to almost everything he wanted to do was *no.* When I did loosen the reins a bit, he had to check in with me. He had a curfew. I sucked, and he let me know it."

"Sucked?" she said, indignant.

"Yeah, we both agreed on that. Not that I let him know I agreed with him in the you-suck department."

"Then you were both wrong. What you did was noble," she said quietly. "The fact that you think you did it imperfectly does not make it less noble."

"Noble!" he snapped, wanting to show only annoyance and not vulnerability. "There's nothing noble about acting on necessity."

But she was having none of it. "It's even noble that you saw it as a necessity, not a choice."

"Whatever," he said. He suddenly disliked himself. He felt as if he was a small dog yapping and yapping and yapping at the postman. He sat up. She sat up, too. He folded his arms over his chest, a shield.

"Given that early struggle, you seem to have done well for yourself."

"A man I worked for gave me a break," Drew admitted, even though he had ordered himself to stop talking. "He was a developer. He told me I could have a lot in one of his subdivisions and put up a house on spec. I didn't have to pay for the lot until the house sold. It was the beginning of an amazing journey, but looking back, I think my drive to succeed also made me emotionally unavailable to my brother."

"You feel totally responsible for him, still."

Drew sighed, dragged a hand through his sun-dried hair. "I'm sure it's because of how I raised him that we are in this predicament we're in now, him marrying a girl I know nothing about, who may be using him. And you. And all of us."

"I don't see that as your fault."

"If I worked my ass off, I could feed him," he heard himself volunteering. "I could keep the roof over his head. I could get his books for school. I even managed to get him through college. But—"

"But what?"

"I could not teach him about finding a good relationship." Drew's voice dropped to a hoarse whisper. It felt as if every single word he had said had been circling around this essential truth.

"I missed them so much, my mom and dad. They could have showed him what he should be looking for. They were so stable. My mom was a teacher, my dad was a postal worker. Ordinary people, and yet they elevated the ordinary.

"I didn't know what I had when I had it. I didn't know what it was to wake up to my dad downstairs, making coffee for my mom, delivering it to her every morning. He sang a song while he delivered it. An old Irish folk song. They were always laughing and teasing each other. We were never rich but our house was full. The smell of cookies, the sound of them arguing good-naturedly about where to put the Christmas tree, my mom reading stories. I loved those stories way after I was too old for them. I used to find some excuse to hang out when she was reading to Joe at night. How could I hope to give any of that kind of love to my poor orphaned baby brother? When even thinking about all we had lost felt as if it would undermine the little bit of control that I was holding over my world? Instead, the environment I raised Joe in was so devoid of affection that he's gotten involved with Allie out of his sheer desperation to be loved."

"Maybe he longs for your family as much as you do."

"It's not that I didn't love him," Drew admitted gruffly. "I just didn't know how to say that to him."

"Maybe that's the area where he's going to teach you," she said softly.

Something shivered up and down Drew's spine, a tingle of pure warning, like a man might feel seconds before the cougar pounced from behind, or the plane began to lose altitude, or the earth began to shake. The remainder of the dam wall felt as if it tumbled down inside him.

"You can say that, even after finding the dress? When neither of us is sure about Allie or what her true motives are?"

"I'm going to make a decision to believe love is going to win. No matter what."

He stared at her. There should have been a choice involved here. There should have been a choice to get up and run.

But if there was that choice? He was helpless to make it.

Instead he went into her open arms like a warrior who had fought too many battles, like a warrior who had thought he would never see the lights of familiar fires again. He laid his head upon her breast and felt her hand, tender, on the nape of his neck.

He sighed against her, like a warrior who unexpectedly found himself in the place he had given up on. That place was home.

"You did your best," she said softly. "You can forgive yourself if you weren't perfect."

She began to hum softly. And then she began to sing. Her voice was clear and beautiful and it raised the hair on the back of his neck. It was as if it affirmed that love was the greatest force of all, and that it survived everything, even death.

Because of the millions of songs in the world, how was it possible Becky was gently singing this one, in her soft, true voice?

It was the same song his father had sung to his mother, every day as he brought her coffee.

Drew's surrender was complete. He had thought his story spilling out of him, like water out of a dam that had been compromised, would make him feel weak, and as though he had lost control.

Instead, he felt connected to Becky in a way he had not allowed himself to feel connected to another human being in a long, long time.

Instead, he realized how alone he had been in the world, and how good it felt not to be alone.

Instead, listening to her voice soar above the roar of the waterfall and feeling it tingle along his spine, it felt as though the ice was melting from around his heart. He felt the way he had felt diving into the water to save her all those days ago. He felt brave. Only this time, he felt as if he might be saving himself.

Drew realized he felt as brave as he ever had. He contemplated the irony that a complete surrender would make him feel the depth of his own courage.

You heal now.

And impossibly, beautifully, he was.

CHAPTER FOURTEEN

NIGHT HAD FALLEN by the time they left the waterfall and found their way back to the castle grounds. He left her with his T-shirt and walked beside her bare-chested, happy to give her the small protection of his clothing. He walked her to her bedroom door, and they stood there, looking at each other, drinking each other in like people who had been dying of thirst and had found a spring.

He touched the plumpness of her lip with his thumb, and her tongue darted out and tasted him.

She sighed her surrender, and he made a guttural, groaning sound of pure need. He did what he had been wanting to do all this time.

He planted his hands, tenderly, on either side of her head, and dropped his lips over hers. He kissed her thoroughly, exploring the tenderness of her lips with his own lips, and his tongue, probing the cool grotto of her mouth.

He had thought Becky, his little bookworm, would be shy, but she had always had that surprising side, and she surprised him now.

That gentle kiss of recognition, of welcome, that sigh of surrender, deepened quickly into something else.

It was need and it was desire. It was passion and it

was hunger. It was nature singing its ancient song of wanting life to have victory over the cycle of death.

That was what was in this kiss: everything it was to be human. Instinct and intuition, power and surrender, pleasure that bordered on pain it was so intense. He dragged his lips from hers and anointed her earlobes and her eyelids, her cheeks and the tip of her nose. He kissed the hollow of her throat, and then she pulled him back to her lips.

Her hands were all over him, touching, exploring, celebrating the hard strength in the muscles that gloried at the touch of her questing fingertips.

Finally, rational thought pushed through his primal reaction to her, calling a stern *no.* But it took every ounce of Drew's substantial strength to peel back from her. She stood there, quivering with need, panting, her eyes wide on his face.

His rational mind was gaining a foothold now that he had managed to step back from her. She had never looked more beautiful, even though her hair was a mess, and any makeup she had been wearing had washed off long ago. She had never looked more beautiful, even though she was standing there in a T-shirt that was way too large for her.

But nothing could hide the light shining from her. It was the purity of that light that reminded Drew that Becky was not the kind of girl you tangled with lightly. She required his intentions to be very clear.

In the past few days, he had felt his mother's spirit around him in a way he had not experienced since her death. It was the kind of idea he might have scoffed at two short weeks ago.

And yet this island, with its magic, and Becky with

her own enchantment, made things that had seemed impossible before feel entirely possible now.

Drew knew his mother would be expecting him to be a decent man, expecting him to rise to what she would have wanted him to be if she had lived.

She knew what he had forgotten about himself: that he was a man of courage and decency. Drew took another step back from Becky. He saw the sense of loss and confusion in her face.

"I have to go," he said, his voice hoarse.

"Please, don't."

Her voice was hoarse, too, and she stepped toward him. She took the waistband of his shorts and pulled her to him with surprising strength.

"Don't go," she said fiercely.

"You don't know what you're asking."

"Yes, I do."

For a moment he was so torn, but then his need to be decent won out. If things were going to go places with this girl—and he knew they were—it would require him to be a better man than he had been with women in the past.

It would require him to do the honorable thing.

"I have to make a phone call tonight, before it's too late." It was a poor excuse, but it was the only one he could think of. With great reluctance, he untangled her hands from where they held him, and once again stepped back from her.

If she asked again, he was not going to be able to refuse. A man's strengths had limits, after all.

But she accepted his decision. She raked a hand through her hair and looked disgruntled, but pulled herself together and tilted her chin at him.

"I have a phone call to make, too," she said. She was, just like that, his little bookworm spelling-bee contestant again, prim and sensible, and pulling back from the wild side she had just shown him.

She took a step back from him.

Go, he ordered himself. But he didn't. He stepped back toward her. He kissed her again, quickly, and then he tore himself away from her and went to his own quarters.

Rattled by what he was feeling, he took a deep breath. He wandered to the window and looked at the moon, and listened to the lap of the water on the beach. He felt as alive as he had ever felt.

He glanced at the time, swore softly, took out his cell phone and stabbed in Joe's number.

There was, predictably, no answer. He needed to tell Joe what he had learned of love tonight. It might save Joe from imminent disaster. But, of course, there was no answer, and you could hardly leave a message saying somehow you had stumbled on the secret of life and you needed to share that *right now*.

Joe would think his coolheaded, hard-hearted brother had lost his mind. So, that conversation would have to wait until tomorrow.

According to the information Becky had, Joe and Allie were supposed to arrive only on the morning of the wedding day. This was apparently to slip under the radar of the press.

Tomorrow, the guests would begin arriving, in a coordinated effort that involved planes and boats landing on Sainte Simone all day.

Two hundred people. It was going to be controlled chaos. And then Joe and Allie would arrive the next day, just hours before the wedding. How was he going to get Joe alone? Drew was aware that he *had* to get his brother alone, that he *had* to figure out what the hell was really going on between him and Allie.

And he was aware that he absolutely *had* to protect Becky. He thought of her tears over that dress that Allie had had specially made, and he felt fury building in him. In fact, all the fury of his powerlessness over Joe's situation seemed to be coming to a head.

"Look, Joe," he said, after that annoying beep that made him want to pick up the chair beside his bed and throw it against the wall, "I don't know what your fiancée is up to, but you give her a message from me. You tell your betrothed if she does anything to hurt Becky English—anything—I will not rest until I've tracked her to the ends of the earth and dealt with it. You know me well enough to know I mean it. I'm done begging you to call me. But I don't think you have a clue what you're getting mixed up in."

Drew disconnected the call, annoyed with himself. He had lost control, and probably reduced his chances of getting his brother to meet with him alone.

Becky went to her room and shut the door, leaning against it. Her knees felt wobbly. She felt breathless. She touched her lips, as if she could still feel the warmth of his fire claiming her. She hugged herself. She could not believe she had invited Drew Jordan into her room. She was not that kind of girl!

Thank goodness his good sense had prevailed, but what did that mean? That he was not feeling things quite as intensely as she was?

She sank down on her bed. It was as if the world had

gone completely silent, and into that silence flowed a frightening truth.

She had fallen for Drew Jordan. She loved him. She had never felt anything like what she was feeling right now: tingling with aliveness, excited about the future, aware that life had the potential to hold the most miraculous surprises. She, Becky English, who had sworn off it, had still fallen under its spell. She was in love. It wasn't just the seduction of this wildly romantic setting. It wasn't.

She loved him so much.

It didn't make any sense. It was too quick, wasn't it?

But, in retrospect, her relationship with Jerry had made perfect sense, and had unfolded with respectable slowness.

And there had been nothing real about it. She had been chasing security. She had settled for safety. Salt and pepper. Good grief, she had almost made herself a prisoner of a dull and ordinary life.

But now she knew how life was supposed to feel. And she felt so alive and grateful and on fire with all the potential the days ahead held. They didn't feel safe at all. They felt like they were loaded with unpredictable forces and choices. It felt as if she was plunging into the great unknown, and she was astonished to find she *loved* how the great adventure that was life and love was making her feel.

And following on the heels of her awareness of how much she loved Drew, and how much that love was going to make her life change, Becky felt a sudden fury with his brother. How could he treat Drew like this? Surely Joe was not so stupid that he could not see his brother had sacrificed everything for him?

Drew's whole life had become about making a life for his brother, about holding everything together. He had tried so hard and done so much, and now Joe would not even return his phone calls?

It was wrong. It was just plain old wrong.

Becky's fingers were shaking when she dialed Allie's number. She didn't care that it was late in Spain. She didn't care at all. Of course, after six rings she got Allie's voice commanding her to leave a message.

"Allie, it's Becky English. I need you to get an urgent message to Joe. He needs to call his brother. He needs to call Drew right now. Tomorrow morning at the latest." There, that was good enough. But her voice went on, shaking with emotion. "It's unconscionable that he would be ignoring Drew's attempts to call him after all Drew has done for him. I know you will both be arriving here early on the morning of the wedding, but he needs to talk to Drew before that. As soon as you get this message he needs to call."

There. She didn't need to say one other thing. And yet somehow she was still talking.

"You tell him if he doesn't call his brother immediately he'll be..." She thought and then said, "Dealing with me!"

She disconnected her phone. Then snickered. She had just used a terrible, demanding tone of voice on the most prosperous client she had ever had. She didn't care. What was so funny was her saying Drew's brother would be dealing with her, as if that was any kind of threat.

And yet she felt more powerful right now than she had ever felt in her entire life. It did feel as if she could whip that disrespectful young pup into shape!

That's what love did, she supposed. It didn't take away power, it gave it.

Becky allowed herself to feel the shock of that. She had somehow, someway, fallen in love with Drew Jordan. And not just a little bit in love: irrevocably, crazily, impossibly, feverishly in love.

It was nothing at all like what she had thought was love with Jerry. Nothing. That had felt safe and solid and secure, even though it had turned out to be none of those things. This was the most exciting thing that she had ever felt. It felt as if she was on the very crest of the world's highest roller coaster, waiting for that stomach-dropping swoop downward, her heart in her throat, both terrified and exhilarated by the pathway ahead. And just like that roller coaster, it felt as if somehow she had fully committed before she knew exactly where it was all leading. It felt like now she had no choice but to hang on tight and enjoy the wildest ride of her life.

In a trance of delight at the unexpected turn in her life, Becky pulled off Drew's T-shirt and put on her pajamas. And then she rolled up the T-shirt, and even though it was still slightly damp, she used it as her pillow and drifted off to sleep with the scent of him lulling her like a boat rocking on gentle waves.

She awoke the next morning to the steady *wop-wop-wop* of helicopter blades slicing the air. At first, she lay in bed, hugging Drew's T-shirt, listening and feeling content. Waking up to the sound of helicopters was not unusual on Sainte Simone. It was the primary way that supplies were delivered, and with the wedding just one day away, all kinds of things would be arriving today. Fresh flowers. The cake. The photographer.

Two hundred people would also be arriving over

the course of the day, on boats and by small commercial jets.

There was no time for lollygagging, Becky told herself sternly. She cast back the covers, gave the T-shirt one final hug before putting it under her pillow and then got up and went to the window.

One day, she thought, looking at the helicopters buzzing above her. She had to focus. She had to shake off this dazed, delicious feeling that she was in love and that was all that mattered.

And then it slowly penetrated her bliss that something was amiss. Her mouth fell open. She should have realized from the noise levels that something was dreadfully wrong, but she had not.

There was not one helicopter in the skies above Sainte Simone. From her place at the window, she could count half a dozen. It looked like an invasion force, but with none of the helicopters even attempting to land. They were hovering and dipping and swooping.

She could see a cameraman leaning precariously out one open door! There were so many helicopters in the tiny patch of sky above the island that it was amazing they were managing not to crash into each other.

As she watched, one of the aircraft swooped down over the pavilion. The beautiful white gauze panels began to whip around as though they had been caught in a hurricane. One ripped away, and was swept on air currents out to the ocean, where it floated down in the water, looking for all the world like a bridal veil.

A man—Josh, she thought—raced out into the surf and grabbed the fabric, then shook his fist at the helicopter. The helicopter swooped toward him, the cameraman leaning way out to get that shot.

Becky turned from the window, got dressed quickly and hurried down the stairs and out the main door onto the lawn. The staff were all out there—even the chef in his tall hat—staring in amazement at the frenzied sky dance above them.

Josh came and thrust the wet ball of fabric at her.

"Sorry," he muttered. Tandu turned and looked at her sadly. "It's on the news this morning. That the wedding is here, tomorrow. I have satellite. It's on every single channel."

She felt Drew's presence before she saw him. She felt him walk up beside her and she turned to him, and scanned his familiar face, wanting him to show her how to handle this and what to do.

He put his hand on her shoulder, and she nestled into the weight of it. This is what it meant to not be alone. Life could throw things at you, but you didn't have to handle it all by yourself. The weight of the catastrophe could be divided between them.

Couldn't it? She turned to him. "What are we going to do?"

He looked at her blankly, and she realized he was trying to read her lips. There was no way he could have heard her. She repeated her question, louder.

"I don't know," he said.

He didn't know? She felt a faint shiver of disappointment.

"How could we hold a wedding under these circumstances?" she shouted. "No one will be able to hear anything. The fabric is already tearing away from the pavilion. What about Allie's dress? And veil? What about dinner and candles and…" Her voice fell away.

"I don't think there's going to be a wedding," he said.

Her sense of her whole world shifting intensified. He could not save the day. Believing that he could would only lead to disillusionment. Believing in another person could only lead to heartache.

How on earth had she been so swept away that she had forgotten that?

She shot him a look. He sounded sorry, but was there something else in his voice? She studied Drew more carefully. He had his handsome head tilted to look at the helicopters, his arms folded over his chest.

Did he look grimly satisfied that there was a very good possibility that there was going to be no wedding?

CHAPTER FIFTEEN

BECKY FELT HER heart plummet, and it was not totally because the wedding she had worked so hard on now seemed to be in serious danger of being canceled.

Who, more than any other person on the face of the earth, did not want this wedding to happen?

Drew took his eyes from the sky and looked at her. He frowned. "Why are you looking at me like that?"

"I was just wondering about that phone call you were all fired up to make last night," she said. She could hear the stiffness in her own voice, and she saw that her tone registered with him.

"I recall being all fired up," he said, "but not about a phone call."

How dare he throw that in her face right now? That she had invited him in. He saw it as being all fired up. She saw, foolishly, that she had put her absolute trust in him.

"Is this why you didn't come in?" she said, trying to keep her tone low and be heard above the helicopters at the same time.

"Say what?"

"You didn't give in to my wanton invitation because you already knew you were planning this, didn't you?"

"Planning this?" he echoed, his brow furrowing. "Planning what, exactly?"

Becky sucked in a deep breath. "You let it out, didn't you?"

"What?"

"Don't play the innocent with me! You let it out on purpose, to stop the wedding. To stop your brother and Allie from getting married, to buy yourself a little more time to convince him not to do it."

He didn't deny it. Something glittered in his eyes, hard and cold, that she had never seen before. She reminded herself, bitterly, that there were many things about him she had never seen before. She had only known him two weeks. How could she, who of all people should be well versed in the treachery of the human heart, have let her guard down?

"That's why you had to rush to the phone last night," she decided. "Maybe you even thought you were protecting me. I should have never told you about the wedding dress."

"There are a lot of things we should have never told each other," he bit out.

She stared at him and realized the awful truth. It had all happened too fast between them. It was a reminder to her that they didn't know each other at all. She had been susceptible to the whole notion of love. Because the island was so romantic, because of that dress, because of those crazy moments when she had wanted to feel unencumbered, she had thrown herself on the altar of love with reckless abandon.

She'd been unencumbered all right! Every ounce of good sense she'd possessed had fled her!

But really, hadn't she known this all along? That love

was that roller coaster ride, thrilling and dangerous? And that every now and then it went right off the tracks?

She shot him an accusing look. He met her gaze unflinchingly.

A plane circled overhead and began to prepare to land through the minefield of helicopters. Over his shoulder, she could see a passenger barge plowing through seas made rough by the wind coming off those blades.

"Guess what?" she said wearily. "That will be the first of the guests arriving. All those people are expecting a wedding."

He lifted a shoulder negligently. What all those people were expecting didn't matter one iota to him. And neither did all her hard work. Or what this disaster could mean to her career. He didn't care about her at all.

But if he thought she was going to take this lying down, he was mistaken.

"I'm going to call Allie's publicity people," she said, with fierce determination. "Maybe they can make this disaster stop. Maybe they can call off the hounds if they are offered something in exchange."

"Good luck with that," Drew said coolly. "My experience with hounds, limited as it might be, is once they've caught the scent, there is no calling them off."

"I'm sure if Allie offers to do a photo shoot just for them, after the wedding, they will stop this. I'm sure of it!"

Of course, she was no such thing.

He gazed at her. "Forever hopeful," he said. She heard the coldness in his tone, as if being hopeful was a bad thing.

And it was! She had allowed herself to hope she could love this man. And now she saw it was impossible. Now, when it was too late. When she could have none of the glory and all of the pain.

Drew could not let Becky see how her words hit him, like a sword cleaving him in two. Last night he had taken the biggest chance he had ever taken. He had trusted her with everything. He had been wide-open.

Love.

Sheesh. He, of all people, should know better than that. Joe had not called him back. That's what love really was. Leaving yourself wide-open, all right, wide-open to pain. And rejection. Leaving yourself open to the fact that the people you loved most of all could misinterpret everything you did, run it through their own filter and come to their own conclusions, as wrong as those might be. He, of all people, should know that better than anyone else.

How could she think that he would do this to her? How could she trust him so little? He felt furious with her, and fury felt safe. Because when his fury with Becky died down, he knew what would remain. What always remained when love was gone. Pain. An emptiness so vast it felt as though it could swallow a man whole.

And he, knowing that truth as intimately as any man could know it, had still left himself wide-open to revisiting that pain. What did that mean?

"That I'm stupid," he told himself nastily. "Just plain old garden-variety stupid."

Becky felt as if she was in a trance. Numb. But it didn't matter what she was feeling. She'd agreed to do a job, and right now her job was welcoming the first of the wedding guests to the island and trying to hide it from them all that the wedding of the century was quickly turning into the fiasco of the century.

She stood with a smile fixed on her face as the door of the plane opened and the first passenger stepped down onto the steps.

In a large purple hat, and a larger purple dress, was Mrs. Barchkin, her now retired high school social sciences teacher.

"Why, Becky English!" Mrs. Barchkin said cheerily. "What on earth are you doing here?"

Her orders had been to keep the wedding secret. She had not told one person in her small town she was coming here.

Her smile clenched in place, she said, "No, what on earth are you doing here?"

Mrs. Barchkin was clutching a rumpled card in a sweaty hand. She passed it to Becky. Despite the fact people were piling up behind Mrs. Barchkin, Becky smoothed out the card and read, "In appreciation of your kindness, I ask you to be my guest at a celebration of love." There were all the details promising a limousine pickup and the adventure of a lifetime.

"Pack for a week and plan to have fun!" And all this was followed with Allie Ambrosia's flowing signature, both the small *i*'s dotted with hearts.

"Isn't this all too exciting?" Mrs. Barchkin said.

"Too exciting," Becky agreed woodenly. "If you just go over there, that golf cart will take you to your accommodations. Don't worry about your luggage."

Don't worry. Such good advice. But Becky's sense of worry grew as she greeted the rest of the guests coming down the steps of the plane. There was a poor-looking young woman in a cheaply made dress, holding a baby who looked ill. There was a man and a wife and their three kids chattering about the excitement of their first plane ride. There was a minister. At least he *might* be here to conduct the ceremony.

Not a single passenger who got off that plane was what you would expect of Hollywood's A-list. And neither, Becky realized an hour later, was anyone who got off the passenger barge. In fact, most everyone seemed to be the most ordinary of people, people who would have fit right in on Main Street in Moose Run.

They were all awed by the island and the unexpected delight of an invitation to the wedding of one of the most famous people in the world. But none of them—not a single person of the dozens that were now descending on the island—actually seem to know Allie Ambrosia or Joe Jordan.

Becky had a deepening conviction that somehow they were all pawns in Allie's big game. Maybe, just maybe, Drew had not been so wrong in doing everything he could to stop the wedding.

But why had he played with her? Why had he made it seem as if he was going along with getting a wedding ready if he was going to sabotage it? Probably, this—the never-ending storm of helicopters hovering overhead—had been a last-ditch effort to stop things when his every effort to reach his brother had been frustrated.

Still, the fact was she had trusted him. She was not going to make excuses for him! She was determined to not even think about him.

As each boat and plane delivered its guests and departed, Becky's unease grew. Her increasingly frantic texts and messages to Allie and members of Allie's staff were not being answered. In fact, Allie's voice mailbox was now full.

Becky crawled into bed that night, exhausted. The wedding was less than twenty-four hours away. If they were going to cancel it, they needed to do that now.

Though one good thing about all the excitement was that she had not had time to give a thought to Drew. But now she did.

And lying there in her bed, staring at the ceiling, she burst into tears. And the next morning she was thankful she had used up every one of her tears, because a private jet landed at precisely 7:00 a.m.

The door opened.

And absolutely nothing happened. Eventually, the crew got off. A steward told her, cheerfully, they were going to layover here. He showed her the same invitation she had seen at least a dozen times. The one that read, "In appreciation of your kindness, I ask you to be my guest at a celebration of love."

Becky had to resist the impulse to tear that invitation from his hands and rip it into a million pieces. Because now she knew the plane was empty. And Allie and Joe had not gotten off it.

Of course, it could be part of the elaborate subterfuge that was necessary to avoid the paparazzi, but the helicopters overhead were plenty of evidence they had already failed at that.

How could she, Becky asked herself with a shake of her head, still hope? How could she still hope they were coming, and still hope that love really was worth celebrating?

She quit resisting the impulse. She took the invitation from the crew member, tore it into a dozen pieces and threw them to the wind. Despite the surprised looks she received, it felt amazingly good to do that!

She turned and walked away. No more hoping. No more trying to fill in the blanks with optimistic fiction. She was going to have to find Tandu and cancel everything. She was going to have to figure out the logistics of how to get all those disappointed people back out of here.

Her head hurt thinking about it.

So Drew had won the headache competition after all. And by a country mile at that.

CHAPTER SIXTEEN

DREW PULLED HIMSELF from the ocean and flung himself onto the beach. His crew had just finished the gazebo and had departed, sending him looks that let him know he'd been way too hard on them. He'd had them up at dawn, putting the final touches of paint on the gazebo, making sure the dance floor was ready.

What did they expect? There was supposed to be a wedding here in a few hours. Of course he had been hard on them.

Maybe a little too hard, since it now seemed almost everyone on the island, except maybe the happy guests, had figured out the bride and groom were missing.

Drew knew his foul mood had nothing to do with the missing bride and groom, or the possibility, growing more real by the second, that there wasn't going to be a wedding. He had driven his crew to perfection anyway, unreasonably.

He had tried to swim it off, but now, lying in the sand, he was aware he had not. The helicopter that buzzed him to see if he was anyone interesting did not help his extremely foul mood.

How could Becky possibly think he had called the

press? After all they had shared together, how could she not know who he really was?

It penetrated his morose that his phone, lying underneath his shirt, up the beach, was ringing. And then he froze. The ring tone was the one he had assigned for Joe!

He got up and sprinted across the sand.

"Hello?"

"Hi, bro."

It felt like a shock to hear his brother's voice. Even in those two small syllables, Drew was sure he detected something. Sheepishness?

"How are you, Drew?"

"Cut the crap."

Silence. He thought Joe might have hung up on him, but he heard him breathing.

"Where the hell have you been? Why haven't you been answering my calls? Are you on your way here?"

"Drew, I have something to tell you."

Drew was aware he was holding his breath.

"Allie and I got married an hour ago."

"What?"

"The whole island thing was just a ruse. Allie leaked it to the press yesterday morning that we were going to get married there to divert them away from where we really are."

"You lied to me?" He could hear the disbelief and disappointment in his own voice.

"I feel terrible about that. I'm sorry."

"But why?"

Inside he was thinking, *How could you get married without me to stand beside you? I might have made mistakes, but I'm the one who has your back. Who has always had your back.*

"It's complicated," Joe said.

"Let me get this straight. You aren't coming here at all?"

"No."

Poor Allie, Drew thought.

"We got married an hour ago, just Allie and me and a justice of the peace. We're in Topeka, Kansas. Who would ever think to look there, huh?"

"Topeka, Kansas," he repeated dully.

His brother took it as a question. "You don't have to be a resident of the state to get married here. There's a three-day waiting period for the license, but I went down and applied for it a month ago."

"You've been planning this for a month?" Drew felt the pain of it. He had been excluded from one of the most important events of his brother's life. And it was his own fault.

"I'm sorry," he said.

"For what?" Joe sounded astounded.

"That I could never tell you what you needed to hear."

"I'm not following."

"That I loved you and cared about you and would have fought alligators for you."

"Drew! You think I don't know that?"

"I guess if you know it, I don't understand any of this."

"It's kind of all part of a larger plan. I'll fill you in soon. I promise. Meanwhile, Allie's got her people on it right now. In a few hours the press will know we aren't there, and whatever's going on there will die down. They'll leave you guys alone."

"Leave us alone? You think I'm going to stay here?"

"Why not? It's a party. That's all the invitations ever said. That it was a party to celebrate love."

"Who are all these people arriving here?"

And when Joe told him, Drew could feel himself, ever so reluctantly, letting go of the anger.

Even his anger at Becky felt as if it was dissipating.

He understood, suddenly, exactly why she had jumped at the first opportunity to see him in a bad light. That girl was terrified of love. She'd been betrayed by it at too many turns. She was terrified of what she was feeling for him.

"Joe? Tell Allie not to call Becky about the wedding not happening. I'll look after it. I'll tell her myself."

There was a long silence. And then Joe said softly, "All part of a larger plan."

"Yeah, whatever." He wanted to tell his brother congratulations, but somehow he couldn't. Who was this woman that Joe had married? It seemed as if she was just playing with all their strings as if they were her puppets.

Drew threw on his shirt and took the now familiar path back toward the castle. What remained of his anger at Becky for not trusting him was completely gone.

All he wanted to do was protect her from one more devastating betrayal. He understood, suddenly, what love was. With startling clarity he saw that it was the ability to see that it was not all about him. To be able to put her needs ahead of his own and not be a baby because his feelings had been hurt.

As he got closer to the castle, he could see there were awestruck people everywhere prowling the grounds. He spotted Tandu in the crowd, talking to a tall, distinguished-looking man in a casual white suit and bare feet.

“Mr. Drew Jordan, have you met Mr. Lung?” Tandu asked him.

“Pleasure,” Drew said absently. “Tandu, can I talk to you for a minute?”

Tandu stepped to the side with him. “Have you seen Becky?” he asked, with some urgency.

“A few minutes ago. She told me to cancel everything.”

So, she already knew, or thought she did. She was carrying the burden of it by herself.

“Impossible to cancel,” Tandu said. “The wedding must go on!”

“Tandu, there is not going to be a wedding. I just spoke to my brother.”

“Ah,” he said. “Oh, well, we celebrate love anyway, hmm?” And then he gave Drew a look that was particularly piercing, and disappeared into the crowd.

“How are you enjoying my island?” Bart Lung was on his elbow.

“It’s a beautiful place,” Drew said, scanning the crowd for Becky. “Uh, look, Mr. Lung—”

“Bart, please.”

“Bart, I think you need to have a qualified first aid person on the island to host this many guests.”

“I have an excellent first aid attendant. That was him who just introduced us. Don’t be fooled by the tray of canapés.”

“Look, Tandu is a nice guy. Stellar. I just don’t think being afraid of blood is a great trait for a first aid attendant.”

“Tandu? Afraid of blood? Who told you that?”

Before Drew could answer that Tandu himself had told him that, Bart went on.

"Tandu is from this island, but don't be fooled by that island boy accent or the white shirt or the tray of canapés. He's a medical student at Oxford. He comes back in the summers to help out." Bart chortled. "Afraid of blood! I saw him once when he was the first responder to a shark attack. I have never seen so much blood and I have never seen such cool under pressure."

Drew felt a shiver run up and down the whole length of his spine.

And then he saw Becky. She was talking to someone who was obviously a member of the flight crew, and she was waving her arms around expressively.

"Excuse me. I have an urgent matter I need to take care of."

"Of course."

"Becky!"

She turned and looked at him, and for a moment, everything she felt was naked in her face.

And everything she was.

Drew realized fully that her lack of trust was a legacy from her past, and that to be the man she needed, the man worthy of her love, he needed to not hurt her more, but to understand her fears and vulnerabilities and to help her heal them.

Just as she had, without even knowing that was what she was doing, helped him heal his own fears and vulnerabilities.

"We need to talk," he said. "In private."

She looked at him, and then looked away. "Now? I don't see that there is any way they are coming. I was just asking about the chances of getting some flight schedules changed."

Despite the fact she *knew* Allie and Joe weren't coming, despite the fact that she had asked Tandu about canceling, despite the fact that she was trying to figure out how to get rid of all these people, he saw it, just for a second, wink behind her bright eyes.

Hope.

Against all odds, his beautiful, funny, bookish, spunky Becky was still hoping for a happy ending.

"We need to talk," Drew told her.

She hesitated, scanned the sky for an incoming jet and then sighed. "Yes, all right," she said.

He led her away from the crowded front lawn and front terrace.

"I just talked to Joe," he said in a low voice.

"And? Is everything okay? Between you?"

This was who she really was: despite it all, despite thinking that he had betrayed her trust, she was worried about him and his troubled relationship with his brother, first. And the wedding second.

"I guess time will tell."

"You didn't patch things up," she said sadly.

"He didn't phone to patch things up. Becky, he gave me some bad news."

"Is he all right?" There it was again, a boundless compassion for others. "What?" she whispered.

"There isn't going to be a wedding."

It was then that he knew she had been holding her breath, waiting for a miracle, because the air whooshed out of her and her shoulders sagged.

"Because of the press finding out?" she said.

"No, Becky, there was never going to be a wedding."

She looked at him with disbelief.

"Apparently this whole thing—" he swept his arm to indicate the whole thing "—was just a giant ruse planned out in every detail by Allie. She sent the press here, yesterday morning, on a wild-goose chase."

"It wasn't you," she whispered. Her skin turned so pale he wondered if she was going to faint.

"Of course it wasn't me."

She began to tremble. "But how are you ever going to forgive me for thinking it was you?"

"I don't believe," he said softly, "that you ever did believe that. Not in your heart."

"Why did she do that?" Becky wailed.

"So that she and my brother could sneak away and get married in peace. Which they did. An hour ago. In Topeka, Kansas, of all places."

Her hand was on his arm. She was looking at him searchingly. "Your brother got married without you?"

He lifted a shoulder.

"Oh! That is absolutely unforgivable!"

"It's not your problem."

"Oh, my God! Here I am saying what is unforgivable in other people, and what I did was unforgivable. I accused you of alerting the press!"

"Is it possible," he asked her softly, "that you wanted to be mad at me? Is it possible it was just one last-ditch effort to protect yourself from falling in love with me?"

She was doing now what she had not done when he told her there would be no wedding. She was crying.

"I'm so sorry," she said.

"Is it true then? Are you in love with me?"

"Yes, I'm afraid it is. It's true."

"It's true for me, too. I'm in love with you, Becky. I am so in love with you. And I'm as terrified as you are. I'm afraid of loving. I'm afraid of loss. I'm afraid I can't be the man you need me to be. I'm afraid..."

She stopped him with her lips. She stopped him by twining her hands around his neck and pulling him close to her.

And when she did that, he wasn't afraid of anything anymore.

CHAPTER SEVENTEEN

"WHY DID SHE do all this?" Becky asked.

"Joe told me that she never told any of these people they were coming to a wedding."

"She didn't! That's true. She told them in appreciation for their kindness they were being invited to a celebration of love. I saw some of the invitations today. It doesn't really answer *why* she did all this, does it? All this tremendous expense for a ruse? There are a million things that would have been easier and cheaper to send the press in the wrong direction so they could get married in private."

"Joe told me why she did it."

"And?"

"Joe told me that people would look at her humble beginnings and share personal stories about themselves. And so she sent invitations to the ones with the most compelling personal stories, a comeback from cancer, a bankruptcy, surviving the death of a child.

"Joe says she has thought of nothing else for months—that she did her homework. That she chose the ones who rose above their personal circumstances and still gave back to others.

"He said those are the ones they want to celebrate

love with them. He said Allie wants her story to bring hope to lives where too many bad things had occurred. He says she's determined to make miracles happen."

"Wow," Becky said softly. "It almost makes me not want to be mad at her."

"Regretfully, me, too."

They laughed softly together.

"It's quite beautiful, isn't it?" Becky said quietly.

He wanted to harrumph it. He wanted to say it was impossibly naive and downright dumb. He wanted to say his future sister-in-law—no, make that his current sister-in-law—was showing signs of being extraordinarily clever about manipulating others.

He wanted to say all that, but somehow he couldn't.

Because here he was, the beneficiary of one of the miracles that Allie Ambrosia had been so determined to make happen.

You heal now, Tandu had said to him. And somehow his poor wounded heart had healed, just enough to let this woman beside him past his defenses. Now, he found himself hoping they would have the rest of their lives to heal each other, to get better and better.

"You know, Becky, all those people are expecting a wedding. Tandu said it's impossible to put a hold on the food now."

"It's harder to reschedule those exit flights than you might think."

"The minister is already here. And so is the photographer."

"What of it?"

"I think any wedding that is a true expression of love will honor why we are all here."

"What are you suggesting?"

"I don't think she ever had that dress made to hurt you."

"Oh, my God." Becky's fist flew to her mouth, and tears shone behind her eyes.

"And I've been thinking about this. There is no way my brother would ever get married without me. Not unless he thought it was for my own good."

"They put us together deliberately!"

"I'm afraid that's what I'm thinking."

"It's maddening."

"Yes."

"It's a terrible manipulation."

"Yes."

"It's like a blind date on steroids."

"Yes."

"Are you angry?"

"No."

"Me, neither."

"Because it worked. If they would have just introduced us over dinner somewhere, it would have never worked out like this."

"I know. You would have seen me as a girl from Moose Run, one breath away from becoming a nun."

"You would have seen me as superficial and arrogant and easily bored."

"You would have never given me a second chance."

"You wouldn't have wanted one."

They were silent for a long time, contemplating how things could have gone, and how they did.

"What time is the wedding?" he asked her.

"It's supposed to be at three."

"That means you have one hour and fifteen minutes to make up your mind."

"I've made up my mind," Becky whispered.

"You should put on that dress and we should go to that gazebo I built, and in the incredible energy of two hundred people who have been hand-chosen for the bigness of their hearts, we should get married."

"It won't be real," she whispered. "I mean, not legal. It will be like we're playing roles."

"Well, I won't be playing a role, and I don't think you're capable of it. We'll go to Kansas when it's all over. In three days we'll have a license."

"Are you asking me to marry you? For real? Not as part of Allie's amazing pretend world?"

"Absolutely, 100 percent for real."

She stared at him. She began to laugh, and then cry. She threw her arms around his neck. "Yes! Yes! Yes!" she said.

All the helicopters had gone away. The world was perfect and silent and sacred.

Despite the fact they were using up a great deal of that one hour and fifteen minutes, they talked. They talked about children. And where they would live. And what they would do. They talked about how Tandu seemed as if he was a bit of a matchmaker, too, leaving Drew to doctor Becky's leg when he had been more than capable of doing it himself, of delivering them to the best and most romantic places on the island, of "seeing" the future.

Finally, as the clock ticked down, they parted ways with a kiss.

Tandu was waiting for her when she arrived back at the castle. He took in her radiant face with satisfaction.

"You need my help to be best bride ever?"

"How do you know these things?" she asked him.

"I see."

"I know you're a medical student at Oxford."

He chuckled happily. "That is when *seeing* is the most helpful."

Tandu accompanied her up the stairs, but when she went to go to her room, Tandu nudged her in a different direction. "Take the bridal suite."

Becky stared at him suspiciously. "Have you been in on this all along?"

He smiled. "Allie has been to Sainte Simone before. I count her as my friend. I will go let the guests know there has been a slight change in plan and arrange some helpers. I will look after everything."

She could not argue with him. All her life she had never been able to accept good things happening to her, but she was willing to change. She was willing to embrace each gift as it was delivered.

Had she not been delivered a husband out of a storybook? Why not believe? She went to the bridal suite, and stood before the dress that she had hung up days before. She touched it, and it felt not unlike she had been a princess sleeping, who was now waking up.

Tandu had assembled some lovely women helpers and she was treated like a princess. Given that the time until the wedding was so brief, Becky was pampered shamelessly. Her hair was done, her makeup was applied.

And then the beautiful dress was delivered to her. She closed her eyes. Becky let her old self drop away with each stich of her clothing. The dress, and every dream that had been sewn right into the incredible fabric, skimmed over her naked skin. She heard the zipper whisper up.

"Look now," one of her shy helpers instructed.

Becky opened her eyes. Her mouth fell open. The most beautiful princess stood in front of her, her hair piled up on top of her head, with little tendrils kissing the sides of her face. Her eyes, expertly made-up, looked wide and gorgeous. Her cheekbones looked unbelievable. Her lips, pink glossed and slightly turned up in an almost secretive smile, looked sensual.

Her eyes strayed down the elegant curve of her neck to the full enchantment of the dress. The vision in the mirror wobbled like a mirage as her eyes filled with tears.

The dress was a confection, with its sweetheart neckline and fitted bodice, and layers and layers and layers of filmy fabric flowing out in that full skirt with an impossible train. It made her waist look as if a man could span it with his two hands.

Shoes were brought to her, and they looked, fantastically, like the glass slippers in fairy tales.

All those years ago this dress had been the epitome of her every romantic notion. Becky had been able to picture herself in it, but she had never been able to picture it being Jerry that she walked toward.

Because she had never felt like she felt in this moment.

She was so aware that the bride's beauty was not created by the dress. The dress only accentuated what was going on inside, that bubbling fountain of life that love had built within her.

"No crying! You'll ruin your makeup."

But everyone else in the room was crying, all of them feeling the absolute sanctity of this moment, when someone who has been a girl realizes she is ready to be a woman. When someone who has never known the reality of love steps fully into its light.

A beautiful bouquet of island flowers was placed in her hands.

"This way."

Still in a dream, she moved down the castle stairs and out the door. The grounds that had been such a beehive of activity were strangely deserted. A golf cart waited for her and it whisked her silently down the wide path, through the lushness of the tropical growth, to the beach.

She walked down that narrow green-shaded trail to where it opened at the beach. The chairs were all full. If anyone was disappointed that it was not Allie who appeared at the edge of the jungle, it did not show on a single face.

If she had to choose one word to explain the spirit she walked in and toward it would be *joy*.

Bart Lung bowed to her and offered her his arm. She kicked off the glass slippers and felt her feet sink into the sand. She was so aware that she felt as if she could feel every single grain squish up between her toes.

A four-piece ensemble began to play the traditional wedding march.

She dared to look at the gazebo. If this weren't true, this was the part where she would wake up. In her nightmares the gazebo would be empty.

But it was not empty. The minister that she had welcomed on the first plane stood there in purple cleric's robes, beaming at her.

And then Drew turned around.

Becky's breath caught in her throat. She faltered, but the light that burned in his eyes picked her up and made her strong. She moved across the space between them unerringly, her eyes never leaving his, her sense of wonder making it hard to breathe.

She was marrying this man. She was marrying this strong, funny, thrillingly handsome man who would protect those he loved with his life. She was the luckiest woman in the world and she knew it.

Bart let go of her arm at the bottom of the stairs, and Becky went to Drew like an arrow aimed straight for his heart.

She went to him like someone who had been lost in the wilderness catching sight of the way home.

She went to him with his children already being born inside her.

She repeated the vows, those age-old vows, feeling as if each word had a deep meaning she had missed before.

And then came these words:

"I now pronounce you husband and wife."

And before the minister could say anything more, Becky turned and cast her beautiful bouquet at the gathering and went into his arms and claimed his lips.

And then he picked her up and carried her down the steps and out into the ocean, and with the crowd cheering madly, he kissed her again, before he wrapped his arms tightly around her and they both collapsed into the embrace of a turquoise sea.

When they came up for air, they were laughing and sputtering, her perfect hair was ruined, her makeup was running down her face and her dress was clinging to her in wet ribbons.

"This has been the best day of my entire life," she told him. "There will never be another day as good as this one."

And Drew said to her, "No, that's not quite right. This day is just the beginning of the best days of our lives."

And he kissed her again, and the crowd went wild, but her world felt like a grotto of silence and peace, a place cut out of a busy world, just for them. A place created by love.

EPILOGUE

"WHO AGREED TO this insanity?" Drew demanded of his wife.

"You did," Becky told him. She handed him a crying baby and scooped the other one out of the car seat that had been deposited on their living room floor.

Drew frowned at the baby and held it at arm's length. "Does he stink?"

"Probably. I don't think that's he. I think it's she. Pink ribbon in hair."

Drew squinted at the pink ribbon. It would not be beyond his brother to put the ribbon in Sam's hair instead of Sally's.

"I've changed my mind," Drew declared over the howling of the smelly baby. "I am not ready for this. I am not even close to being ready for this."

"Well, it's too late. Your brother and Allie are gone to Sainte Simone. They never had a honeymoon, and if ever a couple needed one, they do."

"I'm not responsible for their choices," he groused, but he was aware it was good-naturedly. His sister-in-law, Allie, was exasperating. And flaky. She was completely out of touch with reality, and her career choice of pretending to be other people had made that quality even more aggravating in her. She believed, with a childlike enthusiasm, in the fairy tales she acted out, and was a huge proponent of happily-ever-after.

And yet…and yet, could you ask for anyone more genuinely good-hearted than her? Or generous? Or kind? Or devoted to her family in general, and his brother in particular?

There was no arguing that Joe, his sweet, shy brother, had blossomed into a confident and happy man under the influence of his choice of a life partner.

In that Hollywood world where a marriage could be gone up in smoke in weeks, Allie and Joe seemed imminently solid. They had found what they both longed for most: that place called home. And they were not throwing it away.

"Mommy gone? Daddy gone?"

Drew juggled the baby, and stared down at one more little face looking up at him. It occurred to him now would be a bad time to let his panic show.

"Yes, Andrew," he said quietly, "You're staying with Uncle Drew and Aunt Becky for a few days."

"Don't want to," Andrew announced.

That makes two of us.

Joe and Allie had adopted Andrew from an orphanage in Brazil not six months after they had married. The fact that the little boy was missing a leg only seemed to make them love him more. He'd only been home with them for about a month when they had found out they were pregnant. The fact that they had been pregnant with twins had been a surprise until just a few weeks before Sam and Sally had been born.

But the young couple had handled it with aplomb.

Drew could see what he had never seen before: that

Joe longed for that sense of family they had both lost even more than he himself had. Joe had chosen Allie, out of some instinct that Drew did not completely understand, as the woman who could give him what he longed for.

So, Joe and Allie were celebrating their second anniversary with a honeymoon away from their three children.

And Drew and Becky would celebrate their second anniversary, one day behind Joe and Allie, with a pack of children, because Allie had announced they were the only people she would trust with her precious offspring.

"I wish I had considered the smell when I agreed to this," he said. "How are we going to have a romantic anniversary now?"

"Ah, we'll think of something," Becky said with that little wink of hers that could turn his blood to liquid lava. "They have to sleep sometime."

"Are you sure?"

"It will be good practice for us," she said. She said it very casually. Too casually. She shot him a look over the tousled dandelion-fluff hair of the baby she was holding.

He went very still. He moved the baby from the crook of one arm to the crook of the other. He stared at his wife, and took in the radiant smile on her face as she looked away from him and gazed at the baby in her arms.

"Good practice for us?"

Andrew punched him in the leg. "I hate you," he decided. "Where's my daddy?"

Becky threw back her head and laughed.

And he saw it then. He wondered how he had missed

it, he who thought he knew every single nuance of his wife's looks and personality and moods.

He saw that she was different. Becky was absolutely glowing, softly and beautifully radiant.

"Yes," she said softly. "Good practice for us."

Andrew kicked him again. Drew looked down at him. Soon, sooner than he could ever have prepared for, he was going to have a little boy like this. A boy who would miss him terribly when he went somewhere. Who would look to him for guidance and direction. Who would think he got up early in the morning and put out the sun for him.

Or maybe he would have a little girl like the one in his arms, howling and stinky, and so, so precious it could steal a man's breath away. A little girl who would need him to show her how to throw a baseball so that the boys wouldn't make her think less of herself. And who would one day, God forbid, need him to sort through all the boys who wanted to date her to find one that might be suitable.

How could a man be ready for that?

He looked again into his wife's face. She was watching him with a soft, knowing smile playing across the fullness of her lips.

That's how he could be ready.

Because love made a man what he could never hope to be on his own. Once, because of the loss of those he had loved the most, he'd thought it was the force that could take a man's strength completely.

Now he saw that all love wove itself into the person a man eventually became. His parents were with him. Becky's love shaped him every day.

And made him ready for whatever was going to happen next.

Andrew punched him again. Juggling the baby, he bent down and scooped Andrew up in his other arm.

"I know," he said. "I know you miss your daddy."

Andrew wailed his assent and buried his head in Drew's neck. The stinky baby started to cry. Becky laughed again. He leaned over and kissed her nose.

And it felt as if in a life full of perfect moments, none had been more perfect than this one.

Daddy. He was going to be a daddy.

It was just as he had said to her the day they had gotten married. It wasn't the best day of their lives. All that was best was still in front of him, in a future that shone bright in the light of love. That love flowed over him from the look in her eyes. It flowed over him and drenched him and all of those days that were yet to come in its shimmering light.

* * * * *

What was on her little mind?

She looked like she was about to jump out of her skin. And he needed to know why.

"So why you'd ask me over?"

Avery's fork fell and clattered against her plate.

"I just wanted to follow up… about what happened… on New Year's."

He didn't need a reminder. The heat between them had been undeniable, so strong he'd pulled her into the nearest private spot—a supply closet. He'd waited three years to have her, and the memories of that night still played out in his dreams.

"What *exactly* requires follow-up?" he asked.

She didn't look at him. "Well… it, um, turns out we didn't, um… dodge the bullet."

It took him a minute to figure out what she was saying. Then he felt something deep in his gut. "You're… pregnant?"

She pulled a narrow plastic stick out of her pocket. Two lines showed in the window. Then she met his eyes. "You're going to be a daddy."

* * *

Those Engaging Garretts!:
The Carolina Cousins!

TWO DOCTORS & A BABY

BY

BRENDA HARLEN

First Published in Great Britain 2016
By Mills & Boon, an imprint of HarperCollins*Publishers*
1 London Bridge Street, London, SE1 9GF

ISBN: 978-0-263-91976-9

23-0416

Our policy is to use papers that are natural, renewable and recyclable products and made from wood grown in sustainable forests. The logging and manufacturing processes conform to the legal environmental regulations of the country of origin.

Printed and bound in Spain
by CPI, Barcelona

Brenda Harlen is a former lawyer who once had the privilege of appearing before the Supreme Court of Canada. The practice of law taught her a lot about the world and reinforced her determination to become a writer—because in fiction, she could promise a happy ending! Now she is an award-winning, national best-selling author of more than thirty titles for Mills & Boon. You can keep up-to-date with Brenda on Facebook and Twitter or through her website, www.brendaharlen.com.

This book is dedicated to all the real-life doctors, nurses, EMTs and others who work in the medical field—because you make a difference, every single day. Thank you!

Chapter One

After six years at Mercy Hospital, Dr. Justin Garrett knew that Friday nights in the ER were inevitably frenzied and chaotic.

New Year's Eve was worse.

And when New Year's Eve happened to fall on a Friday—well, it wasn't yet midnight and he'd already seen more than twice the usual number of patients pass through the emergency department, most of the incidents and injuries directly related to alcohol consumption.

A drunken college student who had put his fist through a wall—and his basketball scholarship in jeopardy—with fractures of the fourth and fifth metacarpal bones. A sixty-three-year-old man who had doubled up on Viagra to celebrate the occasion with his thirty-six-year-old wife and ended up in cardiac arrest instead. A seventeen-year-old female who had fallen off her balcony because the Ecstasy slipped into her drink by her boyfriend had made her want to pick the pretty flowers on her neighbor's terrace—thankfully, she lived on the second floor, although she did sustain a broken clavicle and had required thirty-eight stitches to close the gash on her arm, courtesy of the glass vodka cooler bottle she had been holding when she fell.

And those were only the ones he'd seen in the past hour. Then there was Nancy Anderson—a woman who claimed she tripped and fell into a door but whom he recognized from her frequent visits to the ER with various and numerous contusions and lacerations. Tonight it was a black eye, swollen jaw and broken wrist. Nancy wasn't drunk, but Justin would bet that her husband was—not because it was New Year's Eve but because Ray Anderson always hit the bottle as soon as he got home from work.

More than once, Justin had tried to help her see that there were other options. She refused to listen to him. Because he understood that a woman who had been abused by her husband might be reluctant to confide in another man, he'd called in a female physician to talk to her, with the same unsatisfactory result. After Thanksgiving, when she'd suffered a miscarriage caused by a "fall down the stairs," Dr. Wallace had suggested that she talk to a counselor. Nancy Anderson continued to insist that she was just clumsy, that her husband loved her and would never hurt her.

"What did she say happened this time?" asked Callie Levine, one of his favorite nurses who had drawn the short straw and got stuck working the New Year's Eve shift beside him.

"Walked into a door."

Callie shook her head. "He's going to kill her one of these days."

"Probably," Justin admitted grimly. "But it doesn't matter that you and I see it when she refuses to acknowledge what's happening."

"When she lost the baby, I honestly thought *that* would do it. That her grief would override her fear and she would finally tell the truth."

"She fell down the stairs," Justin said, reminding her of the explanation Nancy Anderson had given when she was admitted on that previous occasion.

Then, because talking about the woman's situation made him feel both frustrated and ineffectual, he opened another chart. "Did you call up to the psych department for a consult?"

"Victoria Danes said she would be down shortly," Callie told him. "Did you want her to see Mrs. Anderson?"

"No point," he said. "I just need her to talk to Tanner Northrop so we can figure out what to do there."

"Is that the little boy in Exam Two with Dr. Wallace?"

"Dr. Wallace is still here?" He'd crossed paths with Avery Wallace earlier in the evening when he'd sneaked into the doctor's lounge for a much-needed hit of caffeine and she'd strolled in, wearing a formfitting black dress and mile-high heels, and his eyes had almost popped right out of his head.

She'd barely glanced in his direction as she'd made her way to the women's locker room, emerging a few minutes later in faded scrubs and running shoes. It didn't matter that the more familiar attire disguised her delectable feminine curves—his body was always on full alert whenever she was near.

She'd moved to Charisma three and a half years earlier and started working at Mercy Hospital. Since then, he'd gotten to know her pretty well—professionally, at least. Personally, she wouldn't give him the time of day, despite the definite sizzle in the air whenever they were around each other.

Although she wasn't on the schedule tonight, she'd assisted him with a procedure earlier in the evening because they were short staffed and she was there. He'd expected that she would have gone home after that—making her escape as soon as possible. Apparently, he was wrong.

Callie nodded in response to his question. "She's teaching the kid how to play Go Fish."

He smiled at that, grateful Tanner had some kind of distraction. The eight-year-old had dialed 9-1-1 after his mother shot up a little too much of her favorite heroin cocktail and wouldn't wake up. She still hadn't woken up, and Tanner didn't seem to know if he had any other family.

"Send Victoria in to see Tanner when she comes down," he said. "I'm going to see how Mrs. Anderson is doing."

"Good luck with that."

Of course, it was his bad luck that he'd just opened the door to Exam Four when the psychologist appeared.

"What's *she* doing here?" Nancy Anderson demanded.

"She's not here to see you," Justin assured her. Then, to Victoria, "Exam Two."

"Thanks." The psychologist moved on; the patient reapplied the ice pack to her jaw.

"Are you planning to go home tonight?" Justin asked her.

"Of course."

"Do you need someone to call a cab for you?" he asked.

Nancy shook her head. "Ray's waiting for me outside."

He scribbled a prescription and handed her the slip. "Pain meds—for the wrist."

She had to set down the ice to take it in her uninjured hand. "Thanks."

There was so much more he could have said, so much more he wanted to say, but he simply nodded and left the room.

"Dare I hope that things are finally starting to slow down?" a pretty brunette asked when he returned to the nurses' station. She'd only been working at Mercy a couple of months and he had to glance at the whiteboard to remind himself of her name: Heather.

"I wouldn't," Justin advised. "It's early yet—still lots of champagne to be drunk and much idiocy to be demonstrated."

She laughed. "How did you get stuck working New Year's Eve?"

"Everyone has to take a turn."

"Callie said it was Dr. Roberts's turn."

He shrugged. It was true that Greg Roberts had been on the schedule for tonight. It was also true that the other doctor was a newlywed while Justin had no plans for the evening. He'd received a couple of invitations to parties—and a few offers for more personal celebrations—but he'd declined them all without really knowing why. He usually enjoyed going out with friends, but lately he'd found himself tiring of the familiar scene.

"What's going on with the guy in Exam Three?" Heather asked. "Are we going to be able to open up that room pretty soon?"

He shook his head. "Suspected alcohol poisoning. I'm waiting for the results from his blood alcohol and tox screens to confirm the diagnosis." In the interim, the patient was on a saline drip for hydration.

"Speaking of alcohol," Heather said. "I've got a bottle of champagne chilling at home to celebrate the New Year whenever I finally get out of here."

"You plan on drinking a whole bottle of champagne by yourself?"

Her lips curved in a slow, seductive smile. "Unless you want to share it with me."

What he'd intended as an innocent question had probably sounded to her as if he was angling for an invitation. But honestly, his thoughts had been divided between Nancy Anderson and Tanner Northrop, and Heather's overture was as unexpected as it was unwanted.

"I've got the rest of the weekend off and my roommate is in Florida for the holidays," Heather continued.

"Lucky you," he noted.

She touched a hand to his arm. "We could be lucky together."

He stepped back from the counter, so that her hand fell away, and finished making notes in the chart before he passed it to her. "Sorry," he said, without really meaning it. "I've got other plans this weekend."

"What about tonight?" she pressed. "Surely you're not expected to be anywhere when we get off shift at two a.m.?"

"No," he acknowledged. "But it's been a really long night and I just want to go home to my bed. Alone."

The hopeful light in her eyes faded. "Callie told me that you always go for the blondes."

He wasn't really surprised to hear that he'd been the subject of some conversation. He knew that the nurses often talked about the doctors. He also knew that some of them weren't as interested in patient care as they were in adding the letters *M-R-S* to their names. But the fact that Callie had been drawn in to the discussion did surprise him, and he made a mental note to talk to her. If he couldn't stop the gossip, he hoped to at least encourage discretion.

"My response has nothing to do with the color of your hair," he assured Heather. "I'm just not interested in partying with anyone tonight."

She pouted but turned her attention back to her work.

As he was walking away from the nurses' station, a call came in from paramedics at an MVA seeking permission to transport multiple victims to the ER. Justin forgot about the gossip and refocused his mind on real priorities.

Avery Wallace rolled her shoulders, attempting to loosen the tight muscles that ached and burned. She was an obstetrician, not an ER doctor—and not scheduled to work tonight in any event. But she'd been on her way to a party with friends when she got the call from her answering service about a patient who was in labor and on her way to Mercy. She knew the doctor on call could handle the birth, but the expectant mother—a military wife whose family lived on the West Coast and whose husband was currently out of the country—was on her own and incredibly nervous about the birth of her first child.

Avery hadn't hesitated to make the detour to the hospital. After texting a quick apology to Amy Seabrook—the friend and colleague who had invited her to the party—she'd exchanged her dress and heels for well-worn scrubs and running shoes.

After Michelle was settled with her new baby, Avery headed back to the locker room with the vague thought of salvaging her plans for the evening. She didn't make it far before she was nabbed to assist Dr. Romeo—aka Justin Garrett—with a resuscitative thoracotomy in the ER.

While she might disapprove of his blatant flirtations with members of the female staff, she couldn't deny that he was an exceptional doctor—or that her own heart always beat just a little bit faster whenever he was around. He stood about six feet two inches with a lean but strong build, short dark blond hair and deep green eyes. But it was more than his physical appearance that drew women to him. He was charming and confident, and not just a doctor but also a Garrett—a name with a certain inherent status in Charisma, North Carolina, where Garrett Furniture had been one of the town's major employers for more than fifty years.

After more than three years of working beside him at the hospital, she would have expected to become inured to his presence. The truth was exactly the opposite—the more time she spent with him, the more appealing she found him. She respected his ability to take control in a crisis situation as much as she admired the compassion he showed to his patients and, as a result, she'd developed a pretty major crush on him—not that she had any intention of letting Dr. Romeo know it.

When the patient had been resuscitated and moved to surgery, he'd simply and sincerely thanked Avery for her help. That was another thing she liked about him—he might be in command of the ER, but he never overlooked the contributions of the rest of the staff.

She'd barely discarded her gown and gloves from that procedure when she was steered to the surgical wing to help Dr. Bristow with a femoral shaft fracture. She passed through the ER again on her way out, and that was when she saw Dr. Garrett hunkered down in conversation with a little boy. The child's face was streaked with dirt and tears, but it was the abject grief in his eyes that tugged at her heart and had her slipping into the room after the ER physician had gone. She chatted with him and played Go Fish until Victoria Danes arrived. Once she was confident that he was comfortable in the psychologist's company, she headed back toward the locker room. And ran straight into the one person she always tried to avoid.

"Good—you're still here."

Her heart bumped against her ribs as she looked up at Justin, but she kept her tone cool, casual. "Actually, I'm just on my way home."

"We've got two ambulances coming in from an MVA—one carrying an expectant mother."

"Dr. Terrence can handle it."

"He can, but Callie asked me to find you."

"Why?" she wondered.

"The pregnant woman is her sister."

According to the report from the paramedics, the taxi in which Callie's sister and her husband were riding had been broadsided by a pickup truck that had sped through a red light.

Avery watched the clock as she scrubbed, conscious that each one of the five minutes she was required to spend on the procedure was another minute the expectant mother was waiting. Dr. Garrett was already working on the pregnant woman's husband, who had various contusions and lacerations and a possible concussion.

When Avery finally entered the OR, she was given an immediate update on the patient's condition.

"Camryn Ritter, thirty-one years old, thirty-eight weeks pregnant. Presenting with moderate bleeding and uterine tenderness, BP one-ten over seventy, pulse rate one-thirty, baby's rhythm is steady at ninety BPM."

The numbers, combined with her own observations, supported the diagnosis of placental abruption with evidence of fetal bradycardia, which meant that delivering the baby now was necessary for the welfare of both mother and child. Thankfully, Dr. Terrence had already requested that the anesthesiologist give the patient a spinal block, so she could start surgery almost right away.

She'd lost count of the number of C-sections that she'd performed, but she'd never considered a caesarean to be a routine surgery. Every pregnancy was different and every baby was different, so she was always hypervigilant, never taking anything for granted. But at thirty-eight weeks, both mother and baby had a really good chance as long as she could get in before anything else went wrong.

"Where's Brad?" the patient asked worriedly.

Avery glanced at Callie, who was holding her sister's hand. Ordinarily she would have banned the nurse from the operating room because of the personal connection, but in the absence of the woman's husband, she was counting on Callie to help keep the expectant mother calm.

"Brad's her husband, my brother-in-law," Callie explained. Then, to her sister, she said, "He was a little bumped up in the taxi, but Dr. Garrett's checking him over now and running some tests."

"He was bleeding," Camryn said. "There was so much blood."

"Head injuries bleed a lot," Callie acknowledged. "Remember when you got hit with a baseball bat in third grade—while you were wearing my pink jean jacket? It took mom three washes to get the blood out."

Her sister managed a weak smile. "So he's okay?"

"He's going to be fine," Callie promised, more likely to soothe the expectant mother's worries than from any certainty of the fact. "Dr. Garrett's one of the best doctors on staff here. Dr. Wallace is another."

"Brad really wanted to be here when the baby was born."

"I'm sure neither of you expected that your baby would be born tonight, under these circumstances."

The anesthesiologist was near the head of the bed, monitoring the mother's vital signs and intravenous levels. He nodded to Avery and, after confirming that her patient could feel nothing, she drew the scalpel across her swollen abdomen.

A planned caesarean usually took between five and ten minutes from first cut until the baby was lifted out. In an emergency situation like this one, an experienced doctor could perform the procedure in about two minutes.

Dr. Terrence—who had scrubbed in to assist—worked to keep the surgical field clean, swabbing with gauze and holding the incision open while she worked. They were approaching the two-minute mark when she reached into the uterus. Clear fluid gushed around her gloved hand as she cradled the small skull in her palm and carefully guided the head, then the shoulders, out of the opening.

Her hands didn't shake as she lifted the baby out of the mother's womb. Her hands never shook when she was under the hot lights of an operating or delivery room. She didn't let herself feel any pressure or emotion while she was focused on a task. Her unflappable demeanor was, she knew, only one reason some of the staff referred to her as "Wall-ice."

The baby's color was good, and when Avery wiped his

mouth with gauze and gently squeezed his nostrils, she was immediately rewarded with a soft cry.

"Is that—" Camryn's voice hitched. "Is that my baby?"

"That's your baby," Avery confirmed.

"He's a boy," Callie told her sister, watching with misty eyes as the cord was clamped and cut. "You have a beautiful, perfect baby boy."

"I want to see him," the new mother said.

"You will—in just a moment."

"Seven pounds, five ounces, nineteen inches," another nurse announced from the corner of the operating room, after the newborn had been wiped, weighed and swaddled.

Camryn wiped at a tear that spilled onto her cheek as the baby was placed in her arms. "Where's Brad? I want to see him. I want him to see our baby."

"He'll be here as soon as he can," Callie soothed.

While the nurse and her sister talked quietly, Avery continued to work, suturing up each layer of abdominal tissue. But even as she focused on her task, she was thinking of the awe and wonder on Camryn's face when she saw her baby for the first time—and immediately fell in love with him. Avery had seen it happen countless times, but it never failed to tug at her own heart.

Half an hour later, when she finally left the new mom with her baby, she again crossed paths with Dr. Garrett in the hall.

"How's dad?" she asked, referring to the baby's father whom he'd been working on in the adjacent room.

"Aside from two broken ribs, a punctured lung, mild concussion and a head laceration that required twenty-two stitches to close, he's doing just fine."

"Twenty-two stitches? I just put in more than twice that number *and* delivered a baby."

"Competitive, aren't you?" Though his tone was teasing, his smile was weak.

"Maybe a little," she acknowledged.

"Boy or girl?"

"Boy."

He slung a companionable arm across her shoulders as they headed down the hall. "Good work, Wallace."

"You, too, Garrett."

They walked together in silence for a few minutes, until Avery caught him stifling a yawn. "I imagine it's been a very long night for you," she said.

"It's New Year's Eve," he reminded her.

"Was," she corrected.

He scrubbed a hand over his jaw. "What?"

"It's after midnight now." Afterward, she would wonder what caused her to throw caution and common sense to the wind. But in the moment, it seemed perfectly natural to lift herself onto her toes and touch her lips to his cheek. "Happy New Year."

She could tell he was as startled by the impulsive gesture as she was, but when he looked at her, she saw something more than surprise in his eyes. Something that made her heart pound harder and faster, that made her weary body ache and yearn. Something that warned her she'd taken the first step down an intriguing—and potentially dangerous—path.

He took the next step, pulling open the nearest door—to a housekeeping supply closet—and tugging her inside. She didn't balk or protest. For more than three years, they'd danced around the attraction between them. They weren't dancing anymore.

"Happy New Year," he echoed, then crushed his mouth down on hers.

Chapter Two

His kiss was hot and hungry and demanding. She kissed him back, just as hotly and hungrily, responding to his every demand and meeting them with her own. If she'd been able to think clearly—if she'd been able to think *at all*—she might have drawn back. But the moment his lips touched hers, all rational thought slipped from her mind. In fact, her brain seemed to have shut down completely, letting the hormones that flooded through her veins lead the way.

And they were leading her to a very happy place. A place where his hands were all over her, touching and teasing, giving her so much pleasure and still making her want so much more.

He eased his lips away from hers. "I like the sparkly things in your hair, Wallace—they really dress up your scrubs."

"What?" She frowned as she reached up, startled to realize that her hair was in a fancy twist instead of her usual ponytail. So much had happened since she'd left home, she'd almost forgotten about the party and the decorative pins she'd impulsively added to her updo for the occasion. "Oh."

"You were out celebrating the New Year," Justin guessed.

"I never actually made it that far," she told him.

"I'm sure your date was disappointed."

"It wasn't a date," she said. "Not really."

"Good." He slid his hands up her back, drawing her

closer, and lowered his head to nip playfully at her bottom lip.

This was dangerous. He was hardly touching her and her resistance was melting. He wasn't her type. Not at all. He was a player and a doctor and everything she didn't want in a man.

But right now, she didn't care about any of that. Right now, she *did* want him. Or at least her body wanted to feel the way she knew he could make her feel, the way he *was* making her feel.

"But I am sorry your plans were ruined," he said.

"They were actually Amy's plans—and I was kind of relieved to escape another blind date."

"Then you weren't planning to ring in the New Year with wild, sweaty sex?"

"The thought never crossed my mind." His hands grazed her breasts as they skimmed up her sides, making her breath hitch. "Until now."

"Really?" He smiled against her lips. "You're thinking about it now?"

She slid her hands beneath his scrub top, over the smooth, taut skin of his abdomen. "Yeah, I'm thinking about it now."

"If you want to hold that thought, I'm off shift in a couple of hours."

She scraped her teeth lightly over his jaw. "I'll change my mind in a couple of hours."

"I definitely don't want you to change your mind." He whisked her scrub top up over her head, unveiling her pink lace bra, and his brows lifted. "You sure you didn't put this on for your date?"

"Forget about my date," she suggested. "And focus on me."

"I'm focused," he promised, his thumbs stroking over her rigid nipples through the delicate fabric. "Very focused."

Her head fell back against the door as arrows of sensation shot straight to her core. Her body was on fire. She was burning with want, with need. Desperate, aching need. She was so tightly wound up she was practically vibrating.

Then he dipped his head and found her breast with his mouth, suckling her through the lace. She slid her fingers into his hair, holding him against her as waves of exquisite sensation washed over her.

His mouth moved to her other breast as his hand slid down the front of her pants, his fingertips brushing over the aching nub at her center. The light touch made her gasp and shudder. He parted the soft folds of skin, groaning his appreciation when he found that she was already wet.

"You do something to me, Wallace," he admitted gruffly.

"Do something to me," she suggested, reaching a hand into his pants to wrap around the hard length of him, making him groan again. "Do me."

"I will," he promised.

But for now, he continued to touch and tease her. She bit hard on her lip to keep from crying out, her palms flat against the door to hold herself upright as her knees quivered and her body shuddered.

She was gasping and panting and on the verge of melting into a puddle at his feet when he pushed her panties down to her ankles with her pants, then shoved his own pants and boxers out of the way. Finally he covered her mouth with his and thrust into her, kissing her hard and deep as he took her body the same way.

She was ready for him. More than ready. But it had been a long time, and she'd almost forgotten how good it could feel. How exquisitely and blissfully good.

It was pretty much a consensus among the female contingent of the hospital nursing staff that Dr. Garrett could satisfy a woman's every want and need, and he lived up to that reputation now. He used his hands and his lips and his body to drive her to the ultimate pinnacle of pleasure and far beyond, soaring into the abyss with her.

When she finally floated back to earth, her body was still pinned against the door, still intimately joined with his. She took a minute to catch her breath as he did the same.

"I think I might need the paddles to restart my heart, Wallace."

She forced herself to match his casual tone. "Then it's a good thing you're a doctor."

But even while her body continued to hum with the aftereffects of pleasure, her mind was beginning to remember the hundred and one reasons that giving in to the attraction she felt for Justin was a bad idea. The number one reason was the *MD* that followed his name; the hundred other reasons were the hundred names of other women he'd undoubtedly pleasured in a similar manner.

He brushed his lips against hers—the kiss surprisingly tender and sweet on the heels of their passionate and almost desperate coupling.

"Do you ever wonder how we didn't end up here before now?" he asked her.

Her brows lifted. "Mostly naked in a housekeeping supply closet?"

"I was focused on the mostly naked part," he said. "And thinking that I'd like to take you back to my place and progress from mostly to completely naked."

She shook her head and pushed him away so she could pull up her pants and gather the rest of her discarded clothing. "Not a good idea."

"Why would you say that?"

"Because we have to work together."

"We've always worked well together," he noted. "And now we know that we play well together, too, and—"

She touched a hand to his lips, silencing his words as she shook her head. "No."

He frowned. "You don't even know what I was going to say."

"It doesn't matter," she insisted, refastening her bra.

"You're just going to walk away?"

She tugged her shirt over her head. "Well, someone is eventually going to need something from this closet, so it's probably not a good idea to stay here."

"You know I'm not referring to the closet but what happened between us," he chided.

"It was an impulse, Garrett. Nothing more than that."

"An impulse," he echoed.

He sounded oddly hurt by her characterization of their actions—but she was probably just imagining it. After all, Justin Garrett didn't do emotions or involvement. He moved in and then moved on, and she thought he would appreciate that she didn't want anything more than that.

"It was an intense situation in the ER tonight and we both worked hard to ensure a young couple had reason to celebrate rather than mourn the start of the New Year."

"You think that what just happened between us only happened because of *adrenaline*?" he asked incredulously.

"And proximity," she allowed.

"So this is normal postoperative procedure for you?"

"No!"

"Then it was out-of-character behavior?" he pressed.

"Very," she admitted.

"And probably an inevitable result of the fact that you've been denying the attraction between us for more than three years."

Probably. Although she had no intention of admitting it. To Avery's mind, it was bad enough that she'd succumbed to the attraction she'd tried so hard to ignore without giving him the additional satisfaction of knowing that she'd harbored those feelings for so long.

But he was right—she'd been attracted to him from the

beginning. The day she interviewed with the chief of staff at Mercy Hospital, the first time she'd met Justin, he'd smiled at her and her pulse had skyrocketed.

She wasn't unfamiliar with attraction, but she couldn't remember ever having it hit her so immediately and intensely. On her first day of work, he'd flirted with her a little, and she'd flirted back.

And then, later that same day, she'd seen him flirting with someone else. The day after that, it was someone different again. It had only taken three more days—three more shifts at the hospital—for her to realize that Justin Garrett, aka Dr. Romeo, was not her type. He'd continued to flirt with her—or try to—when their paths crossed, but she'd given him no encouragement.

Not until she'd kissed him.

"I have to go."

He slapped his hand against the door to prevent her from opening it. "And you're still denying it," he noted.

"Let me go, Garrett."

"I'm not holding you hostage. I'm just trying to have a conversation."

"There's nothing to talk about. You got another notch to add to your bedpost—isn't that enough for you?"

"I don't have bedposts," he said. "Which I'd be happy to prove to you if you come home with me when I get off shift."

"No," she said firmly.

He brushed a loose hair off her cheek and tucked it behind her ear, the light touch of his fingertips on her skin making her shiver and want him all over again. *Damn him.*

"What did I do wrong?" he asked her. "Aside from taking you against the closet door with all the finesse of a horny teenager, I mean."

She wished she could blame him for that, but she'd initiated everything. She wished she could dismiss the experience as unsatisfactory, but the truth was, despite the setting and the pace of the event, her body had been very thoroughly satisfied.

"You didn't do anything wrong," she said.

"Then why are you pulling away?" Justin asked, sincerely baffled by her reaction.

Before she could respond, his pager started beeping.

Mentally cursing the untimely interruption, he scooped it up from the floor, where it had fallen when he'd dropped his pants. He glanced at the display and sighed. "Two ambulances are on their way from another MVA."

But there was no response.

Avery was already gone.

With a sigh, Justin tucked the pager back in his pocket and headed to the ER.

He wouldn't be a good doctor if he couldn't set aside personal distractions and do his job. But after he'd finished stitching up another head wound, helped cast the broken arm of a screaming, squirming four-year-old, checked on the college student with alcohol poisoning and confirmed that Tanner Northrop was in the temporary custody of Family Services, it was almost two hours past the end of his shift.

He went to the locker room, physically and mentally exhausted, and let the water of the shower pound down on him. When he finally came out of the shower, he wanted nothing more than his bed.

Then he thought about Avery in that bed, warm and willing and naked, and his body miraculously stirred to life again.

The pretty baby doctor could believe whatever she wanted and make whatever excuses she wanted, but he knew that what was between them wasn't even close to being done.

Avery's apartment was dark and empty when she got home from the hospital, the quiet space echoing the hollow feeling inside her. The physical pleasure she'd experienced in those stolen moments with Justin Garrett had already faded away, leaving her aching and ashamed.

She should never have kissed him. She certainly should never have let him drag her into the closet. And she most definitely should never have succumbed to the lustful desires that stirred deep inside whenever she was near him.

Dropping onto the edge of the sofa, she buried her face in her hands, thoroughly mortified by her own behavior. She had a reputation for being cool and untouchable, but she'd been so hot and desperate for Justin that she'd let him screw her in a housekeeping supply closet.

What if someone found out?

Her cheeks burned with humiliation at the possibility. No doubt the hospital grapevine would love to know that the charismatic Dr. Romeo had succeeded in melting the frosty Dr. Wall-ice.

Of course, the more than two years that had passed since she'd last had sex might have been a factor, too. She missed physical intimacy. She missed the sharing of close personal contact with another person, the rising tension, the exhilarating release. But she'd never been good at sex outside of a relationship, which explained why it had been such a long time since she'd had sex.

Prior to the scheduled setup with Nolan tonight, she couldn't even remember the name of the last guy she'd dated. Was it Simon? Or Mike? Simon was the real estate agent who lived on the ninth floor of her building. Dark hair, darker eyes, sexy smile—but a sloppy kisser. Mike was one of the cameramen on *Ryder to the Rescue*, her brother's TV show. Shaggy blond hair, hazel eyes, great laugh and—she was informed by her brother after she'd agreed to meet Mike for coffee—engaged to one of the show's producers.

Or maybe it had been Kevin. She'd almost forgotten

about him. They'd met on the Fourth of July, having struck up a conversation while they were both in line at the Fireman's Picnic—a charity barbecue for the children's wing of the hospital. He'd asked for her number and he'd even called a few times after that, trying to set up a date, but they'd never actually made it to that next step.

Her life really was pathetic.

Spending time with Amy and Ben, she sometimes found herself wondering if she would ever find that once-in-a-lifetime kind of love that her friend shared with her husband. The kind of love that she'd once believed she shared with the man she'd planned to marry.

Avery had met Wyatt Travers at med school, when she was in her first year and he was in his third. Even then, she'd had reasons for not wanting to get involved with a doctor, but he'd swept her off her feet. Two years after they met, he put an engagement ring on her finger, and six months later, they moved in together.

Their lives were undeniably busy and they were often going in opposite directions, but whenever they had time just to be together, they would talk about their plans for the future, where they would set up a medical practice together, when they would start a family and how many children they would have.

Then he'd decided to go to Haiti as part of an emergency medical response team. Avery had wanted to go with him, but she was just finishing up her residency, so Wyatt went alone. He was gone for six months and when he finally came back, it was to tell her that he'd fallen in love with someone else. When Avery reminded him that he was supposed to be in love with her and that their wedding was scheduled for the following summer, he admitted that he hadn't just fallen in love with Stasia—he'd married her.

Avery had immediately packed up and moved out of their apartment, because it seemed a little awkward to continue to live with her former fiancé and his new wife. She'd crashed with a friend for a few weeks until she figured out what she wanted to do with her life now.

It had taken her a long time to get over Wyatt's betrayal. He'd argued that she couldn't blame him for falling in love with someone else, but she could and she did. If he'd really loved her, he wouldn't have fallen in love with Stasia—and since he'd fallen in love with Stasia, it proved that he'd never really loved *her.*

Either way, what it meant for Avery was that there wasn't going to be a joint medical practice or a wedding in August or a baby born two and a half years after that. Not for her, anyway. Wyatt, on the other hand, had accelerated the timeline he and Avery had mapped out for their life together, becoming a father five months after his return from Haiti.

That was when Avery realized she needed to make some changes, and when her brother, Ryder, was offered a contract to do a cable television show, she decided to go with him to Charisma. She was immediately charmed by the small town and grateful that it was far enough from Boston that she wouldn't worry about running into Wyatt or Stasia at the grocery store. Because as unlikely as that might seem in the city, it was a risk she didn't want to take.

She threw herself into her career and focused on proving herself to the staff at Mercy Hospital. She'd succeeded in building an impeccable reputation, and she'd also made some really good friends, including Amy Seabrook. She even went out on the occasional date, but she hadn't fallen in love again.

And when she went home at the end of the day, it was always to an empty apartment. She tried to convince herself that she liked it that way—that she was glad she didn't have to worry about anyone leaving wet towels in the bathroom or dirty socks on the floor; that she appreciated the freedom of choosing whether she wanted to listen to music or watch TV or simply enjoy the quiet solitude.

But deep in her heart, she couldn't deny the truth: she was alone and she was lonely. She wanted a partner with whom to share her life and build a family, but she was growing increasingly skeptical about either of those things ever happening for her.

In the past six months, she'd attended three bridal showers, four baby showers and two first-birthday parties. All of her friends and contemporaries were at the point in their lives where they were getting married and having babies, and she was sincerely happy for them. But she was a little envious, too.

She was thirty-two years old and her life was so far off track she couldn't see the track anymore. She was so desperate for physical contact with a man that she'd turned to Justin Garrett.

Not that he ever bragged about his conquests—he didn't need to. The women he bedded were only too happy to add their names to the extensive and ever-growing list of those who had experienced nirvana between his sheets.

Now Avery was one of them—one of the nameless, faceless masses who could say that she'd slept with Dr. Romeo. Except that she hadn't actually slept with him; she hadn't even been horizontal with him. No, she'd been so willing and eager, she'd gotten naked with him in a supply closet. Or mostly naked, anyway.

She'd just wanted to feel as if she wasn't completely alone for a few minutes. And while it was true that he'd helped her feel not just connected and desired but incredibly good, now that she was home again she had to face the truth: those stolen moments in the closet didn't change anything.

She was still alone.

But at least there was no one around to see the tears that slid down her cheeks.

Chapter Three

Wellbrook Medical Center was a privately funded clinic that provided medical services primarily to unwed mothers and their children. One of Avery's jobs at the clinic was to talk to young women about the importance of safe sex—reminding them to protect themselves not just against unwanted pregnancies but sexually transmitted diseases. For those who missed coming in for that talk, the clinic also offered the morning-after pill, testing for pregnancy and STDs, and prenatal care.

Avery was making notes in a patient's file when Amy set a mug of coffee on her desk. She glanced up. "Did you say something?"

"I said you seem a little preoccupied today."

"Sorry—I was just wondering how Callie's sister and her baby are doing. I think I'll stop by the hospital to check on them when I'm finished here."

"*If* we ever finish here," Amy noted.

"Brenna and Tess are coming in at two," she reminded her friend.

Amy lifted a hand to cover a yawn. "Why does two seem so far away?"

"Maybe because you had such a good time last night," Avery teased.

Her friend smiled. "What time did you escape from the hospital?"

"It wasn't long after midnight."

"It didn't take you that long to deliver a baby."

Avery shook her head. "No, but the ER was crazy, so I stuck around for a while to help out, which is how I ended up delivering Callie's sister's baby, too."

"You missed a great party," Amy told her.

"I'm sure I did," she acknowledged.

Her friend sighed. "You could at least sound a little disappointed—I really think you would have liked Nolan."

"You say that about every one of Ben's friends that you try to set me up with."

"And I remain optimistic that, one of these days, you'll actually go out with one of them."

"I'm focusing on my career right now."

"I get that, but your focus shouldn't be to the exclusion of all else."

"It's not."

"When was the last time you were on a date?" Amy asked, then she shook her head. "No—forget that question. When was the last time you had sex?"

Last night.

Not that she was going to admit as much to her friend. Of course, even if she did tell Amy the truth, it was unlikely her friend would believe it. Because Avery Wallace didn't have casual sex, and she definitely didn't succumb to the obvious charms of sexy doctors like Justin Garrett.

"Why is it that everyone wants to talk about sex today?" she countered, in an effort to divert her friend's attention.

"Because a lot of people got a little crazy and a little careless last night," Amy admitted. "I don't understand it—we give out condoms for free at the front desk. Why aren't people using them?"

"Don't you remember what it was like to be a teenager? All of the emotions and the hormones?"

"I remember the heady thrill of first love and the exciting rush of sexual desire," Amy acknowledged. "But I was never so overcome by lust—or so intoxicated—that I would have had sex without a condom."

"If everyone was as smart as you, we wouldn't have patients in the waiting room," Avery countered.

"And since we do, I guess we'd better get back to work."

So they did, and a steady stream of patients kept them both busy until Brenna and Tess arrived shortly before two. Avery was almost disappointed when their colleagues showed up, because now she would have time to think about the hard truths her earlier conversation with Amy had forced her to acknowledge.

Most notably that it wasn't only teenagers who made impulsive and stupid decisions about sex—otherwise responsible and intelligent adults could sometimes be just as impulsive and stupid. As she and Justin had proved last night.

Justin often felt as if he spent more time at the hospital than he did in his own apartment, which made him question the amount of rent he paid every month for his apartment overlooking Memorial Park. For the past few years, his parents had been urging him to buy a house—"an investment in real estate"—but Justin didn't see the point in paying more money for more rooms he wasn't going to use.

Besides, his apartment was conveniently located near the hospital—which he particularly appreciated when he had the early-morning shift. And the late-evening shift. And especially after a double shift.

When he was home, he felt comfortable in his space. It was his sanctuary from the craziness of the world. Four days into the New Year, he was enjoying that sanctuary—until his phone rang, indicating a visitor downstairs. He scowled when he glanced at the monitor and recognized the young woman in the lobby, curiously looking around the foyer as she waited for him to respond to the buzzer.

"Yeah?" he said, his tone deliberately unwelcoming.

"Girl Scout cookie delivery," she responded cheerfully.

"If you expect someone to buy that story, you should wear the uniform," he told her.

"Is that what it takes to get an invite to your apartment—a short skirt and a sash?"

"Jeez, no. I'm not a perv."

"You're also not opening the door," his unexpected visitor pointed out.

With a barely suppressed sigh, he punched in the code to release the lock so that she could enter. A few minutes later, there was a knock on his door.

"What are you doing here, Nora?"

His half sister moved past him into the apartment. "You're not a believer in traditional Southern hospitality, are you?"

"Please, come in," he said, his sarcasm contradicting the invitation of his words. "Let me take your coat and offer you some sweet tea."

Ignoring his tone, she took off her coat and handed it to him. "Sweet tea would be nice."

He hung her coat on one of the hooks behind the door. "Sorry, I'm all out."

"A glass of wine?"

"Are you old enough to drink?"

"You know I'm only eleven years younger than you."

He snapped his fingers. "That's right—I was playing Little League when my father was screwing your mother."

"Which isn't my fault any more than it's yours," she pointed out.

He sighed, because she was right. And because he knew his mother would be appalled if she ever found out that Nora had come to visit and he'd been less than welcoming.

His mother was another innocent devastated by her husband's infidelity, although she had forgiven John Garrett a long time ago—before anyone knew that the affair had resulted in a child. And even after learning about the existence of her husband's illegitimate daughter, Ellen had gone out of her way to make Nora feel she was a part of their family—efforts that the woman in question had mostly resisted.

"Red or white?" Justin asked her now.

"Red, please."

She followed him into the kitchen, settling herself on a stool at the island while he uncorked a bottle of Napa Valley merlot. He slid a glass across the counter to her and decided—*what the hell?*—he wasn't on call, and poured a second glass for himself.

"Thank you." She took a tentative sip, then set the glass down. "I'm looking for a job."

"And you want to cash in your DNA results for a cushy office at Garrett Furniture," he guessed.

She shook her head. "I have no interest in your father's company."

"Isn't he your father, too?"

"Well, yes, but that was more by accident than design."

He nodded in acknowledgment as she sipped her wine again.

"Besides, an office job would bore me to tears," she told him. "I like to work with people—that's why I became a registered physical therapist."

Which he already knew but had no intention of revealing to her, because she'd then want to know how and why he knew it, and he didn't intend to share that information. Yet.

"Where'd you go to school?" he asked, pretending he didn't know the answer to that question, either, as he lifted his own glass to his lips.

"The University of Texas at San Antonio. Graduated

with honors." She opened her purse and took out an envelope, offering it to him. "My résumé."

"What do you want me to do with this?"

"Look at it and, if you think it's warranted, consider writing a letter of recommendation for me."

"Why me?"

"Because there's an opening at Mercy Hospital and the Garrett name carries a considerable amount of weight there."

"I'm surprised you didn't go straight to my mother," he commented. "If you've done your homework, you're aware that she's on the hiring committee."

"I'm aware," she admitted.

"So why didn't you knock on her door?" he challenged.

She traced the base of her glass with her finger. "Because a part of me was afraid she'd refuse to give a recommendation...and another part was afraid she *would* give it."

He shook his head. "Every time I think I have you figured out, you say or do something that surprises me."

"I don't need you to understand me—I just need a letter."

"I can't give you that without some understanding of who you are and whether or not you'll fit in with the rest of the staff."

She slid off her seat. "Then I guess I should be going."

He stepped in front of her, blocking her path to the door. "Why Charisma? Why Mercy?"

"Why not?"

"You didn't come here just for a job."

She met his gaze evenly. "I have family here."

"Speaking of family, what do Patrick and Connor think of your decision to move to North Carolina?"

Her eyes narrowed at the mention of her brothers. "What do you know about Patrick and Connor?"

"Quite a lot, actually," he told her. "Patrick is twenty-seven, single and a deputy in the Echo Ridge sheriff's department. Connor is twenty-eight, a graduate of the Thurgood Marshall School of Law currently employed as a prosecuting attorney, which is probably why he's trying to keep his relationship with a certain young woman who works as a public defender under wraps."

"You had my family investigated?" she demanded, her question filled with icy fury.

"Does that bother you?" he challenged. "Does it seem wrong that some stranger could come along and meddle in the lives of the people who matter the most to you?"

"Touché, Dr. Garrett." She reached past him to pick up her glass and tossed back the rest of her wine. "I guess that means I'm not going to get a recommendation."

"I'm not saying no," he told her. Because he was a firm believer in the old adage about keeping friends close and enemies closer, and he wasn't yet sure which category his half sister fit into. "I just want some more information."

"My life's an open book—and one that you've apparently already read."

He ignored her sarcasm. "Can you meet me at the hospital tomorrow?"

"What time?"

"Two o'clock. By the fountain in the courtyard."

She nodded. "I'll be there."

He followed her back to the foyer and plucked her coat off the hook just as another knock sounded. Since no one had buzzed from the lobby, he assumed that it was probably Lianne from across the hall. For a woman who was always baking something—muffins or cookies or banana bread—it baffled him that his neighbor never had all of the ingredients she needed. His brother, Ryan, liked to tease that Lianne asking to borrow sugar was code for her wanting to give him some sugar, but her flirtations were mostly harmless.

But when he opened up the door, it wasn't Lianne on the other side. It was Avery Wallace.

"You're on your way out," she said, noting the coat in his hand.

He shook his head. "It's not mine."

Her eyes flickered past him to Nora, then to the island with the bottle of wine and two glasses. Her color went frosty and her tone, when she spoke again, had chilled by several degrees. "I'm sorry—I obviously should have called first."

He turned to hand the coat to Nora, whose gaze was openly curious as it shifted from him to his new guest and back again. Clearly she was hoping for an introduction, but he wasn't inclined to make it.

"I'll talk to you later," Avery said, already turning away.

He caught her arm. "You can stay. Nora's on her way out."

Thankfully, Nora didn't have to be told twice. She slipped past him. "I'll see you at two o'clock tomorrow."

He nodded, pulling Avery through the door before closing it.

She tugged her arm out of his grasp, looking uncertain and slightly disapproving. "She's a little young for you, isn't she?"

"I don't know," he said mildly. "How young is too young to be my sister?"

"Your—" she looked back at the door through which Nora had departed "—sister?"

He nodded.

She frowned. "I didn't know you had a sister."

"Neither did I until seven months ago."

"Sounds like there's a story there," she mused.

"I'd tell you about it sometime, but you barely stick around long enough to finish a consult never mind an actual conversation."

She flushed but did not respond.

"So why are you here?" he asked. And then, because he couldn't resist ruffling her feathers a bit, he said "Did you come to count the notches on my bedposts?"

She sent him a scathing look. "You said you don't have bedposts."

"Because I don't," he confirmed. "Which I'd be happy to prove to you if you come down the hall with me and—"

She cut him off by shoving an envelope against his chest. "This is why I'm here."

He held her gaze for a long minute before he opened the flap and pulled out a single page. He immediately recognized the logo of Charisma Medical Laboratories at the top, then saw her name in the "patient name" box. "What is this?"

"You did get that MD behind your name from medical school, didn't you?"

"Okay, I guess what I should have asked is '*why* is this?'"

"New Year's Eve."

His brows lifted.

She huffed out a breath. "I should have figured you'd make me spell it out. We didn't just have sex, Garrett. We had unprotected sex."

Justin nodded soberly. While he had no objections to casual sex, he was never careless about protection. Not since that one time when he was a teenager. That one time—one forgotten condom and one terrifying pregnancy false alarm— had been enough to scare the bejesus out of him and make him swear that he would never be caught unprepared again.

And he never had—until he'd found himself in a hospital supply closet with Avery. Then everything had happened so fast, and his desperate need for her had overridden everything else.

"I'm sorry," he said, because although the words were grossly inadequate they were also true.

"Obviously neither of us was thinking clearly that night or what happened between us never would have happened," she said.

He wondered how it was that—despite all the other thoughts screaming in his head—he could be amused by such a prim remark delivered in her characteristically cool tone. Wanting to shake some of that cool, he stepped closer to her.

"We had sex, Avery. Incredible…mind-blowing… ground-shaking sex."

"I was there," she acknowledged, her gaze remaining fixed on the ceramic tile floor. "I know what happened."

He tipped her chin up. "So why can't you say it?"

She jerked her head away. "Because I'm embarrassed."

"Why?"

"Because I used to take pride in the fact that I was one of probably only a handful of women on staff at the hospital who had *not* slept with Dr. Romeo—and I can't say that anymore."

He'd grown accustomed to the nickname so that it didn't bother him anymore. Not that he would acknowledge, anyway. "Honey, I haven't slept with *that* many women who work there."

"I don't care," she insisted. "Or I wouldn't care, except that now I'm one of them."

"It's not as if I've been walking around wearing a sign—I Melted Dr. Wall-ice."

She glared at him. "This isn't funny."

"I agree," he said. "Nor is it anything to be ashamed of. We're two unattached, consenting adults who gave in to a mutual and compelling attraction."

"We had unprotected sex."

He nodded. "My bad. I'm not in the habit of carrying

condoms in my scrub shirt," he said, attempting a casualness he did not feel. "But that still doesn't explain—" he held up the lab report "—this."

"I wanted to reassure you that there's no reason for you to worry—" she bit down on her lower lip "—on my side, I mean."

"But you're worried about mine," he realized.

He couldn't blame her for being concerned. He was well aware of his reputation around the hospital—and well aware that it had been greatly exaggerated. That knowledge had never bothered him before, but now, seeing Avery's misery and distress, he wished he'd clarified a few things. Or a lot of things.

Of course, it was too late now. She'd obviously made up her mind about him and nothing he said was going to change it. He put the lab report back into the envelope and returned it to her. "Most of the other women I've been with just want to cuddle after sex."

"Most of the other women are why I'd like some quid pro quo."

He nodded. "I'll take care of it tomorrow."

Chapter Four

In retrospect, Avery probably could have handled the situation better, but the whole experience with Justin was way outside her comfort zone. She wasn't great with personal relationships in general, and men like Justin—not that there were many men like Justin—flustered her beyond belief.

He was so totally confident and unapologetically sexy, and completely aware of the effect he had on people. Especially women. It was why, for most of the three and a half years she'd worked at Mercy Hospital, she'd put as much distance between them as possible.

Of course, distance wasn't always possible. There were times that they needed to consult and collaborate with respect to the care of patients, and at those times, she did what had to be done, careful to maintain a calm facade and professional demeanor. But when she had a choice, she chose to stay far away from his orbit, because she didn't trust herself to resist the magnetic pull that he seemed to exert on women without even trying. She hadn't been able to resist it on New Year's Eve. She hadn't *wanted* to resist him.

When she'd realized that they'd had sex without a condom, she'd panicked a little. Or maybe a lot. And then she'd started to think about all the possible repercussions of having unprotected sex with a man who'd had numerous other sexual partners. As a doctor, she would have been irresponsible to ignore his history, especially after she'd already been irresponsible in having unprotected sex with him.

She didn't see much of Justin over the next few days after her visit to his apartment, which wasn't unusual. Depending on their schedules, she might cross paths with him numerous times in a day or not at all for several shifts. What was unusual was that she found herself looking for him, wondering when she might see him and even the wondering filled her stomach with an uncomfortable fluttery feeling.

When she did see him, his demeanor toward her was nothing but professional, and she strove to treat him with the same courtesy. But her awareness of him was heightened now, and whenever he was near, her body stirred with not just memories but longing.

Friday afternoon, she'd just finished a consult regarding the course of action for a multiple pregnancy when he caught her in the conference room.

"I've got those test results you wanted," he told her.

She'd been so focused on her work that it took Avery a moment to realize what he was talking about. But when she did, the knots that had been in her belly since New Year's Day tightened.

She looked at him expectantly. His statement suggested that he intended to share the results with her, but his hands were empty. "Are you actually going to let me see them?"

"Of course," he agreed. "At dinner tonight."

She sighed. "Dr. Garrett—"

"Dr. Wallace," he countered, his tone amused.

"I'm *not* going to have dinner with you."

"Yes, you are," he said confidently. "Because you want to hold the lab report in your hands and meticulously scrutinize every letter and digit."

She did, of course. Because she needed to be sure. But she didn't believe he, as a medical professional, would really hold back the results. Certainly not if there was any reason for her to be concerned.

"You're clean," she decided, feigning a nonchalance she didn't feel. "You wouldn't be playing games otherwise."

"And if I'd told you I was clean, that our romantic—" she snorted derisively at that, while he narrowed his gaze and continued "—liaison was the first time I've forgotten a condom since I was a horny, fumbling seventeen-year-old, would you have believed me?"

"Probably not," she admitted.

"Which is why there has to be a tiny niggling of doubt in your mind," he said. "Barely a seed right now, but if you don't hold those results in your hand, that seed will grow…and grow."

She glared at him, because *dammit*, he was right. "What time did you want to eat?"

His smile was smug. "Seven o'clock. Valentino's."

She shook her head. "Seven o'clock works, but I'll cook."

"I'd be flattered by your offer to cook for me if I didn't suspect your true motivation is that being seen in public with me might damage your reputation."

"I suspect you're just as worried about your own, considering that I'm not your usual type."

"And what is my usual type?" he asked curiously.

"Ready, willing and able."

"You've got me there," he acknowledged. "But then it's not really true to say you're not my type, because you were all of those things when we were in SC together."

She frowned. "SC?"

Despite the fact that they were alone in the room, he lowered his voice to a conspiratorial whisper. "I decided that should be our code for the supply closet. That way, if anyone overhears us talking, they'll think we stole away to South Carolina together rather than a six-by-eight utility room."

"No worries," she told him. "We're not going to be talking about it. Not after tonight."

"Seven o'clock at your place?" he prompted.

She nodded and gave him her address.

"You're not worried that being alone with me will tempt you to jump my bones again?"

"I didn't 'jump your bones' the first time," she denied hotly.

"You made the first move."

"It was a kiss. Simple, casual, friendly."

"It was a spark," he countered. "And considering how skillfully you've dodged me for more than three years because of the red-hot attraction between us, you had to know that one little spark would ignite a firestorm."

Thankfully, he didn't stick around for a response, because she didn't know what to say to that. He was right—for more than three years, she had dodged him and the uncomfortable feelings he stirred inside of her. And as soon as she got through this dinner tonight, she would go back to dodging him again.

It was the only way to ensure that the red-hot attraction didn't lead to her getting burned.

Justin immediately recognized the address that Avery had given him because it was on the opposite side of Memorial Park from his own place. He knew their dinner wasn't technically a date, but he picked up flowers for her, anyway, and had the bouquet in hand when he buzzed her apartment at precisely seven o'clock—just as she rushed in through the front door.

"I'm sorry," she said. "I got caught up at the clinic so I'm running a little bit behind schedule."

"That's okay," he said.

She fumbled with her keys. "Why don't you come back

in half an hour?" she suggested. "By that time, I should have everything well under way for dinner."

"Because I'm here now and I can help," he told her.

"I invited you to eat dinner not make dinner," she pointed out, clearly unhappy that he wasn't going away and letting her control the timetable.

"I don't mind." He followed her into the elevator, where she stabbed a finger at the button for the fifth floor.

It was a corner unit of the U-shaped building, with a view of the tennis courts and pool. The interior was exquisitely—and he suspected professionally—decorated, with comfortable furniture in neutral colors, framed generic prints on the walls and a bookcase filled with medical texts. They were no personal touches in the room. No magazines or candles or decorative vases or bowls.

She went directly into the kitchen and, when he followed, he saw that the galley-style cooking area was equally pristine—the cupboards were white with simple steel handles. The white quartz countertops were bare of clutter except for a single-serve coffeemaker. The deep stainless steel sink was literally spotless, without even a spoon or a cloth in sight.

"Can I get you something to drink?" she asked.

"What are you having?"

"Water." She opened a cupboard to take out a glass and filled it with ice then water from the dispenser in the door of the refrigerator.

"That works for me," he said.

She turned to hand him the first glass—and nearly dumped the contents all over him when she discovered that he was directly behind her.

Thankfully, he caught it before it tipped too far. "Relax, Avery."

She managed a strangled laugh as she filled a second for herself, drinking down half of it before setting it aside.

"We can go out if you're not comfortable with me being here."

"It's not you—or not specifically you," she amended. "It's just that I'm not used to other people being in my space."

"Apparently," he noted, offering her the bouquet.

"Oh." She looked at the bright blooms as if she wasn't quite sure what to do with them.

"They probably want some water, too," he told her.

"Of course," she agreed, moving to the cupboard above the fridge to pull down a clear glass vase.

She seemed more comfortable when she was doing something, and she kept her attention focused resolutely on the task while she filled the container with water, trimmed the stems of the flowers, then arranged them in the vase.

"These are really beautiful," she said. "Thank you."

"You're welcome."

She carried the vase to the dining room and set it in the middle of the table. When she returned to the kitchen, she pulled a plastic container—neatly labeled and dated—out of the fridge, then dumped the contents into a glass bowl. He glanced over her shoulder at the thick red sauce with chunks of sausage and peppers, onions, mushrooms and tomatoes.

"That looks really good," he said.

"I don't always feel like cooking when I get home from work, so a couple of times a month I go on a cooking binge where I make all kinds of things that I can throw into containers in the freezer for quick meals later on."

"What do you make besides pasta sauce?" he asked.

She bent to retrieve a large pot from the cupboard beside the stove, then filled it from the tap and set it on the back burner. "Enchiladas, jambalaya, chicken and broccoli—"

He must have instinctively cringed at that, because she

laughed, the unexpected outburst of humor surprising both of them and easing some of the tension.

"You don't like broccoli?" she guessed.

"Much to my mother's everlasting chagrin," he admitted.

"That's too bad, because my chicken and broccoli casserole is delicious."

"Well, it's been my experience that the right company makes any meal taste better, so it's possible I could change my mind if you wanted to make it for me sometime."

She smiled at that. "Let's see if we get through this meal before making any other plans."

He sipped his water as she went back to the fridge and retrieved various items for a salad. She washed the head of lettuce under the tap, then spread the leaves out on a towel to dry. It was apparent that she had a system and she lined up her ingredients and utensils on the counter as if they were surgical instruments.

"I know how to chop and dice," he told her.

She glanced up. "What?"

"I'm offering to help make the salad."

"Oh. Thanks, but it's not really a two-person job."

And he could tell that the idea of letting someone else help—and mess with her system—made her twitchy.

"You're right," he agreed. "So why don't you let me handle it while you go do whatever you usually do when you get home from work and don't have someone waiting in your lobby?"

She hesitated a minute before admitting, "I was hoping for a quick shower."

"So go take a shower," he suggested.

"I will," she decided. "After I get this finished—"

He took her by the shoulders and turned her away from the counter. "Go take your shower—I'll take care of this."

She still looked skeptical. "Are you sure you don't mind?"

"Of course, I don't mind. But if you'd rather I forget about the lettuce and come wash your back—"

"I can wash my back," she interjected. "You handle the salad."

As he tore up the leaves, he tried not to think about Avery down the hall in the bathroom, stripping out of her clothes. As he chopped up celery and peppers, he ordered himself not to envision the spray from the shower pouring over her sexy, naked body. As he sliced cucumber and tomato, he didn't let himself imagine any soapy lather sliding over her breasts, her hips, her thighs.

But damn, all the not thinking, envisioning and imagining made him hot and achy. He shoved the finished salad back into the refrigerator and put the cutting board and utensils in the dishwasher. He could still hear the water running in the bathroom, and the mental images he refused to allow continued to tease at his mind.

Desperate for a distraction from his prurient fantasies, he decided to give himself a quick tour of her apartment. There was the spacious and stark living room, which he'd glimpsed upon entry into her apartment, then the kitchen and the dining room that was connected to the kitchen. The first door in the hall was a second bathroom. Like the kitchen, white was the color scheme in here, dominating the floor tile, the fixtures, even the towels and the liquid soap in the dispenser on the pedestal sink.

Beside the bathroom was a spare bedroom that she'd set up as a home office. Two walls were covered in bookshelves made of pale wood and neatly filled with yet more medical texts and journals. Her desk, also in pale wood, was just as ruthlessly organized—with pens, pencils and highlighters neatly lined up in distinctly separate containers.

The Twilight Zone theme started to play quietly in his head. There were no real personal touches anywhere. No indication of her interests or hobbies or insights into her personality, and if he didn't know better, he'd think her career was the sum total of who she was.

But he did know better. He'd kissed her and touched her, and she'd responded with a passion that had taken his breath away. She'd wrapped herself around him as he'd thrust into her body, shuddering and sighing and completely coming undone. Yeah, there was a lot more to Avery than the impersonal and sterile environment of her home indicated.

A spot of green caught the corner of his eye, and he smiled when he noted the stubby plant on the windowsill, recognizing it as some kind of cactus. Even her plant carried the same hands-off vibe that she did. Except that beneath her prickly exterior, she was warm and soft and shockingly uninhibited.

The challenge, of course, was getting past that exterior, and Justin suspected that scaling her walls once would only make a subsequent breach that much more difficult. He also realized he didn't want to breach her defenses—he wanted to tear them down completely.

He turned away from the cactus in the window to return to the kitchen. That was when he saw it. Another bookcase tucked into an alcove beside the door. He moved in for a closer inspection. The books here were mostly classical literature and popular fiction, with some surprisingly racy titles in the mix, all of them arranged alphabetically by author.

On top of the bookshelf was a framed photograph—the only one he'd seen in the whole apartment—of a little boy and a little girl. The picture had been snapped from behind as the two children walked, hand in hand, away from whoever was in possession of the camera and toward the iconic castle at Disney World. He instinctively knew the children were Avery and her brother, Ryder, even before he looked closely enough to see their names embroidered on the matching Mickey Mouse ears they wore.

It was a snapshot of her childhood, a brief glimpse of a happy moment somehow made more poignant by the realization that she couldn't have been more than eight years old in the photo and there were no other, later pictures to be found anywhere else in her apartment—or at least in any of the rooms he'd visited so far.

"What are you doing in here?" Avery demanded.

He glanced over, his heart doing a slow roll inside his chest when he saw her standing in the doorway, looking so naturally beautiful and sexy. Her face was scrubbed free of makeup, her hair had been released from its habitual ponytail and skimmed her shoulders. She'd dressed in a pair of black yoga pants and a long, fuzzy V-neck sweater in a pretty shade of blue that almost exactly matched her eyes. Her feet were bare, her toenails painted a bold crimson color that seemed out of character for her but which he knew was not.

"I was looking for you," he finally answered her question.

She arched a brow. "You didn't trust I'd find my way back to the kitchen?"

"No, I meant I was looking for a glimpse of you somewhere—anywhere—in this sterile apartment."

She didn't blink at his criticism. Nor had he expected her to. It wouldn't be nearly as much fun to ruffle her feathers if they ruffled easily.

"Remind me not to give you the name of my decorator," she responded lightly.

"I didn't think the white was your choice."

"Did you find what you were looking for?" she asked, in a deliberate change of topic.

"I think I did." He held up the photo.

She took the frame from his hand and carefully set it back into place on the bookshelf. "Dinner will be ready in—" she glanced at the watch on her wrist "—six and a half minutes."

He smiled. "Precisely six and a half? Not six or seven but six and a half?"

"The pasta takes twelve minutes to cook and I dropped it into the pot approximately five and a half minutes ago."

"What would happen if you forgot to put the timer on and cooked it for—" he gasped dramatically "—thirteen minutes?"

"Then we'd have to eat overcooked spaghetti," she said matter-of-factly, but she frowned at the prospect.

He shook his head. "Where did you go to medical school?"

She seemed startled by the abrupt change of topic but, after a brief hesitation, she responded, "Harvard."

"Figures."

"I actually wanted to go to Stanford, but my parents thought Harvard was more prestigious."

"I bet you graduated summa cum laude, too, didn't you?"

"So? I worked hard and studied hard."

"I'm sure you did," he agreed. "And I have no doubt you're a better doctor because of it. But sometimes, instead of blasting a tunnel through a mountain, you should climb to the top and enjoy the view."

"If you have a point, I'm not seeing it," she told him.

"My point is that you're obviously dedicated, focused and driven, and those are great attributes in the practice of medicine. But when they carry over into your personal life, it suggests that something happened that compels you to rigidly and ruthlessly control every aspect of your life."

"You're reading an awful lot into the fact that I use a kitchen timer when I cook my pasta."

"It's not just the pasta," he told her. "You have your highlighters aligned in the spectrum of the rainbow."

"I didn't realize being organized was a character flaw."

"I'm the same way when it comes to every examination and procedure I perform in the ER," he admitted. "But when I walk out of the hospital at the end of my shift, I let that go and relax."

"Good for you."

"You should let go a little, too," he suggested. "You're wound up like a torsion spring and one of these days, all of the energy trapped inside of you is going to let loose. Or maybe that *is* what happened in the supply closet."

"That's a better explanation than anything I could come up with," she acknowledged. "And maybe, after more than two years, it was time to let loose a little."

His brows lifted. "Are you telling me that it was more than two *years* since you'd had sex?"

"I'm sure it's not some kind of celibacy record."

"Sorry, it's just that—wow. Two years." He shook his head. "I can't imagine."

She rolled her eyes. "We both know you can't imagine—that's why I wanted the test."

Chapter Five

"Right. The test."

For a few minutes, Justin had forgotten the reason he was here—the only reason Avery was making dinner for him.

As if on cue, a buzzer sounded from the kitchen.

"That's the pasta," she said, automatically turning away.

He caught her hand, halting her before she reached the door. She glanced over her shoulder, a quizzical expression on her face.

"I just wanted to say thanks—for offering to cook for me tonight."

"You're welcome," she said cautiously.

"I know that you don't really approve of me—"

"And I know you aren't really concerned about my approval."

He lifted a shoulder. "But you should know that only about half of the rumors that circulate around the hospital are true."

"I'll keep that in mind," she said.

"And while I can't control what other people say, I don't kiss and tell. Ever."

"I know," she admitted.

The timer in the kitchen buzzed again.

"I really need to get that pasta off the stove."

But he still didn't release her hand and there was a mischievous glint in his eyes that made her uneasy.

"The noodles are going to be overcooked," she said again, and that was when she realized what he was doing. "You're stalling me on purpose."

"Why would I do that?" he asked innocently.

"To wind up my torsion spring."

"People don't actually have torsion springs—I only said you were *like* a torsion spring."

"If you don't let me get back to the kitchen right now, I'm going to let loose all of my tension in your direction."

He grinned. "Promises, promises."

But this time when she turned away, he let her go.

She had a colander in the sink and a distinctly unhappy look on her face when he returned to the kitchen. She dumped the noodles into the bowl and carried them to the table she must have set when she got out of the shower.

"If dinner is ruined, it's your fault," she told him.

"Dinner is not ruined," he promised, retrieving the salad from the fridge.

But she still looked skeptical as she scooped penne out of the serving bowl and into her pasta bowl. She ladled sauce on the top and waited until he had done the same before she picked up her fork.

"Did your mother teach you how to cook?" he asked, after he'd sampled his first mouthful.

She shook her head. "My mother is a senior research supervisor at the Centers for Disease Control in Atlanta—she can isolate a pathogen but I doubt she knows how to pound or purée."

"So who taught you how to cook?"

"I took a few recreational cooking classes at a small culinary institute in Boston while I was doing my residency."

"Did you graduate with top honors from there, too?"

She shook her head. "It wasn't for grades, it was for fun."

"For fun?" he asked skeptically.

Her lips curved, just a little. “It was more fun than starving.”

“Well, your pasta gets top marks from me,” he told her.

“The sauce was good,” she allowed. “The noodles were overcooked.”

“Maybe by about thirty seconds,” he acknowledged, smiling at her.

She smiled back, a wordless acceptance of the truce he’d offered. “Okay, maybe I could learn to relax a little bit.”

“I’d be happy to teach you.”

She shook her head. “I don’t want to be *that* relaxed.”

He chuckled, unoffended.

“I didn’t make anything for dessert, but I do have ice cream,” she told him.

“I don’t think I have room for dessert—even ice cream,” he told her.

“It’s cookies ’n’ cream,” she said, in a tone that suggested no one could refuse her favorite flavor.

But he shook his head. “No, thanks.”

When she started to stack the dishes, he pulled the lab report out of his pocket and slid it across the table to her.

Avery’s heart pounded as she unfolded the page.

Her eyes skimmed the document quickly the first time, then again, more slowly. She’d been right. Just as she’d suspected, his results were all clear.

She exhaled a grateful sigh. There was nothing to worry about. But she’d needed to be sure—just in case there were other repercussions from that night.

“That’s it, then,” she said, almost giddy with relief as she pushed away from the table to help clear it. “There’s no need for either of us to ever again mention what happened on New Year’s Eve.”

He leaned back against the counter, holding her gaze for a long moment before he finally asked, “Are you sure about that?”

She hugged the salad dressing bottles she carried closer to her chest and eyed him warily.

"There are other potential consequences of unprotected sex," he reminded her.

She nibbled on her lower lip, as if she didn't know where he was going with the conversation. Because she hadn't expected him to go there, she hadn't expected the possibility to cross his mind. And maybe it hadn't. "What do you mean?"

He continued to hold her gaze, his own unwavering. "I mean a baby," he told her. "Is it possible you could be pregnant?"

She shook her head as she turned away from him to put the dressings back in the fridge. "I don't think so."

"That's not very reassuring."

She couldn't see him, but she could hear the scowl in his voice. "Well, that's the best I can do right now," she admitted, shifting around some items in the door of the refrigerator to avoid facing him.

"You're not on the pill or the patch?" he pressed.

"No."

"You didn't take the morning-after pill?"

She shook her head.

He nudged her away from the fridge and firmly closed the door. "Why not?"

"I—I didn't think about it."

His hands settled on the counter behind him, his fingers curled over the edge. "You're a doctor, Avery. You know how babies are made—and you know there are steps that can be taken to prevent a baby from being made, even after the fact."

She felt her cheeks burn, but she nodded. "You're right. And I did get a package of morning-after pills from the clinic—the morning after."

"So why didn't you take them?"

"Because when I stopped at the hospital after I left the clinic, to check on Callie's sister and her baby, something inside of me…yearned."

She'd hoped for some kind of understanding, but the darkness of his scowl warned her otherwise.

"I know it sounds stupid," she continued to explain, "but that's how I felt. Then I got home and I sat at the table with the package in front of me, and I stared at it for a really long time. Because the possibility of an unplanned pregnancy completely freaked me out, but the possibility of a baby…somehow the possibility of a baby didn't freak me out at all."

She looked at him, silently begging for his forgiveness—or at least acceptance. "I mean, I'm not a teenager, and I do want to have a baby someday, so I decided that if I did get pregnant, having a baby might not be the worst thing that could happen to me at this point in my life."

"Not the worst thing that could happen to *you*," he echoed, pinning her with his hard and unyielding gaze. "Did you give any consideration to what it might mean to *me*? Did you think, *for even one minute*, about how a baby would affect *my* life?"

"No." She whispered the admission, ashamed that it was true. She hadn't thought about him at all. She hadn't thought about anything but how the possibility—minuscule as it might be—of having a baby filled her heart and soul with joy. "All I could think about, all that mattered, was that I might finally have the baby I've always wanted."

"You were *trying* to get pregnant?"

"No! I didn't plan any of what happened between us that night," she promised him. "But when I realized it was possible that we might have conceived a child, I just didn't do anything to stop it."

"A decision I'm still struggling to understand," he told her.

She nodded, acknowledging that she owed him a more thorough explanation of her actions. "When I graduated from medical school, I had a fiancé and a five-year plan."

His brows lifted at that, but he remained silent, allowing her to continue.

"The plan included a wedding and, a few years after that, a baby. Then my fiancé decided to go ahead with that plan with someone else, and I moved on with my life without him."

"And moved to Charisma," he guessed.

She nodded again. "I've helped a lot of women deliver a lot of babies, and I always believed that someday it would be my turn. But I'm thirty-two years old and maybe my biological clock isn't actually ticking just yet, but that someday doesn't seem to be getting any closer."

"You still had no right to make a decision that could affect both of our futures without talking to me," he told her.

"I know," she admitted. "But I promise you, if it turns out that I am pregnant, I will take full and complete responsibility for the baby."

"You don't want anything from me?" he challenged. "Not child support? Not even my name on the birth certificate?"

She shook her head, eager to give him the reassurance he seemed to be seeking. "Nothing," she confirmed. "No one will even need to know that you're the baby's father."

"Which only proves you don't know me nearly as well as you think you do."

"What are you saying?"

"I'm saying that if all you wanted was a sperm donor, you should have gone to a clinic."

"Hey, I didn't plan for this, either," she reminded him hotly. "I didn't seduce you or sabotage birth control. We both acted impulsively and *if* it turns out that I am pregnant—and that's still a pretty big *if* at this point—it will be the culmination of various factors that neither of us could have predicted."

"When will you know?"

Her cheeks burned. Somehow, talking about her monthly cycle with him seemed even more intimate than what they'd done in the supply closet. "Sometime in the next seven to ten days."

"Okay," he said. "So between now and then, we're going to spend as much time together as possible."

She frowned. "I don't think that's necessary."

"It's absolutely necessary," he told her. "Partly so that the people around us—friends, family, coworkers—start to see us as a couple. But mostly, and much more importantly, if you are pregnant, we need to know one another a lot better in order to coparent our child."

She stared at him, horrified. "Coparent?"

"I might not have had any say in the choices you've made up to this point, honey, but I promise you, I'll be involved in any decision making that takes place going forward."

He kept his eyes on hers, implacable and unyielding. "If you are pregnant—you don't just get a baby. You get me, too."

His words had sounded more like a threat than a promise, but Avery decided not to worry too much about what Justin had said in the heat of the moment. She understood that he was angry—and that he had reason to be. They'd both forgotten about birth control on New Year's Eve, but she'd unilaterally decided to accept the possible risk of pregnancy.

And maybe it was foolish to want a child under the current circumstances, but she couldn't deny that she did. Even if this wasn't the way she'd envisioned it might someday happen, she refused to have any regrets. She had no illusions that being a single mother would be easy, but she was fortunate to have a job she enjoyed along with a steady income that would pay her bills. She had a lot of patients who lived under much more difficult circumstances on a daily basis.

She'd seen Justin frequently in the week that had passed since the night they'd had dinner at her apartment—and he'd made a point of being seen with her as often as possible—but she'd managed to keep their conversations mostly short and impersonal.

The prospect of coparenting with him made her more than a little uneasy, but there was no point in worrying about that unless and until her pregnancy was confirmed. And even then, nine months was a lot of time. She was confident his determination to be involved would wane long before their baby was born. Maybe that was an unfair assumption to make considering how attentive and solicitous he'd been, but he had a notoriously short attention span when it came to his relationships with women.

She could have taken a test already. The presence of hCG, the hormone that indicated pregnancy, could be found in very low levels within seven days after conception. But she wasn't ready to confirm her pregnancy just yet. Because as soon as she knew for certain that she was going to have a baby, she'd feel obligated to tell Justin, and she wanted to hold the excited anticipation close to her own heart for a while before he trampled all over it.

Three more days.

The words echoed in her head as she waited for sleep to come.

She awoke a few hours later with a crampy feeling low in her belly. Uneasy, she got up to go to the bathroom. That was when she realized her instincts and intuition were wrong.

She wasn't pregnant, after all.

She crawled back under the covers of her empty bed, in her quiet apartment, and cried softly.

* * *

When Justin finally got a break and went in search of a much-needed caffeine fix, he found Avery sitting alone in the cafeteria with a single-serving tub of cookies 'n' cream ice cream in front of her. He took his extralarge cup of coffee over to her table, wondering if the ice cream was evidence of some kind of pregnancy craving or just strange eating habits.

"Do you mind if I join you?"

She glanced up when he stopped by the chair across the table from her. "Of course not."

He lowered himself into the empty seat. "Breakfast?" he asked, nodding toward the ice cream container.

She dropped her spoon into the melting dessert and shook her head. "I was hoping to see you today."

He was surprised and pleased to think that she wanted to see him rather than avoid him, which was her usual modus operandi. "You were?"

"I figured you'd want to know as soon as possible that you're off the hook."

"Off the hook?" he echoed, the implication of her words taking a moment to sink into his brain. "Oh."

She nodded. "I got my period last night."

"Oh," he said again.

"We successfully dodged that bullet."

But her clichéd phrases and the forced cheerfulness warned him that her feelings weren't as simple or straightforward as she wanted him to believe. "How are you doing?" he asked.

"I'm relieved, of course."

"You are?"

She shrugged. "Sure, I'm a little disappointed, too," she admitted. "But considering the circumstances, it's probably for the best."

"You're probably right," he agreed.

He was certainly relieved to have "dodged the bullet," and grateful that their impulsive actions wouldn't have long-term consequences. He liked his life just the way it was and hadn't been thrilled to think of the adjustments he would need to make to accommodate a child. Of course he would have, if it had turned out that she was pregnant, but he was undeniably relieved that wouldn't be necessary just yet.

"Now our lives can go back to normal," she said, her words echoing his own thoughts.

"By normal, you mean that you intend to go back to ignoring me as much as possible," he guessed.

"I mean that you can go back to dating a different woman every weekend," she countered lightly.

He started to protest her erroneous assumption of his habits, but what was the point? She'd made up her mind about him a long time ago and obviously nothing he'd said or done in the past couple of weeks had changed her opinion.

Instead, he nodded his agreement. "There is that."

"Who was that?"

Justin glanced up as Nora slid into the seat Avery had recently vacated. "What are you doing here?"

"Thanks to the introductions you made, I've got an interview with Jovan Crncevic," she explained, naming the supervisor of the hospital's physiotherapy department. "Of course, I came way too early so I decided to stop in here and grab a cup of coffee and I saw you having a deep tête-à-tête with...your girlfriend?"

He shook his head. "No."

"Ex-girlfriend?"

"No," he said again, lifting his own cup to his lips to finish his coffee.

"Really?" she challenged. "Because I'm pretty sure that was the same woman who stopped by your condo when I was there, and there were some serious vibes between the two of you just now."

"We work together," he explained.

Nora laughed. "It was definitely *not* a work vibe."

He scowled. "How long were you watching?"

"Long enough to know it was *not* a work vibe," she assured him.

"We had a thing," he admitted.

"A thing?"

"A shared moment of insanity."

"Ah." She nodded. "A thing." She sipped her coffee. "You still hung up on her?"

"No."

"I think I understand why it didn't work out—she's probably intimidated by your conversational prowess."

"You're a real smart-ass, you know that?"

"I always figured it was better than being a dumb ass."

His lips twitched a little in response to that, but all he said was, "Shouldn't you be preparing for your interview?"

She shook her head. "Even thinking about it makes me nervous—your love life is a great distraction."

"Glad to be of service."

"Do you want my advice?"

"No," he said bluntly.

She frowned. "Just because I'm young doesn't mean I don't have any wisdom to offer. I've got some experience in matters of the heart."

"Good for you."

"I'm only telling you because I recognize the symptoms of a serious infatuation."

"Dr. Wallace is not infatuated with me," he assured her.

Nora laughed. "I wasn't talking about Dr. Wallace."

Chapter Six

Life did go back to normal—eventually.

Although Avery had lived with the possibility of a baby for only a couple of weeks, she'd wanted to be pregnant so much that she'd let her imagination run with it, and it took a few days to shake off her melancholy.

The depth of her disappointment forced her to reevaluate her life and her choices. It was time, she decided, to stop being passive and go after what she wanted. Which meant that she needed to start dating again—and actually make an effort to meet the man who might want to father her future children.

Maybe she'd even ask Amy to set her up again—as soon as she shook the exhaustion that had recently taken hold of her body and which she suspected was a result of some lingering disappointment.

"Are you up for grabbing a drink?" Amy asked, when the last patient of the day had finally exited the clinic.

"I thought you'd be anxious to get home to Henry," Avery said, referring to her friend's fifteen-month-old son.

"He's spending the night with Ben's parents."

"So that you and your hubby can have a romantic evening together?" she guessed.

"That was the original plan," her friend admitted. "Until

his brother snagged a couple of tickets to a Canes game and asked Ben to go with him."

"In that case, a drink sounds good."

"And nachos?" Amy prompted hopefully.

She laughed. "Marg & Rita's?"

"I'll meet you there."

Avery left her white coat on the hook behind the door in her office, untied the fastener around her ponytail, brushed out her hair and added some lip gloss. A quick glance in the bathroom mirror confirmed that she looked better—but she still felt like crap.

She arrived at the restaurant first and didn't wait for her friend. It was Friday night, which meant that if there was a table available, it wouldn't be for long. Shortly after she was seated, the waiter brought two menus. Knowing her friend's preferences, she ordered a Top Shelf margarita for Amy and a virgin classic for herself along with a platter of deluxe nachos.

"Sorry I'm late," Amy said, sliding into the empty seat across the table. "Ben called as I was on my way out to remind me to watch the game so I can see him on TV."

"Maybe we should have gone to the Bar Down," Avery said. "No doubt the game will be on one of the screens there."

Her friend shook her head, then smiled at the waiter who set her frosty drink in front of her. "I have less than zero interest in hockey and I'll see Ben when he gets home." Then she picked up her drink and tapped the rim of her glass against Avery's. "I didn't think this week was ever going to end."

"It's not over for me yet," she said. "I've got morning rounds at the hospital tomorrow."

Her friend made a face. "I'm planning to sleep in late and then have leisurely morning sex with the man of my dreams."

"I'd be happy enough just to sleep in," Avery told her. "I've been exhausted and nauseated for the past several days."

"Maybe tequila isn't the best medicine for that," her friend said worriedly.

"I didn't think so, either," she agreed. "That's why mine is a virgin."

The waiter delivered their heaping platter of nachos and they both dug in.

"Exhausted and nauseated you said?" Amy queried a short while later.

"Trying not to think about that right now," Avery told her.

"Well, I was just thinking that's how I felt when I was pregnant with Henry."

"I'm not pregnant," Avery said quickly.

"I wasn't suggesting that you were," Amy agreed. "Unless you somehow managed to orchestrate an immaculate conception."

When she didn't respond to her friend's teasing comment, Amy's gaze narrowed. "Or is there something you're not telling me?"

"There are a lot of things I don't tell you," she said.

"Such as?" Amy prompted, brushing a jalapeño off her nacho chip.

Avery glanced around to ensure there was no one they knew within hearing range, but still dropped her voice to a near whisper before confiding, "Such as the fact that I had sex with Justin Garrett."

Amy choked on her margarita.

"When did this happen?" she asked, when she finally managed to stop coughing.

"New Year's Eve—actually, in the early hours of the morning on New Year's Day."

"Oh. My. God."

Avery nodded.

"So…" A smile teased at the corners of her friend's mouth. "How was he?"

She took her time selecting another chip. "A colossal disappointment."

Amy's eyes widened. "Really?"

"No. Not really." She sighed. "In fact, it was the single most incredible sexual experience of my life, which probably tells you more than you ever wanted to know about my sexual experience."

"I always wondered if his reputation was exaggerated," her friend confessed.

"It's not," she admitted unhappily. "And now I belong to the not-so-exclusive club that includes almost every other woman who works at the hospital."

Her friend smiled. "Sweetie, if Dr. Romeo slept with even half the women who claim to have slept with him, he'd hardly have time to get out of bed.

"I've known Justin a long time," Amy continued. "There's a lot more to him than most people realize—and he's not nearly as indiscriminate as his reputation would imply."

"So you don't believe he'd get naked with someone in a supply closet in the middle of his shift at the hospital?"

"No way," her friend said. Then her eyes went wide. "Are you telling me that's what happened?"

She nodded.

"Oh. My. God," Amy said again. "You and Justin. In a supply closet. Wow."

"It was wow," she agreed.

"So…are you guys together now?" her friend asked hopefully.

She shook her head. "No."

"Why not?"

"Because he's Dr. Romeo and I don't want to get involved with a man described in either of those terms."

Amy sighed. "Your parents really did a number on you, didn't they?"

"They taught me an important life lesson," she countered. "Which is that two career-focused medical professionals cannot make a marriage work and definitely should not be parents."

"I don't believe that."

"Says the woman married to a newspaper editor."

"I was in love with Ben long before he was a newspaper editor or I was a doctor," Amy pointed out.

"Since I didn't know you in high school, I'll have to take your word for it."

"Now—getting back to the exhausted and nauseated part of our conversation, I have to ask…were you careful?"

She felt her cheeks burn. "You'd think, being a doctor, I wouldn't be anything else."

Amy nodded, accurately interpreting her response as an acknowledgment that she hadn't been. "Then is it possible that you're pregnant?"

Avery shook her head. "I got my period last week."

"Did you take a pregnancy test?" her friend pressed.

"I was going to," she admitted. "And then, there didn't seem to be any point."

"You know as well as I do that it's not unusual for a woman to experience some bleeding in the early months of a pregnancy."

"It was more than that."

"Maybe it was," Amy acknowledged. "But I think you'll feel better if you take a test."

Avery nodded, though she didn't really believe it was true.

Taking a test and confirming that she wasn't pregnant wasn't going to make her feel any better. It would just be one more reminder of how completely her life had gone off track.

* * *

Justin had enough experience with women to know when one was attracted to him, and it frustrated him beyond belief that Avery was continuing to deny the attraction. But that was "back to normal" as far as their relationship was concerned.

He'd wanted her when he first met her and he wanted her now, but he didn't chase women. Not even a woman who stirred his blood and haunted his dreams.

He thought they'd made some real progress over the past couple of weeks. During dinner at her house, they'd talked and laughed and connected on a whole other level. Maybe it was his own fault—maybe he hadn't handled the possibility of a baby very well, but he'd felt angry and betrayed and helpless.

Yeah, there had been two of them in that supply closet, and yeah, the thought of protection had never crossed his mind because he'd been thinking about Avery and being inside Avery and that was all that had mattered. And then, to learn that she'd consciously decided not to take the morning-after pill—a decision that had potential consequences for both of them—without even talking to him, had made him furious.

He didn't have an issue with her choice, just with her complete and total disregard of his thoughts and feelings. She'd deliberately cut him out of the process—as if he wouldn't care. As if he'd walk away from his own child. *That* was what had pissed him off.

But now the possibility and the panic were past. Avery wasn't pregnant. There was no baby and no future for them together. And eight days after their conversation in the cafeteria, he decided it was time to stop obsessing about the woman who didn't want him and enjoy the company of one who did.

He decided to take Heather up on her offer of dinner followed by drinks at a popular club. While they were out, she flirted with him outrageously and rubbed up against him on the dance floor, and Justin found himself wondering why he wasn't tempted. She was offering him a good time without any strings, and he could really use the distraction of a simple fling to help him forget about the impossible woman who was stuck in his mind.

But when he'd walked Heather to her door, she'd put her arms around him and pressed her mouth to his, and he'd felt disgusted. Not with the young nurse but with himself, that he'd considered—for even half a minute—using her to help him forget about Avery. That was one thing he'd never done. He enjoyed women—their company and companionship—but he didn't use them.

So he'd quickly extricated himself from Heather's embrace, thanked her for an enjoyable evening and walked away.

The next day, wanting to ensure there was no repetition of the same scene, he decided to seek out some male camaraderie instead. With his younger brother in Florida and his older brother dealing with his own issues, he headed over to the headquarters of Garrett Furniture to see if anyone was around. He found Nathan in the CFO's office.

"Where's Allison?" he asked, having noted that the desk outside his cousin's office—usually occupied by Nate's wife, who was also his administrative assistant—was vacant.

"Dylan had a dentist appointment so she took off early."

"You dock her pay for the missed time?"

"Nah—she makes it up with sexual favors."

Justin winced. "I don't need to know things like that."

Nathan laughed. "Maybe you do. Maybe you need to realize that being with one woman—the right woman—night after night is far more satisfying than being with a different woman every night."

"I'm not with a different woman every night," he denied.

"That's true—some nights you're working."

"And to think that I came to you for advice."

Nathan leaned back in his chair and crossed his feet on the edge of his desk. "You did? This oughta be interesting."

"I had a date last night," Justin admitted.

"See point above," his cousin noted drily.

"Her name's Heather," he continued, ignoring Nate's sarcasm. "She's a nurse. Young, attractive and apparently willing to get naked with me."

"So far I'm not seeing why you need my advice."

"Because at the end of the evening, I said goodbye at her door and walked away."

His cousin's brows lifted. "Now that *is* a surprise."

"Do you think there's something wrong with me?"

To his credit, Nate didn't offer a flippant reply but took a minute to consider the question. "I think," he eventually said, "that you're finally growing up and realizing that you want something more substantial than a short-term fling, which you're never going to find if you keep dating women who worship the ground you walk on."

"Avery would more likely spit on the ground I walk on," he admitted glumly.

"Avery?" Nate prompted, sounding intrigued.

"Avery Wallace." Justin shook his head. "I need to get her out of my mind."

"This conversation just got a lot more interesting."

"Except that Avery's made it clear she's *not* interested."

"And you, of course, look at that as a challenge."

"Maybe. Partly," he acknowledged. "But it's more than that."

"Is it?"

"I think I could really fall for her—and she won't even go out with me."

Nate chuckled. "I'm sorry," he said. "I know this isn't funny to you. But after having seen so many women fall at your feet for so many years, it's refreshing to learn that there are still some females who are immune to your considerable charms."

"I'm glad you find this amusing," Justin grumbled.

"I can laugh now, because I've been in your shoes," his cousin admitted. "Allison had all kinds of reasons for not wanting to get involved with me—even before I was her boss."

"Really?"

"Really," Nate confirmed.

"What changed her mind?"

"I think it was the chicken soup."

"Huh?"

His cousin grinned. "Long story. Let's just say that some women need to be convinced that a man has staying power—that he'll stick around through good times and bad, in sickness and in health."

"And you managed to do all of that with chicken soup?" he asked skeptically.

"I think it was what the soup symbolized more than the bowl of broth and noodles itself," Nate told him.

"How am I supposed to show Avery that I want to stick around when she keeps pushing me away?"

"That's a dilemma," his cousin acknowledged. "And before you commit to any course of action, you need to decide if she's worth it."

Justin didn't need to think about it. "She's definitely worth it."

The Sixth Annual Storybook Ball—named to reflect both its fantasy theme and the fact that the proceeds benefitted the children's wing of Mercy Hospital—was held annually on the last Saturday in January. It was their biggest fund-raiser of the year and all doctors were invited and encouraged to attend, to mingle with patrons, talk to them about the work that was being done at the hospital and how past donations had been used to benefit their young patients, and explain why their support was needed now.

A handful of staff were always on hand to greet the guests as they arrived, and Avery had planned to be one of them this year—her support of the cause overrode her usual inclination to avoid formal events. Unfortunately, a complicated delivery put her behind schedule so that by the time she got home, showered and dressed for the event, she'd missed dinner. In fact, she was just sliding into her assigned seat as dessert was being eaten and coffee was being served.

No one asked any questions about her tardiness—they all understood that a career in medicine often caused scheduling conflicts with other events. Dr. Terrence, seated beside her, nudged his untouched strawberry shortcake toward her, offering a second dessert to compensate for the other four courses she'd missed. She gave him a grateful smile. The table of ten was rounded out by an accountant and her husband, a software designer and his wife, and a couple of prominent local business owners and their respective spouses.

As a result of her late arrival, it wasn't until after the coffee service was over that Avery realized Justin was in attendance. When she finally did see him, when his eyes skimmed over her even from the other side of the room, her body tingled as if he'd actually touched her.

The man was spectacular in scrubs. Dressed in a shirt and tie, he was mouthwatering. And in black tie, he was breathtaking. Literally. Because when he started across the room, his gaze locked on hers, she could not draw any air into her lungs.

"Dr. Wallace," he said, inclining his head in greeting.

"Dr. Garrett," she returned, grateful that her cool tone

gave no hint of the heat that flooded her system. "I didn't expect to see you tonight."

"I usually prefer to write a check in lieu of attending these kinds of events," he admitted.

"But not this year?"

He lifted a shoulder "I heard that you were going to be here."

"You didn't pay $1500 for a ticket because I was going to be here," she chided.

"You're right—I didn't," he admitted. "I convinced my cousin Nate—the CFO of Garrett Furniture—to pay $1500 for a table in support of a good cause and for the charitable tax receipt. But I only sat at that table because I wanted to see you."

"I should thank your cousin, on behalf of the Mercy Hospital Foundation, for his generous contribution toward the purchase of an EOS imaging machine for the orthopedics department."

He raised his eyebrows. "That's a pricey piece of equipment."

She nodded. "And it will provide clear and detailed images of children's entire limbs–the spine, arms or legs—with a single scan and a lot less radiation exposure."

"I know what it does," he told her.

She flushed. "Of course, you do."

"Are you nervous, Dr. Wallace?"

"A little," she admitted. "These gala events aren't really my thing."

"So it's the event that has you feeling...edgy?"

"What else could it be?"

He just smiled—the slow, sexy curve of his lips making her heart pound even harder.

"You've got those sparkly things in your hair again," he noted.

Again. He was referring, of course, to New Year's Eve.

And though he said nothing more explicit in reference to that night, she could tell by the heat in his eyes that he was remembering what had happened between them.

She hadn't forgotten, either. Not for one minute. But she wasn't prepared to go down that road again. Instead, she shifted her gaze away, scanning the crowd. "Is your cousin here?"

Justin nodded. "That's him on the dance floor—the one in the black tie."

She smiled at that because all of the guests were in black tie—but no other man that she'd seen wore it quite as well as the one standing beside her right now. "Could you be a little bit more specific?"

He moved closer. "His wife is the gorgeous brunette in the fire engine–red dress."

That description helped her narrow in on the couple. His cousin's wife *was* gorgeous, and she and her husband made a striking couple.

"My parents were here earlier," he told her. "But they left right after dinner to attend a showing at the art gallery for a friend's daughter's boyfriend's sister—or something like that."

She smiled. "Well, I hope they enjoyed their meal."

"It was good, but the lobster ravioli was a little overcooked."

"I can't argue with that—I missed the pasta. And the spinach salad. And the beef tenderloin with mushroom risotto. I got caught up at the hospital and arrived late," she explained.

He frowned. "What did you eat?"

"Strawberry shortcake."

"If you're hungry, I can ask someone to heat you up a plate."

She was touched that he would think of it, and tempted to accept his offer. But she wasn't really here for the food.

She was supposed to work the crowd and squeeze every last dime that she could out of their fat wallets.

"Do you want the beef and risotto?" he asked, ready to invade the kitchen.

She laid a hand on his arm. "I'll probably stop for something on my way home, but for now, I'm fine."

He looked at her hand on his arm, then up into her eyes.

She felt it then—the hum that started beneath her palm and spread through her whole body. She snatched her hand away, but it was too late. Awareness crackled and sizzled between them.

He opened his mouth to speak, but before he could say anything, the couple he'd pointed out to her left the dance floor and came over to join them. He made introductions instead.

"So this is Avery," Nate said, sliding a meaningful look toward his cousin as he shook her hand. "Now I understand."

"Understand what?" she asked, glancing from Justin to his cousin and back again.

When Justin didn't respond, Nate decided that he would. "Now I understand the reason my cousin—"

Chapter Seven

"Wants to dance with you," Justin hastily interjected, grabbing for Avery's hand. "Come on—this is a great song."

"I don't want to dance right now," she told him. "I want to chat with Nathan and Allison."

"I'll dance with you, Dr. Romeo," Allison offered, sending a conspiratorial wink in Avery's direction.

Nathan chuckled as his wife dragged Justin away.

"Are you going to finish what you were saying now?"

"Of course not," he said. "That would break the guy code."

"Then why did you let him think you'd tell me?"

"Because it's so rare to see Justin squirm about anything, I couldn't resist needling him a little." He glanced at her. "That was doctor humor, in case you missed it."

"How could I miss an obvious jab like that?"

He grinned at her response. "In any event, all you need to know is that Justin mentioned your name."

"Is that significant?"

"Much more than you might think," he told her. "My cousin's problem—or one of them—is that everything has always come easily to him. He's smart, talented, good-looking and rich. And on top of all of that, he's a doctor. He saves lives on a daily basis, and he does it without breaking a sweat.

"The combination makes him pretty much irresistible to most females, and he has dated a lot of women, but none of them has warranted mention to his family or held his attention for very long."

"Your wife seems to be doing a pretty good job," she noted, watching Justin and Allison dance and laugh together.

"That's because my wife is the most amazing woman in the world." He grinned again. "Not that I'm biased at all."

"Of course not," she agreed.

His gaze shifted back to the dance floor, and she wondered how it would feel to have someone look at her the way Nate looked at Allison—as if she was the center of not just his whole world but the entire universe.

The Rolling Stones gave way to Whitesnake asking "Is This Love?" and several people left the dance floor, including Allison and Justin.

Nate shook his head. "Does this DJ own anything from the last decade?"

"Probably not," Avery said. "He was likely given a specific playlist to appeal to the demographic with the most money."

Allison sidled up to her husband. "Now it's *your* turn to dance with me."

"You know I hate eighties hair bands," he grumbled.

"But you love me," she reminded him.

"With my whole heart," he agreed, letting her lead him to the dance floor.

"Come on," Justin said to Avery. "It's time for you to get out there, too."

"Oh, um, I don't think I should," she hedged.

"Why not?"

"I'm supposed to mingle," she reminded him.

"One dance," he cajoled.

She wanted to refuse, because dancing with Justin—

even one dance—was a bad idea. But if she continued to protest, he would suspect the true reason for her reluctance: she was afraid of the feelings that churned inside her whenever she was near him.

Instead, she let him take her hand and lead her to the dance floor, her heart pounding every step of the way. And then she was in his arms, so close to him that she could feel the heat emanating from his body. So close that every nerve ending in her body actually ached with wanting to be closer.

She forced herself to concentrate on the music and follow his lead, but the muscles in her legs were trembling and her head was spinning—

"Breathe."

She tilted her head to look up at him. "What?"

"You're not breathing," he told her.

"Oh." She managed to drag air into her lungs, which alleviated some of the dizziness. But at the same time, she inhaled the clean masculine scent that was uniquely Justin. Now her head was spinning for a different reason.

Yep, agreeing to dance with him hadn't just been a bad idea, it had been a monumentally bad idea. Like the Taj Mahal, Great Wall and Giza pyramid of bad ideas. And the song was barely half over.

She wanted him. It was pointless to deny it. No other man had ever affected her the way he did, made her want the way he did. And being with him here, somehow so close and not nearly close enough, was wreaking havoc with her system.

But even more dangerous than the attraction between them was her growing realization that she'd misjudged Dr. Romeo. Yes, he was the undisputed playboy of Mercy Hospital, but there was a lot more to him than the title implied, and the more time she spent with him, the more she genuinely liked him.

"This was worth the price of the ticket," he said, the

words whispered close to her ear, making her shiver. "Just being able to hold you like this."

"Don't let Tilly hear you say that," she responded lightly. "The fund-raising chair might decide to add 'dances with the doctors' to the list of auction items for next year."

"It will be our secret," he promised her.

"And speaking of fund-raising, I really do need to talk to some people."

He nodded. "I know."

She stepped away from him as the song faded away.

"Can I see you tomorrow?" he asked.

The Taj Mahal, Great Wall and Giza pyramid loomed over her again. She shook her head. "I'm making no plans for tomorrow—it's my lazy day."

"We could be lazy together," he suggested.

"Why are you doing this, Justin?"

"Because I tried the 'back to normal' thing you suggested and realized it wasn't what I wanted. I want to be with you. I want a real relationship with you."

"You don't do real relationships," she reminded him.

He linked their fingers together. "I think we faked it pretty well—imagine what we could do if we actually tried."

But she shook her head. "I don't want to try."

"Why not?"

She sighed. "Didn't we have a similar discussion a couple of weeks ago and agree that I'm not your type?"

"Apparently we remember that conversation differently," he told her. "As well as what happened on New Year's Eve."

"I'm not going to sleep with you again, Justin. Although what happened between us a few weeks ago might suggest otherwise, I have too much self-respect to let myself become the latest name in a long list of your sexual conquests."

"There isn't a list," he told her. "And maybe I haven't

had a long-term relationship in a lot of years, because I hear enough 'Yes, Dr. Garrett' at the hospital, I don't want that in my personal life.

"I want to be with someone who has her own thoughts and opinions, and who is willing to argue when she disagrees with mine. I want to be with someone who challenges me to think and entices me to try different things, someone who makes me a better person. I think you could be that someone."

She shook her head. "I'm not that someone."

"How do you know?" he challenged.

"I like you," she admitted. "You're smart and funny and charming, and I admire your professional skills and abilities, but I have no interest in dating a doctor."

He looked at her as if she was speaking a foreign language. "Let me see if I've got this right—it's okay that you're a doctor...but you won't go out with someone who's a doctor?"

"It's not personal."

He laughed, but it was without humor. "I don't think it could get much more personal than that."

"There's Dr. Bristow," she said. "I promised to introduce the Langdons to him if I had a chance."

Justin just nodded.

Avery went after the chief of orthopedic surgery and steered him toward the couple that had been seated at her table for dinner.

When she looked around again, Justin was gone.

Avery put a smile on her face and made her way through the crowd, talking to as many guests as possible to ensure they understood how important the coveted equipment would be to the hospital. Many of them wrote checks to the foundation before they left, making her feel good about the success of the event.

Unfortunately, she didn't feel good about the way she'd left things with Justin. But there was no way she could continue to spend time with him without falling for him, and that was a road she refused to go down.

By the time she left the gala, she was exhausted and her stomach felt unsettled. Probably because the strawberry shortcake that had been her dinner had disappeared a long time ago. She stopped to grab a banana-nut muffin and a bottle of juice on her way home.

The food didn't make her feel any better and as soon as she opened her apartment door, she raced to the bathroom and threw up her late-night snack. After her stomach had finished heaving, she scrubbed her face with a cool cloth, brushed her teeth and fell into bed—and dreamed about Justin.

She spent all of Sunday morning in bed, nibbling on saltines and sipping ginger ale to appease her still-queasy stomach. By midafternoon, she was feeling a little better. She went for a walk to the market, bought some chicken and broccoli to make her favorite casserole—and thought about Justin.

Monday morning she was at Wellbrook early to meet with Amy before their patients started to arrive. She grabbed a cherry Danish from the box of pastries that their nurse habitually brought in and filled her favorite mug with coffee. When Amy came in, she filled a second mug and offered it to her friend.

"So tell me," she said, when they were both seated at the table. "How did the interview go?"

Amy grinned. "So much better even than I expected. Olivia is only a third-year resident, but I think she'll be a great addition to our staff. She has a wonderful demeanor—warm and reassuring—and she's not afraid to ask questions when she doesn't know what to do."

"When can she start?"

"Well, I want all of you to meet her before I officially offer her the job. But if you agree, I'd love to get her on the schedule for the middle of February."

"Sounds perfect," Avery agreed. "So why do you have that little furrow between your brows that you always get when you're worried about something?"

Her friend tore off a piece of doughnut. "It has nothing to do with Olivia."

"Okay," she said cautiously.

"It's about… Justin."

"Okay," she said again.

Amy swallowed another mouthful of coffee. "You know what I think about hospital gossip," she began.

"Just tell me what you heard," Avery suggested. Then she shook her head. "On second thought—don't. It doesn't matter."

"Normally I would agree," her friend said cautiously, "but I don't want you to hear it from anyone else."

She sighed. "Okay—hear what?"

"That he spent the weekend with Heather Delgado."

It took Avery a minute to match the name to a face. Heather had only started working at the hospital in the fall—probably not long after she'd graduated from nursing school—but she seemed competent enough. She was also a very attractive woman with dark curly hair and a bubbly personality.

"Oh." She'd have to be blind not to have seen the way Heather looked at Justin—the open admiration and blatant speculation that gleamed in the nurse's dark eyes. She'd watched her flirt boldly with the sexy doctor—and witnessed him flirting right back.

Of course, she hadn't thought anything of it at the time, because Justin flirted with everyone. But the idea of him *with* the young nurse bothered her more than she wanted to admit, as the Danish and coffee churning in her stomach attested.

"It might not be true," her friend said now.

"It doesn't matter," Avery said again.

Amy squeezed her hand. "I'm sorry."

"There's no reason to be sorry. I told you—it was just a one-time thing. He can see whoever he wants to see, sleep with whoever he wants."

"But…weren't you with him at the Storybook Ball on Saturday?"

"Where did you hear that?"

Amy shrugged. "Lucinda Singh told Gabbie Holtby who told Tess that you were dancing with him at the ball."

"It was one dance," she said. "Yes, we were both there, but we weren't together."

"But that proves he wasn't with Heather all weekend."

"No, it only proves that he wasn't with her for the few hours that he was at the ball," she pointed out.

Monica tapped on the door before poking her head into the small kitchenette/staff room. "You've got a five-month prenatal in room one, a physical in two, 'I'm not talking to anyone but the doctor' in three and suspected chicken pox in six."

Amy nodded. "Thanks for keeping that one far away from the expectant mom."

"That's why you pay me the big bucks," Monica joked.

"I guess we'd better get started," Avery said, pushing away from the table.

Amy caught her arm as she started to move past. "Give him a chance to explain."

"There's nothing to explain. We talked last week, agreed that we were lucky to have dodged a bullet and happy to go our separate ways."

"That might have been what you said," her friend acknowledged. "But how do you *feel*?"

"Right now—I'm incredibly grateful that I'm not pregnant with his child."

But she also knew that if she wasn't feeling better by the weekend, she would pick up a pregnancy test—just to be sure.

Justin didn't see Avery again until Wednesday.

He was still a little annoyed and frustrated with her prohibition against dating doctors, but he didn't think she had any reason to be mad at him. But when he passed her in the ER corridor, she immediately dropped her gaze to the chart in her hand, and when she realized that he was in line ahead of her at the sandwich counter, she moved to the salad bar instead.

He made sure he caught up with her as she was leaving the cafeteria and fell into step beside her.

"What did I do?" he asked.

She sent him a sideways glance, but her quick steps didn't slow. "I don't know what you're talking about."

"Well, I know we're not the best of friends, but I thought we'd progressed to the point where we could actually have a civil conversation."

"Isn't this civil?" she asked.

"Sure," he agreed. "Except that I might get frostbite if I move any closer to you."

She pushed open the doors to the ER department. "So don't move any closer."

"Come on, Avery. You're pissed about something—just tell me what it is."

"I'm not pissed," she denied. "And your new girlfriend's trying to get your attention."

He scowled. "What?"

She nodded her head in the direction of the nurses' station and, when he glanced in that direction, he saw that Heather was gesturing for him to come over to the desk.

"She's not my girlfriend," he denied, even as he held up a finger, asking Heather to give him a minute.

"Really? Because that's been the hot topic of conversation at the coffee station for the past few days."

Despite the deliberately low pitch of her voice, the increasingly heated nature of their discussion was starting to draw some curious looks. Not wanting to generate yet more gossip, he took Avery's arm and steered her down the hall and into the doctors' lounge.

"I don't care what the latest gossip is," he said, when the door had closed behind them. "She's *not* my girlfriend—new or otherwise."

"So you didn't go out with her Saturday night?" she challenged.

"I was with *you* Saturday night," he reminded her.

"Only until I told you I wouldn't sleep with you again—then you disappeared pretty quickly."

"I went home," he told her. "But thanks for that confirmation of your lousy opinion of me."

"So when were you with her?" she asked. "Friday?"

"No." He shook his head. "I did go out with her Wednesday night last week, but I *didn't* sleep with her."

"Whether you did or not is none of my business."

"You're right," he agreed. "It's not any of your business. You made it clear that you weren't interested in going out with me, so you have no right to get all bent out of shape when I go out with someone else."

"I'm not bent out of shape," she denied, though the flush in her cheeks suggested otherwise.

"You seem pretty bent to me."

"Well, I'm not," she said again.

"And I wasn't with Heather," he said again. "Not on Saturday or any other night."

"Except Wednesday."

"I went out with her on Wednesday," he acknowledged.

"And then I said good-night to her at her door and went home to my own apartment."

"If that's true—"

"Dammit, Avery. Of course, it's true."

"—she's not going to want that information to get out. Especially when you slept with Madison, Emma and Brooke."

"I didn't sleep with Madison or Emma. I did sleep with Brooke," he admitted wearily. "Once. About four years ago."

"Apparently your legend lives on."

"And I only agreed to go out with Heather because you made it clear that you weren't interested in a relationship with me," he told her. "And even then, the whole time I was with her, I was thinking of you.

"I'm not proud of that fact, but there it is," he told her. "I'm not used to thinking about only one woman, wanting only one woman. But that's the way it's been since New Year's Eve." He shook his head. "No, the truth is, it's been like that since long before New Year's."

She backed away from him. "Why do you do that?"

"Do what?"

"Say things that make me want to believe I'm different from every other woman who ever got naked with you."

"Because you *are* different," he told her. "God knows you frustrate me a hell of a lot more than any other woman I've ever known."

He was furious with Heather for starting the rumors, but he was even more frustrated with Avery for believing them. And he was exasperated by her determination to ignore the attraction between them—especially after what had happened between them on New Year's. And no matter what he did to prove himself to her, she wasn't willing to give him or a relationship between them a chance because she had some ridiculous and arbitrary rule about not dating doctors.

"In that case, you shouldn't have any objections to me cutting this tête-à-tête short so I can get back to work," she said, moving toward the door.

He stepped in front of her. "What I object to is you walking away every time you don't like the direction of a conversation."

"I can't talk to you about this anymore."

"That's fine," he decided. "Because I'm done talking."

Instead, he pulled her into his arms and kissed her.

Chapter Eight

Avery should have seen it coming. It was just the kind of high-handed macho move she should have expected from him. But he'd looked so sincerely frustrated to hear about the latest rumors churning through the hospital gossip mill, and when he'd looked into her eyes—damn, but she was a sucker for those deep green eyes—she'd felt every last ounce of her resistance melt.

She heard a soft, needy moan and realized that it had come from her. She poured everything she was feeling into the kiss. Anger. Frustration. Hurt. Need. Any pretension that she didn't want this—want *him*—was decimated by that sound.

But still, there were so many reasons not to get involved with him. Even aside from the fact that he was a doctor, he was totally wrong for her. And completely out of her league. She believed he was telling the truth about Heather, so maybe he wasn't quite the Casanova that his reputation implied, but he was still a major-league player and she was just learning the rules of rookie ball.

With that thought in mind, she managed to draw away from him, pressing her lips together as if that might stop the exquisite tingling. But when she lifted her gaze to his, the heat and hunger in his eyes made her tremble inside.

"What are we doing here, Justin?"

"I don't know about you, but I'm trying to remember where the nearest supply closet is," he told her.

She shook her head. "I don't know how to do this—how to play these games."

"I'm not playing games with you, Avery."

"This doesn't make any sense to me," she admitted. "None of this. I know all of the reasons that this is a bad idea. And then you touch me—or even just look at me—and I don't seem to care."

"Despite your fondness to control everything, attraction doesn't work that way. You can try to ignore it, but you can't manipulate it."

"I guess I'll just have to ignore it, then," she decided.

He smiled. "You can try."

When his mother called to invite him for dinner and cake Saturday night, Justin was so frustrated and preoccupied by the situation with Avery, it never occurred to him that the simple invitation was anything more than that. Not until he turned onto the street and saw the long line of cars already in her driveway. Apparently "cake" was code for "party," and he was the guest of honor.

His cousin Lauryn met him in the foyer.

"Happy birthday," she said, brushing her lips against his cheek.

"Thanks." He rubbed her pregnant belly, where her second child currently resided, then asked about her firstborn. "Where's Kylie?"

"Off somewhere with Oliver, and I hope Harper's got her eye on them, because I can't keep up anymore."

"Harper and Ryan are here?"

"Of course," she said, as if it wasn't anything out of the ordinary for his brother and sister-in-law to make the trip from Miami, where Harper was the producer of a popular daytime television show. "If you're going to be surprised by anything, it should be the presence of your other brother."

"I thought I recognized Braden's car in the driveway."

She nodded. "Dana's here, too."

"They haven't both been to a family event since…I can't remember," he admitted.

"Well, they're here today," she said.

Then she hooked her arm through his and guided him to the family room where her middle sister, Jordyn, was snuggled up on the sofa with her new husband, Marco. Lauryn released his arm and squeezed onto the other end of the sofa. Her youngest and still-single sister, Tristyn, was across the room in conversation with their cousin Daniel. He didn't see Daniel's wife, Kenna, anywhere, so he suspected she was chasing around after their almost two-year-old son, Jacob. Andrew and Rachel's daughter, Maura, was teaching her cousin Dylan—Nathan and Allison's son—to play poker.

"Don't bet your college fund," Justin warned the boy. "She'll clean you right out."

Dylan looked up and grinned. "Nah, I'm winning."

"Really?" He looked at Maura, who was scowling at the cards in her hand.

"Beginner's luck," she insisted.

"Maybe *you* shouldn't bet your college fund," he told her.

"We're playing for Rayquaza," she told him.

"I don't know what that is, but it sounds dangerous."

Maura giggled. "You're so funny, Uncle Justin."

Of course, the uncle designation was more honorary than accurate, but he'd always enjoyed being "Uncle Justin" to his cousins' kids. There were quite a few of them now, and they were all underfoot today.

"The house seems so big most of the time," his father said, coming up to Justin and offering him a beer. "And then we invite the family over, and your mother starts to fret about where we're going to put everyone."

He accepted the bottle. "Thanks. There is a full house today."

"Your mother thought your thirty-fifth birthday warranted a party."

"I wish she'd told me."

"She obviously told you something to get you here," John noted.

"She said we were going to have a family dinner. And cake."

"It is family," his father assured him. "And there will be cake."

"Who's the woman with Tristyn and Daniel?" He nodded in the direction of a third person he hadn't noticed earlier.

"Emmaline Carpenter."

"Who?"

"Veronica Carpenter's granddaughter," John said, as if that should explain everything.

"She's not family," he noted.

"Well, no," his father admitted.

Justin sighed. "I guess that means Mom's matchmaking again."

"She thinks that thirty-five is time for you to get serious and settle down."

"Why doesn't she believe that I could get my own date if I wanted one?"

"Because you never bring home any of the women you date."

"Because bringing a woman home to meet the parents is the quickest way to give her the wrong idea," Justin pointed out.

"Just talk to the girl," John urged. "You might find you actually like her."

He was sure that she was a perfectly nice woman, and she was undoubtedly attractive—but she wasn't Avery.

"Right now, I'm going to talk to Mom," Justin said.

He found Ellen in the kitchen, where she was sprinkling mozzarella on top of a tray of cannelloni. She wiped her hands on her apron before she enveloped him in her arms. "There's my birthday boy."

He winced visibly, making his aunt Susan laugh.

"I'm thirty-five, Mom," he reminded her.

"As if I didn't know," she admonished. "I was there, you know. In fact, I'm the one who gave birth to you—after twenty-eight hours of labor."

"Ah, the 'twenty-eight hours of labor' story," Tristyn said, having followed him into the kitchen to grab a handful of juice boxes from the refrigerator, no doubt for the various kids spread around the house. "As much a birthday tradition as candles on the cake."

Susan shooed her daughter out of the kitchen.

"It was thirty-six hours with Braden," he reminded his mother.

She nodded. "But only six with Ryan."

"Are you implying that he was the easy one?"

She laughed. "None of you were easy. Not during labor or all of the years since. But you were worth every minute of every day." She opened the oven to check on the chicken drumsticks and roasted potatoes.

"I'm not sure thirty-five is really a milestone that warrants all of this," he said cautiously. "Not that I don't appreciate it."

"Maybe I just wanted an excuse to get the whole family together," she said. "It's been a long time since everyone's been able to coordinate their schedules."

He nodded. "Yeah, it's been a whole five weeks since Jordyn and Marco's wedding."

She swatted at him with a tea towel. "Andrew and Rachel weren't at the wedding," she reminded him. "They were in Florida visiting Rachel's parents."

"Well, you managed to get everyone here today—which hopefully means you also got a really big cake."

"I should have guessed that would be your biggest concern and not realize that we're still missing someone."

"I didn't actually do a head count, but I can't think of anyone who's missing—aside from Rob," he said, referring to Lauryn's husband, who always seemed to be at the Locker Room—the sporting goods store he owned. "But I figured he was working."

"That's what Lauryn said," she confirmed. "And I was referring to your sister."

"You invited Nora?"

"Of course I invited Nora."

He didn't think there was any "of course" about it considering that the woman she so easily referred to as his sister had been born as a result of his father's extramarital affair during a difficult period in his parents' marriage.

"Does Dad know that you invited her?"

"I wouldn't have done so without talking to him first," she chided. "There's been more than enough secrecy about his daughter."

"What did she say?" he asked.

His mother sighed. "She thanked me for the invitation but said that she had other plans."

"She came to see me a few weeks ago," Justin admitted.

"She did?" Ellen sounded surprised but not displeased by this revelation. "Why?"

"She's applied for a PT opening at Mercy and wanted a letter of recommendation."

"Did you give it to her?"

"I did one better—I introduced her to some of the staff in the physio department. She starts on Monday."

Ellen smiled. "You have a good heart, Justin."

He slid an arm across his mother's shoulders. "I wonder where I get that from."

"You need someone to share that heart of yours," she told him.

"Are you really going to start this again?"

"Nate told me that you're seeing someone—another doctor. Is this true?"

He should have known his cousin wouldn't be able to resist telling someone about Avery, but he'd hoped Nate had enough sense not to open his big mouth to Justin's mother. "I'm not sure our relationship is that clearly defined," he hedged.

"You should have invited her to come tonight."

"Then you would have had to uninvite Mrs. Carpenter's granddaughter."

His mother flushed. "All I did was ask a young woman who didn't have any other plans to join us for dinner."

"Would you have asked her if she was married?"

"If she was married, I would have told her to bring her husband, too."

Which, knowing his mother, was entirely possible.

"I invited Josh Slater, too," she pointed out, referring to Daniel's business partner in Garrett/Slater Racing.

"And I'll bet you've arranged the seating so that he's beside Tristyn."

She neither confirmed nor denied it, saying only, "Get out of here now so we can finish up and get dinner on the table."

Avery's stomach was being uncooperative again. Of course, staring at Justin's phone number might have had something to do with the nerves tangled into knots in her belly.

She had to call him—and she was going to. She just

wanted to be sure that she wasn't going to throw up in the middle of their conversation before she dialed.

She looked at the stick on the table—at the two parallel lines in the narrow window. She'd bought the test because she was still feeling fatigued and occasionally queasy, but she'd expected it to rule out a pregnancy. Seeing those two lines… She wasn't sure how she felt, but she knew that she wanted her baby.

Not just her baby, but hers and Justin's. And if her own emotions were in turmoil, she couldn't begin to imagine how he might react when he learned that he was going to be a father. He'd made it clear that he would be involved if there was a baby, but he'd also been obviously relieved when she told him that they'd dodged the bullet.

Now she had to tell him that she'd been wrong.

And she had to be prepared for the fact that those words would change everything for both of them.

She took a few more slow, steady breaths and punched in his number.

She could hear voices in the background when he connected the call. Voices and laughter.

"I'm calling at a bad time," she realized.

"No, it's okay," Justin said. "It's good to hear from you."

He sounded as if he meant it, which only made her feel guiltier about the reason for her call.

"What's up?"

"I was hoping we could get together, to talk about some things," she admitted. "But obviously you're busy so—"

"I'd say 'stuck' rather than busy," he told her. "But I should be able to get away in about an hour, two at the most."

"Where are you?"

"Family birthday party," he said. "Did you want to meet somewhere or do you want me to stop by your place?"

"Why don't you come here?" she suggested. "That way it doesn't matter if you're an hour—or two."

"I could probably get away sooner, if it's important," he offered.

It was more than important—it was terrifying and exhilarating and life changing. But all she said to Justin was, "I'll see you when you get here."

She disconnected and set the phone back in the cradle. Only then did she realize how much her hands were shaking. Now that she'd made the call, there was no going back.

But she had an hour—or maybe two—and no idea how to pass the time. Her apartment was clean, her laundry done, the dinner dishes washed up and put away. She tried to read, but she couldn't focus on the words on the page. She turned on the television, but nothing held her attention there, either.

She picked up the plastic stick again and stared at the two narrow lines in the window.

Yes, from this point forward, everything was going to change.

Avery immediately released the lock on the door when Justin buzzed, as if she'd been waiting for him. He'd been surprised by her call—even more so by the invitation to stop by her apartment, especially in light of the way their previous conversation had ended.

He wanted to believe that she'd reconsidered, that she'd realized it was pointless to continue to ignore the attraction between them and had decided to explore it instead. Yeah, it was probably wishful thinking on his part—or maybe it was his birthday wish come true.

"What's that?" she asked, when she opened the door and saw the plate in his hands.

"Birthday cake."

"You took the leftover cake?"

"It's my cake," he told her, stepping into the foyer.

"I didn't realize—" She dragged a hand through her hair. "The birthday party was for *you*?"

He nodded. "Apparently thirty-five is some kind of milestone in my mother's world, so she invited the whole clan—aunts, uncles, cousins, spouses and kids."

"Sounds…fun," she said, a little dubiously.

"It was fun. And chaotic. And lucky that there was any leftover cake, which I brought to share with you."

"I should refuse, but I have no willpower when it comes to chocolate cake."

"I thought your weakness was cookies 'n' cream ice cream," he said, following her into the kitchen.

"Okay, so I have more than one weakness," she admitted. "Do you want a glass of milk with your cake?"

"I'd rather have coffee—if it's not too much trouble."

"It's no trouble at all," she told him.

She took a mug out of the cupboard, popped a pod into her home brewing system and pressed the button. Her movements were usually smooth and effortless—indicative of a woman who was confident in herself and her abilities. But she seemed a little jumpy today, and unwilling to hold his gaze. It was as if she was anxious about something, and her nervousness was starting to make him nervous.

Justin found plates and forks in the cupboard, and divided the slab of cake into two pieces. Avery carried his mug of coffee and her glass of milk to the table.

"Cream? Sugar?"

He shook his head. "Black is fine."

They sat at the dining room table and ate their dessert. Actually, he ate his while Avery—despite her declared weakness for chocolate cake—picked gingerly at hers.

"So, why did you call?" he asked, swallowing his last bite.

Avery's fork slipped from her grasp and clattered against

her plate. She pushed her half-eaten dessert away and picked up a napkin, her attention focused on wiping each and every finger. "Maybe we should do this another time."

"Why?"

"Because it's your birthday and there's probably somewhere else you'd rather be."

"I want to be here, Avery," he said patiently. "I want to know what's on your mind."

She folded her napkin in half once, and then again. "I just wanted to follow up our earlier conversation…about what happened…on New Year's."

She wasn't the type to meander through a conversation rather than get straight to the point, but she was meandering now. "What—*exactly*—requires follow-up?"

"Well…it, um, turns out that we didn't, um…dodge the bullet."

It took him a minute to figure out what she was saying, probably because his brain didn't want to figure it out. They'd had a close call, she'd assured him he was "off the hook."

And he'd been grateful—so incredibly grateful—because he knew there was no way he was ready to be a father. Now, he felt that hook slice deep into him, lodging painfully in his gut.

"You're…pregnant?"

She nodded and pulled a narrow plastic stick out of her pocket to show him the two lines in the window.

"You're going to be a daddy."

Chapter Nine

Justin stared at the plastic stick for a long minute.

"Well," he finally said, "this is an even bigger surprise than my mother's party."

Avery nodded again. "I'm sure you need some time… to process."

Yeah, processing would probably be good, because right now, his mind was blank except for the *holy crap* going around and around inside his head.

When she'd told him that she got her period, he'd breathed a sigh of relief that they were in the clear and chalked up the birth-control faux pas to an "oops" that he promised himself would never happen again. And over the past couple of weeks, he'd mostly managed to put the whole pregnancy scare out of his mind.

Now…he wasn't sure what to think or how to feel. He'd already told her how he felt about the decisions she'd made without any communication or consultation, so there was no point in rehashing all of that again.

But—*holy crap*—he really hadn't been prepared for this.

And though he was certain he already knew the answer to the question, he had to ask, "You're going to have the baby?"

Avery tilted her chin and narrowed her gaze on him. Maybe it was a question he felt compelled to ask, but after their previous discussion on the topic, she couldn't help but feel angry and annoyed. "Yes, I'm going to have the baby."

He drew in a deep breath and nodded. "Do you want to get married?"

She stared at him, certain she hadn't heard him correctly.

"Did you just ask—" She shook her head.

"I asked if you wanted to get married," he repeated.

The question was so completely unexpected, even the second time, that she wasn't sure how to respond.

"I always thought I would get married someday," she finally told him. "But not because I'm pregnant and not to a man who doesn't understand the meaning of commitment or long-term."

"Just because I haven't had a long-term relationship in a while doesn't mean I'm incapable of making a commitment."

"Then what does it mean?" she challenged.

"Maybe I just haven't wanted to commit to any of the other women that I've dated."

"But I'm supposed to believe that you're willing to commit to a woman you haven't dated at all?"

"The only reason we haven't dated is that you have some nonsensical ban on dating doctors," he told her.

"It's not nonsensical," she denied.

"Then explain it to me," he suggested.

She shrugged, figuring she probably owed him that much. "Both of my parents were doctors—more committed to their careers than either their marriage or their children—and I decided a long time ago that that's not what I want for my life."

"Except that we are both doctors and we're having a baby together, so that pretty much decimates your logic, doesn't it?" he challenged.

"I don't expect you to make any decisions right now," she said, striving to remain calm and reasonable.

"When should I make them?"

"When you've had a chance to think about what this means for you."

"You said it yourself—it means I'm going to be a father," he acknowledged bluntly.

"That's true," she agreed. "But the last time we talked about this, I told you that it was my decision to accept the potential consequences of what happened between us and I'm not asking for anything from you."

"And I told you that if you were pregnant—and now we know that you are—you don't just get a baby. You get me, too."

She frowned at the grim determination in his tone. "I thought that was just…an emotional outburst."

"I'm not prone to emotional outbursts," he assured her. "I say what I mean and mean what I say. I want to be part of our baby's life, and that would be easier to do if we were married."

"And a lot harder on both of us and the baby when we decide it isn't working, we can't stand to live together anymore and can't figure out who's going to get stuck with the kids," she argued.

It was her use of the plural pronoun that made Justin realize she was projecting her own childhood experience onto the current situation and made him want to throttle both of her parents. But at the moment, the best he could do was proceed cautiously.

"You might want to consider the possibility that we *could* make a marriage succeed," he told her.

"If you're serious about coparenting, we need to be able to work together for the sake of the baby. Which means we need to keep our focus on the baby and not get distracted by other stuff."

"Other stuff?" he echoed, amused despite the guilt and

responsibility weighing on him now. "As in the attraction between us? The reason we're going to be parents?"

"Maybe we're not ready to talk about this," she decided, pointedly ignoring his questions.

"When do you think we will be ready to talk about it?"

"I've had about—" she glanced at her watch "—four hours to think about this. You've had twenty minutes."

"To think about the baby," he agreed. "I've been thinking about us for a lot longer."

"There is no 'us,'" she snapped.

But beneath the frustration, he heard the desperation in her voice. She obviously wanted to believe what she was saying, to establish some control over the situation—because he knew how important it was to Avery to be in control.

"Maybe we both need some time," he suggested.

"That's probably best," she agreed, relief evident in her tone.

"I'll give you a call in a couple of days."

She nodded, apparently willing to be agreeable and reasonable now that he was on his way out the door.

But if she expected him to back off, she was going to be disappointed. Because their future was too important—to both of them and their baby.

She told Amy about her pregnancy a few days later, in part because she continued to be plagued by fatigue and queasiness and it wouldn't take her friend long to put the pieces together, but also because she wanted Amy to know that she'd need to reduce her hours later in her pregnancy and after the baby was born.

Amy was unreservedly thrilled by the news. She knew how much her friend wanted a child and she was convinced that Avery and Justin would be fabulous parents. When Avery pointed out that she and Justin weren't together, Amy reaffirmed her belief that that would change before their baby was born. Avery didn't argue with her friend—preferring to save her energy to have that battle with her baby's father.

After sharing the news with Amy, she thought about telling her family. And when she thought about family, she thought about Ryder, her brother and—aside from Amy—her best friend. She sent him a text message inviting him to come over for dinner, because she'd never known Ryder to turn down a free meal.

She decided on pulled pork, because she could put it in the slow cooker before she went to work and also because she knew how much he liked it. When she got home, she made garlic mashed potatoes and corn—more of her brother's favorites.

He was appreciative of her efforts and was on his second helping when Avery said, "I haven't seen much of you over the past few weeks."

"Our filming schedule has been pretty chaotic," Ryder told her. "The director wants to wrap up the season before the beginning of April so that he can take an extended vacation, which means that all of the crews are working around the clock to finish projects before then."

"I've been busy, too," she said. "In addition to my usual shifts at the hospital, we've extended the hours at the clinic to accommodate our growing list of patients. It's amazing how many women are having babies and, coincidentally, I'm going to have one, too."

She'd hoped that sharing her news as a footnote might diffuse the impact of the words, at least a little. When Ryder paused with his fork halfway to his mouth to stare at her, she realized it had not.

"You're pregnant?"

She forced a smile. "Isn't that great?"

"I don't know." He continued to hold her gaze. "Is it?"

"It is," she assured him. "I'm ready for this, and I really want this baby."

"And the father?" he prompted.

"We're...figuring things out."

"I didn't know you were dating anyone."

"You've been busy," she reminded him.

"So you have been seeing someone?"

She nodded.

"For how long?" Ryder asked.

"Not very long," she admitted.

"Does he have a name?"

"Of course," she said, "but I'm not going to give it to you—not until I'm sure that you won't go all Neanderthal on me and beat him over the head with a club for messing with your sister."

"Then you better give me some more information," he suggested.

"Such as?" she asked warily.

"The date of the wedding."

She shook her head. "Jesus, Ryder—what century do you live in?"

"Hopefully a century in which my sister wouldn't screw around with a guy who doesn't believe in doing the right thing."

She sighed. "Then you'll be happy to know he did offer to marry me."

"And the date of the wedding?" he prompted again.

"I said no."

"Why?"

"He's a doctor."

Ryder sighed and shook his head. "You don't learn, do you?"

"Apparently not."

"But you obviously like the guy—at least well enough to get naked with him."

"Yeah, I like him," she admitted.

"So maybe you could make it work," he said, though not very convincingly.

"Liking someone is hardly a foundation for marriage."

"Maybe not," he allowed. "But you need to think about your baby, too."

"I *am* thinking about the baby. And we both know that putting the responsibility of kids on top of a shaky foundation is a blueprint for disaster."

Her brother reluctantly nodded. "I just want you to be happy, sis. After what happened with Wyatt—"

"I'm over Wyatt," she told him. "My broken heart is mended, fully and completely, and now I'm going to have a baby, and I'm happy about that. I wish you could be, too."

"I am happy for you," he said. "I just wish you were planning to marry the baby's father."

"Because a woman having a baby out of wedlock offends your sense of propriety?"

"I'm not worried about propriety—I'm worried that you've closed off your heart."

"My heart's not closed," she denied. "It's just not open to the baby's father."

The clinic was decorated for Valentine's Day with hearts and flowers and adorable little cupids. When Avery finished for the day, her only thoughts were of dinner and bed—and then she got home and found Justin standing outside of her apartment door with several bags at his feet and a bouquet of flowers in his hand, and her traitorous heart swelled up inside her chest.

"What are you doing here?"

"I brought dinner and flowers for Mr. Gunnerson across the hall, but he already had a date for Valentine's Day so he suggested that I bring everything over here to you."

"Mr. Gunnerson let you into the building," she guessed.

"And Mrs. Gunnerson said you were lucky to have such a handsome and thoughtful beau to share this special day with, because you're a lovely young woman who works too hard and needs someone to take care of *you* every once in a while."

Avery shook her head as she unlocked the door. "This was a really thoughtful gesture, but I had leftover chicken and broccoli in the freezer that I was planning to have tonight."

"Then you should be doubly grateful the Gunnersons sent me over here," he said solemnly, handing her the flowers so he could pick up the rest of the bags to carry into her apartment.

Her heart gave a little jolt inside her chest when she unwrapped the dozen long-stemmed red roses mixed with lush greens and starry gypsophila. "These are...gorgeous," she told him, tracing the edge of a velvety soft petal with the tip of her finger.

"I know you want to pretend this is all about the baby," he told her. "But it's not. There's something going on between us that has nothing to do with the child you're carrying—or maybe it would be more accurate to say it's the reason for the child you're carrying."

She sighed. "I really just want to focus on what's best for the baby right now."

"You don't think having two parents who are together would be the best thing for our baby?"

"I think a lot of things can happen in nine months and we should just take things one day at a time."

"Fair enough," he said, and began to unpack the food.

"How many people were you planning to feed?" she asked, when she saw the number of containers on the table.

"I wasn't sure what you liked, so I got manicotti, lasagna, fettuccine Alfredo, and penne with sausage and peppers. Plus salad, garlic bread and dessert, because you're eating for two now."

"That's a myth," she told him, as she snipped the stems of the flowers. "A pregnant woman only needs about three hundred additional calories a day. Too much weight gain during pregnancy can increase her risk of gestational diabetes, high blood pressure and caesarean delivery."

"I was teasing, Avery," he said patiently. "Believe it or not, I did learn some things during my obstetrics rotation in medical school." He found plates and cutlery and carried them to the table. "How are you feeling?"

"I'm okay. Tired, but that's common in the first trimester."

"Any morning sickness?"

She carried the vase to the table and placed it at the center. "Rarely, and not usually in the morning."

"Have you been to see a doctor?" He held her chair for her to be seated.

"I see doctors every day," she assured him.

"You know what I mean," he chided, settling into the chair beside hers.

She nodded. "Yes, I've seen Dr. Herschel."

"And she doesn't have any concerns about anything?"

"He," Avery told him, lifting a manicotti onto her plate. "Dr. Richard Herschel."

He frowned at that as he reached for the lasagna. "Why did you pick a male doctor?"

"Because he was highly recommended. In fact, he delivered Amy and Ben's son, Henry."

"Is Dr. Herschel at least old and bald?"

She tapped her chin with a finger as she considered the question. "I'd guess early forties, curly blond hair, blue eyes, great bedside manner."

His scowl deepened.

She laughed as she added a slice of garlic bread to her

plate. "Even if I did date doctors—which I don't," she reminded him, "Dr. Herschel is happily married with four kids."

"You could have mentioned that at the beginning."

"I could have," she agreed. Then she said, "I had a consult in the ER this morning, and I saw Heather's name on the schedule."

He nodded. "She was there."

"She didn't invite you to celebrate Valentine's Day with her tonight?"

"She did," he admitted. "And I told her I had other plans. I was tempted to tell her that I was going to be with you, but I wasn't sure how you'd feel about that."

"I'd rather not be the hot topic of conversation at the nurses' station tomorrow."

"You do know that people are eventually going to find out that you're pregnant—and that I'm the father."

"Eventually," she acknowledged. "But I don't want to tell anyone else about the baby until I'm past the first trimester."

He nodded. "Will you come to dinner with me at my parents' house next Saturday?"

"Were you listening to anything I just said?"

"I heard every word," he assured her. "I'm not suggesting that we tell my parents next weekend—I just want them to meet you, to get to know you before they know that you're going to be the mother of my child."

"You want to pretend we're in a relationship," she realized. "You don't want them to find out about the baby and then have to explain that we had a quickie in a closet."

"I don't want to pretend anything," he denied. "I want to give us the chance to actually build a relationship."

She stood up from the table and began clearing away the dishes. "We had this conversation already," she reminded him.

"Actually, we didn't, because you said we weren't ready to have the conversation."

"And I'm still not ready."

"I'm not asking for anything more than one day at a time," he told her. "And I don't think wanting you to meet my parents—our baby's grandparents—is unreasonable."

She nodded. "You're right, it's not."

"Then you'll come to dinner next Saturday?"

"Don't you think you should clear it with your parents first?"

He waved a hand dismissively. "I'll let them know, but it won't be a problem. My mother always cooks more than enough food."

"Okay," she relented. "I'll go to dinner next Saturday."

"Good." After they finished their dessert, he helped her tidy up the kitchen.

"Thank you for tonight," she said, as she walked him to the door. "I was planning on leftovers when I got home—this was better."

"I thought so, too." He settled his hands on her hips and drew her toward him.

She put her hands on his chest, determined to hold him at a distance. "What are you doing?"

"I'm going to kiss you goodbye."

"No, you're not," she said, a slight note of panic in her voice.

"It's just a kiss, Avery." He held her gaze as his hand slid up her back to the nape of her neck. "And hardly our first."

Then he lowered his head slowly, the focused intensity of those green eyes holding her captive as his mouth settled on hers. Warm and firm and deliciously intoxicating. Her own eyes drifted shut as a soft sigh whispered between her lips.

He kept the kiss gentle, patiently coaxing a response. She wanted to resist, but she had no defenses against the masterful seduction of his mouth. She arched against him, opened for him. And the first touch of his tongue to hers was like a lit match to a candlewick—suddenly she was on fire, burning with desire.

It was like New Year's Eve all over again, but this time she didn't even have the excuse of adrenaline pulsing through her system. This time, it was all about Justin.

Or maybe it was the pregnancy.

Yes, that made sense. Her system was flooded with hormones as a result of the pregnancy, a common side effect of which was increased arousal. It wasn't that she was pathetically weak or even that he was so temptingly irresistible. It wasn't about Justin at all—it was a basic chemical reaction that was overriding her common sense and self-respect. Because even though she knew that he was wrong for her in so many ways, being with him, being in his arms, felt so right.

She pulled him closer, so that her breasts were crushed against his chest, but still it wasn't close enough. She wanted to tear away her clothes and his, so that there was nothing between them. She wanted to feel his warm, naked skin against hers; she wanted to feel his hard, sexy body intimately joined with hers.

It was almost as if he could read her mind, because he slid a hard thigh between hers, the exquisite friction dragging a low, desperate moan from deep in her throat. Her fingers curled in the fabric of his shirt, holding on to him, as she rocked her hips against his, silently begging for more. He pressed into her, the hard evidence of his arousal sending happy little sparks dancing through her system.

"You make me crazy," he said, muttering the words against her lips.

"I'm feeling pretty crazy right now, too," she admitted.

"Which is precisely why I need to go."

"Go?" she echoed, confused—and more than a little hurt—by his sudden withdrawal.

He nodded.

"What was this?" She gestured between them. "Just a quick demonstration of how easily you can turn a woman on? How easily you can turn *me* on?"

He rubbed his thumb over her bottom lip, swollen from his kiss. "Do you think you're the only one turned on?" he asked her. "I want you so badly I ache."

"Then why did you stop?" she demanded.

"Not because I don't want to make love with you," he assured her. "Because I want you to realize and accept that I want more than a few stolen hours with you. I don't want you to wake up in the morning and justify your actions on the basis that it was Valentine's Day and you were feeling lonely, and then push me away again because you're angry with yourself for giving in to the attraction between us."

"I wouldn't do that," she denied. Then, in response to his skeptical look she added, "Probably not."

"This way we'll be sure," he said, and brushed his lips against hers again. "Good night, Avery."

Chapter Ten

Avery didn't like to call Amy at home because she never knew when Henry might be napping—or when Henry's parents might be taking advantage of the fact that their little guy was napping. Instead, she sent her friend a brief and concise text message.

Help.

Amy immediately called her. "What's wrong?"

"I'm sorry—I didn't mean to make it sound urgent, like I was trapped in the back of a closet with a knife-wielding maniac outside the door."

"There's no knife-wielding maniac?" Amy asked, sounding just a little disappointed.

"No," Avery assured her. "Although I do feel like I'm trapped by my closet."

"Why?"

"Justin's taking me to meet his parents and I have nothing to wear."

"You're going to meet his parents?" Amy sounded intrigued. "That's an interesting turn of events."

Avery continued to push hangers on her closet rod, shaking her head. "I don't know why I agreed to this. I don't know what I was thinking. And I have no idea what to wear. Are pants too casual? Is a skirt and jacket too businesslike?"

"How about a dress? Something informal but pretty."

"Informal but pretty?" Avery echoed, shaking her head. "I don't own anything like that."

"I'll be over in fifteen minutes."

"You don't have to come over—I just need you to talk me out of my insanity."

"More easily done in person," Amy said.

"But it's Saturday, and I'm sure you're busy with Ben and Henry."

"It's good for Ben to be busy with Henry sometimes," her friend said. "Besides, they'll both still be here when I get back."

True to her word, Amy was there in fifteen minutes—with a garment bag and several shoe boxes in hand.

"Because you knew there was nothing appropriate in my closet," Avery noted.

"I just wanted you to have a few more options," Amy said.

"I'm not sure anything from your closet will fit me—I've got bigger boobs than you do."

Amy dumped the shoe boxes on the sofa. "Stop bragging and I won't hold that fact against you."

"Merely stating the facts."

"You've got longer legs, too," Amy admitted, unzipping the bag. "You should show them off more."

"I don't—" Whatever Avery had intended to say was forgotten when Amy pulled out a deep blue dress. "Oh."

"This is my favorite," Amy told her. "And I think the color will look great on you."

"You must be my fairy godmother."

Her friend grinned. "Go try it on."

She did and was pleasantly surprised to find that the garment looked even better on her than it had on the hanger.

The dress had a round neckline, cap sleeves and twisted pleating at the waist that added a nice touch of detail.

Amy nodded approvingly. "It's feminine and flattering without being too much for a casual dinner—and you really do have bigger boobs."

"Can we talk about shoes instead of boobs?"

"Okay. What size do you wear?"

"An eight."

"Then we better look at what's in your closet because your feet are bigger than mine, too."

They found appropriate footwear to go with the dress, then Amy looked through Avery's admittedly limited selection of jewelry to help her accessorize. She found a pair of hammered silver hoop earrings and a couple of silver bangle bracelets.

"You have no idea how much I appreciate this," Avery said. "Not just letting me borrow your dress but being here to distract me so that I didn't go crazy watching the clock."

"Happy to help," Amy said. "Are you okay now?"

"Actually, I feel like I'm going to throw up."

"Morning sickness?" Amy asked, immediately concerned.

She shook her head. "It's the thought of meeting Justin's parents that's making me feel nauseated. Tell me again why I agreed to this."

"Because Justin's parents are your baby's grandparents," Amy reminded her gently. "And they're lovely people."

"You know them?"

Her friend nodded. "Ellen Garrett is on the hospital board so they attend a lot of functions. She's an absolutely wonderful lady, and her husband is incredibly charming—not unlike his son."

"So they're lovely people who will probably hate me when they find out I'm pregnant with Justin's baby."

"Are you telling them tonight?"

"No. Justin wanted them to meet me before we said anything about the baby."

Her friend glanced at her watch. "And I should get out of here before your boyfriend shows up."

She rolled her eyes. "You know he's not my boyfriend."

"That's right—you're not dating, you're just having a baby together."

"Thanks for the dress," Avery said, pointedly ignoring the teasing comment.

Amy kissed her cheek. "Be home by midnight or you'll turn into a pumpkin."

Dinner at his parents' house wasn't a big deal. Taking a woman to dinner at his parents' house, on the other hand, was.

A very big deal.

Justin had tried to downplay the significance of it to Avery, certain she would have refused his invitation if she suspected what it meant—or what his mother would interpret it to mean. But it was important to him that his parents meet her. He wanted them to know her before they found out about the baby. He wanted them to know not just the mother of their future grandchild but the woman who had captivated him from the day he first met her.

He knew his parents would like her because he did. He wasn't so sure what Avery would think about his family. It was hard to get a handle on what she was thinking or feeling. He thought he was starting to know her pretty well, but there were still parts of herself that she kept closed off, not just from him but from everybody.

He heard the door unlatch and opened his mouth to speak, then she stepped into view and his brain shut down.

He was accustomed to seeing her at the hospital, with a long white coat covering up whatever else she was wearing. Tonight she didn't look like a doctor but a woman.

The dress she was wearing gently hugged her tantalizing curves, the knee-length skirt showcasing shapely legs that were further enhanced by the slim heels. Her hair fell in loose waves over her shoulders and her lips shone with a hint of gloss. He'd always thought she was beautiful, but now she was absolutely breathtaking.

He managed to roll his tongue back into his mouth to speak. "I want to say something charming and clever about how great you look, but all I can think is 'wow.'"

"'Wow' works," she said, offering a shy smile. "So long as it's a 'wow, she looks perfect to take home to meet my parents' rather than 'wow, I'm making a huge mistake here.'"

"It's definitely a 'wow, you look perfect.'"

"I borrowed the dress from Amy," she admitted. "I didn't have anything in my closet that seemed appropriate. To meet your parents, I mean. I have clothes, of course, but it's been a long time since I've met anyone's parents and I didn't know what to wear. And now I'm babbling like an idiot."

He smiled at that. "You seem a little bit nervous."

"Of course I'm nervous."

"I didn't think anything ever fazed you," he admitted.

"I wouldn't be a very good doctor if I fell apart at the sight of blood," she pointed out. "But those two lines on the pregnancy test fazed me. Big-time."

"Well, you don't need to be nervous about meeting my parents," he promised her.

"What time are we supposed to be there?"

He glanced at his watch. "In about fifteen minutes."

"Do they live very far from here?"

"About a ten-minute drive," he told her.

"Then I guess we'd better get going." She opened the closet to get her coat. He was sorry that she was covering up the dress, but it was still February and although it had been a sunny day, the temperature tended to drop significantly after the sun went down.

"Ready?" he asked, when she picked up her purse.

"I think so." She took her keys out of her pocket. "Oh, wait—I almost forgot the pie."

"Why do you have pie?"

"Because when you're invited to someone's house, you don't show up empty-handed." She detoured into the kitchen to pick up the dessert.

"I do. At least once a month when I go over to beg a meal."

"That's different—they're your parents."

He looked at the covered glass dish in her hand. "You actually *made* a pie?"

"I told you that I took cooking classes," she reminded him.

"But you didn't tell me that you could make pie," he said, undeniably impressed. "So..." He put his hand on her back as they made their way to the elevator. "What kind of pie?"

When they arrived at his parents' house—a sprawling bungalow of stone and brick—Justin gave a perfunctory knock on the front door before he walked in.

"They're here," Avery heard a female voice call out. "Come on, John."

"I'm coming," a male voice, sounding eerily similar to Justin's, replied.

"They don't get much company," Justin said, his dry tone making her smile.

Then his parents were there and he made the introductions. John Garrett shook her hand warmly; his wife, Ellen, pulled her into her arms for a quick hug.

"Avery brought pie," Justin said, holding out the plate he'd carried from the car.

"You didn't have to do that," Ellen said.

"That's what I told her," Justin pointed out.

"But it's very much appreciated," his mother said.

Her husband peered over her shoulder. "What kind of pie?"

The echo of his son's question made Avery smile. "Pecan."

John winked at her. "My favorite."

"What's for dinner?" Justin asked.

"Beef Wellington." Ellen looked apologetically at Avery. "I'm sorry—I didn't even think to ask Justin if you were a vegetarian or had any food allergies."

"I definitely eat meat and I don't have any allergies," she assured the other woman.

"I never worry about what I'm feeding Justin," his mother explained. "He'll eat almost anything that's put in front of him."

"Any food I don't have to cook is a favorite," he acknowledged.

"Except broccoli," Avery noted.

Ellen chuckled. "You know about that, do you?"

She realized that she'd inadvertently given the impression that she and Justin were closer than they really were. Aside from his abhorrence of broccoli and his affection for pasta, she really didn't know much about his likes and dislikes.

"Did you know that he can cook, too?" Ellen asked her. "I made sure that each of my boys knew enough of the basics to put a meal on the table, but he'll pretend that he can't if it means someone else will cook for him, so don't you let him fool you."

"No one fools Avery," Justin said.

"But I've cooked for you and not had my efforts reciprocated."

"It sounds like you owe Avery a home-cooked meal," his mother said.

"I brought her here tonight," he pointed out.

"That doesn't count."

"It should count for something," he insisted.

Ellen shook her head. "John, take your son into the den and turn on the television to see what's happening in Daytona—I want to know how Daniel's driver is doing."

"You want us to leave you alone with Avery so you can interrogate her?" Justin guessed.

"Of course," his mother agreed easily. "But don't worry—I'll save the waterboarding for after dinner."

"After dessert," he suggested. "I want to make sure I get a piece of that pecan pie."

Avery didn't panic when Justin left the room. To her surprise—and profound relief—her earlier nervousness had dissipated almost immediately upon entering John and Ellen's home. Justin's parents were simply the kind of people who knew how to make a guest feel comfortable and welcome, and even Ellen's teasing promise of an interrogation didn't worry her.

At least, not too much.

Ellen started mashing the potatoes. "Can you get the milk out of the fridge, please?"

As Avery did so, her attention was snagged by the numerous photographs on the refrigerator door, affixed by magnets advertising everything from pizza delivery to Pier 39. But it was one picture in particular that caught her eye—a couple with four children, including two boys who couldn't be anything but identical twins.

"My nephew's family," Ellen said, when she saw what Avery was looking at.

She swallowed, suddenly uneasy. "Do twins run in your family?"

The other woman shook her head, and Avery exhaled a quiet sigh of profound relief.

"Quinn and Shane are Georgia's boys from her first marriage," Ellen explained. "Pippa was born a few months after her husband died, then she married Matt and they added Aiden to the family."

"They must be very busy."

"I'm sure they are," she acknowledged. "Unfortunately,

I don't get to see them nearly as often as I like because they live in upstate New York. Both of Matt's brothers are there, too, along with their wives and families."

"They're all married?"

"All within twelve months of one another," she admitted. "Justin's cousin Nate almost didn't go to Lukas's wedding—he was afraid there was something in the water up there.

"Now that I think about it, I don't think he did drink any water that weekend. Of course, Nate's married now, too, and not too long after both of his brothers, so maybe he should have worried about the water here."

Avery smiled. "I actually met Nate and Allison at the Storybook Ball."

Ellen frowned. "John and I were there, too. I wonder why Justin didn't introduce you to us that night."

"I arrived late and he said you left early—something about a friend's cousin's boyfriend's show at the art gallery?"

"Oh, that's right," Ellen remembered. She shook her head. "We never should have wasted our time. We've always believed in supporting the arts, and young artists in particular, but I'm not sure that what we saw that night would fit even the broadest definition of art. However, I heard the ball was a tremendous success."

"It was," Avery confirmed. "And the orthopedics department is going to get its EOS imaging machine."

"That is wonderful news." Ellen opened the oven to check on the beef Wellington. "But I've got myself sidetracked again—I wanted to know more about you."

"Well, you know that I'm a doctor."

"Harvard Medical School followed by a residency at Massachusetts General."

"You're on the hiring committee," Avery suddenly recalled.

Justin's mother nodded. "I remember when your résumé came in—no one could understand why you'd leave a major hospital in a big city to come to Charisma, and many didn't believe, even if you did come, that you'd stay."

"I had some doubts myself," Avery confided. "Charisma is a different world from Boston, but Mercy is an excellent hospital, and within six months, I knew I didn't want to be anywhere else."

"How quickly did Justin hit on you?" his mother asked.

She felt her cheeks flush. "The day of my interview."

"And now, three-and-a-half years later, he finally got you to go out with him."

"I know I'm not his usual type," Avery began.

"I wouldn't know his usual type," Ellen admitted. "Justin doesn't typically bring home any of the women he dates."

"He doesn't?"

"Not since college. So when Justin told me that he was bringing a guest to dinner—I didn't know what to think. Now that I've met you…I'm so glad that you're here—that he found you."

The sincerity in the other woman's voice made Avery uneasy. "I'm afraid you're thinking this dinner means more than it does," she told her.

Ellen smiled. "I think it means more than you're willing to admit."

"Mrs. Garrett—"

"Call me Ellen."

"Ellen," she said, trying again. "Justin and I are friends and coworkers, but our relationship really isn't much more than that."

"Not much more means that it is something more."

Trapped by her own words, Avery reluctantly nodded. "I guess it does."

"That's good enough for now," Ellen said, handing her the bowl of mashed potatoes to carry. "Now let's get this food out before the men start banging their fists on the table."

Chapter Eleven

Justin slid his arm across Avery's shoulders as they made their way down the walk toward his car. He was disappointed but not really surprised when she immediately tensed in response to his touch. But she didn't shrug it off, which he took as a sign of progress.

He opened the passenger door for her and offered a hand to help her into her seat.

"Thanks for doing the dinner thing with me," he said, when he'd slid behind the wheel of the car.

"I enjoyed meeting your parents," she told him. "But you could have warned me that it's a big deal for you to take a woman home with you."

"It's not *that* big of a deal," he hedged.

She slid a look in his direction. "That's not what your mother said."

"I'm sorry you were disappointed to discover that I don't take a different woman home every week."

"I wasn't disappointed," she denied.

"But you were surprised."

She nodded.

"What else did my mother say to you?"

"Before or after she pulled out your baby pictures?"

He looked at her, horrified.

She laughed.

"I can't imagine your mother would ever embarrass you in such a way—if your baby pictures are even embarrassing, which I'm sure they're not."

"I was a pretty cute kid," he acknowledged.

"Whoever would have guessed?" she asked drily.

He grinned. "Are your parents the type to pull out baby pictures when I meet them?"

"I don't know that you'll have the opportunity to meet my parents. It's even more unlikely that they have any baby pictures."

"You're kidding."

She shook her head. "I told you that my mother works at CDC and my father's a cardiac surgeon at Emory. They married seven months before I was born and divorced seven years later."

"I'm sure it wasn't as simple and straightforward as you make it sound."

She shrugged, but Justin wasn't fooled by the gesture. "There really wasn't a lot of drama—they both had very busy lives, demanding careers. Truthfully, I'm not sure how they decided that they wanted to live separate and apart, because I don't really remember them ever being in the same place together." She shrugged. "For whatever reason, they decided to split and share custody of me and Ryder. We spent one week with Mom, the next with Dad, and alternated holidays. It was all very civil and reasonable."

And confusing, he imagined, for a child who might never feel sure where she belonged—or if there was anywhere she did.

"Did both of them being doctors have anything to do with your decision to go into medicine?"

"My brother thinks so. He claims it was a last and desperate attempt to get them to notice me—to finally do something that was worthy of their attention.

"I'm ashamed to admit that it might have been true, at

least in the beginning. But once I started med school, I knew I'd found what I was meant to do. And I didn't need their approval so much as I needed to succeed for myself, because I couldn't imagine any other career."

"It shows," he told her. "The way you are with your patients and coworkers—there's no doubt medicine is your calling."

She glanced away, as if uncertain how to respond, but finally murmured softly, "Thank you."

"So why obstetrics?" he asked.

"I guess that was partly a way of proving that I was different from both of them. I might have followed generally in their footsteps, but it was a specialty that was uniquely mine. And it's a lot of fun to deliver babies."

"Why do you think your brother chose to pursue a career outside of the medical field?"

"I would have said pure obstinacy," she said. "Ryder is brilliant. His marks in high school were far superior to mine. He could have done anything he wanted—he could have been a doctor or an engineer, a college professor or an astrophysicist. It took me a long time to accept that he didn't throw away his choices to spite our parents, that he's doing exactly what he wants."

"Now that wasn't so bad, was it?" he asked, when he pulled into a visitor's parking spot beside her building.

"What?"

"Making conversation, getting to know one another."

"No," she agreed. "It wasn't so bad at all."

"Then maybe we could do this again."

"Dinner with your parents?"

He smiled. "That, too."

It was almost one thirty by the time Avery stripped off her soiled gloves and gown, and she was on the schedule at Wellbrook for two o'clock. She'd been called in to the ER to deal with a suspected ectopic pregnancy that ended up rupturing while the patient was undergoing an ultrasound exam. The patient had lost a lot of blood and one of her fallopian tubes, but she was going to be fine. Avery was relieved—and exhausted.

She took a quick shower in the women's locker room in a desperate effort to revive her flagging energy. When she exited into the staff lounge, she found Justin waiting for her.

He held up a prepackaged sandwich and a carton of milk from the cafeteria. "I brought you lunch."

"I'm not hungry."

"I don't care if you're not hungry," he told her. "You have to eat."

"I don't have time to eat right now. I've got to be at Wellbrook—"

"You have to take care of yourself," he admonished, his tone gentle but firm as he nudged her toward a chair. "Sit."

"I have to go," she said again.

"Is there an emergency at the clinic?"

She huffed out a breath. "No, but—"

"Then sit."

She hated being pushed around. She hated men who thought they could push women around. But the fact was, she was so hungry she was feeling a little dizzy, and she was afraid if she didn't capitulate and sit down voluntarily, she might fall down. So she sat.

He peeled back the plastic wrapping and handed her half the sandwich.

She took a bite. "Where's the mustard?"

He took a handful of packets—both mustard and mayo—out of his pocket and tossed them onto the small table beside her.

She didn't really want mustard. She'd only asked for it because she was being difficult and ungrateful, but she opened a packet, peeled the bread away from the roast beef, and squirted the condiment onto the meat.

She ate the sandwich, dutifully drank the milk. “Can I go now?”

“That depends.”

“On what?” she asked warily.

He took a huge chocolate chip cookie out of his other pocket. “On whether or not you want dessert.”

Her gaze locked on the cookie and her mouth started to water. “I definitely want dessert.”

He grinned and passed her the cookie. “Feeling better now?”

“I am,” she admitted. “Thanks.”

“You do know that the world’s not going to stop turning if you slow down a little?”

She nodded. “I know. And I am taking care of the baby—I promise.”

“Do you really think all I care about is the baby?”

She frowned as if she didn’t understand the question.

Justin hunkered down beside her chair and laid his hands on her knees. He immediately felt the muscles in her thighs tighten—Avery withdrawing. He’d thought it was just him, but watching her over the past several weeks, he realized that she wasn’t freezing only him out—she froze almost everyone out. Aside from her best friend and her brother, she didn’t seem to let anyone get too close. The realization challenged rather than discouraged him.

“Has no one ever taken care of you?” he asked gently.

She was silent for a minute before she responded. “Hennie.”

“Who?”

“Henrietta was the nanny we had when Ryder and I were little, but we called her Hennie.”

“And if Hennie said to you, ‘Avery Wallace—you need to eat,’ what would you do?”

"I'd eat," she admitted.

"So eat," he suggested.

She unwrapped the cookie.

"I know you have a job to do," he said to her. "But it's also your job to take care of yourself and our baby."

Our baby.

He said the words so casually, so easily.

Then he touched his lips to hers, the kiss as casual and easy as his words.

And she thought—at least in the moment—that maybe they could do this.

Just because her hormones immediately went into overdrive every time he was near didn't mean that she had to do anything about it. They could be friends and coparents of their baby without muddying things up with unnecessary attraction or emotions.

Maybe.

Justin was generally pretty good at reading people, and he was confident that Avery would come to accept that he was going to be part of her life. Unfortunately, he wasn't confident that it would happen before their baby was born.

He deliberately stayed out of her way for a few days, to give her a chance to relax. He knew she was sensitive to hospital gossip, and even he was aware that there had been some talk about the two of them spending time together. There would be a lot more when word got out that she was going to have his baby so, for now, he backed off a little.

Until he got a call on the afternoon of February 29 that drew him to the maternity ward.

"You're a little far from the ER, aren't you, Dr. Garrett?"

"I had to come and take a peek at my cousin's baby," he said, gesturing to the bassinet with a tag that said 'Schulte' on it.

"Almost nine pounds and twenty-two inches, and Mom barely batted an eyelash," Avery told him.

"You delivered him?"

She shook her head. "I just caught him—Mom did all the work."

"Lauryn's second," he explained. "Although I seem to recall that Kylie didn't give her much trouble when she was born, either. Of course, those are the ones that my mother always says you need to worry about when they hit their teen years."

"Which of her sons did she need to worry about the most?" Avery asked.

"Probably me," he admitted.

"Why am I not surprised?"

He grinned and slid an arm across her shoulders. "Was Lauryn's husband there when the baby was born?"

She shook her head.

"Figures," he said. "It's the story of his life—expecting his wife to handle everything on her own."

"She wasn't alone," Avery told him. "Her sister—Tristyn—was with her."

He chuckled. "I would have paid to have seen that. Tristyn practically passes out if she gets a paper cut."

"Well, she held up very well in the delivery room. She did look a little green at first, but after I suggested that she stay at the head of the bed, away from all of the activity, she was fine."

"Is it different now?" he asked.

Despite the apparent disconnect from their previous topic, she understood what he was asking and nodded in response.

"Delivering babies has always been my favorite part of the job," she told him. "There's something incredibly satisfying about helping to bring a new life into the world—especially when the mothers do most of the work.

"It was only today that I realized it's not going to be so long until I'm the one actually pushing a baby out of my body. And suddenly, it wasn't just amazing—it was a little scary."

"I'll be there with you," he told her.

"You can't guarantee that. You could be—"

"I'll be there with you," he said again.

She was quiet for a minute before she said, "What if I don't want you there?"

"You don't know what you want."

Her brows lifted but she didn't deny it.

"So I'll be there," he said again. "Every day, every step of the way, until you realize it *is* what you want."

The original plan not to tell anyone about Avery's pregnancy until she was past the first trimester changed when she registered to attend the Spring Conference on Women's Sexual Health Issues in Atlanta the second weekend in March. Deciding that it would be the opportune time to share the news with her parents, they agreed to tell Justin's family about the baby the weekend prior.

Ellen cooked another delicious meal—baked lemon-and-herb chicken breasts served with a creamy risotto and green beans. Avery had again brought dessert, this time an apple crisp.

After everyone had consumed their fill, Justin reached for her hand and linked their fingers together. She might have thought his action was a show of togetherness for his parents' sake except that their hands were beneath the table where no one else could see. For some reason, that fact made the gesture all the more reassuring.

"We've got some news to share," he told his parents.

"You're getting married?" his mother guessed, her expression hopeful.

"No," Avery said quickly, sending a panicked look in Justin's direction.

He squeezed her fingers reassuringly. "We're going to have a baby."

Ellen drew in a quick breath. "A baby," she echoed, her whispered tone almost reverent. Then her attention shifted to Avery for confirmation. "Really?"

She nodded.

"Oh, that's even better than a wedding," Ellen decided, sounding sincerely thrilled by the news. "Although a wedding *and* a baby would be even better still."

This time Avery squeezed Justin's hand—a silent and desperate plea.

"Let's just focus on the baby right now," he suggested.

"Of course," his mother agreed. "This is definitely cause for celebration. John—is there any champagne downstairs? Wait—what am I thinking? We don't want champagne but sparkling grape juice. Do we have a bottle of that?"

"I can go check," her husband told her.

"Please do," Ellen urged. Then, when John got up from the table, she said, "Justin, go help your father. Half the time he can't find his nose on his face."

He looked at Avery. She knew he wasn't actually asking for permission so much as seeking confirmation that she didn't mind him abandoning her with his mother. She managed a weak—and probably not very convincing—smile.

"I'll be right back," he promised.

"Glasses," Ellen said, popping up from her seat. "We'll need glasses."

Avery got up from the table to start clearing away the dessert plates while Justin's mother opened the cabinet for the champagne glasses.

"No, no," Ellen admonished. "I'll take care of that later. Please sit and rest—and tell me how you're feeling. Are you experiencing any morning sickness?"

She shook her head. "Some occasional queasiness, but nothing too serious."

"I was sick as a dog through the first trimester with each of the boys," Justin's mother confided. "It started somewhere around week three and didn't let up until week twelve, but then I never had any further problems." She brought the crystal flutes to the table. "How far along are you? When is the baby due?"

"Almost ten weeks. The baby is due September twenty-fourth."

"September seems so far right now, but really, the months will fly by." Her eyes misted. "And we'll have a new grandbaby before Christmas."

"You're really not upset about this?" Avery asked cautiously.

"I'm not going to lie," Ellen said. "I would have preferred if there had been a wedding *before* a baby, but I understand that things don't always work out the way we plan.

"I've always worried about Justin," she continued. "Because despite his active social life, I could tell that he was lonely. Not that he would ever admit it, of course, but I was anxious for him to find the right woman, to finally realize how much he wanted to share his life with someone."

She reached across the table and took Avery's hands. "I'm so glad he found you, and I'm overjoyed that you're going to have a baby together."

While Ellen was talking to Avery, her husband was silent as he made his way down the stairs.

"You haven't said anything about the baby," Justin said, when they reached the climate-controlled wine cellar.

"I'm not quite sure what to say," his father admitted.

He nodded. "My initial reaction was pretty much the same."

"Then this wasn't planned?"

Justin shook his head.

"Have you talked about getting married?" John asked.

"Avery likes to take things one step at a time."

"Having a baby doesn't give you the luxury of leisure," his father warned as he scanned the labels. "Sparkling grape juice, apple grape, sparkling cider, cranberry-orange and fizzy peach-pomegranate juice."

"Why do you have so many choices?" Justin asked.

"Your mother insists on having it on hand for the kids."

"Avery likes cranberry juice, so let's go with that one."

John opened the door and pulled the bottle from the shelf. "How much else do you know about her?"

Something in his father's tone got his back up. "What are you asking?"

"Where's she from?"

"Atlanta originally, but she attended med school and did her training in Boston."

"How did she end up in Charisma?" John pressed.

"I don't know," he admitted.

"Did she chase after you?"

The question was so outrageous he couldn't help but laugh. "No, Dad. *I* chased *her*. For more than three years."

His father frowned at that. "Some women play hard to get on purpose—it's part of the game to snag a wealthy husband."

"Not Avery. If you want the truth, she'd probably prefer if I wasn't the father of her baby."

John didn't look convinced. "Does she know that you have an interest in Garrett Furniture?"

Justin sighed. "I promise you, she's not after my company shares."

"You should think about a prenup, anyway."

"A prenup assumes there are going to be nuptials," he pointed out, already not liking the direction of this conversation.

"You need to protect your assets," John warned. "And your parental rights."

"Whether or not Avery and I get married, I will be part of this baby's life from the beginning," he said, trying to keep his escalating anger in check. "My child won't need to come looking for me on Father's Day twenty-something years from now."

His father's face flushed. "You know damn well I would have been in Nora's life from the beginning if I'd known she was my daughter."

He nodded. "I guess I just wonder if you would still have been in mine. If your lover had told you that she was pregnant with your child, would you have left Mom to be with her?"

"How can you even ask that question?" John asked indignantly. "You know I love your mother."

"Did you love her even when you were screwing around on her?"

A muscle in his father's jaw ticked. "I'm not going to discuss this with you."

"That's fine," Justin agreed. "Because I really don't want the details—and I don't intend to take relationship advice from a man who couldn't honor his own wedding vows."

"I made a mistake," John said wearily.

"Locking your keys in the car is a mistake. Washing whites with colors is a mistake. A ten-month affair while your wife is raising your three kids and caring for her ailing mother?" He shook his head. "That's selfish and self-indulgent behavior."

He didn't wait for his father's response—he wasn't willing to listen to any more of his excuses. He turned and carried the bottle of juice upstairs.

Chapter Twelve

"Is everything okay?" Avery asked Justin as they were driving away from his parents' house.

"Sure," he said.

"There seemed to be some…tension," she said cautiously, "between you and your dad when you came back to the dining room."

"It wasn't about the baby," he promised. "My parents are both thrilled that they're going to be grandparents again."

"I have to admit, I wasn't expecting that."

"Because you haven't seen them when the whole family is together. My mother is never happier than when there are a bunch of little ones around. It nearly broke her heart when Ryan and Harper moved to Florida with Oliver last year."

"You're lucky to have such a close family," she told him.

He could tell that she was thinking ahead to the following weekend, when she would be in Georgia for a medical conference—and to share the news with her parents.

"Do you want me to go to Atlanta with you?"

She seemed surprised that he would offer and, after only the briefest hesitation, she shook her head. "You have to work Saturday night."

"I can get someone to cover for me," he offered.

"There's no need."

"Would you tell me if there was?" he asked her.

"I'm not going to pretend that my parents will be even half as excited or supportive as yours, but I can handle it."

Of course she could. Avery didn't need anyone to help her with anything. Not only could she handle everything on her own, she preferred it that way—a truth that continued to frustrate him. "I'd really like to be there with you when you share the news with your parents," he said.

She shook her head. "Having you there will only shift attention from the baby to our relationship."

"And that's a problem?"

"Yeah, because right now, I'm not prepared to face questions that I don't know how to answer."

"All the more reason for me to be there," he suggested.

"Not this time," she said.

"Okay," he finally agreed.

They rode in silence for another few minutes before she said, "If the tension between you and your dad wasn't about the baby—what was it about?"

He should have realized she wouldn't be distracted from her original inquiry. "Old wounds," he said simply.

"Anything to do with your sister?"

He frowned. "What hat did you pull *that* out of?"

"It makes sense," she said. "Your father had a child out of wedlock and now you are, too."

"It's hardly the same thing. For starters, I wasn't married—or even involved with someone else—when I was with you."

She nodded in acknowledgment of that fact.

"Because regardless of what you think of me and my reputation, I don't juggle women."

"I know," she said.

"But you still think I'm a bad bet," he guessed.

He was surprised by the shake of her head and even more so by the response that followed.

"I don't think you're a bad bet," she denied. "I think *I* am."

* * *

As Avery got ready to go out for dinner with Justin Wednesday night, she couldn't stop thinking about her last patient of the day. Karen Greer's fourth child had died in utero at twenty-eight weeks as a result of listeriosis and although an induction was scheduled for the following morning, Avery was still apprehensive.

She called the clinic to get Karen's home number so that she could check on her patient. It rang six times before the young mother answered, and she sounded harried and out of breath when she finally did. Of course, chasing after three young boys, she was often harried and out of breath.

"Your procedure is booked for eight a.m. tomorrow," Avery reminded her. "I just wanted to make sure that works for you."

"That's fine," Karen said. "I've made arrangements for my sister to come and watch the boys."

"I'll see you in the morning, then," she said.

But even after she hung up the phone, Avery couldn't shake the uneasy feeling in the pit of her stomach. She considered that there might be another cause for her preoccupation—maybe she was worried about her date with Justin and desperately trying not to think about it.

She saw him almost every day, and they occasionally had lunch or dinner together. But grabbing a bite after work was casual and easy, tonight was a DATE. Tonight he was taking her to a restaurant that required reservations, and for some reason that put their relationship on a completely different level—a level she wasn't entirely sure she was ready for or even wanted.

No, that wasn't entirely true. She did want to take the next step with Justin, and that scared her almost as much as her growing feelings for him. She wanted to believe that he could make a commitment to her and that they could raise their child together as a family, but personal experience warned her otherwise.

Amy kept urging her to give him a chance, but giving Justin a chance meant risking heartbreak, and that was a risk she wasn't willing to take. So she'd go out for dinner with him, and she'd work with him to figure out what was best for their baby, but she wasn't going to be foolish enough to hand him her heart.

She'd just fastened her earrings when her phone rang. She automatically checked the display, more curious than concerned until she saw R&K Greer. She dropped the lid on her jewelry box and connected the call.

Ten minutes later, she was on her way to the hospital.

Justin had made reservations at Casa Mercado, an upscale tapas bar and restaurant that had been highly recommended by his brother, Ryan. While he and Avery had made some slow and steady progress in getting to know each other, he'd deliberately kept their dates low-key: casual meals, movies at home, walks in the park. Tonight, he was determined to wow her.

And maybe tonight, when he kissed her good-night, he would turn up the heat a little. And then, if she invited him inside, he wouldn't walk away. The chemistry between them was one more reason he believed they could make a relationship work, and he was prepared to exploit it if necessary.

Except that when he arrived at Avery's building just after seven to pick her up for their seven-thirty reservation, there was no response when he buzzed her apartment. He called her cell phone next and sent a text message, but got no answer to either. It was then that he returned to the parking lot and saw her car was missing from its designated spot. He called the restaurant and canceled their reservation.

He wasn't upset or angry. Being a doctor meant that the best-laid plans often went awry—he understood that as much as anyone. A medical emergency required immediate response—he wouldn't expect her to take the time to call him and, in fact, he would have been surprised if it had occurred to her to do so. She would have been focused on caring for her patient and that was how it should be.

But when the emergency had been dealt with, when she had a minute to catch her breath and focus on other matters, he hoped that she would call to explain. His phone remained silent.

Avery sank down onto one of the overstuffed sofas in the doctors' lounge, drawing her knees up to her chest and wrapping her arms around them. Her chest felt tight and her eyes were burning, but she didn't cry.

She hadn't let herself shed many tears since she was nine years old and found out that her grandmother had died. Dr. Cristina Tobin—Avery's mother—had tolerated a few sniffles, then she'd told her daughter to dry her eyes, because if she ever wanted to have a career in medicine, she was going to have to accept that death was a fact of life and learn not to give in to her emotions.

Avery had broken down a few times since that day, but not ever again in front of her mother. The first time was when she'd broken up with Mason Turner, her first love and first lover; the next was when she'd lost a twenty-five-week-old baby during her obstetrics rotation in medical school.

She'd known the baby's chances of making it were slim, but the neonatal team had worked so hard to get the nearly two pound baby through the first and most critical twenty-four hours after birth and he'd seemed to be doing well when she went home at the end of her shift. But when she returned to the hospital the next day, he was gone. It wasn't the first patient she'd failed to save, but for some reason losing that baby—an infant that she'd helped deliver, that she'd held in her very hands—had really shaken her.

Tears were a sign of weakness, Cristina had told her. She was already fighting an uphill battle as a woman. She couldn't afford to be weak and she especially couldn't afford to show any sign of weakness.

She wasn't crying now, but the tears were there—burning her eyes and clogging her throat. She'd known that Karen's baby was gone, of course, but holding on to the tiny lifeless body, she'd been overwhelmed by a wave of grief and frustration and fear. Karen had carried and delivered three other children without any difficulty, but an undercooked burger had introduced dangerous bacteria to her system and ultimately cost the life of this one.

And suddenly Avery was in a panic about her own unborn child, overwhelmed by the knowledge of how many things could go wrong in a pregnancy and swamped by a feeling of complete helplessness. Because even if she did all of the right things—and she was trying—there were no guarantees that her pregnancy would go to term or that the baby would be born healthy.

She heard the door open and footsteps enter the room, but she didn't look up. The footsteps drew nearer, and then Justin lowered himself onto the battered coffee table, facing her.

"It's cookies 'n' cream," he said, offering her a single-serving tub of ice cream and a spoon.

She looked at him blankly.

"There's conflicting evidence about the safety of herbal teas during pregnancy and I know you hate decaf coffee," he explained. "I figured this was a more appealing option."

"Thanks." She accepted the frozen offering. "But what are you doing here?"

"Well, my plans for the night fell through so I thought I'd hang out at the hospital and try to pick up a hot doctor."

She tried—and failed—to muster a smile for him. "Good luck with that," she said, peeling the lid off the tub to dip the spoon into the ice cream.

He settled his hands on her thighs. "It seems to be working out so far."

"I should have called you," she said, before she shoved a spoonful of cookies 'n' cream into her mouth.

"I'm a doctor, too," he reminded her. "I know how it works."

She dipped the spoon into the container again and nodded.

"How's your patient?"

"Stable," she answered around the mouthful of ice cream.

"How are you?"

Her eyes filled with tears again. She shook her head as she swallowed. "Apparently not so stable."

He moved to sit beside her on the sofa, putting his arm across her shoulders. She didn't know why, but it felt natural to tip her head back, so that she was leaning against him. He was so solid and warm and, for some inexplicable reason, just being close to him made her feel safe enough to finally let go of the grief that she'd been holding inside. Justin didn't say anything as the tears spilled onto her cheeks, only held her close while she cried.

"I knew the baby was gone," she told him when she'd gathered her composure enough to speak again. "We did an ultrasound earlier today and confirmed an intrauterine death. She was scheduled for induction tomorrow morning, and although she started to bleed around four o'clock, she thought she could hold off until the morning."

Avery closed her eyes and sighed wearily. "She didn't call me until after she'd made dinner for her other kids. I immediately called 9-1-1 but she was unconscious even before the paramedics arrived."

"But she's okay now," he reminded her gently.

She nodded. "Physically, anyway. The emotional scars will take longer to heal."

"They always do."

"I'm not sure if it's a blessing or a curse that she's got three other kids to take care of at home."

"Is there a dad in the picture?" he asked.

"A great dad—devoted to his wife and kids but busy working two jobs to keep a roof over their heads, so he doesn't get to spend much time with any of them."

"A common dilemma for a lot of parents," he noted.

She nodded again and scooped up some more ice cream.

"Are you going to share any of that?" Justin asked her.

"I thought you bought it for me."

"I did," he agreed. "But I missed dinner, too."

She offered the spoon to him.

There was something incredibly sensual about sharing an eating utensil, about watching his lips close around the spoon that had been inside her own mouth. And a slow growing awareness pushed through the bubble of grief that had enveloped her.

She tore her gaze away. "I am sorry about our date."

"We'll reschedule," he promised.

She wanted to, because she enjoyed being with him—so much more than she knew was smart. It was crazy how quickly and completely he'd infiltrated her life, how much she looked forward to seeing him every day, and how much she missed him when she didn't.

Being with him was exciting and scary, because her feelings for him were already so much stronger than she'd ever intended. He had this uncanny ability to know when she needed him—even if she wouldn't admit it. And the more time she spent with him, the more she was in danger of not just relying on him but falling in love with him. Despite her earlier promise to herself not to give him her heart, she was afraid that she'd already done so.

"What are we doing here?" she asked softly.

"Sharing ice cream."

She shook her head. "I didn't mean at this particular moment."

"What did you mean?"

"I'm just wondering why we're going through the motions."

He scooped up another spoonful of ice cream. "Is that what you think we're doing?"

"We had sex and I got pregnant and now we're trying to turn that into a relationship, and I'm not sure that's a good idea."

"I know you're accustomed to having a life plan," he acknowledged. "But not everything can be scheduled and organized according to your timetable. Sometimes you just have to let things happen and be willing to deal with the consequences."

"Isn't our baby proof that I'm doing that?"

He tightened his arm around her. "I think that's the first time you've said that."

"Said what?"

"*Our* baby."

She frowned. "I say it all the time."

He shook his head. "You say 'the baby'—you don't usually acknowledge that we're both responsible for the life growing inside of you."

"Maybe I was subconsciously trying to absolve you of responsibility."

"I don't think it was subconscious at all."

"Maybe not," she admitted. "When I first suspected that I might be pregnant, I was certain you wouldn't want to have anything to do with the baby—*our* baby."

"And now you know you were wrong?" he prompted.

"Now I'm starting to believe I was wrong," she acknowledged.

He kissed the top of her head and hugged her close. "Then we're making progress."

Chapter Thirteen

The next day, Avery was carrying her lunch tray into the atrium when she spotted Callie. She hadn't seen the nurse in several weeks and started automatically toward the long table where she was seated with several other nurses. As Avery drew nearer, their conversation faded away.

"I didn't mean to interrupt," she said. "I just wondered how Camryn and Brad are doing with their new baby."

"You're not interrupting," Callie said, speaking loudly enough to ensure that she could be heard by everyone at the table. "Nothing more than the usual hospital gossip, anyway."

Heather shot her a venomous look as she picked up her tray and left the table. A couple other nurses commented that they were due back at their stations and followed suit.

"I guess the talk was about me," Avery said, which didn't really surprise her.

Anyone who had seen her with Justin would be able to tell that the relationship between them had changed. And people were watching, because Dr. Romeo had always been the subject of much scrutiny and speculation around the hospital. People liked to talk about who he was dating and guess how long a relationship would last. Some of the nurses ran a pool—anything outside of two weeks was always considered a long shot—and bonus points were awarded to anyone who correctly identified the lucky woman chosen as his next companion.

No one would have guessed that he would pick Avery, and she could tell that they were as baffled as they were envious that he was with her now. Of course, only she and Justin knew the truth—that they were only together because she was pregnant with his child.

She hated that people assumed she was sleeping with him—which was both ridiculous and hypocritical, because while she wasn't actually sleeping with him now, she had been naked with him. She had no right or reason to be upset that they were judging her for the truth.

The worst part, though, was that her body had apparently not gotten the memo from her brain that what had happened between them that night was not going to happen again. Every time he touched her or kissed her, her hormones started clamoring for more.

"Heather's all bent out of shape because she saw you and Dr. Garrett in the lounge together last night," Callie explained, gesturing for her to sit down.

"And?" Avery prompted, setting her tray on the table.

The nurse shrugged. "She said he was—" she made quotation marks in the air with her fingers "—consoling you."

"I almost lost a patient last night," she explained. "Dr. Garrett could tell I was upset, and we sat and talked for a while."

"You don't have to explain," Callie assured her. "Everyone thinks the two of you would be great together. Well, almost everyone. Not that *everyone* is talking about you," she hastened to explain. "Because that would be completely unprofessional and inappropriate."

Avery managed a smile. "Well, thanks for the heads-up about the gossip that's not gossip."

The nurse smiled back. "Anytime."

"And your nephew?" she prompted.

"He's fabulous." Callie opened the camera app on her phone. "Let me show you some pictures."

Friday night, Avery was in Atlanta and Justin was alone at home, contemplating his dinner options. Because he didn't have neatly labeled containers in his freezer, those options were pizza and Chinese, both of which he could have delivered to his door.

He opted for a large pizza that would fulfill his requirements for dinner tonight and lunch the following the day. He'd just hung up the phone after placing his order when the buzzer sounded from downstairs.

He knew it couldn't be his pizza delivery already, and a quick glance at the lobby display made him frown. He picked up the phone again, answering the summons.

"It's Ryder Wallace—Avery's brother."

Justin figured the man would show up somewhere, and he was grateful he hadn't tracked him down at the hospital. Of course, it was probably out of deference to his sister that he'd avoided a showdown in that arena. No doubt she'd told him that she didn't want anyone at work to know about her pregnancy yet—or the identity of her baby's father at all.

"Come on up," he said, releasing the lock on the downstairs door.

He'd never met Avery's brother, but he'd seen him on TV. The guy seemed taller in person—about Justin's own height, but broader. His shoulders seemed to fill the doorway, and the muscles in his arms confirmed that his job required him to wield tools much heavier than a scalpel or stethoscope. Not that he felt intimidated, exactly, but Ryder's grim expression was hardly reassuring.

"Are you going to invite me to come in?" he asked, when Justin continued to block the door.

"It depends," he said. "Are you planning to hit me?"

Ryder shrugged his broad shoulders. "I thought we'd try talking first."

"Talking works for me," Justin said, stepping back so Avery's brother could enter. "Do you want something to drink?"

"I wouldn't say no to a beer."

He pulled a couple of bottles of his favorite microbrew from the fridge, twisted off the caps and handed one to the other man.

Ryder glanced at the label, then lifted the bottle to his lips and sipped cautiously. "Not bad," he decided.

"Thanks, but I'm guessing you didn't come over here to critique my beer selection."

"I didn't," he confirmed. "I'm here because Avery told me about the baby."

"I suspected as much," Justin said.

"My sister's a smart woman," Ryder noted. "She likes to gather facts and evidence before she decides on a course of action. She's never careless or impulsive, so you can imagine how surprised I was when she told me that she was pregnant."

"Me, too," he admitted.

"I don't know what your relationship is, and Avery would say it's none of my business—"

"I disagree," he interjected. "She's your sister and the child she's carrying is your niece or nephew. It's understandable that you'd be concerned."

"I am concerned," Ryder said. "She thinks she's prepared to do this on her own—from everything she's said to me, she's determined to do this on her own—but a child should have two parents."

"Our child will have two parents," Justin assured him.

"I'd be more convinced of that if you were planning to marry her."

"I am."

Ryder frowned. "Well, that was a lot easier than I expected."

"Easy?" Justin laughed. "It doesn't matter that you and I are in agreement. Try convincing your sister—*that's* the hard part."

"You've talked to her about this?"

He nodded. "And she said she wants to get married someday—but not to me."

Ryder winced. "Sorry."

Justin shrugged. "I understand some of her reservations."

"If you met our parents, you'd understand a lot more."

"Maybe you could fill in some of the details for me," he suggested.

Ryder tipped the bottle to his lips again, considering what—or maybe how much—to say. "For starters, they got married in May and Avery was born in November the same year—and she wasn't a preemie."

"So they got married because your mother was pregnant," Justin acknowledged. "That's hardly an unusual situation."

"You're right. But the unplanned pregnancy forced them to detour from their plans. Whenever either of us would make the mistake of asking if they could attend a school activity or sporting event, Mom would remind us that she had to work to make up for the time she lost giving birth."

"And your dad?" Justin prompted.

"He always said he would try to be there," Ryder admitted. "Which made it even harder when he never showed up."

"It sounds like you had lousy parents," Justin said. "But there are plenty of couples who manage to have successful careers and happy families."

"Sure," the other man agreed. "But a doctor doesn't punch a clock—people's lives depend on them being available."

"But not every minute of every day," he countered. "And I think that both Avery and I have been doing this long enough that we've found some necessary balance."

"Until a baby throws the scale out of whack."

"I'm confident that we can figure it out together."

Ryder tipped his bottle to his lips again. "You're not at all what I expected when Avery told me about you."

"What did you expect?" he asked curiously.

"I expected to want to hit you," Ryder admitted. "But now, I actually think you could be good for her."

"If I can convince your sister to give me a chance."

"If you've got another beer, I might be persuaded to share some insights."

"I've got more beer *and* pizza coming."

Ryder grinned. "Now I'm really glad I stopped by."

Avery had decided to attend the Spring Conference in Atlanta because the trip would also give her the opportunity to see both of her parents. Not that she expected either of them to adjust their own schedules to accommodate hers—and her mother did not disappoint in that regard.

When Avery called to set up a time for Saturday, Cristina advised that she had a lunch meeting with a pharmaceutical rep at one o'clock, and then she was presenting a research paper on new vaccines that were in development for sexually transmitted diseases at four. She offered to squeeze out some time for Avery in between these commitments.

At two-thirty, Avery was seated at the hotel bar, waiting. Her stomach was tangled in knots and her hands were clammy because, despite the fact that she was thirty-two years old, apparently she was still reluctant to disappoint her mother.

The knots in her stomach tightened when her mother walked into the bar. Cristina air-kissed Avery's cheek before sliding onto the vacant stool beside her daughter.

"G&T, extra lime," Cristina told the bartender.

"I'll have the same," Avery said. "Hold the G."

Her mother frowned. "That's just tonic."

"With lime."

"You said you wanted to meet for a drink," she said, her tone disapproving of the fact that her expectations had not been met.

Avery was all too familiar with that tone. "No, *I* said I wanted to meet for dinner," she reminded her mother. "*You* said you didn't have time for dinner but we could do drinks."

"Tonic water isn't a drink."

"Well, gin isn't good for the baby," she said bluntly, unable to endure any more of her mother's nitpicking.

"The—" Cristina's mouth dropped open. "You're pregnant?"

Avery nodded. "Yes, I am."

"How far along?"

"Ten weeks."

Cristina immediately lifted the glass the bartender set down in front of her and took a healthy swig. "It's not too late, then."

"Too late for what?" she asked, a sinking feeling in the pit of her stomach. But she pushed the uneasiness away, because there was no way her mother was saying what she thought she was saying.

"To terminate the pregnancy."

The blunt statement felt like a physical blow, but Avery lifted her own glass and sipped. Her throat was tight and her eyes burned, but she refused to give in to her emotions—refused to give Cristina that ammunition to use against her.

"I don't want to terminate the pregnancy," she said, pleased that her voice was clear and calm.

"You can't honestly think that it's a good idea to have a baby at this point in your life."

"I didn't plan to get pregnant," she acknowledged. "But I want this baby."

"Because you have no idea how demanding a child can be—especially an infant," Cristina warned. "And you're not married, so you won't have any support system to help you through the long nights and other difficult times."

"I know there will be challenges, but Justin and I will figure it out," she said, with more conviction than she felt.

"He's the father?" her mother guessed.

"Yes, he's the father."

"So you have a…relationship?"

She nodded.

"Are you planning to get married?" Cristina asked. "Or live together?"

"We haven't worked out all of the details yet."

Her mother sipped her drink. "Is he pressuring you to do this?"

"What?"

"Is he pressuring you to have the baby?"

"No, Mom. This was *my* decision."

"Because I have a friend—she works at a private women's clinic in Forest Park. I can give her a call and get you in to see her this weekend. Then you can go back to Karma and tell him that you lost the baby. Ten to twenty percent of women miscarry in their first trimester."

She drew in a slow breath and mentally counted to ten. "It's Charisma," she reminded her mother. "And I'm well aware of the statistics about miscarriages—and I want to have this baby."

Cristina lifted her glass again, frowning when she saw it was empty.

"Can I get you a refill?" the bartender asked.

"No," Avery responded before Cristina could, because she didn't want to prolong this painful encounter a single minute longer than necessary. Then, to her mother, she said, "I appreciate you squeezing in some time to see me, but I know you're busy and anxious to get back to the conference."

"I do have to review my notes for the presentation," Cristina acknowledged, taking out her wallet to pay for their drinks.

Avery just nodded.

"Think about what I said," her mother advised, tucking the money under her glass. "I'm happy to make the call for you, if you change your mind."

"I won't change my mind," she promised. "But what is even more important, I won't ever let my child doubt that she was both wanted and loved from the minute I learned of her existence."

After meeting with her mother, Avery took off her conference badge, tucked it into her bag and headed up to her room on the eighth floor.

Her mother's reaction to the news didn't just bother her—it worried her. Cristina Tobin was the only example of a mother Avery had ever had. Anything she thought she knew about parenting had been learned from her own parents, and neither of them had been the warm, fuzzy type.

Justin's family was different. Even in her limited interactions with them, she could tell that much. She could tell even more by the way he talked about them—the easy but unmistakable affection in his voice. And it wasn't just his parents and his brothers that he was close to. When he talked about his family, he meant all of his aunts, uncles and cousins, too. Even his half sister.

There were still a lot of months before their baby would be born, but she realized that she no longer wanted him to lose interest. Instead, she was hoping his family could be an example that she and Justin might emulate for their child, because she had no intention of basing her parenting style on her own family.

Thinking about Justin now, she impulsively pulled her cell phone out of her purse and called his number. He answered on the second ring and the sound of his voice, so strong and familiar, brought tears to her eyes. And because no one was around to see, she didn't worry about holding them back.

"Avery? What's wrong?"

"Nothing's wrong," she lied. "I just…I wanted to hear your voice."

"Then I'm glad you called," he said. "How's the conference?"

She swiped at the tears that spilled onto her cheeks. "It's good."

"That doesn't sound very convincing," he said gently.

"I was just thinking…and wondering…do you…do you think we're doing the right thing?"

"About what?"

"The baby."

He was silent for a minute. "Well, I'd prefer if we got married—"

"No," she said. "I mean…do you wish I had taken the morning-after pill?"

"No," he said, his immediate and vehement response soothing some of her anxiety. "Maybe in the beginning, before we knew that you were pregnant, I might have thought that was the right choice. But now, I'm so glad that you didn't. I *want* this baby—*our* baby."

The tears were falling in earnest now.

"What's this about?" he asked.

"I saw my mother today and told her that I was pregnant," she admitted.

"And she didn't respond well to the news," he guessed.

"She told me…" She swallowed around the lump in her

throat. "She told me that it wasn't…too late…to terminate my pregnancy."

"Tell me you're joking."

She shook her head, though she knew he couldn't see her. It was all she could manage without sobbing.

"Avery?" he prompted.

"I'm not joking," she told him. "She said that I have no idea how—" she drew in a shuddering breath "—how difficult it will be to juggle the demands of a baby with my career."

"It won't be easy," he agreed. "But I know we can do it."

We can do it.

The words, combined with his unwavering conviction, helped steady her. She only wished he was there with her so she could feel the solid warmth of his arms around her and not feel so alone. But that, of course, was the danger she was fighting against—needing him, relying on him, loving him.

"Please tell me you're not considering what she suggested," he pleaded.

"I'm not," she told him. "Of course not."

"Good."

"You really do want this baby?"

"More than I ever thought I would," he admitted. "And more and more every day."

And me? She wanted to ask.

But, of course, she didn't. Because she had no idea what his answer might be, and she wasn't prepared to open herself up for yet another rejection.

They talked awhile longer and she felt a lot better about everything when she finally disconnected the call. Not good enough to want to go back downstairs and risk running into her mother again, but better.

Though it was only four o'clock, she took a shower, put on her pajamas, fell asleep on top of the covers and woke up three hours later to realize it was past dinnertime and she was hungry. She ordered room service, then booted up her computer to look at changing her return flight to Charisma. She'd originally planned to see her father for brunch the following day, but she wasn't sure she could deal with a second round of what she'd gone through with her mother.

Maybe that wasn't fair. Maybe her father would be more supportive of her choices. She honestly didn't know, and that alone said everything about their relationship.

And now that the insult wasn't quite so fresh, Avery found it interesting that Cristina didn't believe her daughter would be able to balance her career with the responsibilities of a child. Because, as far as Avery could tell, neither of her parents had ever really tried to do so, preferring to work longer hours to pay someone else to raise their children.

A knock sounded at the door, dragging her attention away from those unhappy memories. Her stomach growled in anticipation of her dinner, but when she opened the door it wasn't room service on the other side.

It was Justin.

Chapter Fourteen

It seemed like forever that she just stood there, staring at him. Certainly it was long enough for Justin to question the wisdom of rearranging his schedule and hopping on a plane just because she'd called and he thought she might need him.

"I was in the neighborhood," he began, and her lips curved, just a little.

It wasn't even really a smile, but it was all he needed to be glad that he'd made the trip.

"Are you going to let me come in?" he asked.

"I was waiting for the rest of the story—" she stepped away from the door, gesturing for him to enter "—about why you were in the neighborhood."

"Because I needed to see you," he admitted, setting his overnight bag inside the door. "To be sure that you were okay."

The warmth in her eyes dimmed a little. "You thought I was going to do it."

"Do what?" he asked, baffled by the accusatory tone.

She folded her arms over her chest. "Get rid of our baby."

"No, I didn't." He stroked his hands down her arms. "I promise you, Avery, the possibility never even crossed my mind."

"It didn't?" she asked uncertainly.

"Of course not," he told her. "There may be a lot I still don't know about you, but I know you want our baby as much as I do."

"Then why are you here?"

"Because you sounded like you needed a friend."

She unfolded her arms and splayed her palms on his chest. "You flew four hundred miles because I sounded like a needed a friend?"

"And because it would have taken too long to drive," he said logically.

She shook her head, but she was smiling again. "You constantly surprise me."

"Good, then I shouldn't have to worry about you getting bored with me," he said, and lowered his head to touch his lips to hers.

It was a fleeting kiss—friendly, casual—that might have led to something more if another knock hadn't sounded at the door.

"Room service."

She pulled away from him, drew in a breath. "That's my dinner."

He went to the door and slipped some bills from his pocket in exchange for the tray. He set it on the table and lifted the lid to uncover two slices of bread with thinly-sliced roast beef in between and a scoop of potato salad on the side. "*This* is your dinner?"

"I didn't know what I wanted," she admitted. "Then I remembered the day you showed up in the doctors' lounge with the roast beef sandwich, demanding that I take care of myself."

"A sandwich is fine for lunch when you're rushing from the hospital to the clinic, but you need something more substantial for dinner," he said, putting the lid back on the plate. "Let's go out and get some real food."

She glanced pointedly at her plaid pajama pants and rib-knit Henley. "I can't go out like this."

"Why not?"

"Because these are my pajamas."

"Then put some clothes on," he suggested.

"And I've cried off all of my makeup."

He cupped her face in his hands. "I hate to think of you here, by yourself, crying," he admitted.

"I think it's the pregnancy hormones," she said. "I feel like I don't have any control over my emotions anymore."

He thought it was probably as much the fault of her mother, but he wasn't going to go there now. "How about pregnancy cravings?" he asked instead. "What are you in the mood to eat?"

"A whole cow."

"Okay, I'll call the concierge and ask for a nearby cattle ranch recommendation while you get dressed."

She gathered up her clothes and moved toward the bathroom, pausing in the doorway. "Justin—"

He turned back.

"Thank you," she said quietly.

He smiled. "My pleasure."

He took her to a restaurant called the Chophouse. The decor was simple: sturdy tables covered with neatly pressed linen cloths, leather booth seating and muted lighting. But it was the mouthwatering scent of grilled meat that really appealed to Avery and made her stomach growl so loudly that Justin turned to look at her.

She started with a field greens salad with a tomato-parmesan vinaigrette, followed by a ten-ounce filet mignon with roasted fingerling potatoes and grilled asparagus. He had the same type of salad, then the New York Strip with sautéed sweet corn and mashed red-skinned potatoes.

"I can't believe I ate all of that," she said, after she'd cleared her plate.

"It was too good not to," Justin said, having polished off his own meal. "And you look better now that you've got some food in you."

She managed a wry smile. "I probably couldn't look much worse than I did when you showed up at the door of my hotel room."

"You're always beautiful," he told her. "But you looked a little tired and a lot sad."

"I was feeling a little tired and a lot sad," she admitted.

"And now?"

"I feel better." And maybe a little foolish that she'd let her mother's insensitive remarks get to her. Maybe she should have been stronger. Maybe she shouldn't have called Justin. But she couldn't deny that she was glad he was there with her now.

"Dessert?" he asked.

She managed a laugh. "You've got to be kidding."

He nudged the dessert menu that the waiter had left on the edge of the table toward her. "They have homemade ice cream."

"You are the devil."

He just grinned. "I'm going to try the raspberry mango cheesecake."

"Some women lose weight in the first trimester, but I've gained three pounds already," she told him.

"Gaining weight is necessary when you're growing a baby," he said matter-of-factly.

She looked at him across the table, his gaze steady even in the flickering light of the candle. He was so incredibly handsome—and so much more than his playboy personality had led her to believe.

"You know, a few weeks ago I was thinking that I'd completely screwed up, getting pregnant with your baby," she confided. "I've only recently started to realize that if I had to get pregnant, I'm so glad it was with *your* baby."

He reached across the table to take her hand. "Me, too."

"Does that mean you'll come with me to see my dad tomorrow?"

"I was just waiting for you to ask," he told her.

"And if I didn't ask?"

"I was going, anyway."

His answer didn't surprise her. What did surprise her was that she was grateful for his determination to stand by her side. Over the past few weeks, he'd proven that he was a man she could count on and trust—maybe even a man she could fall in love with—which was why she was trying very hard to keep her balance.

When the waiter came back to the table, Justin ordered the cheesecake and Avery opted for the ice cream.

By the time they left the restaurant, it was after ten o'clock. He took her hand again as they walked to the hotel. It was a cool night, but she didn't feel the chill in the air with Justin beside her.

"I need to stop at the desk," he said, when they entered the lobby and she started automatically toward the bank of elevators.

"Why?"

"I was in such a hurry to get here, I didn't book a room," he admitted.

Until that moment, she hadn't given a single thought to where he might be sleeping. Of course, he needed his own room—offering to share hers would be tempting fate. Despite his claim that he'd come to Atlanta because she'd sounded as if she needed a friend, there was more between them than friendship. And the more she grew to like Justin, the harder it was to ignore the attraction.

So she nodded and followed him to the desk. Unfortunately, the clerk informed him, there was a medical conference in the hotel and no rooms were available. He offered to contact the Sheraton across the street, but Avery shook her head.

"I have a room here," she reminded him, trying to sound casual. "It has two beds—and I'll only be sleeping in one of them."

Justin appreciated the offer, especially because he knew it couldn't have been an easy one for her to make. "Are you sure that won't be…awkward?" he asked cautiously.

She shrugged. "You said you plan to be there when I have the baby. In comparison, I don't think sharing a hotel room for one night even registers on the scale of awkward."

"In that case, I'll say thank-you."

When they got back to her room, Avery went directly to the bathroom with her pajamas. She came out again a few minutes later, wearing the same plaid pants and rib-knit Henley she'd had on when he arrived. And she didn't have anything on beneath the top, because he could see the outline of her nipples clearly—two hard points pushing against the fabric, making all the blood in his body head south.

Which reminded him of another problem: he hadn't worried about bringing something to sleep in because he hadn't considered the possibility that they might end up sharing a room. So he waited until she was under the covers, then he turned out the light and stripped down to his boxer briefs before slipping between the sheets of the other bed.

He'd gotten up early that morning to help his cousin Daniel put together the backyard climbing apparatus he'd bought for his almost two-year-old son, so he should have been exhausted. And he was. He was also conscious of Avery's every movement, every breath. About an hour after the lights had been turned off, she shoved the covers away and padded into the bathroom.

He sat up in bed, waiting for her to return. "Can't sleep?"

She started at his question, obviously not having realized that he was awake. "I'm sorry—I didn't mean to disturb you."

"You didn't," he told her. "I wasn't sleeping, either."

She hesitated for a second, then she came over and perched on the edge of his bed. She was facing him, with one knee bent on the mattress and the other leg hanging over the edge. She was close enough that he only had to lift a hand to touch her, but he didn't.

"I still can't believe you dropped everything to come to Atlanta," she said softly. "No one has ever done anything like that for me before."

"I didn't just drop everything," he said, hoping to score even more points. "I had to call Greg Roberts to cover my shift in the ER."

"Did he grumble?"

"A little, but he owed me for New Year's Eve."

"You weren't supposed to work that night?" she asked.

He shook his head. "No."

"And if you hadn't taken that shift for him…"

"We wouldn't be where we are right now," he completed the thought. "I guess maybe I owe him."

She smiled at that. "I wanted you here," she admitted to him now. "I would never have asked you to come, but I really wanted you here."

"I want you to ask—if you ever need anything," he said.

"It's not easy for me."

"I know—you always want to do everything on your own. But you're not on your own anymore."

"Amy was right."

His brows lifted. "What was she right about?"

"There's a lot more to you than most people realize."

"She said that?"

"She did," Avery confirmed. "She also told me that she didn't believe you'd slept with Heather—despite the rumors."

"I always did like Amy," he said. "She's a smart woman."

"Did you and she ever…?" She trailed off, as if unable to put the question into words.

"No," he answered immediately. "I might have thought about making a move, but she's been in love with Ben for as long as I've known her—even when he was on the other side of the world."

She nodded. "She told me that he was gone for twelve years, and she never stopped loving him."

"Distance and time don't matter when you love someone."

"Do you really believe that?" she asked skeptically.

"I do," he confirmed.

"I guess that tells me everything I needed to know about why my fiancé fell in love with someone else only a few months after he went to Haiti."

"Are you still in love with him?" Even as the question spilled out of his mouth, Justin wanted to pull it back. Because if the answer was yes, he didn't want to hear it.

But she shook her head. "No. Definitely not."

"Then I'm inclined to think that neither of you was one hundred percent all the way in love," he suggested.

"Maybe not," she acknowledged. "But how do you know? It's not like your heart has one of those meter things with an arrow that shifts from 'casual affection' to 'all the way in love.'"

He smiled at the mental image. "You're right—it's not something you can see. It's something you feel." He slid his arms around her, drawing her into his embrace. "It's wanting to spend every possible minute with the other person and missing them every second that you're apart. It's knowing that your life is better, richer and fuller with that other person in it."

"It almost sounds like you know what you're talking about," she said lightly.

"I'm starting to." He brushed his lips against hers, a whisper-soft kiss. "I'm crazy about you, Avery."

"You make me crazy," she said. "Whenever I'm with you, I get all tangled up inside so that I don't know what I'm thinking or feeling."

"What are we going to do about that?"

She lifted her gaze to his. "You could take me to bed."

"You're already in my bed," he pointed out to her.

"So I am." She let her lips graze his jaw, his unshaven skin rasping beneath her soft mouth. "Can I stay?"

Forever, he wanted to say, but he suspected that kind of response would send her running. Instead, he said lightly, "I'd never kick a beautiful woman out of my bed."

"That's the rumor," she agreed. "But I'd rather not talk about all the other women now."

He tipped her chin up. "There's no one but you now. I don't want anyone but you."

"You do want me?"

It killed him that she even had to ask, that she had any doubts about his feelings for her. But he knew the question was rooted in deeper history. "More than you can imagine."

"I can imagine a lot," she said, lifting her arms to link them behind his head and draw his mouth close to hers again.

His arms tightened around her. "Then let me show you."

And finally he kissed her.

No—it was completely inadequate to describe the feel of his lips on hers as a kiss. It was a seduction of her mouth: patient, thorough, devastating. And Avery's mind was spinning around one single thought: *yes*. Her body was aching and straining toward one single goal: *more*.

And he gave her more. His tongue swept into her mouth, tasting and teasing. His hands slipped under her pajama top, touching and tempting. Her palms slid over his bare shoulders—those strong, solid shoulders, down his chest to his stomach—learning and loving all those hard, rippling muscles.

He lifted his mouth from hers only long enough to dispose of her pajama top, then he eased her down onto the mattress and stripped away the bottoms, too. He straddled her naked body, his knees bracketing her hips, holding her in position while he worshipped her body with his hands and his mouth. He seemed to instinctively know where to touch, where to linger.

No, it wasn't instinct—it was experience. The man had a wealth of experience in the bedroom, but she wasn't going to let that bother her now. She wasn't even going to think about that now. In fact, with his hands and his lips moving over her body, she could hardly think at all.

She reached down to stroke his hard length, and he jerked in her hand. "I don't know what it is about you that makes me respond like a horny seventeen-year-old."

"I wouldn't know—I didn't have sex until I was almost twenty."

"But I bet you drove all of the guys at your high school crazy, anyway."

"I doubt it. I was something of a nerd."

He nibbled on her lips. "I always thought smart girls were sexy."

"Prove it," she said, pushing his briefs over his hips.

"I will," he promised. Then, "I have condoms."

"What?"

"In my toiletry kit," he explained. "I haven't been with anyone else since you, and you've seen the test results so you know there's nothing to worry about, but if you don't believe me, I can go—"

"I believe you," she said, because it was true. Because—his reputation aside—he had never given her any reason not to trust him, and she no longer questioned that she did.

He kissed her again, long and slow and deep, while his

hands continued to touch and tease. It amazed her, how quickly and effortlessly he could make her body respond, make her yearn.

"You make me feel…so much."

"There's more," he promised, sliding farther down her body.

"Don't you want—"

He touched his fingertips to her lips, silencing her words. "I definitely want," he said. "And I will. But first, I want to show you some of the things we missed out on in the closet."

"I have no complaints about what happened in SC."

He smiled at her use of his code and slid his hands between her legs, urging them apart as he lowered himself between them. "Then you won't have any complaints tonight, either."

She felt his breath on her first—a whisper of warmth that made everything inside her tense and tighten. Then his fingers, parting the soft folds of flesh at her center. And then his tongue, just the barest flick of his tongue. Her hips bucked instinctively, a wordless plea for more. *Yes. More.*

He clamped onto her hips, holding her immobile while he took her with his mouth, licking and nibbling and sucking while she gasped and moaned. He took his time, drawing out her pleasure. And then, finally, her body flew apart, shattering into billions of shards of exquisite sensation, and he held her while all those sparkling pieces free-fell from the heavens.

"Open your eyes, Avery."

She managed to do so, though her gaze was still unfocused, the world still spinning. He rose up over her, then he slid into her—one slow, deep thrust that filled her deeply, completely.

This time, he moaned, a low sound of satisfaction. She tilted her hips, taking him just a little bit deeper, and though she would have sworn it wasn't possible, her body went from loose and languid to primed and ready again in a heartbeat.

He began to move in a slow and steady rhythm, stroking deep, deeper, causing the pressure to build inside her. Gradually he increased the pace. Faster. Harder. His skin was damp beneath her palms, his breath rasping out of his lungs in shallow pants.

She could tell he was close to his own release, but he was holding back, waiting for her. She'd never had a lover who was so completely unselfish, so single-mindedly focused on making her feel good. She wanted to reciprocate, to give back to him even a fraction of the pleasure that he'd given to her, but she was already caught up again in another maelstrom of desire, a myriad of sensations battering at her, overwhelming her.

Finally he stiffened, every muscle in his body going rigid, and then he emptied himself inside of her. When he could finally summon the energy, he shifted to lift his weight off her, but he didn't let her go. He tucked her head against his chest, where she could feel his heart beating in tandem with her own.

She should have been satisfied with what had happened in the closet, because being with him like this made her believe they could have more, made her want more…

But for now, at least, they had this. So for now, this would be enough.

Chapter Fifteen

Avery fell asleep naked in Justin's arms and awoke the same way. She wondered if she should feel embarrassed about her request to share his bed, and maybe she would have if he'd turned down her entreaty. But in the warmth of his embrace, she didn't feel anything but contented. Maybe even happy.

And while she suspected that she could easily get used to this, she knew she had to be careful. Whatever was happening between them now, she couldn't let herself hope that it would last. Justin had been great since he learned of her pregnancy and he seemed committed to being a father to their child. But his recent behavior didn't change the fact that he didn't do long-term relationships, and it would be foolish to expect that his commitment to their baby extended to encompass her.

But right now, she wasn't going to worry about any of that. Right now, he was with her, and she was going to enjoy the status quo for as long as it lasted.

His hand skimmed over her torso, from her thigh to her hip to her breast. He found her nipple and rubbed his thumb over the taut peak. She sighed softly.

He snuggled closer to her, so she could feel the rigid length of him pressed against her backside. "I love the sounds you make when I touch you."

"I love the way you touch me," she admitted.

"I love touching you," he said, nibbling on her earlobe as his hands continued their leisurely and sensual exploration of her body.

She turned in his arms so that she was facing him. "I want to touch you, too," she said, wrapping her fingers around the hard length of him and stroking gently.

His throaty groan signaled his appreciation and further stirred her own blood.

"I haven't had morning sex in a long time," she admitted. "Actually, I hadn't had any sex in a long time, prior to New Year's Eve."

"New Year's Day," he reminded her.

"So it was technically morning sex," she realized. "But not sleepy morning sex."

"Is that what we're having?" His mouth, warm and moist, closed over her breast, and waves of sensation flooded her body.

She gasped and arched. "I don't know," she said. "Suddenly I'm not feeling so sleepy."

"Me, neither," he admitted, parting her thighs with his knee.

She opened for him, embracing him fully and completely as he slid into her wet, welcoming heat.

Yes, she could definitely get used to this.

George Wallace lived with his second wife and her two daughters in a newer two-story brick home in North Fulton. Justin and Avery rented a car so that they'd be able to leave directly from there to the airport for their flight back to North Carolina.

Sharon met them at the door, her eyes lighting up with genuine pleasure as she hugged Avery close.

"It's so good to see you," she said. "George is upstairs on the phone. Just before you pulled up, he got a call from some cardiologist in England wanting to discuss a patient's treatment.

"I told him he could have ten minutes. If the call required more time than that, he had to call back later because he wasn't going to spend your entire visit on the phone." She turned to Justin. "I'm sorry—I've been rambling on and on without even introducing myself. I'm Sharon Wallace."

He offered his hand. "Justin Garrett."

"Come in," she invited. "I've got a pot of coffee on, or fresh juice if you prefer, and everything is ready to go on the table as soon as George comes down."

While Justin drank his coffee and Avery sipped her juice—because she was trying to cut back on her caffeine intake—Sharon set another place at the table to accommodate the unexpected guest.

"Where are Molly and Ruby?" Avery asked, referring to Sharon's daughters.

"They're with their dad this weekend." She moved the chairs around the table. "Another reason why the timing of your visit is so perfect—the house is far too quiet without them."

Avery knew what it was like to be shifted from the house of one parent to the next, but she'd never considered how it might feel from the other side, as a parent who only got to be with her child for half of the time—and she didn't like thinking about it now.

Footsteps sounded on the stairs and Sharon immediately started putting food on the table. There were scrambled eggs, bacon and sausages, home-fried potatoes and pancakes—and that was in addition to the fresh fruit, yogurt and pastries that were already on the table.

Avery introduced Justin to her father. She could tell George wanted to ask who Justin was—to inquire about his relationship to her—but didn't feel as if he had the right.

Over the past several years, their relationship had faded so there was little tying them together aside from biology.

"I hope you're hungry," George said instead. "Sharon's been cooking all morning in anticipation of your visit."

His wife waved a hand dismissively. "We don't get to see Avery very often—I just wanted to be sure she didn't go away hungry."

"The buffet breakfast at the conference didn't look this good," Avery said to Sharon. "Thank you."

Her stepmother smiled. "You're welcome—dig in."

"How was the conference?" George asked, latching on to a topic of conversation that seemed safe for both of them.

"No shoptalk at the table," Sharon interjected before Avery could respond.

Her husband sighed. "She doesn't have a lot of rules, but she's strict with that one."

Sharon offered a further explanation. "The difficulty with both of us being doctors is that we often get caught up in our work and forget that there's a whole world outside of the hospital."

"Some people would say that's only one of many difficulties," Justin noted, slanting a look at Avery.

A phone rang in the other room, prompting Sharon to push her chair away from the table. "Excuse me," she said.

They continued to eat more than talk while she was gone. The problem with Sharon's no-shoptalk rule was that Avery didn't have a lot of other things in common with her father—and she wasn't quite ready to share her big news just yet.

"I'm so sorry," Sharon said, returning to the dining room with her purse and keys in hand. "That was Molly on the phone. I need to go pick her up now."

"Davis is supposed to bring both of them back after dinner," George reminded her.

"Molly asked me to come now."

"But Avery's here and we were—"

"George," she said patiently. "I'm sure Avery understands that there are certain times in a preteen girl's life when she'd rather be with her mother."

"Oh," he said, his cheeks turning red as he finally clued in to what she wasn't saying.

"If you're gone before I get back, it was really good to see you, Avery. And to meet you, Justin."

"I'm sorry Sharon had to rush off," George said when his wife had gone. "She was really looking forward to spending some time with you."

"I'm sorry, too," Avery admitted. "But I'm glad Molly and Ruby can count on her to be there when they need her."

"She's a great mom," George agreed. "Certainly a much better parent than I ever was."

"Molly posted pictures on Facebook of her science fair," Avery noted.

"She won first prize," her father said proudly.

"It's nice that you were there with her."

He didn't have any trouble deciphering the subtext. "And I never was when you were growing up, was I?"

"Water under the bridge," Avery said.

"Is it?" her father challenged.

She shrugged.

George glanced at Justin. "Did she tell you what a lousy father I was?"

"No, sir," he said. "She told me that you were an excellent cardiac surgeon."

"Same sentiment, different words," her father acknowledged. "And I'll confess, I wasn't sure anyone could be a good doctor and a good parent until I met Sharon."

"She's a pediatric oncologist," Avery told Justin. "And she's never missed a school play or gymnastics competition."

George nodded, his attention shifting back to his daughter. "You can't know how many times I've wished I could go back and do things differently—be a better father to you and your brother."

"Maybe you'll be a better grandfather," Avery suggested.

Her father paused with his coffee cup in the air. "Am I going to be a grandfather?"

She nodded.

He took a moment to absorb the news. "Well, this is... unexpected," he finally said. "When?"

"September twenty-fourth."

"Are you planning to be there when the baby's born?" he asked Justin.

"Of course."

George sipped his coffee. "I was there when Avery made her grand—and loud—entrance into the world," he confided.

That was news to Avery. "You were?"

He nodded. "I hadn't planned on it and certainly wouldn't have rearranged my schedule to accommodate it, but afterward, I was so humbled and amazed and grateful that I'd had the opportunity to share the experience. Because there is absolutely nothing more incredible than seeing a child come into this world, especially when that child is your own."

"Why did you never tell me that before?" she said.

"It's not the type of thing that usually comes up in conversation," George replied.

"Maybe it should have," Justin suggested.

The older man nodded. "You're right. There are a lot of things that should have been said and done over the years and, as a result, I've had to live with the knowledge of everything that I missed out on."

"You know, Charisma isn't that far away," Avery told him.

George seemed surprised by her statement. "Are you inviting me to visit?"

She lifted a shoulder. "If you need an invitation. And if you can fit it into your schedule."

"I'll figure out a way," he promised, his eyes growing misty. "My baby girl's going to have a baby of her own, and that is something I definitely don't want to miss."

The whole weekend had been physically and emotionally exhausting, and as Avery settled into her seat on the plane beside Justin, she was grateful to finally be going home.

"I know I already said it, but thank you again, for everything."

He flipped up the armrest that separated their two seats so that he could take her hand. "It was my pleasure."

"You have an odd definition of pleasure."

He smiled. "Come on—it wasn't so bad, was it?"

"The second act was much better than the first," she told him.

"And the intermission?" he prompted.

Thinking about the night they'd spent together, she couldn't help but smile. "The best part of the show."

He smiled back. "I certainly thought so. And, as a bonus, your dad did acknowledge that he was a lousy father."

"Mostly because, I realize now, he didn't have the first clue about what he was doing."

"It does make you wonder," Justin mused. "They won't give anyone a driver's license until they've proved they can operate a motor vehicle, but there aren't any restrictions on who can be a parent."

"Pretty much any two people willing to get naked in a supply closet can make a baby," she agreed.

"I wasn't talking about us," he chided. "I happen to think we're going to make pretty good parents."

"I appreciate your optimism, though I'm not sure it has any foundation in fact."

"We both want this baby and are committed to doing what is best for our baby."

"Okay, that's true," she acknowledged.

"Plus we've got the whole sizzling sexual chemistry thing happening."

"I'm not sure that's going to help us be good parents."

"Maybe not, but at least you didn't deny the sizzling sexual chemistry. And since I don't have to work until two o'clock tomorrow, when we get back to Charisma there will still be a lot of hours that we could—"

"I *do* have to work in the morning," she interjected.

"Okay, so I won't keep you up *all* night," he said, his eyes and his voice filled with wicked promise.

She was more tempted than she wanted to admit, but she was wary of setting a precedent. Making love with him, even sleeping with him in Atlanta hadn't made her uneasy, because they were outside of their usual world. If she invited him to spend the night in her apartment, in her bed, that would be too much like letting him into her life. And then she'd be all the more aware of how empty her life was when he was gone.

She shook her head. "I've got some reading to do when I get home."

"Reading?" he echoed.

"All the materials I picked up at the conference."

He sighed regretfully. "I guess back to Charisma means back to normal again."

"I didn't think our normal was so bad."

"No," he admitted. "But last night was a hell of a lot better."

It was good to be home and in her own bed, but it was funny how the same mattress she'd been sleeping on for years suddenly seemed so big and empty. After only one night in Justin's arms, she felt as if she didn't ever want to sleep without him, and that was a very dangerous road to go down. Especially with a man like Justin Garrett.

He claimed that he'd never been with a woman that he wanted to be with long term—until her. And as much as she wanted to believe him, she wouldn't let herself fall into the trap of thinking that he could change. Despite his assertion that he wanted only her, she didn't know how long that would last.

But maybe she could just enjoy being with him for a while. Her body was certainly an enthusiastic supporter of that plan, but her brain—now that it was capable of functioning again—warned her of the danger to her heart.

She decided to heed the warning, knowing that she'd never been able to enjoy a purely physical relationship without wanting more. And it wasn't just her own heart she needed to worry about. In just over six months, they would have a baby, and she had to consider what was best for their child.

She was preoccupied with these thoughts so that when her phone rang Wednesday morning, she didn't even check the display before connecting the call. "Hello?"

"Avery, hi. It's Ellen Garrett calling."

"Hello, Mrs. Garrett."

"I thought we agreed you were going to call me Ellen."

"Right," she said. "Sorry, Ellen."

"I'll forgive you," the other woman said. "So long as you agree to have lunch with me."

"Lunch?"

"Is one o'clock good for you?"

"Oh, um." Her mind was a blank as to her schedule. "I guess one o'clock would work."

"That's wonderful," Ellen said. "What do you like to eat? Have you been craving any particular kinds of food?"

"Hamburgers," she admitted. "Big, thick, juicy hamburgers."

The other woman laughed. "How about the Grille?" Ellen suggested. "They have burgers on the menu but plenty of other choices, too, if you want something different when you get there."

"The Grille sounds good," she agreed.

Ellen Garrett was already seated in the restaurant waiting for her when Avery arrived.

"Am I late?" she asked, slipping into the chair across from Justin's mother.

"No, I was early. I was so eager to see you that I couldn't wait to get here."

"I was pleased you invited me," Avery said politely.

"And wondering why I did," Ellen guessed.

She nodded.

"My motives aren't complicated or nefarious," the other woman assured her. "I just wanted to spend some time getting to know the future mother of my grandchild and the woman my son hopes to marry."

Avery didn't know exactly what Justin had said to his mother, but she mentally cursed him for getting Ellen's hopes up—and making her be the one to deflate them again. "Justin only suggested that we get married because he thinks it's the right thing to do."

Ellen smiled. "You don't know my son nearly as well as you think you do if you believe he would be motivated by a sense of propriety."

"Actually, I don't know him very well at all," she acknowledged. "Which is one of the reasons that a marriage between us would be a mistake."

"One of the reasons?" his mother prompted curiously.

Avery looked away. "We're very different people—I'm not sure we'd be compatible."

Of course, Ellen was a very astute woman and she had no trouble reading between the lines.

"I can understand why you'd have concerns about marrying a man with Justin's reputation," she admitted. "He hasn't always been discriminating or discreet when it comes to his personal life, but he is unfailingly honest. He doesn't cheat and he doesn't lie and he has little tolerance for anyone who would."

"He has many wonderful qualities," Avery agreed, because she was talking to his mother and what else was she supposed to say?

"Have you met Nora Reardon?" Ellen asked. "Justin's half sister who works in PT at the hospital."

She nodded.

"Then you must have heard—or figured out—that John had an affair. It was more than twenty-five years ago and a tremendous betrayal of our vows and our family. It took me a long time to forgive him, to realize that I could."

Ellen unfolded her napkin and laid it across her lap, taking a moment to gather her composure. "When he told me about the affair, he didn't tell me—because he didn't know—that his mistress was pregnant. It was only last year that he found out he had a daughter, and though he immediately shared the news with me, the boys didn't learn about Nora until she showed up at our house on Father's Day."

"That must have been awkward," Avery said.

Ellen managed a smile. "Incredibly awkward and uncomfortable," she agreed. "And although Nora didn't stay long—and stayed out of touch for a long time afterward—it shook the whole family. But I think it affected Justin even more than either of his brothers.

"Because despite his faults and flaws—and I know he has them," his mother assured her, "he also has a very strong moral compass. And it took him a long time to forgive his father for breaking his vows and hurting me."

Ellen lifted her water glass to her lips and sipped. "My purpose in telling you this is to help you understand that Justin wouldn't have asked you to marry him if he wasn't prepared to commit himself to you, heart and soul. He would never make a promise he didn't believe he could keep."

"Maybe finding out about his half sister has something to do with his desire to marry me," Avery suggested. "To ensure that he doesn't miss out on his child's life the way John missed out on Nora's."

"If that was all he was concerned about, he would have hired himself a lawyer," Ellen said matter-of-factly. "Any decent attorney could protect his parental rights. If Justin asked you to marry him, it's because he *wants* to marry you.

"And, of course, you already know that I'd love for there to be a wedding before the baby is born, but for more reasons than the child you're carrying."

"What other reasons are there?"

Ellen smiled again. "That's something you need to figure out for yourself," she said gently. "But regardless of what happens between you and Justin, I want you to know that John and I are thrilled about becoming grandparents again, and we hope you'll let us help out in any way that we can. Whether that's watching the baby for a few hours so you can sleep after a long shift at the hospital or helping out with a few meals or just throwing in a couple of loads of laundry—whatever you need."

Her words were sincere and heartfelt, and Avery's eyes filled with tears.

Ellen rummaged in her pocketbook for a packet of tissues, which she passed across the table. "Justin's not going to be happy if he finds out that I made you cry."

Avery dabbed at her eyes. "It's not your fault—I think pregnancy hormones are running amok through my system, and you and John have both been so accepting and supportive. I guess I'm just feeling lucky and grateful and a little overwhelmed."

"Why would we be anything but accepting and supportive?" Ellen asked her.

Avery could only shake her head. "I haven't begun to figure out my feelings for Justin," she confided. "But I can tell you that I've fallen in love with his family."

Now it was Ellen's turn to tear up. "That's a Garrett baby you're carrying," she said, "which means that we're your family now, too."

Chapter Sixteen

"I'm thinking of getting a name tag that says, Don't Hate Me—I'm His Sister," Nora said, wrapping her hands around her mug of coffee.

Justin finished the text message to a colleague and set aside his phone to give her his full attention, because clearly he'd missed something. "What are you talking about?"

She shook her head. "Do you really not see it?"

"See what?"

"The looks I get every time we come in here together."

He glanced around the atrium but didn't notice anything or anyone out of the ordinary. "What kind of looks?"

"Let's just say, if looks could kill, I would have been on my way to the morgue on my first day."

Nora had been working in the PT department for six weeks now and he tried—if their schedules allowed—to meet her for coffee at least every couple of weeks. The first time he'd invited her because he felt a strange sort of obligation, but the more time he spent with her, the more he found that he actually enjoyed his sister's company. "You have quite a flair for drama, don't you?"

"And you have blinders on," she countered. "The women here *all* want to be with you. Of course, if the rumors are to be believed, more than half of them already have been."

"The rumors are *not* to be believed," he told her firmly. "And you shouldn't pay attention to hospital gossip."

"So is there anything to the rumors about you and Dr. Wallace—or 'Wall-ice' as she's otherwise known?"

He winced at the unflattering nickname. "Don't call her that."

"I'm not the one who does," Nora told him.

Justin took a bite of his chocolate-glazed doughnut.

"And you sidestepped."

He chewed, swallowed. "What?"

"You sidestepped the rumors about you and Dr. Wallace," she explained. "If they were unfounded, you would have said so. The fact that you said nothing suggests otherwise."

"Did you ever think about becoming a lawyer instead of a physiotherapist?"

She shook her head. "My brother Connor is a lawyer—one in a family is enough. And you're sidestepping again."

"The rumors are unfounded," he told her. "I'm not having a torrid affair with Dr. Wallace. We are, however, going to have a baby together."

She gaped at him. "Seriously?"

He nodded.

"Why would you tell me that?" she demanded. "Don't you realize how quickly I could elevate my standing in the hospital community by sharing such a juicy tidbit of information?"

"I do," he confirmed. "But I know you won't."

She frowned. "You're right—but how do you know I won't?"

"Because you're my sister," he said simply. "And regardless of whatever differences we may have, family looks out for family."

"Not all families," she told him.

"Maybe not. But ours does."

"Ours, huh?" She smiled, just a little, as if pleased to be included but still uncertain.

"When you barged into our Father's Day family barbecue last year, you made a statement. Like it or not, you're one of us now."

"You guys take some getting used to," she said. "But I think I like being one of you."

"In that case, I'll tell you another secret. I'm not just the father of Avery's baby—I'm hoping to marry her."

Nora didn't seem nearly as surprised or impressed by that revelation. "Because she's pregnant?" she challenged. "Because Dr. Wallace doesn't strike me as the type of woman who would worry about having a baby without a ring on her finger."

"The baby's only part of the reason," he said. "The biggest reason is that I love her."

"The halls will be littered with broken hearts when that gets out," she warned him.

"Then it's a good thing I don't have to worry about it getting out, isn't it?"

After her lunch with Ellen, Avery was on her way home when she saw her brother's truck parked outside of the office of Renovations by Ryder. She pulled into the parking lot beside his vehicle and made her way into the building.

"Do you actually still work here?" she asked from the doorway of his office.

Ryder looked up from his computer and offered a quick smile. "Less and less all the time," he admitted.

She ventured into the room and gestured to a pile of envelopes on his desk. "What's all of that?"

"The network has decided to shift the show's focus next season. They're offering home renovations to three lucky viewers who write in to explain why they need *Ryder to the Rescue*."

"I heard something about that," she admitted. "How many entries have you got?"

"Over three hundred legitimate ones, so far."

She lifted a brow. "Are you getting illegitimate offers?"

He pulled an envelope from a smaller pile and passed it to her. "Check it out."

Curious, she opened the flap and pulled out a neatly clipped document. The front page was an official contest entry form, with the applicant requesting a makeover of the master bath. The next three pages were photos of the current bathroom—with the homeowner in each one. Naked. Lounging in the soaker tub; standing in the shower; sprawled on the granite counter.

"That's a gorgeous bathroom," she remarked. "I particularly love the glass-tiled shower enclosure with the body jets."

He nodded. "Absolutely no renovation required."

"So you just tossed the contest entry aside? Because I'm pretty sure that's a phone number beneath the lipstick kiss on the page."

"Not interested," he said bluntly.

"It must be tough being you," she teased. "A decently good-looking and moderately famous guy with women throwing themselves at you at every turn."

"It's tougher than you think," he acknowledged.

His obvious discomfort made her think about Justin and the way women were always throwing themselves at him. Because he handled the situation with such apparent ease, she hadn't considered that he might not want all the attention. Or maybe she was only considering the possibility now because she wanted to believe he was the man she needed him to be.

"Have you narrowed down your choices?" she asked Ryder.

"Not really. I've discarded some of the obviously unsuitable ones, but more and more are coming in each day. Thankfully, the contest closing date is Friday."

"I bet you put them all in a bag and draw out three at random."

He grinned. "You know me so well." Then his smile faded. "Except that the producers really want to push the local angle, so at least one of the chosen properties has to be in or near Charisma."

"So one bag for the local entries and another bag for the rest," she suggested.

"There's an idea." He turned away from his computer now to give her his full attention. "Tell me what's going on with you."

"Nothing too interesting. I saw the folks when I was in Atlanta."

"Did you tell them about the baby?"

She nodded. "Mom warned me that I didn't know what I was getting myself into. Dad was equally surprised—but surprisingly supportive. He actually sounded as if he was looking forward to becoming a grandfather."

"How are *you* feeling?" Ryder asked her.

"Actually, I feel great."

"How are things with the dad?"

She thought about the weekend she'd spent with Justin in Atlanta. She couldn't deny that her feelings for him were growing, but she was still afraid to risk her heart—and even more afraid to risk their baby's future. "Fine."

"You want to expand on that at all?"

"Nope."

"You might want to give him a break," her brother suggested. "He's not really a bad guy."

Her gaze narrowed. "How do you know he's not a bad guy?"

"I went to see him last week."

She shook her head. "This is exactly why I didn't want to

tell you who the father was, because I knew…" Her words trailed off and her gaze narrowed. "Wait a minute—I *didn't* tell you who the father was."

"No, you didn't," he confirmed.

"So how did you find out?" she demanded.

"Amy."

She frowned at that. "Where and when did you see Amy? And how did you get her to give up his name?"

"I ran into her in the paint department at the hardware store. She wanted to do the trim in her bedroom but she didn't know what kind of brush to use with the paint she'd picked, so I helped her out and we chatted for a bit." He shrugged. "In between our discussion about natural versus polyester bristles, I casually mentioned that you had some concerns about your baby's father sticking around and she immediately assured me that 'Justin' would never walk away from his child. In fact, 'the whole Garrett family' would support you and the baby."

"You think you're pretty clever, don't you?"

"I *am* clever," he reminded her. "And Amy left the hardware store with everything she needed."

"And you left there and decided to track down Justin." She shook her head again. "I can't believe he didn't tell me."

"It wasn't a big deal—we just had a couple of beers and pizza."

"You had beer and pizza with Justin?"

"And as we talked, I realized that Amy was right," Ryder told her. "There's no way that man is going to bail on you or your kid."

"Oh, well, what am I worried about, then?" she asked, her voice fairly dripping with sarcasm.

He slid an arm across her shoulders. "I know it's not easy for you to trust—especially after Wyatt and especially with this guy being a doctor, too. I'm just suggesting that you give him a chance—I think you'll be surprised."

"I don't want to be surprised," she insisted stubbornly. "I want him to be the irresponsible and unreliable Casanova I expected him to be."

Ryder kissed the top of her head. "I love you, sis, but you've got some serious issues to work out."

If Avery could face her father and tell him about the baby after what she'd been through with her mother, Justin knew that he had to talk to his brother. He made arrangements to meet him at the Bar Down, their favorite hangout, when they were both finished work.

"I haven't been here in a long time," Braden noted, sliding into the booth.

"You haven't been anywhere in a long time," Justin pointed out.

"Dana and I have been sticking pretty close to home," his brother admitted. "But it sounded like there was something important you wanted to talk about."

"There is." He nodded his thanks for the two glasses of beer that Chelsea set on their table.

Braden waited until the bartender was out of earshot before he guessed, "Avery's pregnant."

Justin frowned. "Where did *that* come from? You don't even know Avery."

"True," his brother admitted. "But I know that you took her home to meet Mom and Dad, and you haven't taken a woman home to meet Mom and Dad since...Darcy?" He waited for Justin's nod at the mention of his college girlfriend before continuing. "I figured you were either planning to marry her or she was pregnant."

Justin sipped his beer. "Or maybe I just wanted her to meet my family."

"So she's not pregnant?"

He sighed. "No, she is pregnant. But I was hoping to ease into sharing that news with you."

"No need," Braden said, lifting his glass to his lips.

"And I do want to marry her," Justin added.

"Wow. She must be something special."

"She's unlike any other woman I've ever known."

"Considering how many women you've known, that says a lot."

Justin growled his frustration. "I really haven't been with as many women as everyone seems to believe."

"No need to take offense. The rest of us mere mortals are simply awed and amazed by your legendary reputation."

"Avery isn't," he said, picking up his glass again.

"And yet she slept with you, anyway," Braden noted drily.

"It only took three years."

His brother chuckled. "She's really got you hooked, doesn't she?"

The choice of words reminded Justin of the feeling he'd had when Avery first told him about her pregnancy—of a hook lodging painfully in his gut. Maybe the hook was still there, but his feelings about the baby and for Avery were different now.

"I haven't thought of another woman—wanted another woman—since the first night we spent together," he confessed.

"So when's the wedding?"

"I'm still working on that."

"You asked her to marry you and she turned you down?" Braden's tone was incredulous.

He nodded.

His brother picked up his beer coaster, held it several inches above the table, then let it drop.

"What are you doing?" Justin asked him.

"Testing gravity, because apparently the laws of nature have been turned upside down."

"Ha-ha," he said. "And by the way, gravity isn't a law of nature but a principle of physics."

Braden waved a hand dismissively. "Whatever. I'm more interested in why she turned you down."

"She thinks I'm only trying to do the right thing, and she keeps insisting that it isn't necessary. She's promised that we can work out the details of a coparenting arrangement, if that's really what I want, but she has no desire for a legal union that's doomed to fail."

His brother winced. "She actually said that?"

He nodded.

"Ouch."

Justin nodded again.

"She'll come around," Braden assured him.

"I know," he said, attempting to project a confidence he didn't actually feel. "I just hope it doesn't take her another three years."

"My money's on you."

"So what's new in your life?" Justin asked.

"I'm trying to talk Dana into taking a vacation."

"Anywhere in particular?"

His brother stared into the bottom of his glass. "Wherever she wants to go," he said. "For the past few years, it seems that we haven't had a conversation about anything but babies. I just want to get away somewhere so that we can focus on us. I want my wife back."

"Have you told her that?"

Braden nodded. "She insists she hasn't changed, and I can tell she really believes that, which makes me wonder if the woman I fell in love with even exists anymore."

Justin found himself thinking about his conversation with his brother for a long time after Braden had gone. He knew marriage wasn't easy, but being surrounded by so many happy newlyweds at family events had allowed him to temporarily lose sight of the difficult realities.

His parents were a case in point. He'd always believed their marriage was solid. He never would have suspected that his father had cheated on his mother, because his father wasn't that kind of man. The ten-month affair he'd carried on with Fiona Reardon—regardless of the circumstances—wasn't just a betrayal of the vows he'd exchanged with his wife but their whole family.

Justin had been angry with Nora when she'd shown up, unexpected and unannounced, at their traditional Father's Day barbecue the previous year, demanding to see the father she'd never known. And then he'd been angry with his father for what he'd done to their family. But now he could also feel some regret and remorse for him.

John Garrett had missed out on the first twenty-four years of Nora's life because Fiona had chosen not to tell him about their daughter. He and Avery had fought their share of battles—and would inevitably fight many more—but she hadn't hidden her pregnancy from him and he was confident that she wouldn't ever try to cut him out of their child's life.

He was sincerely grateful for that, but it wasn't enough. He wanted more. He wanted to share all of the joys and responsibilities of parenthood with the mother of his child—the woman he loved.

Just when Avery was starting to feel confident that she'd successfully made it through the first trimester of her pregnancy, she went to the bathroom and discovered that she was bleeding. When she saw the bright red blood, panic rose up inside and her heart dropped into the pit of her stomach. She immediately called her doctor's office, only to learn that Richard Herschel was on holidays until the following week.

"If this is an emergency, please hang up and dial 9-1-1," the recorded voice advised.

Avery hung up and drove herself to Wellbrook instead.

"You're not on the schedule today," Amy said, when she walked in through the staff entrance at the back of the building.

"I know."

"So what are you doing here?"

"I'm—" She blinked back the tears that filled her eyes. "I'm afraid I might be having a miscarriage."

Chapter Seventeen

Amy immediately hustled Avery into an exam room and helped her up onto the table. "Why didn't you go to the hospital?"

"Because I haven't told anyone there that I'm pregnant and I didn't want them to find out this way."

"Did you call Dr. Herschel?"

She nodded. "He's on vacation until next week."

"Then I guess we're going to do an exam here," Amy agreed. "Tell me what's going on."

"I'm…I was bleeding."

"How much?"

"Not a lot," she admitted. "But more than what I would consider light."

"But it's stopped?" Amy prompted, picking up on her use of the past tense.

Avery nodded.

"How far along are you now?"

"Almost fifteen weeks."

"How do you feel?"

"Scared."

"I know," her friend said gently. "I meant physically. Any pain or cramping?"

"I don't think so," she admitted. "But maybe I'm blocking it out because I don't want to admit what either of those symptoms could mean."

"Okay. I'll get Monica to bring in the sonogram machine."

Avery nodded, because she wasn't sure she could say anything else through the tightness in her throat. While she waited for the nurse to come, she checked her cell phone for messages, but there were none.

She'd tried to reach Justin before she went to the clinic, but her call had immediately gone to voice mail. So she'd left a message, trying to keep her voice steady and calm as she explained that she was going to the clinic, and asking him to get in touch when he got her message. Obviously he hadn't received it yet.

After the ultrasound and a quick exam, Amy seemed much less concerned. "The bleeding has stopped and everything looks fine," she said. "Your placenta is in good position and your cervix is closed. The baby's heartbeat is strong and steady and he—or she—is very active, so there's no immediate cause for concern."

Avery exhaled a shaky sigh.

"But we don't know what caused the bleeding," Amy reminded her. "And although we have no reason to suspect it will happen again, if you want to do everything possible to ensure that it doesn't, you're going to have to focus on taking care of yourself for the next several days."

She understood what her friend was saying. It was the same advice she would give to any of her own patients, but those patients were the reason she felt compelled to protest. "But I have responsibilities—"

"No," Amy interjected firmly. "You're a fabulous doctor, but you're not indispensable. Your shifts at the hospital can be covered, your shifts here can be covered. But no one else can do what you need to do to take care of your baby."

She nodded. "Okay."

Amy's gaze narrowed. "Really okay? You're not just pretending to go along with what I'm saying?"

"I won't do anything to jeopardize my pregnancy," she assured her friend, laying a protective hand on the slight swell of her belly.

"Good. Then I only have one more thing to say."

"What's that?"

"You should call—"

Before she could finish, there was a brisk knock on the door. Frowning, Amy went to open it. Of course, Avery couldn't see who was on the other side, but she immediately recognized Justin's voice when he said, "The receptionist told me that Avery was in here."

"She is," Amy confirmed. "We just need another two minutes."

"I want to see her—"

"Two minutes," Amy said firmly again, closing the door with him on the other side.

Then she turned to face her friend, her expression contemplative. "I was going to suggest that you call Justin, but apparently you already did."

"Of course, I did," Avery said. "This is his baby, too."

"I know that," Amy acknowledged. "But you don't ask for help from anyone. Ever. You don't lean on anyone. Ever."

"Why are you making such a big deal out of a phone call?"

"Because it *is* a big deal. Because it proves that you're actually opening up to Justin, letting him into your life."

"It's not like he's really given me much choice."

Amy smiled at that. "Knowing Justin, I'm sure that's true. And I'm proud of you, anyway."

"It was just a phone call," Avery said again.

"And he came over here as soon as he got your message," Amy pointed out to her.

"So it would seem," she agreed.

"Because he's the type of person who will be there for you—whatever you need."

Before Avery could respond to that, Amy opened the door and gestured for Justin to come in. He immediately crossed the room to her and took both of her hands in his. "Are you okay?"

"I'm okay, and the baby's okay," she told him.

He turned to look at Amy, as if for confirmation.

She nodded. "The bleeding's stopped and the baby's vital signs are all good. But I want Avery to stay off her feet for a few days and to follow up with Dr. Herschel early next week when he gets back into the office."

"Has she agreed to stay off her feet?" he asked.

"She has, but I'd feel better if she had someone to stay with her and look after her."

"She doesn't appreciate being spoken about as if she's not in the room," Avery interjected. "And she's perfectly capable of looking after herself."

Justin shifted his attention back to her, and she could see the worry etched in his face. "I know you are," he admitted. "But I'd feel a lot better if you let me take care of you."

"Why?"

"Because it's the only thing I can do while our baby is growing inside of you."

"It's not necessary," Avery said again.

"Please."

She sighed, because she couldn't resist the plea that was in his eyes as much as the word. On the way to his condo, they made a brief stop at her apartment so that she could pack a few things in a bag.

"Are you hungry?" he asked, after settling her on his sofa.

"Starving," she admitted.

"I could heat up a can of chicken soup."

She made a face. "I'm not sick—I'm pregnant."

"So tell me what you want."

"A cheeseburger? From Eli's?" she said hopefully.

"I can get you a cheeseburger," he agreed. "Do you want fries, too?"

She shook her head. "Onion rings."

"Anything else?"

"Extra pickles on the burger but no onions."

He looked at her quizzically. "You want onion rings but no onions on the burger?"

"I don't like raw onions."

"Maybe I should write this down." He found a notepad in the kitchen and wrote down her order. "Anything else?"

She shook her head.

"Are you comfy there?" he asked her.

"Why?"

"Because I don't want you moving until I get back," he told her. "If the phone rings, ignore it. If someone comes to the door, ignore that, too."

She should have been annoyed by his bossiness but the truth was, she was touched that he was so determined to take care of her and their baby.

He was back within twenty minutes, with two cheeseburgers, two orders of onion rings and two chocolate shakes.

"This one meal probably contains more calories than I should be consuming in three days—especially since you won't even let me walk across the room," Avery said, unwrapping her burger.

"I'll make a salad for you for supper," he promised.

"The baby says thank-you, too," she told him. "Especially for the shake—apparently she has quite the sweet tooth."

"She?" he queried.

Avery shook her head as she chewed, then swallowed. "I don't know. I just don't want to refer to our baby as 'it' and most people automatically invoke the masculine pronoun, so I decided to go with 'she.'"

He smiled. "Why doesn't that surprise me?"

"Are you okay with 'she'?"

"Sure," he agreed, popping a crisp onion ring into his mouth. "The pronoun works just fine, and I think it would be fun to have a daughter."

"I thought most men wanted sons, as a testament to their masculinity."

"Doesn't the fact that I got you pregnant prove my masculinity?"

"I guess it does," she agreed, and took another bite of her burger.

"And truthfully, the sex of the baby doesn't matter to me. All that matters is that both you and 'she' are taken care of."

She smiled at his use of the feminine pronoun. "It's strange," she admitted. "I've known you for three and a half years but over the past couple of months, I've realized that I didn't really know you at all."

"Maybe because you didn't want to know me."

She nodded. "Because I was so sure I knew your type. And because I knew your type, I was sure you wouldn't want to have anything to do with a baby conceived in a reckless and impulsive moment of passion."

"I guess I can't really blame you for believing that. I've done everything possible to live up to my reputation."

"And people—myself included—often see what they expect to see. Until a couple of weeks ago, when I saw something at the hospital that made me revisit some of my assumptions." She picked up her cup and took a long sip of her milkshake.

"What was that?" he asked a little warily.

"You were with an elderly gentleman, sitting on those horrible plastic chairs outside of the ER, and he was crying."

"Mr. Ormond," Justin said. "He'd just lost his wife of sixty-eight years."

Anyone could pay lip service to those who were grieving, and often that was all doctors had time for or were capable of doing. Despite recent advances in medicine, doctors still weren't given much education or practical advice on how to deal with surviving family members after the death of a patient. They were taught the appropriate phrases, but compassion was something else entirely—and often lacking.

Avery had witnessed Justin offering sincere and heartfelt empathy to an old man who'd desperately needed it. The fact that, more than two weeks later, he remembered not just the man's name but the reason for his grieving showed her the capacity of his heart and unlocked something inside her own.

"She was with us for fourteen hours," Justin told her. "And he sat with her the whole time, holding her hand, brushing her hair, reading aloud to her from a favorite book. That kind of love and devotion, after sixty-eight years, is amazing. And humbling."

"Sixty-eight years," she echoed, amazed.

He nodded. "He had just turned twenty when they got married, and she was a year and a half younger."

"You listened to him."

"It was a slow night."

And maybe it had been, but she knew that wasn't the reason he'd taken the time. "You're an incredible man, Dr. Garrett."

He just shrugged, obviously uncomfortable with her praise, as he immediately proved by shifting the topic of conversation. "Does that mean I get to choose what we watch on TV tonight?"

She polished off her burger, then crumpled up the wrapper and tossed it into the take-out bag. "That depends on what your choice would be," she said.

Of course, they argued about what to watch. There was a classic Clint Eastwood Western that he wanted to see; she was more interested in a Sandra Bullock rom-com. In the end, she let him have his way and the movie did hold her attention—at least for a while.

She woke up when Justin carried her to the bedroom.

"I didn't get to see the end," she protested.

He sat her down on the bed and rummaged through the duffel bag she'd packed. "I TiVo'd it so that you can watch it tomorrow."

She looked around, as if trying to get her bearings. "This looks like it's your bedroom."

"Because it is."

"I can't sleep in your bed."

"It's the only one I've got," he told her. "Unless you want to sleep on the sofa—and I'm not letting you sleep on the sofa."

"You're going to sleep on the sofa?"

He shook his head. "It's a king-size, which is bigger than the bed we shared in Atlanta."

She wished that he hadn't mentioned Atlanta, because now they were both thinking about that bed—and the things they'd done in it. And suddenly the air was snapping and crackling with sexual tension.

He started to unbutton her shirt; she slapped his hand away. "What are you doing?"

"Helping you get ready for bed."

"I can manage."

"I think I can get you undressed without succumbing to my baser instincts." But his movements slowed when he pushed her shirt away, and he lowered his head to kiss her bare shoulder. Then his lips moved lower, trailing kisses down to the curve of her breast, above the scalloped edging of her bra.

"You said you wouldn't succumb to your baser instincts," she reminded him, a little breathlessly.

"Apparently I lied." He brushed his mouth over her nipple, through the lacy fabric, and she gasped as little darts of pleasure arrowed through her veins.

"We can't do this, Justin."

"I know." He drew in a long, deep breath, then released it.

When he reached for her again, his movements were brisk and efficient. He unhooked her bra, slid the straps down her arms and quickly tugged her pajama top over her head. The only signs that he wasn't as unaffected as he appeared were the ticking of a muscle in his jaw and the heat in his gaze when it met hers.

"Lie down so I can take off your pants."

"Usually a guy has to buy me dinner before he gets into my pants," she said, attempting to lighten the mood.

"I did buy you dinner," he reminded her. "And dessert."

"So you did." She leaned back on her elbows and lifted her hips off the mattress so he could slide her pants down her legs. Then he reversed the process with her pajama bottoms.

"Are you really going to hang out here for the next few days babysitting me?"

"Why not? I happen to like your company."

"Do you realize that you've spent every weekend that you haven't been working, for the past eight weeks, with me?"

"I wasn't actually keeping track," he told her. "Why—are you growing bored with me?"

"No, I just—" She changed her mind about what she was going to say and shook her head. "No."

"You figured I would be growing bored with you," he guessed.

She shrugged. "Even when I was younger—and not pregnant—I was never the life of the party."

"Well, despite your advanced age and cumbersome condition," he teased, "I happen to like the life we're building together."

"You don't want to build anything with me," she warned. "I can't hammer a nail in straight."

"That's okay—I can." And then, because he knew that wasn't really what she was worried about, Justin took both of her hands in his. "I'm not going to leave you. I'm not going to abandon you or our baby, not ever. I promise you that."

She shook her head. "You can't make that kind of promise."

"Yes, I can," he insisted. "Because I love you."

Avery shook her head, and the tears that filled her eyes slashed at his heart like shards of glass.

He forced himself to stay where he was, to let her see the truth of his feelings—even if it was a truth she wasn't ready to admit. He hadn't really expected that she would say the words back to him. Maybe he'd hoped, but he knew that it would take her time to process what he'd said, and longer still to believe he meant it.

He blamed her parents for that. From the little that she'd told him, and the little bit more he'd managed to glean through his conversation with her brother and meeting her father, not only had her parents been too preoccupied with their own lives to ensure their children knew they were loved, they'd also made them feel as if their love and attention had to be earned. If Avery got good marks at school, her father would take her out for ice cream. If she promised to be quiet while mommy was working in her office at home, she might be allowed to do her homework on the opposite side of the big desk.

Justin had never appreciated his own parents so much as he did after hearing Avery talk about her childhood. And while he knew there was no way to undo the damage that had been done by her parents' disinterest and neglect, he hoped he could heal it by loving her. Because he refused to give up on her or the family he wanted them to build together.

Except that Avery's response to his declaration proved that she wasn't ready to acknowledge or accept his feelings. He cupped her face gently between his hands and used his thumbs to brush away the tears that spilled onto her cheeks.

"I didn't expect a declaration of my feelings would make you cry," he said, trying to keep his tone light.

"It's been an emotional day."

"I know."

"I'm scared," she admitted. "I don't want to look too far ahead or make any specific plans when everything could change in the blink of an eye."

He knew that she was worried about their baby, and he was, too. So he let the subject drop—for the moment.

Chapter Eighteen

Tuesday morning, Avery had her appointment with Dr. Herschel. Justin went with her, and the doctor reassured both of them that everything was fine and there was no reason to suspect that she would have any further complications. He also reminded Avery to take her cues from her body—to eat when she was hungry, rest when she was tired—and to let the baby's father do as much for her as he was willing to do.

"You bribed him to say that, didn't you?" Avery asked, when she and Justin left the doctor's office.

"I didn't," he denied. "Although I might have if I'd thought of it."

She shook her head at that, but she was smiling.

"Are you going back to work tomorrow?"

"I am," she confirmed. "But I'm going to do fewer shifts at the hospital and shorter shifts at the clinic."

"I know you're more than capable of taking care of yourself," he acknowledged. "But maybe you could consider staying at my place for a while longer."

"Why?"

"Because knowing you're capable doesn't mean I won't worry about you," he admitted. "And because I want to watch your body change and grow along with our baby, and because I'd love to be there when you feel her move for the first time."

"A lot of first-time mothers don't feel their babies move until after twenty weeks," she told him.

"I'll try to be patient."

She shook her head. "That's not what I meant. I meant that I'm only in my sixteenth week right now—the novelty of having a pregnant roommate might wear off long before you can feel anything."

"I'll let you know if it does," he promised.

Still, she hesitated. Not because she didn't want to stay with him, but because she did. Over the past few weeks, she'd started to rely on him, his company and companionship more than she ever would have expected. And even though they hadn't had sex since they'd returned from Atlanta, she loved falling asleep beside him at night and waking up with him in the morning.

"I guess I could stay a little longer," she agreed.

It was three weeks later, after she woke up to go to the bathroom in the middle of the night, that she felt tiny flutters in her belly. When she realized it was their baby, she immediately nudged Justin awake to share the news. Of course, the movements were so subtle that he wasn't able to feel anything from the outside, but he seemed as happy as she was, anyway.

She continued to see Dr. Herschel on a weekly basis, and every week Justin was there with her. The baby continued to grow and thrive, and her belly continued to get bigger. Justin seemed to be fascinated by the changing shape of her body, but when he touched her—as he did frequently—it was with the cautious awe of an expectant father rather than the passionate desire of an ardent lover.

She knew that he was being considerate of her feelings and showing concern for their baby, but her body ached for him. So at her next appointment, four weeks after Dr. Herschel had given her permission to go back to work, she asked—without looking at Justin—if there were any restrictions on sexual activity.

The doctor seemed surprised by her question. No doubt he assumed that she, being an obstetrician, would understand that the danger had passed and there was no cause to worry that sex would jeopardize her pregnancy. Which she did know, of course, but she wanted Justin to hear from another professional.

He took the hint. That night, he made love to her passionately but tenderly. Afterward, he snuggled up behind her with his hand splayed on the curve of her belly, their baby nudged against his palm. He felt it that time, and when she saw the awe and wonder on his face, Avery acknowledged that all of her efforts to protect her heart had been for naught.

She wasn't just starting to fall in love with Justin—she was more than halfway there. All she could do now was brace herself and hope that her heart wouldn't shatter into a million pieces when reality hit.

Early in June, Avery and Amy were on opposite schedules but decided to meet at the Corner Deli for lunch.

"Things are slightly chaotic at the clinic," Amy warned, as she picked up her turkey club wrap. "Pam just broke up with her boyfriend."

Avery nibbled on a French fry that she'd stolen off her friend's plate. She'd ordered a salad for her own lunch because she'd already gained sixteen pounds and had promised herself that she would try to eat more healthy foods, but she figured one or two fries weren't really cheating. "They were together for a long time, weren't they?"

"Five years," Amy confirmed. "And because she moved

in with him last year, he's insisting that she be the one to move out. I suggested that she ask you about your place."

Avery shook her head. "There aren't any vacant units in my building."

"I didn't mean your building but your actual apartment."

She lifted her brows. "You mean the one that I live in?"

"I mean the one that you pay rent for," Amy clarified. "Which seems a waste of money when you're living with Justin."

"I'm not living with Justin," she denied.

"Really?" Amy's voice was tinged with amusement. "When was the last time you slept at home?"

The furrow in her brow deepened as she tried to remember and realized that she hadn't spent a night in her own bed since the miscarriage scare more than seven weeks earlier. She'd gone back to her own place periodically, to pick up a few things when she needed them, but Amy was right—she *was* living with Justin.

"Tonight," she declared. "I'm going back to my place tonight."

"But why?" Amy was clearly baffled by the decision.

"Because this wasn't supposed to happen." Avery said, referring not just to their current living situation but her feelings for Justin. "And I'm not even sure how it did. I agreed that we could figure out a way for us to work together for the sake of the baby, but I never agreed to live with him."

"Wouldn't living together make it a lot easier to work together—for the sake of the baby?"

"Sure," she admitted. "And if I continue to go along with this, the next thing I know, I'll end up married to him without ever planning for that to happen, either."

"There are worse things than being married to a sexy doctor," Amy pointed out.

"I don't want to get married, and I especially don't want to marry a doctor." Except that she did. In her heart, that was exactly what she wanted—a future with Justin and their baby. But the wanting scared her, so she buried it deep inside.

"We're not talking about any doctor," her friend pointed out. "We're talking about Justin—the father of your baby, the man who's wildly in love with you and wants to spend his life with you."

"Did he tell you that?"

Amy shook her head. "Sweetie, he didn't have to tell me. It's obvious in everything he says and does that he's head over heels. And I've known you long enough to know that you wouldn't be in such a panic about his feelings if you didn't feel the same way."

Her friend was right, of course.

But that knowledge did nothing to alleviate Avery's anxiety, because she believed that loving Dr. Romeo couldn't end in anything but heartbreak. And the longer she continued to pretend otherwise, the more devastating that heartbreak would be.

She was packing up the last of her clothes when Justin got home from the hospital later that night. As she folded and stacked, she realized that most of her wardrobe had found its way to his condo, along with her toiletries and cosmetics and all three of the suitcases she owned.

"Do you want to go out for dinner tonight?" he asked as he made his way toward the bedroom. "We haven't yet tried..." His words trailed off when he saw her bags lined up by the door.

Avery closed the closet.

"What are you doing?" Justin asked her.

"I didn't realize how much stuff I'd dragged over here," she said, her tone deliberately light. "I thought you'd appreciate me moving it out again so you could have your closet back."

"I don't want my closet back," he told her. "I want *you*."

As she'd transferred her belongings to her suitcases, she'd reminded herself that this was inevitable, that Justin would be relieved by her decision to move out and grateful not to have to nudge her in that direction. She hadn't expected him to protest, and she definitely hadn't anticipated the hurt and confusion she could see in his eyes.

She tried to explain. "When you first invited me to stay here… I don't think either of us expected this to go on like this for as long as it has."

He was quiet for a minute, considering his response. Then he nodded. "You're right. I thought we would have moved to the next stage of our relationship before now, but I didn't think you were ready."

"The next stage?" she echoed.

He took her hand and led her over to the bed, sitting down on the edge of the mattress facing her. "I want to marry you, Avery. In fact, I planned to ask you tonight." He pulled a small jeweler's box out of the inside pocket of his jacket. "That's why I was late—I had to go pick this up."

She felt the sting of tears in her eyes. "We talked about this, Justin. When you first found out about the baby and suggested that we should get married, I said no."

"That was five months ago," he pointed out.

"Why would you expect my answer to be any different now?"

"Because of everything that's happened over the past five months," he said patiently.

She shook her head. "Nothing has changed."

"*Everything* has changed, Avery. Why can't you see that?"

"We had an agreement," she reminded him, refusing to let herself be swayed by the frustration in his tone. "This was supposed to be temporary."

"I tried to give you time, to accept how I feel—to believe that I want to be a husband to you and a father to our baby."

He hadn't told her how he felt—not in words—since

the first night she'd spent here at his condo, when they'd both been so worried about her health. As a result, she'd managed to convince herself that his feelings for her had changed—or maybe even that he'd been mistaken to ever think that he was in love with her.

But he said the words again now. "I love you, Avery. And I want to spend the rest of my life—every single day of it—proving that to you."

Every word he spoke made her heart soar a little higher, but she was determined to keep her feet firmly planted on the ground. "I think what's going on here is that our feelings for the baby are getting tangled up with our growing respect and affection for one another."

Justin shook his head sadly. "I watch you at work, and I'm continually amazed by how strong and fearless you are. But when it comes to your personal life—our life together—you're a complete coward."

"Maybe I'm overly cautious at times," she allowed. "But I'm thinking about our baby now and trying to do what's right for her."

"And you believe that leaving is the right thing for our baby? For us?"

"I believe it's inevitable." Deep in her heart, she knew that she was being unfair, that she was using the heartache from her past as a shield against him, but she couldn't help it. The scars of those ancient wounds were too deep—she couldn't risk her heart again.

"Okay," he finally said. "If that's what you really believe, I'm not going to try to convince you to stay."

"Thank you," she said, though the victory felt hollow.

This was what she wanted, so why wasn't she happy? Had she really been foolish enough to hope that he would fight for her?

He cupped her face in his hands. "I know what you're thinking," he said gently. "And you're wrong."

"What am I thinking?"

"You think I'm letting you go because I don't want you anymore."

"It doesn't matter," she said.

"It does," he insisted. "The only reason I'm not fighting you on this is that I need you to realize my feelings for you aren't about proximity or about the baby. They aren't about anything but you and me, and they're not going to change just because you're not living under the same roof with me.

"I know you've got scars," he continued. "I know it's hard for you to trust me when I tell you I love you, harder still to believe that those feelings are being offered without any strings or conditions. I thought five months was enough time—obviously I was wrong.

"But you need to understand that turning down my proposal and moving out aren't going to change anything. When I say that I love you, I mean that I love you forever."

She wanted—almost desperately—to believe him. But the strong and fearless woman he loved didn't exist in this world, and the weak and terrified one didn't belong.

He helped her load her suitcases in her car, because even when she was walking out on him, he was still determined to take care of her. Of course, when she got back to her own apartment, she'd be on her own with her luggage. Or so she believed until she saw her brother waiting for her.

"What are you doing here?" she asked.

"Your doctor called and asked me to come over here to give you a hand with some things."

"He's not *my* doctor," she said wearily.

"Is that why you moved out?"

It seemed ridiculous, when he was laden down with three suitcases, to deny that she'd ever moved in, so she said nothing as Ryder carried her bags into her apartment.

"Are you going to tell me what happened?"

"He asked me to marry him," she admitted.

Ryder sighed. "And you trampled all over his heart, didn't you?"

"He'll get over it."

"I don't know if he will—he loves you, sis."

"Do you really believe that?"

"I get that it's hard for you to recognize and accept his feelings," he said, dumping the luggage beside her bed. "We got screwed over pretty good in the parent department and I couldn't say for sure whether Mom and Dad loved us, or even if they're capable of those kinds of emotions. But that's on *them*—not *you*."

"I know," she said softly, but acknowledging the truth in her head was a lot easier than accepting it in her heart.

He tipped her chin up so that she had to look him in the eye. "Do you believe that I love you?" he asked.

She nodded.

"And do you love me, too?"

"Of course."

He wrapped his arms around her, offering the comfort he knew she would never ask for. "So why don't you believe that Justin could love you as much as you love him?"

Justin called her every day, just to see how she was doing. Even if he was working, he would find a couple of minutes to steal away to make a phone call. Sometimes they only chatted for a few minutes and other times they talked for much longer. Avery enjoyed talking to him and she found herself looking forward to their daily conversations, but she missed being with him.

Three and a half weeks after she moved back into her own apartment, she was on her way to the hospital cafeteria to grab a bite when she realized that many of her colleagues were looking at her differently. As if they were in on some kind of secret that she knew nothing about.

Then she walked into the cafeteria and saw it: an enormous banner stretched out across the back wall, over the seating area, proclaiming: Justin Garrett Loves Avery Wallace.

She closed her eyes for a second, but when she opened them again, it was still there. For not just her but everyone else who walked into the cafeteria to see. She wanted to turn around and walk out again, but she forced herself to ignore the stares and whispers and pick up a tray. She'd lost her appetite, but she moved toward the salad bar, anyway.

"The man sure knows how to make a statement, doesn't he?" Amy picked up the tongs to pile lettuce on her plate.

Avery had never been so grateful to see her friend, and her presence made her feel a little bit steadier as she added a few cucumber slices and cherry tomatoes to her own salad.

"Any idea what brought this about?" Amy asked.

"I'm guessing a severe head injury." She grabbed a bottle of water from a refrigerated display case and—because the salad was healthy enough to warrant dessert—a tub of cookies 'n' cream, then headed toward the cash.

Amy followed her to an empty table in the atrium, as far away from the banner as possible without actually leaving the dining room. "Do you believe it?"

"That he has a head injury?"

Amy rolled her eyes. "That he loves you?"

She picked up her fork and poked at her salad. "I believe he thinks he does."

"How do you feel about him?"

"I...miss him," she said.

"What do you miss?"

She missed seeing him every day, falling asleep in his arms at night and waking up beside him in the morning. She missed kissing him and touching him and making love with him. She missed their middle-of-the-night conversations, their playful disagreements and their spirited discussions. And she missed just being with him, even when they didn't have anything to say.

"Everything," she finally responded. "I miss everything about him, every minute of every day."

Amy nodded approvingly. "The question now is—what are you going to do about it?"

Apparently if a man decided to spell out his deepest feelings on a three-foot-by-ten-foot banner, he should expect a fair amount of ribbing and ridicule. None of it bothered Justin. What bothered him was that the banner had been up in the cafeteria for four days and, as far as he knew, Avery still hadn't seen it.

And how could a grand gesture be grand if the recipient was unaware?

The banner had been a last, desperate effort to help her realize the true depth of his feelings for her. And, so far, a futile one.

He was reviewing a patient's chart with a second-year resident when Avery showed up in the ER. He glanced at her briefly, and his heart hammered against his ribs as he refocused his attention on the resident to explain the next steps in the patient's treatment. She waited patiently until he turned to face her again.

Activity at the nurses' station had practically come to a standstill, with all eyes focused in their direction. She didn't seem to notice; he didn't care.

"Is there something I can help you with, Dr. Wallace?"

"I hope so," she said. "Do you have a few minutes to take a walk with me?"

He couldn't read much in her expression. She seemed a little nervous, but after studiously avoiding any personal contact over the past few weeks, that didn't surprise him.

He glanced at his watch. "I'm waiting on a report from radiology regarding a possible tibia fracture in Exam Six."

"Dr. Roberts is finished up in Two," Callie piped up

helpfully from the nurses' station. "I can see that he gets the report when it comes in."

"That would be great—thanks."

Avery didn't say anything as they made their way down the corridor toward the cafeteria, and he wasn't sure what to say to her. He knew how much she hated being the subject of gossip, and he considered that maybe the banner hadn't been such a great idea. Maybe he should warn her—

But before he could say anything, she walked directly through the food service area to the atrium. The strong, fearless woman, who could handle any medical emergency with a steady hand but who hated to be the center of attention and trembled when he touched her, didn't halt until she was standing directly beneath the banner he'd hung up four days earlier—and he'd never loved her more.

And that was before he realized a length of examination bed paper had been taped to the bottom of the banner. Her response, written with a Sharpie marker, read: She Loves You, Too.

He looked from the paper to Avery, who was watching him and chewing on her bottom lip, as if she wasn't quite sure of his response.

He put his arms around her and drew her close. "How did you finally figure it out?"

"I remembered something someone once said to me," she confided. "That love is wanting to spend every possible minute with someone, missing him every second that you're apart, and knowing that your life is better, richer and fuller with him in it. That's how I feel about you."

He lowered his mouth to hers, kissing her with all the pent-up emotion of the past few weeks and all the love in his heart. And she kissed him back exactly the same way.

"So where do we go from here?" he asked, when he finally eased his mouth from hers so they could each catch their breath.

"Well, I've offered to sublet my apartment to a colleague who needed a place, so I was hoping you might let me move back into your condo and share that king-size bed again."

"That sounds like a good start," he agreed.

"And my prenatal classes begin in a few weeks," she told him. "I could use a partner for those."

"Done."

"Then I'll want you there for the actual birth, too."

"I already told you that I'd be there for that," he reminded her.

She nodded. "And I was thinking it might be good for us to stick together after."

"How long after?"

"A long time," she decided.

"I like that plan."

"Okay, then." She nodded again. "That's good."

"It is good," he agreed, holding her close. "And it will only get better."

"I do love you, Justin. The feeling terrifies me, but it scares me even more to imagine my life without you in it."

"You don't have to imagine that," he promised. "Because I love you, too, and I'm not ever going to leave your side."

"I still want to take things slow."

"We can take them as slow as you want," he assured her.

"I'm not saying I don't *ever* want to get married, but I don't want to rush into it. I need to be sure."

"Then we'll wait until you're sure."

"Thank you," she said, and brushed a soft kiss across his lips. "In the meantime, will you do me a favor?"

"Anything," he promised.

"Will you please take down this banner that's hanging over our heads?"

He chuckled softly. "I'll take it down and put it up in our bedroom—to make sure you never forget how I feel about you."

Epilogue

Three months later

"I think I'm ready," Avery told him, zipping up the duffel bag she'd packed for the hospital.

"I hope so." Justin stood in the doorway with his keys in hand. "I've already called Dr. Herschel to meet us at the hospital."

Her labor had started several hours earlier, but her contractions were—she insisted—still mild and inconsistent. He wasn't sure how mild they could be when she sucked in a breath every time one started. She was gritting her teeth now and holding her belly as another pain hit. He immediately glanced at his watch, timing the contraction as she panted through it.

She nodded, indicating that it had passed.

"Thirty-eight seconds."

She nodded again as he picked up the duffel and slung it over his shoulder.

"I meant I'm ready to get married," she said.

He stared at her, not sure he understood what she was saying. "You're ready to get married?"

"Yes," she confirmed.

"When?"

She headed toward the door. "I was thinking that I'd like to do it before the baby's born."

"Wait a minute—are you honestly saying that you want to get married *now*?" he asked incredulously.

"I know the circumstances aren't ideal," she admitted, "but the more I think about it, the more I realize you're right. We should be married before we become parents."

"I love you, Avery, with all of my heart and soul," he said, punching the button to summon the elevator, "but there are times that I am completely baffled by your thought processes."

"I'm not asking for a church wedding with a hundred guests in attendance—more of a quick, informal ceremony, maybe performed by the hospital chaplain."

"What if *I* want the church wedding with a hundred guests in attendance?" he asked her.

"We can have a big reception at a later date, if it means that much to you," she promised.

He shook his head as the elevator dinged to signal its arrival. "You know the only thing that really matters to me is being with you."

"Is that a yes?"

"That's an 'I'll try to find the chaplain when we get to the hospital.'"

She smiled and brought his mouth down to hers for a quick kiss. "That's good enough."

But he did better than that.

He called his mother while they were on their way to the hospital, to tell her that Avery was in labor and that they were hoping to get married before the baby was born. He wasn't surprised that his parents arrived at the hospital only moments after they did. He *was* surprised to discover various other family members were already gathered in the hospital chapel—including his cousin Andrew and Andrew's wife, Rachel, who brought a hand-tied bouquet of white roses for the bride and a matching boutonniere for the groom.

But Avery's labor had progressed rapidly, and by the time they were ready to begin, her contractions were much more painful and intense and coming every five minutes. The chaplain expedited the proceedings as much as he could, but Justin could tell by the death grip Avery had on his hand that she was struggling with the transition stage.

"Breathe," he said softly.

She nodded.

When it was time for his vows, he recited them as quickly as he could. Then it was her turn.

"I, Avery Vanessa Wallace, take you, Justin Aaron Garrett, to be my—" She broke off on a gasp and squeezed his hand so hard he worried that she was going to break a bone.

"We can finish this later," he reminded her.

She shook her head fiercely as she breathed through the contraction, then picked up right where she'd left off.

"To be my husband. To have and to hold, from this day forward, for better, for worse, for richer, for poorer, in sickness and in health—and in labor," she ad-libbed, squeezing his hand again but much less painfully this time, "to love and to cherish, till death do us part."

Moved beyond words, Justin leaned forward and touched his lips to hers. "I love you."

"We haven't got to that part yet," the chaplain admonished.

"Sorry," Justin apologized automatically.

Avery smiled at him, because she knew he wasn't sorry at all, then mouthed the words back to him. *I love you, too.*

"By the power vested in me by the state of North Carolina, I now pronounce you husband and wife." He closed his book and peered over the rim of his glasses at Justin. "*Now* you may kiss your bride."

He drew her as close as her belly would allow and

brushed his lips over hers again, just as another contraction started.

"Can we move you up to maternity now?" he asked her.

She nodded. "I think that's probably a good idea."

Amy immediately came forward with the wheelchair she'd kept at the ready. Justin helped his bride into it, then pushed her toward the door.

On her way out of the chapel, she seemed to realize that she was still holding her bouquet. She tossed it over her head—and it smacked straight into her brother's chest. But Avery didn't have time to wonder what that could mean—she had a baby to deliver.

Thirty-nine minutes later, at 8:52 p.m., Vanessa Erin Garrett was born. The baby girl weighed in at almost eight pounds and measured twenty inches. Her proud parents celebrated the birth—and their wedding—with family, friends and cookies 'n' cream ice cream from the hospital cafeteria.

* * * * *

MILLS & BOON®

Why not subscribe?

Never miss a title and save money too!

Here's what's available to you if you join the exclusive **Mills & Boon® Book Club** today:

- ✦ *Titles up to a month ahead of the shops*
- ✦ *Amazing discounts*
- ✦ *Free P&P*
- ✦ *Earn Bonus Book points that can be redeemed against other titles and gifts*
- ✦ *Choose from monthly or pre-paid plans*

Still want more?

Well, if you join today, we'll even give you ***50% OFF your first parcel!***

So visit **www.millsandboon.co.uk/subs** to be a part of this exclusive Book Club!

SUBS_2015